Praise for Laila

THE MOOR'S

Winner of the Ameri

A *Kirkus Reviews* Best Book of the Year

"Compelling. . . . Necessary. . . . Laila Lalami's mesmerizing *The Moor's Account* presents us a historical fiction that feels something like a plural totality . . . a narrative that braids points of view so intricately that they become one even as we're constantly reminded of the separate and often contrary strands that render the whole."
—*The Los Angeles Review of Books*

"A bold and exhilarating bid to give a real-life figure muzzled by history the chance to have his say in fiction." —*San Francisco Chronicle*

"[A] rich novel based on an actual, ill-fated sixteenth-century Spanish expedition to Florida. . . . Offers a pungent alternative history that muses on the ambiguous power of words to either tell the truth or reshape it according to our desires." —*Los Angeles Times*

"[Lalami's] Estebanico is a superb storyteller, capable of sensitive character appraisals and penetrating ethnographic detail."
—*The Wall Street Journal*

"Feels at once historical and contemporary. . . . For Lalami, storytelling is a primal struggle over power between the strong and the weak, between good and evil, and against forgetting. . . . Lalami sees the story [of Estebanico] as a form of moral and spiritual instruction that can lead to transcendence." —*The New York Times Book Review*

"Meticulously researched and inventive. . . . Those interested in the history of the Spanish colonization of the Americas will find much to like in *The Moor's Account*, as will lovers of good yarns of faraway lands and times." —*The Seattle Times*

"Excellent historical fiction. . . . The way the Moor's account differs from the Spaniards' is amazing. It's a play on perspective in more ways than one."
—*Ebony*

"Artfully conveys the politics and power dynamics of bondage. . . . Eloquently examines the subjectivity of narrative and the creation and manipulation of the truth. . . . With this magnificent novel, Lalami, through fiction, has penned a revelation and tribute to truth."
—*The Millions*

"Tremendous and powerful, *The Moor's Account* is one of the finest historical novels I've encountered in a while. It rings with thunder!"
—Gary Shteyngart, author of *Super Sad True Love Story*

"Laila Lalami's radiant, arrestingly vivid prose instantly draws us into the world of the first black slave in the New World whose name we know—Estebanico. A bravura performance of imagination and empathy, *The Moor's Account* reverberates long after the final page."
—Henry Louis Gates, Jr.

"Richly rewarding."
—NPR

LAILA LALAMI

THE MOOR'S ACCOUNT

Laila Lalami is the author of the short story collection *Hope and Other Dangerous Pursuits*, which was a finalist for the Oregon Book Award, and the novel *Secret Son*, which was on the Orange Prize long list. Her essays and opinion pieces have appeared in the *Los Angeles Times*, *The Washington Post*, *The Nation*, *The Guardian*, and *The New York Times*, and in many anthologies. She is the recipient of a British Council Fellowship, a Fulbright Fellowship, and a Lannan Residency Fellowship and is an associate professor of creative writing at the University of California at Riverside. She lives in Los Angeles.

www.lailalalami.com

THE MOOR'S ACCOUNT

THE MOOR'S ACCOUNT

A NOVEL

LAILA LALAMI

VINTAGE BOOKS
A Division of Penguin Random House LLC
NEW YORK

FIRST VINTAGE BOOKS EDITION, AUGUST 2015

Copyright © 2014 by Laila Lalami

The Library of Congress has cataloged the Pantheon edition as follows:
Lalami, Laila.
The Moor's account / Laila Lalami.
pages cm
Includes bibliographical references.
1. Narváez, Pánfilo de, –1528—Fiction.   2. Cabeza de Vaca, Álvar Núñez, active 16th century—Fiction.   3. America—Early accounts to 1600—Fiction.   4. America—Discovery and exploration—Spanish—Fiction.   5. Morocco—Fiction.   I. Title.
PS3612.A543M66   2014   813'.6—dc23   2013045255

Vintage Books Trade Paperback ISBN: 978-0-8041-7062-8
eBook ISBN: 978-0-307-91167-4

Book design by Iris Weinstein

www.vintagebooks.com

Printed in the United States of America
12   14   16   18   20   19   17   15   13

FOR MY DAUGHTER

THE MOOR'S ACCOUNT

In the name of God, most compassionate, most merciful. Praise be to God, the Lord of the worlds, and prayers and blessings be on our prophet Muhammad and upon all his progeny and companions. This book is the humble work of Mustafa ibn Muhammad ibn Abdussalam al-Zamori, being a true account of his life and travels from the city of Azemmur to the Land of the Indians, where he arrived as a slave and, in his attempt to return to freedom, was shipwrecked and lost for many years.

Because I have written this narrative long after the events I recount took place, I have had to rely entirely on my memory. It is possible therefore that the distances I cite might be confused or that the dates I give might be inexact, but these are minor errors that are to be expected from such a relation. In all other ways, I testify here that I have described these events as I have witnessed them, including those that, by virtue of their rarity, may seem to the reader to be untrue.

I intend to correct details of the history that was compiled by my companions, the three Castilian gentlemen known by the names of Andrés Dorantes de Carranza, Alonso del Castillo Maldonado, and especially Álvar Núñez Cabeza de Vaca, who delivered their testimony, what they called the Joint Report, to the Audiencia of Santo Domingo. The first was my legal master, the second my fellow captive, and the third my rival storyteller. But, unlike them, I was never called upon to testify to the Spanish Viceroy about our journey among the Indians.

I consider the three Castilian gentlemen I have mentioned to be men of good character, but it is my belief that, under the pressure of the Bishop, the Viceroy, and the Marquis of the Valley, and in accordance with the standards set by their positions, they were led to omit certain events while exaggerating others, and to suppress some details while inventing others, whereas I, who am neither beholden to Castilian men of power, nor bound by the rules of a society to which I do not belong, feel free to recount the true story of what happened to my companions and me.

What each of us wants, in the end, whether he is black or white, master or slave, rich or poor, man or woman, is to be remembered after his death. I am no different; I want to survive the eternity of darkness that awaits me. If, by a stroke of luck, this account should find its way to a suitable secretary, who would see fit to copy it down without any embellishment, save for those of calligraphy or, in the manner of the Turks and the Persians, colorful illumination, then perhaps, someday, if that is to be the will of God, my countrymen will hear about my wondrous adventures and take from them what wise men should: truth in the guise of entertainment.

1.

THE STORY OF LA FLORIDA

It was the year 934 of the Hegira, the thirtieth year of my life, the fifth year of my bondage—and I was at the edge of the known world. I was marching behind Señor Dorantes in a lush territory he, and Castilians like him, called La Florida. I cannot be certain what my people call it. When I left Azemmur, news of this land did not often attract the notice of our town criers; they spoke instead of the famine, the recent earthquake, or the rebellions in the south of Barbary. But I imagine that, in keeping with our naming conventions, my people would simply call it the Land of the Indians. The Indians, too, must have had a name for it, although neither Señor Dorantes nor anyone in the expedition knew what it was.

Señor Dorantes had told me that La Florida was a large island, larger than Castile itself, and that it ran from the shore on which we had landed all the way to the Peaceful Sea. From one ocean to the other, was how he described it. All this land, he said, would now be governed by Pánfilo de Narváez, the commander of the armada. I thought it unlikely, or at least peculiar, that the Spanish king would allow one of his subjects to rule a territory larger than his own, but of course I kept my opinion to myself.

We were marching northward to the kingdom of Apalache. Señor Narváez had found out about it from some Indians he had captured after the armada arrived on the shore of La Florida. Even though I had not wanted to come here, I was relieved when the moment came to disembark, because the journey across the Ocean of Fog and Darkness had been marred by all the difficulties to be expected of such a passage: the hardtack was stale, the water murky, the latrines filthy. Narrow quarters made the passengers and crew especially irritable and almost every day a quarrel erupted. But the worst of it was the smell—the indelible scent of unwashed men, combined with the smoke from the braziers and the whiff of horse dung and chicken droppings that clung to the animal stalls in spite of daily cleanings—a pestilential mix that assaulted you the moment you stepped into the lower deck.

I was also curious about this land because I had heard, or overheard, from my master and his friends, so many stories about the Indians. The Indians, they said, had red skin and no eyelids; they were heathens who made human sacrifices and worshipped evil-looking gods; they drank mysterious concoctions that gave them visions; they walked about in their natural state, even the women—a claim I had found so hard to believe that I had dismissed it out of hand. Yet I had become captivated. This land had become for me not just a destination, but a place of complete fantasy, a place that could have existed only in the imagination of itinerant storytellers in the souqs of Barbary. This was how the journey across the Ocean of Fog and Darkness worked on you, even if you had never wanted to undertake it. The ambition of the others tainted you, slowly and irrevocably.

The landing itself was restricted to a small group of officers and soldiers from each ship. As captain of the Gracia de Dios, Señor Dorantes had chosen twenty men, among whom this servant of God, Mustafa ibn Muhammad, to be taken on one of the rowboats to the beach. My master stood at the fore of the vessel, one hand on his hip, the other resting on the pommel of his sword; the posture seemed to me so perfect an expression of his eagerness to claim the treasures of the new world that he might have been posing for an unseen sculptor.

It was a fine morning in spring; the sky was an indifferent blue and the water was clear. From the beach, we slowly made our way to a fishing village one of the sailors had sighted from the height of the foremast, and which was located about a crossbow shot from the shore. My first impression was of the silence all around us. No, silence is not the right word. There was the sound of waves, after all, and a soft breeze rustled the leaves of the palm trees. Along the path, curious seagulls came to watch us and departed again in a flutter of wings. But I felt a great absence.

In the village were a dozen huts, built with wooden poles and covered with palm fronds. They were arranged in a wide circle, with space enough in between each pair of homes to allow for the cooking and storing of food. The fire pits that dotted the perimeter of the clearing contained fresh logs, and there were three skinned deer hanging from a rail, their blood still dripping onto the earth, but the village was deserted. Still, the governor ordered a complete search. The huts turned up tools for cooking and cleaning, in addition to animal hides and furs, dried fish and meat, and great quantities of sunflower seeds, nuts, and fruit. At once the soldiers took possession of whatever they could; each one jealously clutched what he had stolen and traded it for the things he wanted. I took nothing and I had nothing to barter, but I felt ashamed, because I had been made a witness to these acts of theft and, unable to stop them, an accomplice to them as well.

As I stood with my master outside one of the huts, I noticed a pile of fishing nets. It was while lifting one up to look at its peculiar threading that I found an odd little pebble. At first, it seemed to me that it was a weight, but the nets had smooth stone anchors, quite unlike this one, which was yellow and rough-edged. Then I thought it might be a child's toy, for it looked like it could be part of a set of marbles or that it could fit inside a rattle; it might have been left on the fishing nets by mistake. I held it up to the light to get a better look, but Señor Dorantes saw it.

Estebanico, my master said. What did you find?

Estebanico was the name the Castilians had given me when they bought me from Portuguese traders—a string of sounds whose foreign- ness still grated on my ears. When I fell into slavery, I was forced to give up not just my freedom, but also the name that my mother and father had chosen for me. A name is precious; it carries inside it a language, a history, a set of traditions, a particular way of looking at the world. Losing it meant losing my ties to all those things too. So I had never been able to shake the feeling that this Estebanico was a man conceived by the Castil- ians, quite different from the man I really was. My master snatched the pebble from my hand. What is this? he asked.

It is nothing, Señor.

Nothing?

Just a pebble.

Let me see. He scratched at the pebble with a fingernail, revealing, under the layer of dirt, a brighter shade of yellow. He was an inquisi- tive man, my master, always asking questions about everything. Perhaps this was why he had decided to set aside the comfort of his stately home in Béjar del Castañar and make his fortune in an uncharted territory. I did not resent his curiosity about the new world, but I envied the way he spoke about his hometown—it was, always, with the expectation of a glorious return.

It is nothing, I said again.

I am not so sure.

It must be pyrite.

But it might be gold. He turned the pebble around and around between his fingers, unsure what to do with it. Then, suddenly making up his mind, he ran up to Señor Narváez, who was standing in the village square, waiting for his men to complete their search. Don Pánfilo, my master called. Don Pánfilo.

I should describe the governor for you. The most striking thing about his face was the black patch over his right eye. It gave him a fearsome look, but it seemed to me his sunken cheeks and his small chin did not particularly reinforce it. On most days, even when there was no need for it, he wore a steel helmet adorned with ostrich feathers. Over his breast-plate, a blue sash ran from his shoulder to his thigh and was tied with flourish over his hip. He looked like a man who had taken great pains with his appearance, yet he was also capable of the same coarseness as the lowliest of his soldiers. I had once seen him plug one nostril with a finger and send out a long string of snot shooting out of the other, all while discussing shipping supplies with one of his captains.

Señor Narváez received the pebble with greedy fingers. There was some more holding up to the light, some more scratching. This is gold, he said solemnly. The pebble sat like an offering in his palm. When he spoke again, his voice was hoarse. Good work, Capitán Dorantes. Good work.

The officers gathered excitedly around the governor, while a soldier ran back to the beach to tell the others about the gold. I stood behind Señor Dorantes, shaded from the sun by his shadow and, although I could not see his face, I knew that it was full of pride. I had been sold to him a year earlier, in Seville, and since then I had learnt how to read him, how to tell whether he was happy or only satisfied, angry or mildly annoyed, worried or barely concerned—gradations of feelings that could translate into actions toward me. Now, for instance, he was pleased with my discovery, but his vanity prevented him from saying that it was I who had found the gold. I had to remain quiet, make myself unnoticed for a while, let him bask, alone, in the glory of the find.

Moments later, the governor ordered the rest of the armada to disembark. It took three days to shuttle all the people, horses, and supplies to the white, sandy beach. As more and more people arrived, they somehow huddled around the familiar company of those closest to them in station: the governor usually stood with his captains, in their armor and plumed helmets; the commissary conversed with the four friars, all wearing identical brown robes; the horsemen gathered with the men of arms, each of them carrying his weapon—a musket, an arquebus, a crossbow, a sword, a steel-pointed lance, a dagger, or even a butcher's hatchet. Then there were the settlers, among whom carpenters, metalworkers, cobblers, bakers, farmers, merchants, and many others whose occupations I never determined or quickly forgot. There were also ten women and thirteen children, standing in throngs beside their wooden chests. But the fifty or so slaves, including this servant of God, Mustafa ibn Muhammad, were scattered, each one standing near the man who owned him, carrying his luggage or watching his belongings.

By the time everyone had congregated on the beach, it was late afternoon on the third day, and the tide was low. The waves were small, and a dark strip of shoreline was exposed. The weather had cooled; now the sand was cold and sticky under my feet. High clouds had gathered in the sky, turning the sun into a faint, distant orb. A thick fog drifted in from the ocean, slowly washing the color out of the world around us, rendering it in various shades of white and gray. It was very quiet.

The notary of the armada, a stocky man with owlish eyes by the name of Jerónimo de Albaniz, stepped forward. Facing Señor Narváez, he unrolled a scroll and began to read in a toneless voice. On behalf of the King and Queen, he said, we wish to make it known that this land belongs to God our Lord, Living and Eternal. God has appointed one man, called St. Peter, to be the governor of all the men in the world, wherever they should live, and under whatever law, sect, or belief they should be. The successor of St. Peter in this role is our Holy Father, the Pope, who has made a donation of this terra firma to the King and Queen. Therefore, we ask and require that you acknowledge the Church as the ruler of this world, and the priest whom we call Pope, and the King and Queen, as lords of this territory.

Señor Albaniz stopped speaking now and, without asking for permission or offering an apology, he took a sip of water from a flask hanging from his shoulder.

I watched the governor's face. He seemed annoyed with the interruption, but he held back from saying anything, as it would only delay the proceedings further. Or maybe he did not want to upset the notary. After all, without notaries and record-keepers, no one would know what governors did. A measure of patience and respect, however small, was required.

Unhurriedly Señor Albaniz wiped his mouth with the back of his hand and resumed speaking. If you do as we say, you will do well and we shall receive you in all love and charity. But if you refuse to comply, or maliciously delay in it, we inform you that we will make war against you in all manners that we can, and shall take your wives and children, and shall make slaves of them, and shall take away your goods, and shall do you all the mischief and damage that we can. And if this should happen, we protest that the deaths and losses will be your fault, and not that of their Highnesses, or of the cavaliers here present. Now that we have said this to you, we request the notary to give us his testimony in writing and the rest who are present to be witnesses of this Requisition.

Until Señor Albaniz had arrived at the promises and threats, I had not known that this speech was meant for the Indians. Nor could I understand why it was given here, on this beach, if its intended recipients had already fled their village. How strange, I remember thinking, how utterly strange were the ways of the Castilians—just by saying that something was so, they believed that it was. I know now that these conquerors, like many others before them, and no doubt like others after, gave speeches not to voice the truth, but to create it.

At last, Señor Albaniz fell silent. He presented the scroll and waited, head bowed, while Señor Narváez signed his name on the requisition. Facing the crowd, the governor announced that this village would henceforth be known as Portillo. The captains inclined their heads and a soldier raised the standard, a green piece of fabric with a red shield in its center. I was reminded of the moment, many years earlier, when the flag of the Portuguese king was hoisted over the fortress tower in Azemmur. I had been only a young boy then, but I still lived with the humiliation of that day, for it had changed my family's fate, disrupted our lives, and cast me out of my home. Now, halfway across the world, the scene was repeating itself on a different stage, with different people. So I could not help feeling a sense of dread at what was yet to come.

. . .

MY FEARS WERE CONFIRMED early the next morning, when we heard a commotion behind the village storehouse. Señor Dorantes had wanted me to give him a haircut, and I had just begun to trim the edges of his thick, wheat-colored hair. His beard had grown, too, but he had not asked me to shave it. Perhaps he felt that he did not need to worry about matters of grooming now that he had reached the edge of the empire. Or he grew his beard because he could and the Indians, it was rumored, could not. I confess I did not ask him why; I was relieved to have fewer chores. But when we heard the cries of soldiers, Señor Dorantes shot to his feet, with the white linen cloth still tied around his neck, and ran across the square to see what had happened. I followed him, with the Sevillian scissors still in my hand. The soldiers, it turned out, had found some Indians hiding in the bushes and had captured four of them.

All four were men. All four were naked. I had seen Indians before, on the islands of Cuba and La Española, where the armada had stopped to purchase more supplies, but never at such close range. I was unused to seeing men walk about in their natural state, unashamed of their bodies, so my first impulse was to stare. They were tall and broad-shouldered, with skin the color of earth when it has rained. Their hair was glossy and long, and on their right arms and left legs, they had tattoos in shapes I did not recognize. One of them had a lazy eye, just like my uncle Omar, and he blinked in order to focus his gaze on his captors. Another was surveying the village, taking stock of all that had changed since our arrival: a large cross had been set up by the temple; the governor's standard hung from a pole in the square; and, along the perimeter, horses were tethered to newly built posts. The stories I had heard about the Indians had me expecting something incredible, fire-breathing jinns perhaps, but these men looked harmless to me—especially next to the Castilian soldiers. Still, they were tied up and brought to Señor Narváez.

From his pocket, the governor retrieved the pebble of gold I had found. Holding it up in his palm, he asked them about it. Where did you find this gold?

The captives looked at him levelly and two of them said something in their mother tongue. I could not detect a pattern yet to the stream of sounds that emerged from their lips—where did one word end and another one begin? My upbringing in a trading town like Azemmur had instilled in me a love of language and, if I may be forgiven for this moment of immodesty, a certain ease with it. So I was curious about the Indians' tongue, even though it had none of the clues that had been helpful to me when I learned new idioms: familiar sounds, a few words in common, a similar intonation. But, to my surprise, the governor nodded slowly, as if he understood the Indians perfectly and even agreed with them.

Still, he repeated his question. Where did you find this gold?

Behind him, the soldiers watched and waited. Up in the trees, birds were singing, determined in their trills despite the oppressive heat. The soothing sound of waves came from the beach nearby and I could smell smoke in the air—someone had already started a fire for the almuerzo. Again, the Indians answered the governor in the same way as before. At least, I assumed they were answering; it was just as likely that they were asking the governor a question of their own, or challenging him to a fight, or threatening him with death if he did not release them.

The governor listened politely to their answers and then he turned to his page. Lock them up in the storehouse, he said, and bring me a whip.

Señor Dorantes returned to his seat, and again I had to follow. Neither one of us spoke. I finished cutting his hair, handing him a small mirror and holding another one behind him. I saw both of our reflections on these opposing mirrors. My master looked satisfied with the haircut, nodding appreciatively as he turned his face this way and that. His beard nearly hid the scar on his right cheek, a scar, I once heard him proudly tell one of his dinner guests, he had sustained years earlier in Castile, when he had helped put down a rebellion against the king. As for me, my bondage had taught me to keep an impassive face, but in the mirror I noticed that my eyes betrayed my anxiety. I told myself that I had merely been curious about the kind of fishnets the Indians used. I had not been looking for gold. Yet the pebble I had found had caused these four men, men who had done me no harm, to be whipped. I had to pretend, like my master, not to hear the cries that had begun to emerge from the store-house. Within moments, they had turned into howls, so long and so filled with pain that I felt they were echoing in the depths of my own soul. And then, interrupted by the periodic and terrifying crack of the whip, there was only silence.

Later, when I was helping Señor Dorantes into his boots, I overheard his younger brother, Diego, a quiet lad of sixteen or seventeen years of age, ask him about the governor's encounter with the Indians. Diego was so different from Señor Dorantes it was a wonder to me that they were blood brothers. Where one was shy and guileless, the other was bold and crafty. Where one was selective in his friendships, the other was quick to love and quick to hate. And yet Diego patterned himself after his older brother in whatever way he could. He wore his doublet unbuttoned at the top and his helmet tilted back, like a weary soldier. He had tried to grow his beard, too, but so far only scattered patches of hair had sprouted on his cheeks. Hermano, Diego said. When did Don Pánfilo learn their language? Has he been to La Florida before?

Señor Dorantes gave Diego an amused look, but he must have thought the question harmless, for he answered it presently. No, this is his first time here, just like us. But he has a lot of experience with the savages. He can make himself understood quite well by them, and he rarely fails to obtain the facts he seeks.

This made no sense to me, yet I remained silent, for I knew that my master would not take kindly to being challenged about the governor's fluency in the Indian tongue. The elders teach us: a living dog is better than a dead lion.

But why must he whip them? Diego insisted.

Because the Indians are known liars, Señor Dorantes replied. Take these four. They are likely spies, sent here to watch us and report on our movements. Slowly, almost imperceptibly, my master's tone had shifted from amusement to mild irritation. He stood up and ran a finger along the top edge of his boots, making sure his breeches were properly tucked in. To get the truth, he said, it is necessary to flog them.

THE GOVERNOR HAD WHIPPED the four prisoners until he was satisfied that they had given him the whole truth. Armed with it, he called a gathering of all the officers that evening. They met in the largest lodge in the village, a kind of temple that could have easily accommodated a hundred people, though only a dozen high-ranking men had been invited: the commissary, the treasurer, the tax inspector, the notary, and the captains, among whom was Señor Dorantes. Wooden statues of panthers, their eyes painted yellow and their arms bearing war clubs, had been removed earlier in the day, along with the hand drums that, I imagined, were used in heathen ceremonies. So the temple was bare now. But the ceiling attracted my eye: it was decorated with a multitude of inverted seashells that cast a faint gleam on the ground.

One by one, the Spanish officers took their seats on Indian stools that had been arranged in a circle. The governor's page had covered a long bench with a white tablecloth and placed lit candelabras on either end of it. Now he served dinner—grilled fish, boiled rice, cured pork, and fresh and dried fruit from the village storehouse. At the sight of the food, I felt hungrier than I had in many days, but I had to wait until after the dinner before I could eat my meager rations.

Standing before his officers, Señor Narváez announced that the pebble of gold came from a rich kingdom called Apalache. This kingdom was located two weeks' march north of this village, and its capital city had great quantities of gold, as well as silver, copper, and other fine metals. There were large, cultivated fields of corn and beans around the city, and many people who tended them, and it was also near a river filled with fish of all kinds. The Indians' testimony, which the governor asked Señor Albaniz to record, had convinced him that the kingdom of Apalache was as rich as that of Moctezuma.

This word had the effect of a cannon shot. It seemed to me that the entire party greeted it with awe, and I admit that I, too, gasped with wonder, for in Seville I had heard many stories about the rich emperor whose palace was covered with gold and silver. The captains' excitement was so contagious that I found myself daydreaming. What if, I thought, the Castilians conquered this kingdom? What if Señor Dorantes were to become one of the richest men in this part of the empire? The reckless hope came to me that he might, as a gesture of gratitude or goodwill, or even as a celebration of his gold and glory, free the slave who had set him on this path. How easily I slipped into this fantasy! I would be able to leave La Florida on a vessel bound for Seville, and from there travel back to Azemmur, the city at the edge of the old continent. I would be able to return home to my family, to hold them and be held by them, to run my fingers along the uneven edge of the tiled wall in the courtyard, to hear the sound of the Umm er-Rbi' when it is swollen with spring runoff, to sit on the rooftop of our home on warm summer nights, when the air is filled with the smell of ripening figs. I would once again speak the language of my forefathers and find comfort in the traditions I had been forced to cast aside. I would live out the rest of my days among my people. The fact that none of this had been promised or suggested did not dampen my yearning. And, in my moment of greed, I forgot about the cost of my dream to others.

The officers raised their glasses to the governor, to thank him for the good tidings he had brought, and the slaves, including this servant of God, Mustafa ibn Muhammad, refilled them with wine. (Reader, it is not easy for me to confess that I served the forbidden drink, but I have decided in this relation to tell everything that happened to me, so I must not leave out even such a detail.) However, the governor said, raising his palms to quiet the assembly, there was one complication. The armada was too large: four caravels and one brigantine, six hundred men and eighty horses, fifty thousand arrobas of supplies and weapons. It was not suitable for the mission at hand.

So he had decided to split it into two contingents, each roughly the same size. The first of these was the sea contingent, with the sailors, the women and children, and anyone who suffered from a cold or a fever or was otherwise too weak to continue. These people would sail along the coast of La Florida to the nearest town in New Spain, which was the port of Pánuco, at the mouth of the Río de las Palmas. There, they would set their anchor and wait. The second contingent, that is to say, the able-bodied men who could walk, ride a horse, or carry food and water, weapons and ammunition, would march inland to Apalache, secure it, and then send forward a smaller group to meet the sea party. The governor invited the captains to select the best men from among those who had traveled on their ships.

Silence fell upon the assembly. Then, all at once, several captains raised their objections to this plan, particularly a young man who was a close friend of my master's. His name was Señor Castillo and he had joined the expedition on a whim, after hearing about it at a banquet in Seville. His voice had a nasal tone that made him sound like a child, and indeed he was a slight man who looked barely out of his teenage years. I remember he stood up from his seat and asked if it was not too risky to send all the ships and supplies away while we went on a mission to the interior.

We have no map, he said. No means to resupply ourselves if the mission takes longer than we expect. And no agreement among our pilots about how far Pánuco is. Señor Castillo spoke with candor and without a hint of animosity; the others who had also objected to the plan were quiet now, tacitly allowing him to speak for them all.

We may not have maps, Señor Narváez replied pleasantly, but we have the four Indians. The padres will teach them our language, so that they can serve as guides and translators. As for the length of the mission, you have seen with your own eyes how poorly armed the savages are. It will not take us long to subdue them. The governor was not in his armor that night. He wore a black doublet, whose sleeves he periodically tugged and straightened. Now, he said, let us discuss how we will divide our numbers.

Señor Castillo ran his fingers through his mass of brown hair—a nervous habit. Forgive me, Don Pánfilo, he said. But I am still not convinced that we should send away the ships when the three pilots disagree about how far we are from New Spain.

We are not far from the port of Pánuco, the governor said. The chief pilot said it is only twenty leagues from here. The other pilots think it might be twenty-five. I would not call that a disagreement.

Surely you are not suggesting that we send the ships away, just like that?

Out of his good eye, the governor gave Señor Castillo a piercing look. That is precisely what I am suggesting.

What if the ships get lost on the way to the port? Some of us have invested large sums in these ships. We cannot afford to lose them.

I will not be lectured about the cost of the vessels, Castillo. I have put all my money in this expedition, too. The governor looked around him, enjoining all the officers who were present to share in his bafflement. Señores, my plan is simple. We march to the kingdom of Apalache, while the ships wait for us at a safe and secure port, where the crew can procure any supplies we might need. I used the same strategy in my Cuba campaign, fifteen years ago. Now the governor smiled nostalgically at the memory of his past glory and then, addressing himself only to Señor Castillo, he added: Probably when you were still a baby.

Señor Castillo sat down, his face the color of beets.

The governor's plan may have seemed bold to the young captain, but I knew that it had been tested. Before marching to Tenochtitlán to claim the riches of Moctezuma, Hernán Cortés had scuttled his ships in the port of Veracruz. And, seven centuries earlier, Tariq ibn Ziyad had burned his boats on the shores of Spain. In truth, Señor Narváez's plan was quite cautious, for he was only sending the ships to wait for us at the nearest port, where they could resupply. So I did not share Señor Castillo's fears, and a part of me even resented him for wanting to delay the journey to the kingdom of gold and thereby defer my dreams of freedom.

But Señor Castillo appealed to Señor Cabeza de Vaca, who sat across from him. Do you not agree that we are taking an unnecessary risk? he asked.

Señor Cabeza de Vaca was the treasurer of the expedition, charged with collecting the king's share of any wealth acquired in La Florida. Rumor had it that he was close to the governor, so most of the men feared him, even as they made jokes behind his back about his unusual name, calling him Cabeza de Mono, on account of his ears, which protruded like that of a monkey. Señor Cabeza de Vaca laced his fingers together; they were white and smooth and his nails were clean. He had the hands of a nobleman.

There is indeed a risk, he said. There is always a risk. But the Indians of this territory know about our presence now. We must start marching right away, before the king of Apalache can raise a large army against us or make alliances with any neighbors. We cannot squander a chance to take Apalache for His Majesty. Señor Cabeza de Vaca spoke with the innocence of a man in thrall to lofty ideas, ideas that could not be tainted by banal concerns about ships. Some of the captains nodded in agreement, for the treasurer was a thoughtful and experienced man who wielded a lot of influence among them.

The rest of the council was quiet now. Señor Narváez cleared his throat. I need someone to take charge of the ships while we march to Apalache. So if Castillo would rather not venture inland . . .

The insult in the governor's offer was barely hidden.

Don Pánfilo, Señor Castillo said, his manner completely changed. He stood up, ready to defend his honor. No, he said.

He will go, Señor Dorantes added, his hand on his friend's elbow, to stop him from saying anything to further damage his reputation.

So it was that the governor sent the ships to the port of Pánuco, while he led the officers and the soldiers, the friars and the settlers, the porters and the servants deep into the wilderness of La Florida—a long procession of three hundred souls looking for the kingdom of gold.

ALL AROUND US, the land was flat and dense. In places where the sunlight penetrated the canopy of trees, it was colored a faded green, or sometimes a sickly yellow. The sound of the horses' hooves was muffled by the soft ground, but the soldiers' songs, coarse and loud, the creaking of the officers' armor, the clanging of the tools inside the settlers' bags—

all these announced the passage of our company in the lush sea of green. Behind the trees, a quiet swamp often awaited, surrounded by exposed roots and overhung with slimy branches. After each crossing, I emerged covered with gray mud, which caked on my legs and in between my toes, making me nearly mad with the urge to scratch.

Once, when we were crossing a large swamp, a slave by the name of Agostinho—a man like me, whom greed and circumstance had brought from Ifriqiya to La Florida—called for help with the heavy burlap bag he was carrying over his head. I walked toward him, past a clump of white flowers whose fragrance I found intoxicating. The swamp bubbled around us, as if it were taking a deep, restful breath. My hands were almost on the burlap bag when a green monster leapt out of the water and sank its teeth into Agostinho. There was a clear snap of bones breaking, a gush of blood hitting the surface, and Agostinho went down with a gasp. I ran out of the swamp as fast as my legs could carry me, my heart consumed with the same boundless terror I had felt as a boy, when my mother told the ghoulish tales she reserved for the early evenings of winter, tales in which, unfailingly, children who dared to go into the forest were eaten by strange creatures. I reached dry land and collapsed, in time to see the beast disappear, beating its tail in the muddy water.

In the language of the Castilians, as in mine, there was no word yet for this animal, no way to talk about it without saying, the Water Animal with Scaly Skin, a cumbersome expression that would not work for long now that the Spaniards had declared their dominion over La Florida. So they gave new names to everything around them, as though they were the All-Knowing God in the Garden of Eden. Walking back to the edge of the swamp, the governor asked whose slave that was and what was in the burlap bag. Someone told him: the dead slave belonged to a settler; the bag was full of pots, dishes, and utensils. All right, the governor said, his voice tinged with annoyance. This animal, he announced, would be called El Lagarto because it looked like a giant lizard. It was not a name the expedition's notary needed to record. Everyone would remember it.

But the lagartos were not the only impediments to the governor's march. The rations he had assigned were not large: each man was given two pounds of biscuit and half a pound of cured pork, and each servant or slave, half that. So the men were always looking for ways to supplement their meals, particularly with hare or deer, but very quickly the governor forbade those who had bows or muskets from using them; he wanted them to save their ammunition in case the Indians of Apalache offered any resistance. I had no weapon; I had only my walking staff. With it, I could occasionally disturb a bird's nest and eat the eggs it held. Sometimes, I picked the fruit of the palm trees, which were smaller and thicker than those of my hometown, or I tried the berries of unfamiliar bushes, tasting only one or two before daring to eat them in greater quantities.

Señor Dorantes, of course, had no such troubles. Because he had invested some of his own money in this expedition, he and others like him received larger rations. He rode comfortably on his horse, Abejorro—a gray Andalusian with smart eyes, dark legs, and a good carriage—and tried to stave off the boredom by chatting with his younger brother Diego. On the whole, however, he seemed to prefer the company of Señor Castillo, often nudging his horse to keep up with his friend's white mare. As for me, I walked where Señor Dorantes had told me to: at all times, I was to be one step behind him. He was not satisfied just to travel through this wondrous land and to seek a share of its kingdom of gold, he wanted a witness for his ambitions; he felt himself at the center of great new things and so he needed an audience, even when there was nothing for him to do but march.

One fine morning, about two weeks into the march, we came upon a wide river. The sun glazed its surface a blinding white, but if you stood at the edge of the water you could see that it was very fast and so clear that you could count all the black pebbles at the bottom. The governor announced that this river would be called the Río Oscuro, on account of its multitude of black rocks, but the men barely paused to listen. Agua, por fin, they said, and Gracias a Dios and Déjame pasar, hombre!

Señor Dorantes dismounted, and I led Abejorro to the water, wading in myself to wash the gray mud off my legs and sandals. I thought we would rest on the riverbank for a while, but the governor ordered his carpenters to begin constructing rafts immediately, in order to transport those who could not swim—that is to say, most of the men—across the water. It was late spring and the days were longer, but sunlight had already begun to turn amber by the time the rafts were finally ready and the first groups of men crossed the river.

The other bank was flat and bare, with only a few tufts of grass jutting out here and there, but farther ahead a screen of green stalks showed where the wilderness began again. A cool breeze blew, rustling the edges of the pine trees in the horizon. I could feel it through the coarse fabric of my shirt as I adjusted the saddle on Abejorro and rubbed his neck. The officers and soldiers, who had been the first to be shuttled across the river, huddled together: the governor was having a long conversation with the commissary, his head inclined sideways toward the short friar, as if he could hear from only one ear; Señor Dorantes was showing Señor Castillo how to tie his cuirass so that it would not chafe against his skin; two men were arguing about a set of horse spurs.

Then a band of Indians emerged from behind the wall of trees, silently gathering on the field. Some were naked, but others wore, over their shameful parts, animal hides painted in patterns of blue and red. They held weapons made of animal bone and fire-hardened wood—lances, bows, or slingshots—but they did not threaten us. There were as many as a hundred of them. For a moment, each side regarded the other with the curiosity of a child who sees his reflection in the mirror for the first time. Then, unhurriedly, the governor climbed on his horse and the officers who had their mounts did the same. The page pulled the flagpole from the ground where it had been stuck and lifted it up; the standard of the governor whipped in the breeze.

Albaniz, the governor called.

In addition to being the official notary of the expedition, charged with the safekeeping of all its contracts and petitions, Señor Albaniz was also responsible for chronicling its progress for the next few months. His presence at this moment, our first encounter with an Indian nation, made me think of my father, who had dreamed of me becoming, like him, a notary public, a witness and recorder of major events in other people's lives. I felt as though my father's aspiration, which I had so easily and so carelessly brushed off many years ago, would never let go of me, that I would be reminded of it wherever I went, even here, in this strange land. But perhaps my father's dreams for me have come true in the end, for here I am setting down, for my own reasons, a relation of the Narváez expedition.

Tell the savages, the governor said, to take me to Apalache. He considered it beneath him to speak directly to the Indians.

With the look of a servant who has found himself chosen for a tedious chore, Señor Albaniz dismounted and stepped forward. This, he said, pointing behind him, is Pánfilo de Narváez, the new governor of this terra firma, by virtue of the bequest made to him by his Holy Imperial Majesty. He wishes to go to the kingdom of Apalache and to meet with its leader in order to discuss matters of great importance to our nations. He wants you to take him there.

Whether the Indians did not understand the notary's command or refused to comply with it, I could not guess. They remained silent. I looked for their leader, but I could not make out if it was the man who wore a headdress of stiff animal hair or the one who had the greatest number of tattoos.

Take us to the kingdom of Apalache, Señor Albaniz said, louder this time, his hands cupped around his mouth so that his voice could carry farther. One of the Indians sat on his haunches, enjoying the spectacle of this man in a metal costume and a feathered hat, crying and gesticulating before him.

Kingdom of Apalache! Señor Albaniz yelled again.

By then, the rafts had made another crossing, and more people disembarked—soldiers, settlers, servants, and captives. They joined our party without speaking; now we outnumbered the Indians.

You can stop, Albaniz, the governor said. He looked behind him. Bring me the captives.

The order was passed down, and a foot soldier brought forth the prisoners. Because I was always with my master, near the head of our long procession, I had not seen the prisoners since our departure from Portillo, the fishing village. They shuffled forward now, their hands bound by a length of rope that was tied to the soldier's belt. Their bodies were crisscrossed by lash marks and their limbs thinned down by the smallest of all the rations. One of the prisoners bowed his head in a way that struck me as unnatural until I noticed the hole where his nose should have been. Snot and blood caked at the edges of the gap. Flies darted around him relentlessly, but he could not swat them because his hands were tied. I averted my eyes from the horror, feeling as if I were witnessing something I should never have seen.

The prisoners came to stand next to Señor Albaniz, who spoke directly to one of them. Pablo, he said. Tell them to take us to Apalache.

The man Señor Albaniz had called Pablo, a lad whose long, glossy hair had been sheared and whose shoulders were covered with blisters, commenced to speak in his mother tongue, but almost immediately a lance surged in the air from the Indian side and the foot soldier who had been holding him by the arm lurched forward and tumbled to the ground, clutching his throat. An arrow had gone through his neck, its tip coming out on the other side. The soldier opened his mouth wide, but the only sound that came out was the bubbling of the blood inside. Now the Indians let out great howling cries, cries that sparked in me a nearly paralyzing fear.

My God, Señor Albaniz said, turning around and looking for his horse.

Ándale! the governor shouted.

Señor Dorantes nudged his horse forward and I felt Abejorro's tail swish across my chest as I turned to look for cover, though there was no place to hide. I tried to run back toward the river, but the crowd of Castilians who were moving forward pressed against me, their bodies bearing down on mine with such strength that I had no other choice but to sink to my knees. The air above me exploded with the sound of muskets. One of the soldiers next to me, a boy of no more than fifteen or sixteen years of age, raised his weapon and fired, but it was one of his own comrades who fell down. I could hear the Indian warriors advancing behind me, their unintelligible cries no longer in need of any translation.

Somehow, I made my way to a pack load, crates that held carpentry tools, and I cowered behind them. I would be safe here, I thought. Then I heard a labored grunt. Past a thicket of weeds on my left, not ten steps away from me, a settler was fighting an Indian. The settler had a trowel, which he was trying to land somewhere on the Indian. He missed. But the Indian's aim was unswerving and when he brought his hatchet down, he severed the settler's arm neatly at the elbow. Another blow to the head and the settler fell to the ground, eyes still open.

The Indian turned around, looking for another adversary. I flattened my back against the pack load. He seemed surprised when he saw me— a black man among white men. The color of my skin, so different from that of the others, made him pause. And I, as I said, had no weapon. He seemed unsure whether to leave me or kill me, but he decided on the latter, for he took a step forward with his hatchet raised. As he brought it down, I rolled to the side and he fell on top of me, his weight landing on my hip, his long hair falling on my eyes and blinding me. I could smell him—his sweat, his breathless anger, the snakeskin belt tied around his loins. We wrestled on the ground and I pressed the heel of my hand against his jaw, though my palm slipped against his hairless face. He punched me; I punched back. Still, he managed to right himself up and stand, with his hatchet drawn again. I thought my hour had come, but

God willed that a stray musket ball brought him down. He fell forward and his hatchet grazed my leg, leaving a shallow cut along my shin. I cried out. I do not remember what I said, I imagine it was nothing at all, just a cry of relief at having survived the attack. Then I took the weapon by its handle and, trying to contain the fear inside me, I resolved to defend myself.

I raised myself upon my knees to peer over the stack of crates at the battlefield. Soldiers in armor were firing their crossbows and muskets, and the Indians were fighting back with their lances and arrows. Here and there, a few Indians had managed to inflict grievous harm—a Castilian in a rusty helmet tottered from his mount, his hands gripping the lance that had landed on his thigh; another had fallen from a slingshot strike—but more often, the Indians suffered injury. I remember that one of them, his bowels slipping out from his stomach, was holding on to himself with both arms. Another one screamed as a soldier straddled him and smashed his body with a mace.

I was not a man of arms and I knew nothing of battles, but I could see that this was not a fair match, that the Indians had no hope of winning. Soon, I found myself searching the dusty field for my master, the man to whom my mortal fate was tied. Where was he? Then I saw him, past the line of crossbowmen, riding on his horse. With his sword, he hacked an Indian on the shoulders until blood sprayed out from him. The man fell down to his knees, and Señor Dorantes trampled him as he moved on to the next. The other horsemen, too, had come upon the same solution; they crushed the Indians before them on the field in a savage stampede.

Then there came the sound of a horn and the Indians began to retreat. The sun had set now and it was difficult for me to make out the faces of all those who lay on the ground. As I walked, I was guided more by the sound of soldiers knocking the Indians about and the smell of dust and smoke than I was by sight alone. O Lord, I thought, what am I doing here in this strange land, in the middle of a battle between two foreign peoples? How did it get to this? I was still standing there, stunned and motionless, when torches were lit and names were called. Settlers and friars trickled in from wherever they had found some cover—a crate, a tree, or even a corpse. Behind us, the Río Oscuro rumbled, flowing unceasingly toward the ocean.

2.

THE STORY OF MY BIRTH

My mother once told me that I had been destined for a life of travel. The signs, she said by way of proof, had been there on the day of my birth. At that time, my father was a newly credentialed notary, with ambition to match his youth, but he found it nearly impossible to earn decent wages in Fes. You see, the city was overrun with refugees from Andalusia, Muslims and Jews who had fled the forced conversions. Among these exiles were many famous jurists and experienced notaries. So when news reached my father that the town of Melilla—less than three days away by horse—had fallen to the Crown of Castile, his first thought was that there would be even more refugees in the city and even less work. He decided that he and my mother should move south to Azemmur, where he was born, where his brothers still lived, and where he could, without shame, call upon them if ever he needed help.

But the story of my birth began long before I tumbled forth into this world. It began when one empire was falling and another was rising. It began, like a thousand other stories, in Fes. My mother, Heniya, was the youngest of nine children, the only girl, and my grandfather's favorite. When she turned fifteen, he had agreed to let her marry a wealthy rug merchant, someone he thought would take good care of her, but the merchant died just three months later in a fight with two of the sultan's mekhazniya. Her second husband, an old and wise tailor, died of a high fever less than a year after their marriage. Of course, accidents and disease were a part of life, but it seemed that Heniya had received an unusual share of them at an early age. People began to talk about the unlucky bride, twice widowed by the time she was seventeen. As the gossip was told and retold around town, it acquired the embellishments any good story deserves: my mother was a young maiden of unparalleled beauty, unrivaled virtue, and uncommon talent, she could play the lute and recite poetry, but, oh how unlucky she was in matters of matrimony!

When the story came back to my grandfather, he was the first to believe it, in spite of the fact that my mother was rather plain and had no special musical talents. He had been given to despair, but now he decided that there was a simple way to break her curse. Instead of an old and wealthy husband, she needed a young and healthy one. My grandfather was a chandler by profession, a popular man whose clients included the hospice of el-Maristan, the madrassat el-Attarine, and the hammam es-Seffarine. He was delivering a batch of candles to the college of the Qarawiyin one morning when he saw my father, Muhammad, reclining against a pillar in the main hall.

My father was resting his aching back, but in the half-light of the early morning, he looked like a pensive, earnest student. As my grandfather lowered the bronze chandelier and began to replace the candles, he struck up a conversation with the young scholar. He learned that my father studied shari'a, that he planned on becoming a notary, and, most interesting of all, that he was a boarder. For my grandfather, these details had an advantageous interpretation: Muhammad was ambitious, he would soon have an income, and, since he had no relatives in Fes, he would surely agree to live with his wife's family. My grandfather concluded that Muhammad was the perfect match for Heniya.

It was true that my father was tall and well built, but his appearance belied his true nature. As a child in Azemmur, he had barely survived the measles, and he had subsequently caught every other disease that swept through town. If he swam in the Umm er-Rbi' River, he caught a cold, even in the summer. If he raced with his friends through the alleyways of the medina, he was the one to fall and sprain his knee. If he walked around barefoot, his big toe was sure to find a stray nail. He came from a family of carpenters, but early on his father had decided that there was no point in training him, like his other children, into the craft. That was how Muhammad had ended up at the town school and, later, at the Qarawiyin. Studying seemed to be the only activity that caused him neither sickness nor injury.

When my father met Heniya's father, each saw in the other something he desired. Muhammad had already heard about Heniya's legendary beauty and her many talents, so he was keen to satisfy his curiosity. My grandfather, meanwhile, thought that this handsome young man would finally break his unlucky daughter's curse. There followed an invitation to tea, a quick glimpse behind a curtain, and in short order my parents were married. After my father recovered from the shock of discovering that my mother was not Scheherazade, he tried to make the most of it. He finished his studies and, between bouts of cold, fever, or fatigue, he looked for work. That was when he noticed that Granadans were everywhere. Not only did they have credentials and experience, but they also had an exotic appeal my father could never match. With the fall of Melilla to the Crown of Castile, he decided to move back to Azemmur with my mother, now pregnant with me. This caused great consternation among his in-laws, who, incidentally, were also recovering from the shock of discovering that my father was not Antara on his steed.

When they set out on the long road to Azemmur—my father on foot, my mother on the black pannier-laden donkey that had been given to her as a wedding gift—dark clouds followed them all the way to the coast, so that it seemed to them they were being chased from one end of the country to the other. It was an early fall that year. The weather was cooler than usual and frequent showers impeded their progress. They did not reach the mouth of the Umm er-Rbi' River until late afternoon two days later. Across the water, the eleven minarets of Azemmur must have seemed to them like so many welcoming hosts. They must have been eager to get to my uncle's house, where they could have a bowl of hot soup while they warmed themselves by the side of the brazier. They sat under a cluster of fig trees to wait for the barge. My mother began to feel uncomfortable, but she did not want to alarm my father because, by her calculations, she was not due for another two months.

Ordinarily, the crossing of the river does not take much time at all, but on that particular day, after my father and the other travelers haggled about the price of their passage and loaded their belongings, it was almost dusk. Just as the barge was ready to depart, two Portuguese horsemen arrived, trailing a prisoner. The city of Azemmur had been under vassalage to Manuel the Fortunate for a few years already and none of the travelers, burdened by Portuguese taxes, could abide the sight of these two men of arms. Still less could they bear to see that the prisoner was one of their own, a young woman whose veils had been removed and whose hands were bound by chains. Red, blistered strokes ran down her face and arms.

The two soldiers were tall and their helmets and armor looked heavy, perhaps too heavy for the current trip. The barge itself was not very large—the wooden platform built between two feluccas and towed from either side of the river could fit only a dozen passengers—and it soon became clear that one animal had to be let out if the soldiers and their horses were to get on board. The head ferryman asked the soldiers to wait until he returned, but they refused.

My father intervened; he was one of only two travelers with a donkey and, if anyone were to disembark, it might have to be him. Addressing the soldiers haltingly in their native language, he explained that he and my mother had been on the road since before dawn, that their luggage had already been loaded, and that it would not take long for the ferry to return. The soldiers replied that they were expected at their garrison and, in any case, they should have priority over civilians—vassals, at that.

The sun had begun to set now and the call for the evening prayer resonated from the minarets across the river. A cold wind blew. My father pulled the hood of his jellaba over his head. He was a soft-spoken man who was known for his ability to negotiate—after all, that was what his occupation often demanded—but on that day he suddenly and inexplicably opted for confrontation. Why should you have right of way? he demanded. He put his left hand on one of the horses' bridle as he spoke. His voice croaked, so unused was he to speaking to soldiers. And what has this poor girl done? Why do you have her in chains?

How dare you question me? one of the soldiers replied. He drew his sword and, despite cries of Wait, wait, from his companion, he struck my father on the shoulder.

All at once, my father fell to the ground, my mother ran off the barge screaming, and the soldier sheathed his sword. My mother dropped to her knees next to my father. Sidi Muhammad, she called. Sidi Muhammad, are your hurt?

On my father's gray jellaba, the neat hole made by the sword was blooming red. The travelers and ferrymen gathered around, giving advice, clucking their tongues, or elbowing each other for a better look.

He needs to be taken across the river right away.

Lift him up against that fig tree.

Take off his turban, it looks too tight.

Brother, give him some water to drink.

What good will water do? He is bleeding, not fasting.

At least I am offering advice, not just standing there like some people.

My mother pressed her palms on the wound and called for a candle from her basket so she could take a better look. My grandfather, may God have mercy on his soul, had sent her on the road with plenty of his stock. The Portuguese soldier calmly tethered his horse to a post and went to pull the donkey off the barge, but the poor animal twitched its long ears, turned its head sideways, and refused to move.

Come help me, the soldier said to his companion. The two men, each one with a strap in his hand, dragged the donkey forward, but the travelers held it back from its saddle. First, you kill a man, they said, and now you want to steal his donkey? Meanwhile, the head ferryman searched the donkey's panniers for the bundle of candles my mother needed.

The commotion must have flustered the animal, because it began to bray. Out of solidarity, the other donkey on the barge took up the call. Donkeys, as anyone who has owned one will tell you, are loud. They can be heard for leagues around. If you happen to be near a particularly vocal one, it can be very unpleasant, which is exactly what everyone on the eastern bank of the Umm er-Rbi' experienced on that fall evening of the year 903 of the Hegira. The deafening noise made everyone cover their ears, so no one heard my mother say that she was feeling the early contractions of labor.

One of the travelers, perhaps remembering the saying of our Messenger, as recorded by Abu Huraira—when you hear a cock crow, ask for God's blessing, for their sound indicates they have seen an angel, and when you hear a donkey bray, seek refuge in God for their sound indicates they have seen Satan—picked up a heavy stone and threw it at the soldiers. Others soon joined him, though it was dark by then and no one could see anything. The wind moaned, the horses heaved, the donkeys brayed, people shrieked.

At last, one of the ferrymen managed to light a candle. He lifted it up. The horses had somehow untethered themselves and ambled away, dragging their prisoner. The soldiers dropped the man they had been beating and ran after them. The travelers sat up, rubbing their heads or limbs where the stones of fellow travelers had struck them. As for my father, he still lay where he had fallen, contemplating the scene with impotent fury.

The ferrymen told everyone to get back on the barge immediately, before the Portuguese soldiers returned. The travelers carried my father aboard, seating him gingerly next to his belongings. With difficulty, my mother walked on. Hurry, she told the ferryman, this child is on its way.

The anchor was hoisted, and the barge glided on the river, now as dark as olive oil in a jar. By then, my mother's pain had grown so intense that she settled herself on her knees and began to push. My father asked her whether she needed anything. I need to be home, she said.

So it was that she pushed me out into the world, on the barge that carried her from one bank to the other, my father bleeding by her side. She said that she did not cry, that the violence that had been visited on my father had silenced her pain.

When they arrived in Azemmur, a porter helped my mother, my father, and me onto his cart and took us home, while our belongings followed behind on the donkey. As they walked through the gate of the medina, my mother turned to my father and said, I want to name him Mustafa. My father did not reply; he had fainted.

All three of us—father, mother, and newborn child—were carried into our new home. My uncle Abdullah went to fetch the doctor while the neighbors on either side of the house came to help: the men lifted my father onto his bed, where he would be more comfortable; the women washed and dressed me, then handed me to my mother to nurse; the children moved our belongings out of the doorway and into the courtyard.

The doctor was a Jew, a man by the name of Benhaim al-Gharnati, whose reputation had extended throughout the city in just a few short years. (Knowing of my father's resentment of refugees, however, no one told him that his doctor was originally from Granada.) Benhaim wore the customary black and had a long beard, white save for a few strands of dark hair. Unwrapping the haik my mother had used to tie the wound, he cut through the jellaba and undershirt with scissors. The wound was very deep, the sword having gone through all the way to the other side, and strips of skin were floating in the puddle of blood. The doctor cleaned the wound and dressed it, but warned that my father was showing signs of disease. This muscle, he said, pointing to the shoulder, is becoming rigid. This is not a good sign. Not good at all.

It surprised neither of my uncles to hear this diagnosis. If there had been even a small chance of getting an infection, my father, they knew, would not miss it. In spite of the torrential rain, the doctor returned every day for a week to check on my father, the expression on his face getting grimmer each day.

On the seventh day after our return to Azemmur, our house filled with guests to celebrate my birth. The men gathered around my father, read verses from the Qur'an, and asked the Most High to bring His blessings upon me. The women gathered around my mother, painted her hands with henna, and brought her amulets to protect me against evil and injury. But the following morning, the doctor returned, this time to amputate my father's left arm. And so my mother spent the next few weeks attending to her men folk, both of them helpless and wholly dependent on her.

The first time my mother told me this, the Story of My Birth, I was only a boy of five, still prone to hide in the folds of her caftan, reluctant to leave her side and venture out alone into the streets of Azemmur. She said that I was born on a river, which could only mean that I was fearless then, and that I should be brave now. I should run to the stall around the corner and buy her the lamp oil she needed, even though it was getting dark.

But the second time she told me this story, it was many years later, when she had despaired of making me listen to reason, when she had lost hope that I would remain in Azemmur. She said I had been destined for a life of travel. But she could just as easily have prophesied that, having been born on the day my father stood up to the Portuguese soldiers, I had been destined for a life of war, or that, having endured a riot before my arrival, I had been destined for a life of survival, or that, having been born to a crippled father, I had been destined for a life of loss. If only I could see her now, I would tell her that all these destinies were mine in the end, and that God, in His bountiful mercy, had sent multiple signs, though in her desire to prepare herself and me for what was yet to come, she had noticed only two.

OF THE TEN YEARS that followed my birth, I can only say that they were happy, maybe even the happiest of my life. We lived with my uncle Abdullah and his family in an old house with whitewashed walls and a creaky blue door, down the street from the gates of the medina. The air

inside smelled of bread and wood, and it was full of a constant, comforting noise—someone was always calling out for a child, or grinding
herbs in the mortar, or running up the stairs in slippered feet, or sharing
a story around the evening brazier. My uncle Abdullah was older than my
father by five years, though he treated my father with the deference and
respect due to an older sibling. My uncle Omar, the middle brother, had
recently gained admission into the carpentry guild and lived with us, too,
occupying one of the four rooms around the center courtyard. He had
never married, a fact that filled both my mother and my aunt Aisha with
disquiet. They often wondered out loud what was wrong with him, why
he had not taken a wife. It was true that he had a lazy eye, but that alone,
they said, could not account for his reluctance. Later they clucked and
argued with each other about whose turn it was to wash his clothes, mend
his jellabas, or serve his meals. And later yet they felt only relief, because
his bachelorhood meant fewer mouths to feed.

After my father lost his left arm, he became known around town as
Muhammad the Lame. You might think this was an impediment to his
business, but the opposite was true: his nickname made it easier for him
to stand out among all the other notaries and to be remembered whenever his services were needed. Do you need to record a deed? people
said. Just go to Muhammad the Lame, he will take care of it. Or: If you
wish to divorce that wife of yours, at least go to Muhammad the Lame, he
will be discreet. Or: Talk to that shifty judge if you must, but make sure
Muhammad the Lame is there to record what he said.

Over the years, my father gained a reputation as a reliable and faithful
notary, whose demeanor mirrored the feelings most appropriate for the
occasion—joy at a wedding, disappointment in a divorce, delight at a new
sales contract, or sadness at the severing of a partnership. In this way, he
came to know nearly everyone on our side of the medina, speaking with
them on the most significant days of their lives and witnessing their most
private emotions.

Sometimes, my father hired out his donkey to farmers or merchants
in the area, either to supplement his earnings or to help out a friend.
Other times, my mother found work as a bridal attendant at lavish weddings, but my father rarely let her because he disapproved of such osten-
tatious displays of joy. My parents were further blessed with the birth of
three other healthy children—my sister, Zainab, and my twin brothers,

Yahya and Yusuf. My uncle Abdullah, who had four daughters of his own, treated my brothers and me as the sons he never had. We were not rich but, as I said, we were happy.

When I turned seven, my father bought me a jellaba made from the finest wool in Azemmur, and took me to meet the fqih of our mosque. My father wanted me to learn how to read, memorize the Holy Qur'an, and later attend the Qarawiyin, in the hope that I might take up the same profession as him. Azemmur was a growing town, my beloved father reasoned, and a growing town required deeds and contracts, which he could easily and frequently imagine me drafting by the light of a candle. This image of me as a dutiful recorder of events in other people's lives did not particularly inspire me. At the msid, I listened to the day's lessons, but all too often I wondered why I was not allowed to go play on the street, like all the other children in the neighborhood.

My sense of this injustice was especially strong on Tuesday, which was market day, because the other boys were able to run around, exploring stalls, eating sweetmeats, watching a dancer or a snake charmer, or otherwise getting into mischief, while I had to sit in a dark, musty classroom with my fqih. Before long, I began to skip school in order to indulge in my favorite pastime—visiting the souq. There, I watched fortune-tellers, faith healers, herbalists, apothecaries, and beggars. They promised a healthy child, a painless life, a pliant husband, a dutiful wife, or a path to heaven, perhaps different versions of the same things, but the stories they told or foretold comforted people, inspired them, allowed them to imagine a future they had denied themselves.

One Tuesday, I noticed a new tent at the market. It was made of a ghostly black fabric and, unlike the other tents in its row, it was closed. Eager to satisfy my curiosity, I lifted a side flap and slipped inside without being seen. It took a moment for my eyes to adjust to the darkness and the suppressed heat. The rank odor of men's sweat mixed with the smell of steaming tripe that drifted from the stall across the way. But, after a moment, I was able to make out two dozen spectators, men of different ages and stations, merchants in linen cloaks, farmers in patched jellabas, or Jews in customary black. They sat in a circle around a narrow cot, on which a man, naked save for his seroual, lay facedown. He looked asleep. Over him stood a tall and turbaned healer, with piercing eyes and large nostrils.

The healer spoke with a lilting voice and had an accent I was too young to place. This poor man, he said, suffers from constant pain in his shoulders and neck. By day, it torments him and prevents him from doing his work. By night, it tortures him and keeps him from sleep. Oh, what kind of a life is this? I ask you. How can a man endure so much grief? The elders teach us: if you are a peg, endure the knocking, but if you are a mallet, proceed with the strike. Today I will show you that you do not have to be a peg. I will begin by preparing this man for treatment.

He rubbed his hands together—I noticed that one of them had an additional finger, sprouting from the thumb—and ran them on the patient's neck and shoulders, massaging them deeply for a few moments. Though I listened to him, I could not take my eyes off his extraneous finger. I wondered if it hurt him, if he used it for grabbing things, if it made it easier or harder for him to eat or to wash. And I suppose I also wondered why a healer could not find a way of curing himself before he attended to other people's ailments.

Now the healer took a glass cup, turned it upside down, and placed a candle inside it until he was satisfied that the glass was hot. In the name of God, he whispered, and, in a swift motion, he removed the candle and placed the hot glass on the man's back. The skin lifted inside the glass like fine dough on a hot pan.

Hijama, the healer said, can relieve pain, whether old or new. It improves the flow of blood in your body, it builds up your endurance, it restores your youth. If you fall from a horse and sprain your knee, if you slip on the floor of the hammam and hurt your back, if you carry crates in the port and injure your shoulders—all these things can be helped with hijama.

Now the patient was covered with hot glasses, little towers of different colors on the black field of his back. Though it was unbearably hot in the tent by then, he did not move or complain—a good sign, I thought. When the healer began taking the glasses off, each one left behind it a raised circle.

The tent was silent now, united in its desire to see whether the treatment would work. The patient took a deep breath, as if waking from a long and pleasant dream. It was only when he sat up that I noticed he had only one arm, but before I could turn on my heel, I came face-to-face with my father. We stared at each other, each surprised to have found the other in such a place. The healer gave my father a glass of water. Drink, he said, to your health.

But my father pushed the glass away. With his one good hand, he pulled me up by the hood of my jellaba and kicked me all the way back to the msid, where, upon receiving custody of me, the fqih proceeded to cane my feet until they swelled—my punishment for skipping school.

It was often like this with my beloved father. His years of training at the Qarawiyin had instilled in him a deep belief in the importance of learning, the necessity of discipline, and the rightness of our faith. Unlike my mother, who nourished me with stories, both real and imagined, my father, though he loved me, often spoke to me only to correct me or to advise me, and so I learned to keep my peace whenever I was in his presence. Hoping to cure me of my love for the souq and to breed in me an interest in the law, he began to take me with him whenever he met his customers. But I maintained my silence. Silence taught me to observe. Silence made me invisible to those who speak. Year after year, I witnessed my father write contracts for other people, and I began to wonder what it would be like to be a rich merchant, instead of a simple recorder.

3.

THE STORY OF THE ILLUSION

The three Castilians who were killed in the Battle of the Río Oscuro were buried under the pale light of a crescent moon, in a ceremony overseen by the commissary. In the bushes, the grasshoppers were singing, so the old friar had to raise his voice over their frenetic chants in order to be heard. My brothers, he said. These men of faith and honor were devoted to God our Lord and to His Majesty the King, for it was in the service of both that they came to the Indies. They have fallen in battle, but their courage and sacrifice will remain. The commissary spoke in the level voice and practiced formulas of a cleric who had spent much of his life in the farthest corners of the empire, where death was at once spectacular in its violence and common in its frequency.

The young friars standing behind him looked on with terror, especially the one who was swinging the incense, a wispy lad by the name of Father Anselmo. I remember him well, not just because of what happened much later on the Island of Misfortune, but because he stood out immediately among his brothers in brown robes. He was the youngest of them and yet the tallest; he had thick, carrot-colored hair around his shaved crown; and he was afflicted with a terrible and unpredictable stutter. This impediment made him the occasional target of jokes—good-natured jokes, for the most part, though sometimes people's impatience with him was colored by meanness.

I did not stay to witness the three bodies being lowered into hastily dug graves because I had to prepare the evening meal for Señor Dorantes. When I went to draw water at the Río Oscuro, I found that the Indians killed in the battle, some fifteen of them, had been piled under a cypress tree. The dark heap of bodies, with arms and legs jutting out at odd angles, smelled of decaying flesh. The odor wrapped itself around my throat like a noose and made it impossible for me to breathe. Some of the bodies had been mutilated, I noticed, their noses, ears, or fingers cut out by the soldiers and hung from strings as keepsakes. Flies hovered around in a constant and unnerving drone. Altogether the heap gave me the impression of some creature of the underworld, lying in wait for whoever might cross its path. And indeed the Castilians moved carefully around it, without looking at it or speaking of it, as if they might wake it by sight or speech.

I went about my tasks that night, but all the while I kept thinking that it could have been me in one of the three graves, shovelfuls of earth thrown upon my unwashed and unshrouded body, my soul unprepared for my meeting with the Angel of Death, while a group of Christians above me delivered prayers in a foreign idiom. Or, if the battle had ended differently, if the Indians had won, perhaps I would have been piled with others under a cypress tree, my mortal flesh food for vultures and vermin. Either of these fates was repulsive to me—all I wanted was to return home, where I could die among my own kind.

Sleep eluded me that night. Holding on to my newly acquired hatchet, I tossed and turned, listening to the sound of unfamiliar animals in the distance and trying to ignore the smell of the dead bodies, which had begun to spread all around the camp. As soon as the moon began its descent in the west, I rose to start the fire and prepare the morning meal. Sunlight found me on the bloodstained riverbank, gathering my master's things and getting ready for the march to Apalache.

Señor Dorantes was a light traveler. Many of the items he had chosen to bring from the Gracia de Dios—his clothes, linens, dishes, a few jars of salve, some cotton padding for his armor, a set of scales—fit in one traveling bag, which this servant of God had to carry on his back. But the other noblemen were less practical. In his saddlebag, the young Señor Castillo carried his treasured but cumbersome chessboard, which was a gift from his deceased brother. For this reason, he never lent it to others who might wish to play with it, but only used it for himself and his closest friends. As for Señor Cabeza de Vaca, the treasurer, he had brought with him several leather-bound books of poetry. Whenever he found the time, he would open one of his books at a random page and begin to read, sometimes declaiming the verses of Garcilaso de la Vega for the enjoyment of the other officers: cuando me paro a contemplar mi estado, y a ver los pasos por do me han traído . . .

Once the company was ready to depart, the governor forced his Indian captives down a native path that led deep into the wilderness. Take us to Apalache, he commanded. He followed them on horse, with his officers trailing behind him, their armor clanging and creaking in the quiet morning air. The gray metal of their livery looked out of place in the wilderness, alien and uncomfortable.

As the sun rose in the sky, the air grew hot and damp. Farther away from the river, the horses began to kick up dust, which made it even more difficult to breathe, so I wrapped a rag around my nose and mouth, in the style of the caravan merchants who came to Azemmur from the south. They would dismount in the marketplace, calling out to one another to water the animals or set up a tent, and then they would slowly unwrap their blue scarves from their heads and faces, revealing a dyed beard or a beaked nose or a surprisingly young face. My friends and I would run up to them to find out what they were bringing for sale on market day, whether it was jars of indigo and argan oil, or trinkets of gold and silver, or something else entirely, something exotic we could puzzle over as we sat in throngs, cracking sunflower seeds and watching the tents being set up. Memories of my hometown came to me at odd moments, just like this, when I least expected them, as if my grief liked to ambush me. I tried to push the images to the back of my mind, telling myself I would think of them only when I had a quiet moment alone.

Are they any good? Señor Dorantes asked suddenly. He was speaking of the fruits of the Florida palm trees, which I picked as we marched, collecting them in the pocket of my breeches so that I could eat them at mealtimes. Their strange taste had already grown ordinary on my tongue.

I pulled the rag from my face. They are fine, Señor.

My master's hair had already started to grow, shooting out in tiny spikes from beneath his helmet. He rode with his back very straight, one fist holding the reins and the other resting on his thigh. We were in a clearing now, but in spite of the sun and the heat the horse shivered.

Abejorro's ears are leaning sideways, Señor Dorantes said.

He loved that horse dearly, had been riding him since he was a young lad on his father's estate near Salamanca, and was particularly sensitive to his moods and needs. I stepped out of my master's shade to get a better look at Abejorro; it was true, his ears were lowered.

I hope, Señor Dorantes said, his tone halfway between a warning and a threat, that you haven't been giving him some of that fruit you keep eating.

No, Señor.

A horde of mosquitoes moved drunkenly toward me, and I untied the red rag from my neck to swat at them. They were diabolically persistent, a species unlike any I had seen before, a torment for every one of us. All day long, the mosquitoes hummed and the men slapped their arms and legs, like a procession of penitents. I yearned for some lemon and garlic, a mixture my mother used to rub on me to protect me from these parasites in the summer, but despite its richness the Land of the Indians did not have any lemon trees.

That palm fruit could make him sick, my master said.

I did not give it to him, Señor.

As if to expose my lie, Abejorro's stomach growled loudly, to which my master responded by casting me a grim look. I had grown attached to Abejorro during the journey across the Ocean of Fog and Darkness, so I hated to see him remain hungry after he had finished his feed. I had given him only a small handful of fruit. Now I put my ear on his belly, just behind his ribs, but the gurgling sounds I heard seemed ordinary to me.

If anything happens to my horse, my master said, I will flog you.

The memory of the Indians being whipped came to me, unbidden. It seemed to me I could still hear their howls of pain reverberating against the walls of the storehouse in Portillo.

Just then, Abejorro defecated; Señor Dorantes and I both turned to look. It is hard and dry, I said. He needs more water, Señor. That is all.

Señor Dorantes chewed on his lower lip. Although the horses had been watered at the river, they were kept on strict rations during the march, because the porters could not carry large amounts of water and it was impossible to know how long we would have to walk before we came to another clean source.

I will find him some more water, I said.

How?

The ration master is Portuguese. I will speak to him.

Very well.

As I turned to go, my master called after me. Estebanico.

Señor?

Do not get caught.

The governor was exceedingly strict about rations, so of course I had to be discreet. I walked back to the end of the procession until I found the ration master. He was a man of middle age, with a sweaty forehead and a thick beard. I did not know him well, having conversed with him only when necessity demanded it. Still, I made my request, speaking to him not in Spanish but in his native language, which I had learned as a child in Azemmur. I hoped that this would earn me some goodwill, but his only reply was to ask me, Why should I give you more water?

I told you. My master's horse is ill.

You know the rules.

The horse could die in this heat. Have some mercy, I beg you.

Mercy is from God. I only ration the water.

But I have no money.

You have this.

The ration master reached for the hatchet I had tied around my neck, and which I had taken from the Indian who had tried to kill me. As a slave in Seville, I had not been allowed to carry a weapon, but here in the Indies, Señor Dorantes had not asked me to relinquish this native ax. Its blade was made of limestone, so finely sharpened it could easily cut through thick pinewood, and its handle was painted in a pattern of white and blue stripes. I put my hand on the weapon to stop the ration master from taking it. It was the only means I had to defend myself in case of an attack. But when I thought of what might happen if Abejorro fell ill—and what might happen to me as a result—I relented. Gingerly, the ration master put his finger on the blade, and when it cut a sliver of his skin, he whistled in admiration. Let him take the hatchet, I said to myself. Let him take the hatchet if it means I can help Abejorro and elude the whip.

Well done, Señor Dorantes said when I reported to him that I had secured a larger ration for the horse. He did not ask how I had managed that feat. Instead, he turned back toward the sunlight and I took my usual place, one step behind him, in his shadow.

THE GOVERNOR HAD ORDERED the Indian captives to take us to the kingdom of Apalache, but they led us into a village of thatched-roof dwellings, arranged in a half-moon against a horizon of pine trees. It was barely larger than Portillo, the fishing settlement where I had found the gold. Inside the firepits, I noticed, the ash was fine and white. Animal bones, all of them picked clean, were drying in the sun. A lone sandal sat in the middle of the square. The colors of the village—the brown of thatched roofs, the red of doorway blankets, the green of ripening corn in the field—seemed to blend together in the hazy heat. I felt dizzy and had to steady myself against Abejorro's saddle.

From the height of his horse, with his hand shielding his eyes from the light, Señor Narváez spoke: Search the village.

His page repeated the order in a loud voice, so that no one would miss it. Search the village!

The soldiers fanned out through the settlement. They turned the blankets upside down, patted the animal hides that hung on rails, ran their hands through stored beans, checked water urns, and looked inside cooking pots, but none of them reported any trace of gold.

By then, I had tethered Abejorro to a tree and was following Señor Dorantes and Señor Castillo as they walked about. They went in and out of a few homes—simple huts that contained little more than bedding made of animal fur, baskets for storing food, or a few children's toys. Then they entered the largest lodge, which was the temple. It had a high ceiling and a dirt floor, now covered with the soldiers' bootprints. A few wooden idols sat along the far end of the lodge, three in the shape of eagles and two in the shape of panthers. Hanging from the ceiling on opposite walls were a dozen ceremonial headdresses, of the same kind as those we had seen in Portillo.

The two señores were walking back and forth along the temple walls, looking for anything of value, when suddenly Señor Castillo stopped in front of one the headdresses; it stood out from the others because it had red and yellow parrot feathers instead of black and brown hawk feathers. The leather strap that maintained the parrot plumes in place was decorated with a multitude of beads and charms, arranged in several neat rows. Señor Castillo unhooked the headdress from its string and in a voice high with excitement he called out: Dorantes. Look at this.

In three strides, my master was standing beside his friend. Señor Castillo dislodged one of the charms with his thumbnail and held it up to the light that came in from the doorway. Motes of dust floated in the air, which carried with it the faint smell of pine trees. In the distance, a horse moaned with exhaustion.

Gold? Señor Dorantes whispered.

His tone was conspiratorial. Instantly, I was reminded of the time he had asked this servant of God to commit a sin on his behalf: to eavesdrop on a private meeting. This happened in Santo Domingo, on the island of La Española, where the armada had stopped for supplies on its way to La Florida. Señor Cabeza de Vaca, the treasurer, had asked to speak to Señor Narváez in private, a request that made my master think he was trying to arrange for a position as lieutenant governor of the new territory. While the treasurer and the governor ate their lunch in the dining room of an inn, I sat underneath the open window and listened. If I had been found, I knew, my master would have denied any knowledge of my mission and instead would have beaten me for spying on his gentleman friends.

It was a hot, humid day, but even as sweat trickled down my back and with a fly exploring the spaces between my toes, I did not dare move a muscle. I could hear the governor complaining about how difficult it was to find an experienced pilot. None of those I have spoken to, he was saying, are familiar with the western seas.

He threw a chicken bone out of the window—uncouth behavior, but it did not surprise me coming from him—and it landed in one of the bushes on my left. I flattened my back against the wall even further.

I have heard of one pilot, Señor Cabeza de Vaca replied, by the name of Miruelo, who claims he was part of the voyage of Ponce de León, and that he can take us to La Florida.

For the remainder of the meal, they discussed hiring this man. I did not hear Señor Cabeza de Vaca ask for the position of lieutenant and I did not hear the governor promise him one, yet when I reported the conversation to Señor Dorantes, his doubts grew stronger, not weaker. My master was an ambitious man, and ambition made him suspicious of his rivals.

Señor Castillo had trouble removing the rest of the golden charms with his thumbnail, for they were sealed to the leather with glue.

Here, I said, offering him my rusty pocketknife.

Perfect, Señor Dorantes said, patting me on the back. This gesture, this little gesture, nourished the dream I had conceived when I found the pebble of gold.

Once the headdress was stripped of its spangles, we returned to the square, just in time to hear the governor say that he had given the name Santa María to the village. He received the charms from Señor Castillo's cupped hands and examined them under the harsh afternoon sun. Then he sent spit shooting out of his mouth in a long, straight line. This is gold, he confirmed.

The charms were passed around to the handful of officers and friars who were standing near the governor. A mosquito flew into one of Señor Cabeza de Vaca's ears and he slapped himself, tilting his head sideways to get it out, but all the while he held on to one of the golden charms, turning it between his fingers. The commissary was saying something about the urgency of destroying the heathen idols in the temple. Quietly, the governor spoke. Did anyone else find any gold?

The captains stopped talking and looked at each other. One of them had found an arrowhead made of gold and another had come across what looked like a small silver earring, but no one had brought back as much gold as Señor Castillo. So this is all of it, Señor Narváez said.

Señor Castillo cleared his throat and seemed about to say something when the governor held up his palm to stop him. In a thin voice, he ordered one of the carpenters and one of the prisoners brought to him. From the carpenter, a Portuguese man with a slight limp and a bushy beard, who went by the name of Álvaro Fernándes, he borrowed a hammer and nails. Then he had two of his soldiers force the Indian prisoner to sit on his knees, with his hands before him, in a pose that reminded me of a man at prayer.

Listen to me carefully, the governor said. Is this Apalache?

The prisoner nodded. He was thin and very long-limbed, and on his right shoulder there was a birthmark in the shape of a circle.

This is Apalache? The governor crouched in front of the man, so that he could look him in the eye.

The prisoner nodded again. His eyes were like dark pools, filled to the brim with attention.

It cannot be Apalache. There is little gold here.

The man seemed to hesitate now. Then he nodded again.

Are you telling me the truth? And with this, the governor brought the hammer down on the man's little finger.

Howling with pain, the man yanked his hand, but the soldiers restrained him and put it back down on the ground. The shattered nail oozed blood, and the knuckle was broken.

Fernándes, the carpenter whose innocent tools had been turned into instruments of torture, walked away toward the huts, but all the officers stood, waiting for an answer to the governor's question. Where is Apalache?

I wish I could say that I protested. I wish I could say that I enjoined the governor to leave the poor man alone. But I was afraid to speak. I am a slave now, I told myself, I am not one of them. I cannot interfere in matters between the Spaniards and the Indians.

The governor hammered another finger, blind to the blood that now streaked the earth.

Señor, I whispered, shall I go prepare you something to eat? I wanted to walk as far away from the square as I could, to go someplace where I would not have to see what was being done to the prisoner. Señor Dorantes did not hear me or did not wish to answer. I tried again—louder this time. Señor.

My master finally turned toward me, but before he could answer, someone called out, Don Pánfilo, please. Please. It was the youngest of the friars, Father Anselmo, leaning so far forward he seemed about to fall. With all eyes on him now, his voice rose to a higher register, and he began to stutter. P-p-please stop, he said. Th-th-this man d-d-does not know a-a-anything.

The commissary gave Father Anselmo a deeply censuring look, and the red-haired friar bit his lower lip, as if to force himself to say no more. His face, already burned by the sun, turned a dangerous shade of pink. Now he cast his eyes down on his sandaled feet, like a reprimanded child. From somewhere near the village came the call of a strange animal—I could not tell if it was beast or fowl—but otherwise it was quiet, all the officers waiting for the governor to say something in return.

Señor Narváez stood up slowly and, rubbing the soreness from his knees, handed the hammer to his page. Take the prisoner away, he said.

BUT THE INTERROGATIONS DID not stop—they continued for several days, in the privacy of a special hut. Señor Narváez was nothing if not a patient and thorough man. In the presence of at least one of his officers, he spoke to each prisoner and then compared the prisoner's answers to the ones that had been given by the others. After he had questioned all of them, he did it again, perhaps to see if they had changed their minds. Whenever the guards walked a prisoner back to the holding cell, the commissary and one of his friars would appear. The first would go to the governor to inquire about the progress of the investigation; the other would wash the Indians' wounds and dress them in strips of cloth.

So for a few days, I was spared the sight of pain. I heard the howling, but I did not have to see it. Still, as I swept the hut that had been requisitioned for Señor Dorantes, as I picked corn for his meals or washed his clothes with the last scrap of Castile soap I still had—women's tasks, tasks my bondage had reduced me to and from which I longed to be freed—I had ample time to imagine the prisoners' pain. I knew what it was like to be whipped, to protest, to proclaim one's innocence only to be whipped with greater fury, and to find that the beatings subside only in the face of complete and unquestioning surrender. On my neck, I still had a scar made by the heel of my first owner, a man everyone in Seville regarded as kind and devout and generous. Señor Dorantes had not beaten me, but that did not mean that he would not start—all it meant was that I had managed to avoid his ire thus far.

It took me a day and a half to gather the courage to smuggle some food to the Indians. I could not give them nuts or fruit, because I feared that the guards would find an errant nut or a fallen seed, and would question the prisoners about its provenance. Using an Indian pestle and mortar, I ground some corn and made flatbreads, which I hid until the prison guard had to go to the necessary.

The night was warm and dark. The only light came from the torches that had been placed along the path that led to the river. When I slipped inside the cell, I heard the movements of the prisoners and smelled their presence before my eyes adjusted to the darkness. Two of them lay on blankets in the corner, asleep or pretending to sleep. The others were huddled together, with their knees against their chests. The man whose nails had been hammered in the village square recognized me and recoiled when he saw me reach into my pocket. I brought out the flatbread and pressed it into his bandaged hands. Seeing this, the others reached out for the bread, too. I wanted to speak their language, but I would have needed to spend time with them in order to learn the cadences of their native tongue. For now, silence was our only idiom.

How strange I must have seemed to them: not a conqueror, but the slave of a conqueror, who had brought them the small comfort of a little food. Perhaps this led them to think of me as a good man, a decent man. But these prisoners did not know, and I could not explain to them, that I had once traded in slaves. I had sent three men into a life of bondage, without pausing to consider my role in this evil. Now that I had become a slave myself, it shamed me that, even without meaning to, I still caused the suffering of others. It was my find—the pebble of gold—that had unleashed the violence of Señor Narváez upon them. They had bruises everywhere, on their faces, their chests, their arms, and their legs. Did they know where the kingdom of Apalache was? And would they tell the governor? If I could have spoken their language, I would have counseled them to tell the governor everything, because he was the sort of man who would only desist after he had gained his heart's desire. But not a word passed between us that night. I stepped out carefully and ran back to my sleeping mat, outside Señor Dorantes's lodge, hoping that no one had seen me.

HAVING HAD SO LITTLE SLEEP, I felt especially tired the next morning, and was dozing under the shade of an oak tree. It was warm, but a merciful breeze blew. A few paces away from me, Señor Dorantes was playing a game of chess with Señor Castillo and whenever one of them scored a point, his squeals of delight would jolt me awake. Take that, Gordo, Señor Dorantes said, moving his knight on the board. Gordo was his nickname for Señor Castillo, a little joke at the expense of a young man who, in reality, was very thin.

He had a way with nicknames, my master. Mochuelo was Señor Albaniz, because of his deep-set eyes. Zanahoria was poor Father Anselmo, on account of his red hair. Cabeza de Mono had been my master's little invention, too, though of course he never said it to the treasurer's face. And he had several nicknames for his brother, Diego: Chato, because of his pug nose; Flaco, because he was a little thick around the middle; El Tigre, because he was shy and sometimes even fearful.

Señor Castillo rubbed his chin in an exaggerated manner, as if Señor Dorantes's move had puzzled him, then he slammed his rook down and discarded the knight. And what do you think of that? His voice was filled with childish joy.

I was woken up for good when Señor Narváez walked by, returning from the interrogation cell. For some reason, he was alone, without his page. He wore a red doublet and his boots looked freshly shined in spite of the dust. Buenos días, he said with a friendly smile.

He was already on his way when Señor Castillo stood up suddenly and called after him. Don Pánfilo, if I may have a moment.

The governor gave the young señor a sharp look. Even on the best of days, his black eye patch gave his face a forbidding air, but when he was annoyed the effect could be repulsive. What is it, Castillo?

Don Pánfilo, I noticed that the Río Oscuro had a strong current.

It did indeed. But we managed.

Yes. But I thought—I thought—what if it is a tributary of the Río de las Palmas or even the Río de las Palmas itself? I could take a few men with me and go to where the river meets the ocean. We would look for the port of Pánuco, where we can tell our crews about our location and procure more rations for our march.

The response of Señor Narváez was a mix of disbelief and mockery: You want me to spare rations so you can procure more rations?

It was a mystery to me why a man like the governor, who always welcomed the opinions of his officers, felt the need to belittle the young Señor Castillo, or indeed why Señor Castillo did not respond angrily to the provocations. He was either incapable of noticing them or unwilling to respond to them. Or perhaps he was just young—so young that he had not yet learned to greet the orders of his superiors with meekness and respect.

Don Pánfilo, Señor Castillo said, obviously this is not about the rations.

What is it, then? We will go to the port after we reach Apalache, not before.

Señor Castillo ran his hands through his hair and turned toward Señor Dorantes, who was still seated on an Indian bench beside their game of chess. It was a beautiful board, made with polished ebony and ivory, a bright, clean pattern of white and black. The wind picked up now, rustling the branches of the trees around us and disturbing the shadows on the ground.

Señor Dorantes stood up. I think what Castillo is trying to say is that, as we get farther away from the coast, it is just a good precaution to chart a way to the ships and back.

And what if the Río Oscuro is not a tributary of the Río de las Palmas? the governor asked.

At the very least, Señor Castillo said, the river will lead us to a harbor. We can leave a message on the shore to signal our location. Maybe tie it to a flagpole, so that any passing ship can see it. Just as a precaution.

Fine. Take twenty-five men and go to the port. We will remain in this village for a few more days until I am finished with my investigation.

The governor left, and Señor Dorantes returned to his game of chess. Pavo Real, he said between his teeth.

Pavo Real was the nickname Señor Dorantes had given to Señor Narváez, because the governor took as careful care of his appearance as a peacock. But my master had no nickname for me. A nickname is something you use to tease someone, whether out of spite or out of affection, whereas all the things he called me were said without a hint of humor or irony: El Moro, El Negro, El Arabe. On most days, he did not even call me anything. He did not need to—I was always right behind him.

4.

THE STORY OF AZEMMUR

Listen, my mother said. Let me tell you a story.

She was sitting on a stool, shelling beans into a bowl wedged between her knees. Beside her, on the brazier, the grease from a shoulder of lamb crackled in the cooking pot; from time to time, she prodded the meat with a long-handled spoon and turned it over. Her shadow danced on the kitchen wall, where jars of oil and barrels of wheat and barley were arranged in a neat row. In the space between us, my twin brothers were crawling on the floor, while my sister, Zainab, was kneading dough for the bread, her kerchief slipping halfway down her hair with the force of her movements. When the loaves were ready, I would have to take them to the neighborhood oven, but for now I could still sit by the fire.

It was an afternoon in winter, and the light from the doorway was dim. I had come straight from my father's bedroom, running in my slippers across the wet courtyard to the kitchen; I craved the warmth of the brazier as much as I needed my mother's company. Once again, I had disappointed my father—I had deserted the msid for the souq, where our neighbor Moussa had seen me. With a promptness born of malice, he had reported my whereabouts to my beloved father, who duly questioned me about the day's lessons and found that I had failed to learn them. He had given me a look full of displeasure, which was much worse than if he had punished me, the way he used to when I was a younger boy. Now that I was thirteen, nearly as tall as him, he had taken to quietly shaking his head at my stubborn folly.

Mustafa, my mother said.

I did not reply. I sat with my knees drawn into my chest and, after a moment, I lowered my forehead upon my knees. The scholar's life, which my father worked so hard to provide for me, held neither the dangers nor the delights of the marketplace; I found no enjoyment in it. Worse: I felt guilty for not enjoying it. It seemed to me that I could never measure up to my father's ambitions.

Mustafa, my mother said again.

I looked up. Her face had begun to show signs of middle age, but her eyes were still luminous and kind. My brother Yusuf, perhaps sensing my sadness, had crawled toward me and now he thrust up his stubby fingers in the air, begging to be picked up. I seated him on my knees. He was still teething, and I let him gnaw on one of my fingers.

Listen, my mother said. Once there was and there was not, in olden times, a poor slipper-mender whose wife died in childbirth, leaving him with two boys and an infant girl. The boys he took with him to his work-shop, but the girl he placed with her aunt, who was an embroiderer. The aunt taught the girl everything she knew: how to choose fabric, how to select threads, how to marry colors, how to disguise an imperfect stitch behind a looped one. Best of all, she taught the girl all the embroidery patterns that had been passed down from generation to generation, patterns that could not be trusted to paper, but had to be committed to memory. By the time she was fourteen, the apprentice surpassed the mistress. She even began to invent new patterns. Her fame spread through-out our fortunate kingdom until, one day, a company of women musicians from the sultan's court came to commission caftans from her.

The girl set to work immediately. She chose a dark blue silk, upon which she embroidered eight-pointed stars in silver thread, giving the fabric the appearance of a starry night sky. The caftans, she hoped, would look beautiful on the musicians. But the more she thought about the court, the more curious she became. What did the sultan's palace look like? Was it true, as the musicians had said, that the marble in his court-yard was so clear that you would mistake it for a mirror? Had it really taken ninety-two artisans a year to decorate the ceilings of his reception rooms? Were there truly grapevines hanging over the walls of his court-yard, so that passing guests could eat from them?

To a girl who had spent her entire life bent over her embroidery scrolls, the musicians' stories seemed too good to be true. But Satan, may he be cursed, continued to tempt her. She was so tormented by her curiosity that, surreptitiously, she made one additional caftan—this one for herself—and when the musicians came to pick up their garments, the girl donned the precious caftan and followed them into the palace.

How right the musicians had been! The palace was dazzling. Mouth agape, the girl stared at everything around her. The arched ceilings and colorful rugs were unlike anything she had ever seen in the city. Dozens of guests sat on the divans, attended to by servants who brought in platter after silver platter of succulent dishes. But, while the girl was still entranced by the riches around her, the sultan came in. With his dark turban and his long, green cloak, he was as imposing as a monarch could be. He sat down on the throne and, with a snap of the fingers, asked for wine and entertainment.

The musicians came forward. A hush fell on the assembly at the sight of the magnificent caftans, though the sultan barely took any notice. Then each of the ladies picked up her instrument—the flute, the guenbri, the kamanja. Hoping to keep up her deceit, the girl took up the lute. She knew nothing about music and could not have guessed that she had chosen the most difficult of all instruments. As soon as the company started performing, the sultan frowned. Who dared to play such discordant notes in his presence? The musicians themselves stopped and looked. And the girl, who had foolishly continued to pluck at her strings, was unmasked.

The sultan's mekhazniya fell upon her and, beating her this way and that, threw her out of the palace. Caftan in tatters, feet bare, hands broken, the girl returned home, where her aunt tried to nurse her back to health. But the fractures did not heal properly and the girl's precious fingers became deformed. She could no longer make the delicate patterns that had made her so famous.

My mother had come to the end of her story. Only then did I notice that she had finished shelling the beans and tossed them into the cooking pot. The smell of the meat stew now filled the kitchen. My brother had fallen asleep on my lap, his legs dangling on either side of my knees, his little hand still gripping my finger; now it was covered with baby spittle.

My mother had accustomed me to fairy tales in which it was easy for me to imagine myself, so I remained quiet as I thought about the Story of the Embroiderer and the Sultan. Was I the embroiderer, who should have been content with her gift and not sought out that which was beyond her reach? Or was the story about my father? Was he like the sultan, so enamored with his entertainment that he fails to notice the embroiderer's talent? I could not be sure, but I knew better than to ask her, because my mother would have told me that stories are not riddles; they do not have a simple answer. All I knew was that the weight on my chest no longer felt as heavy, because my mother's stories always entertained me, and, by so doing, soothed me.

You have a story for every occasion, I said. I meant it as a compliment, though I disguised it as a complaint.

Nothing new has ever happened to a son of Adam, she said. Everything has already been lived and everything has already been told. If only we listened to the stories.

Zainab washed the dough from her hands in a bowl of water. She took my brother Yusuf into her arms. The bread is ready, she told me.

But I was still trying to make sense of my mother's story about the embroiderer. If I was like her, then what was my talent? Was it really to become a notary public or could it be something—anything—else?

Still, I picked up the bread tray and, swiftly pulling the hood of my jellaba over my head, went out into the street. The world outside was cloaked in darkness. The lamplighter's rounds had not yet brought him to our street, but I managed to find my way by the glow of the oil lamps in the shops that were still open. A pair of Portuguese soldiers passed me, quarreling in their nasally tongue about something or other. In my pocket was the money my mother had given me, though I did not need it because I had convinced the baker to let me sweep his floors in exchange for baking our bread. With my mother's coins, I thought, I could go to the souq on Tuesday.

IF MY FATHER WAS ASKED about the circumstances under which he lost an arm, he never failed to finish his story by saying he was not sorry to have spoken up about the Portuguese tax. He had reason to repeat this when, one summer afternoon in the year 919 of the Hegira, town criers announced that the governor of Azemmur had refused to pay the tribute to the Christians. Finally! my father said when I told him the news. He was sitting under the pomegranate tree in the courtyard, but even in the shade of its branches I could see his eyes glinting with delight. He drew on his pipe, savored the taste of his kif for a long moment, then tilted his head back to blow out the pale lavender smoke. It was rare for me to see my father display his pleasure in anything, let alone the physical pleasure of smoking. So I sat down across from him and, resting my back against the tiled wall, watched him.

Let me tell you, Mustafa, he said. He launched into the Story of How He Lost His Arm—an account of the events that had taken place on the day I was born and that in my mother's telling I had come to know as the Story of My Birth. My father's tale ended at the moment when his arm was being severed and he lost consciousness. Now he smiled grimly and pointed the stem of his pipe toward me. My son, he said, this country is besieged by Castilians in the north and Portuguese in the west. I tell you, I would give up my other arm if it would free our city from intruders.

I remember being amused by my father's pledge and thinking it nothing more than the bravado of a scholar. But, for several weeks, he was a changed man. He did not haggle over the price of his services; he did not check on my attendance at school; he managed to escape a vicious cold that my brother Yahya had caught; and, rather than rush to the mosque for tarawih prayers, he took the time to linger with us after dinner. And all this, I thought, because the governor had refused to pay the Portuguese? My father and uncles had always paid the tax when it was asked of them, even though they did it grudgingly. My uncles' workshop thrived. All of my cousins had made good marriage matches and a successful metalworker had come that year to speak to my father about Zainab. Our family was known and respected everywhere in Azemmur. Was that not enough? But I had just turned fifteen and I did not yet understand that there are things far more valuable than private comfort or public admiration.

My father's new enthusiasm was dampened only slightly when five hundred Portuguese caravels appeared on the blue horizon of Azemmur. From the rooftop of our home, I saw the ships gliding closer, their billowing white sails dotting the line where the sky touched the ocean. With his usual bluster, my father said: If they want a fight, they will have it.

But in the days that followed, their cannons stayed silent—the Portuguese had chosen the way of the siege. Now we had to live in a state of uncertainty.

That night, I joined my father and uncles for dinner, taking my seat around the copper tray table that was set up in a shaded corner of the courtyard. My twin brothers, who were old enough now to eat their meals with us men, arrived late. Yahya carried the pitcher and the bowl, while

Yusuf had the towel, though they argued about whose turn it was to pour the water over our hands.

But you did it yesterday, Yusuf said, his voice rising to a shrill.

Without spilling half of it on the way, Yahya replied.

I never spill.

Yes, you do.

There is no need to quarrel, I chided. Yusuf, you can carry the pitcher tomorrow, God willing.

We all took turns washing our hands. To put a stop to their squabbling, I separated my brothers, making Yusuf sit on my right side and Yahya on my left.

In the name of God, my uncle Abdullah said, reaching into the dish filled with couscous. Steam rose from the chicken and carrots that lay in the middle, their sweet and savory smells mingling in the air. We began to eat, and, while listening to my father talk about the siege of the harbor, I cut my brothers' meat into pieces small enough for them to handle.

Of course the Portuguese want to hold on to Azemmur, my father was saying, now for the third time. But we will defeat them. You will see. He raised his forefinger in the air, with grains of couscous still stuck to it.

My uncle Abdullah regarded my father with the keen indulgence he always reserved for him, but it seemed he could not hold himself back. How will we defeat them? he asked.

With our soldiers.

Whose soldiers?

The governor's soldiers, of course.

Brother, the governor does not have enough soldiers.

My father was quiet for a moment as he thought about this. Then he sat back against the wall. We can join the governor's forces, he said.

Who will join them?

I will, he said fiercely, his only thumb pointed at his chest.

Come now, Brother, you are not a soldier. This was not said in meanness or in anger, and yet my father remained quiet, as though he had been insulted.

I can fight, I said hotly. And so can you, I told my uncles.

It was my younger uncle, Omar, who replied. My son, what will we fight the Portuguese with? They have eighteen thousand men. They have cannons and weapons and powder and armor and horses, and we have only our tools. The governor barely has three hundred men to his name. We must wait for the sultan in Fes to send his army.

Yes, my father said, his face alight with reckless hope. The sultan will come to our aid. God willing, he will send reinforcements.

Then my father began to tell us how, five and seventy years earlier, the sultan had sent his vizier Yahya al-Wattasi to rescue the city of Tangier from the Portuguese. Al-Wattasi had rallied troops from around the country, forced Henry the Navigator to retreat, and even starved him into submission. It was a story of courage and determination and it sounded so simple, the way he told it: round up all the soldiers and throw out the intruders.

I was about to reply when Yahya found a wishbone. He reached over me to hand it to Yusuf, who innocently took the side presented to him and tugged on it—when the bone broke, he was left with the short end. He put it on the table in front of him and quietly started eating again, ignoring Yahya's mocking smile. Yusuf had a very gentle soul; he always fell for his twin brother's rigged games.

I looked at my father then. His face shone with such hope that I did not have the heart to tell him that when I went to the souq on Tuesday, I had heard rumors that the sultan had sent his army to quell a rebellion in the south. Already, the siege of our harbor had ground all trade with the Christians to a halt and made it impossible to get to the merchandise that sat on the other side of the Umm er-Rbi' River. Even the chicken we were eating I had procured from a merchant for whom I sometimes ran errands, though my father, perpetually engaged in conversations with other notaries and scholars, never suspected it.

A week later, when the Portuguese soldiers started their assault, the governor's forces could offer them little resistance.

Azemmur fell.

Only then did my father's mood turn somber. We should have known better than to rely on that devious sultan, the burtuqali, he said. Muhammad al-Burtuqali had earned his nickname because, as a child, he had been held hostage for seven years by the Portuguese while a treaty between our two kingdoms was negotiated. My father doubted both the will and the ability of a man named Muhammad the Portuguese to actually fight them. Over the next few months, my father and I watched helplessly as a fort was built at the edge of the town, hiding our horizon behind high walls, and a white flag with the red shield of the infidel king was hoisted over the tower. The tax was levied again.

Patience, my father counseled. They will leave. They must.

My beloved father was right.

They did leave, though neither he nor I would be there to witness it.

AFTER THE BATTLE OF AZEMMUR, my father's dark eyes acquired a melancholy expression that never left them. Wrapped in his white linen cloak, he floated quietly in and out of our bustling house, absorbed in thoughts he did not share with any of us. Nothing pleased him—an invitation from my grandfather to visit Fes drew only a shrug of the shoulders; a bowl of pomegranate fruit, lovingly peeled and sprinkled with rosewater, was left untouched next to his pipe; a close shave in the barber's chair no longer brought a smile to his face; a new shirt with silver trimming and black velvet buttons was put on with the same hurry as any old house shirt. And nothing vexed him, either—not my brothers getting into mischief, not my aunt Aisha's terrible cooking, not even my sister playing the tambourine. It is a terrible thing to see your father a broken man, a terrible thing, but I was young and selfish and did not fully understand what was happening to him.

In spite of my lackluster attendance and poor performance, I had eventually learned the principles of Arabic grammar, memorized the Qur'an, and was ready to graduate from the msid. Or perhaps the fqih had tired of me: I was the oldest student in his school now, all of the boys my age having long ago earned their credentials. Either way, I was thrilled to be finished and I hoped that the celebrations we were planning in my honor would lift my father's spirits. It was a spring day, I remember, and the air was filled with the promise of rain. I waited at the door of the msid, surrounded by my schoolmates and my fqih until my uncle Omar brought the horse, a white stallion rented for the occasion and adorned with colorful green garlands. I mounted it and was led through the crooked streets of my hometown, with friends and strangers alike cheering me on, until we reached our house, where my father awaited me. Behind him, the blue door was wide open—I could see our guests and neighbors filling our courtyard, all of them calling out congratulations or trilling joy-cries as I dismounted. I walked into our receiving room and sat on an elevated cushion, surrounded by our guests.

May God bless you, they said.

May He grant you a long life.

I remember the day you were born.

I was the one who carried him through that door.

Look at him now!

A learned man.

Recite something for us, son.

My father offered our guests cakes and sweets, and danced when the guenbri was played, but a part of him, a part more vibrant and more vital than a limb, seemed to me to be absent, as clearly as if it had been severed by a knife. He remained in this contemplative mood all evening, emerging from it only after everyone had left, and it was to ask me what it was I wanted to do with my life. We were alone—my uncles were walking the fqih home and my mother and aunt were cleaning up in the kitchen. All around us were empty platters, half-filled glasses, and cushions strewn on the floor.

I gave my father the dutiful answer he expected of me. Father, I said, I will do whatever you think is best.

But tell me, my son. What do you wish to do?

His eyes seemed softer now and, encouraged by the kindness in them, I managed to say, Father, I want to be a merchant.

A merchant?

If I had said I wanted to become a hammam attendant or a street musician, he would not have looked more surprised. He stared at me speechlessly. The elders teach us: if you must drown, let it be in a deep well, not in a shallow pond. So I went on, Father, I have always liked the souq. I like watching merchants convince buyers with the yarns they spin, how they persuade someone to buy something he did not know he wanted. And then the offer, the haggling, the resolution: all the give-and-take of a sale. That is what I would enjoy doing.

My son, he said, the life of a notary is a noble one. You practice the law that God and His Messenger have laid down for us and you serve the people of your town. You receive honest earnings that can support a home.

A fine occupation, I said.

But you do not wish to be a notary?

No.

Then why not join your uncles in carpentry?

I have no inclination for carpentry, Father.

My father spoke to me at length that day. He told me that I would do well to choose law or carpentry, that law was the labor of the mind and carpentry the labor of the hands, whereas trade was neither. He warned me that trade would open the door to greed and greed was an inconsiderate guest; it would bring its evil relations with it. I should consider, he said, an occupation for which I would be well prepared by my family and which would honor them. But, just as a deaf man cannot heed a warning to watch out for the horse cart, I would not listen to his appeals. And it seemed he no longer had it in him to compel me. I tried to put some sense into you, he said, but I failed.

So my father asked a friend of his, a notary who often worked with the famous al-Dib family, to introduce me to them. The sons of al-Dib were the most successful merchants in town, being the descendants of refugees from Portugal, and therefore fluent in the country's language and familiar with its customs. They warehoused the merchandise they purchased from the Christians and sold it to the Muslims in the Dukkala region, or stored the merchandise they bought from the Muslims and sold it to the Christian merchants. In this way, wheat and barley grown in Dukkala was shipped to Portugal, while Azemmur received glass, cotton, and weapons.

Over the next few years, I learned how to preserve wax from the heat and how to parcel it out, how to tell if a roll of linen was from England or from Flanders, how to transport glass from one end of town to the other without breaking it, how to select the kind of woven materials that would sell in Portugal or Spain, how to clean a weapon of its powder so it would look new, and most of all, how to get the best price for any of the goods in which I traded. I learned a lot from my apprenticeship and eventually I became a trusted partner of al-Dib, earning commissions that made me rich. I had a fireplace built in the largest room of our house; I bought fine rugs and silver chests; I paid for Zainab's wedding.

I felt that I had finally realized my dream, that I had become exactly the sort of man I wanted, a man of means and power, a man whose contracts were recorded by flattering notaries. But as time went on, I fell for the magic of numbers and the allure of profit. I was preoccupied only with the price of things and neglected to consider their value. So long as I managed to sell at a higher price, it no longer mattered to me what it was

I sold, whether glass or grain, wax or weapons, or even, I am ashamed to say, especially in consideration of my later fate—slaves.

THE COMMERCE OF HUMAN FLESH came to tempt me one spring morning when I was negotiating the price of seven loads of wheat destined for Lisbon. The farmer selling the grain, a middle-aged man with a narrow face and thin lips that gave the impression of avarice, brought with him three slaves he had unexpectedly inherited from an old uncle. Do you know of a buyer? he asked me, lifting his skullcap and scratching his head. His accent hinted to an upbringing deep in the country, somewhere east of Khenifra.

Why do you want to sell them? I asked.

I know not what else to do with them, he replied. They are too old to be of much use to me on the farm. Still, this one is a good cobbler and the other two can work metal.

The cobbler had small, heavy-lidded eyes that seemed to take no interest in the world they beheld. But the two metalworkers watched me, their eyes pleading silently as I dug my hands inside each bag of wheat to gauge its quality. The sun was in my face. Beads of sweat rolled down my cheeks in a continuous stream. And in my ears was the din of the marketplace: carts creaked, vendors quarreled, water-sellers rang their bells.

The farmer spoke again. How about it? Seventy-five for all three.

I stopped appraising the grain and began to appraise the farmer. Strands of white ran through his beard. He held the strap of his leather satchel with two hands, as if he feared someone might snatch it from him at any moment. Did he really want to sell three skilled slaves for that little? Did he not know how much they were worth? The Portuguese were buying slaves by the hundreds from all their trading posts along the continent, and he could surely sell these three at the port before nightfall. Or he could free them and allow them to return home and live out their lives among their people. I opened my mouth, but instead of an admonition to release these men from bondage, out came a price. Sixty for all three, I said.

From that sale, I derived a profit of one hundred and fifty reais, the most I had made in a single transaction. I was stunned at how easy it had been and how high the proceeds. If I felt any guilt, I quieted it by telling myself that I had not done anything that others had not done before me.

The sultan of our kingdom, the governor of our province, and the nobles of our city—they all owned slaves. I ignored the teachings of our Messenger, that all men are brothers, and that there is no difference among them save in the goodness of their actions. With neither care nor deliberation, I consigned these three men to a life of slavery and went to a tavern to celebrate.

MY MOTHER WAS HUDDLED OVER her embroidery when I walked in one summer afternoon. I had spent the day delivering and registering twelve loads of barley to the port, from where they would be shipped to Porto, but I had finished much earlier than I had expected and, rather than spend the evening out, as was often my habit, I had decided to come home. The walk from the port to the house was always pleasant, but at this time of day the streets of Azemmur were still bustling with activity—men sold steamed chickpeas or cooked snails from creaky carts, their voices hoarse from the effort of calling out the price of their wares; women hawked woven baskets or fine linens, holding them before each passerby with one hand, while keeping their haiks in place with the other; children ran to or from the water fountain, bearing pitchers. Then I came across my old teacher. How is your father? he asked me.

He is well, I said, by the grace of God.

Give him my regards.

God willing.

A few more steps, and I was stopped by the silversmith. What a fine tunic you have, he said teasingly. He took the licorice stick out of his mouth and spit straight into the puddle of mud on his right. Be careful, he said, you might get it dirty if you do real work.

I laughed. If you want it so much, just tell me, I replied, and I will sell it to you.

As I rounded the corner toward the house, I came across the baker. Mustafa, he said, can you help me with this load?

Of course. I lifted the baskets and placed them on top of his wheelbarrow.

A beggar boy appeared out of nowhere. A coin, uncle, he asked me.

Run along, I said.

I closed the door of our house behind me and walked straight to the courtyard. My mother looked up from the yellow fabric mounted on her scroll frame, her needle poised in the air, her little finger gracefully maintaining the thread in a taut line. She was sitting with her legs stretched before her. She had the feet of a little girl, small and thin, and her soles were tinted orange from years of henna use. Beside her were a pitcher of water and a plate of figs, the last of the summer season.

Peace be with you, I said.

And upon you be Peace, my son.

I poured myself some water from the pitcher and savored the taste of the lemon slices that floated inside it. Sitting down across from my mother, I asked: Is Father home yet?

He never left, she said. He is in his room, asleep.

It saddened me to hear this. My father had once been the most diligent man in the house—up before the dawn prayer, working on letters and contracts and then meeting with judges and clients until evening— but lately his days were getting shorter and his naps longer. I felt responsible in some way for the melancholy mood he was always in and wished there was something I could do to shake him out of it. Should I buy him a new silk cloak? Or perhaps another pair of leather slippers?

And where are the boys? I asked.

Upstairs, on the roof, my mother said. But you are home early.

The customs clerk arrived on time for once, I said. (The man was new to his position and had not yet learned, like some of his colleagues, to delay everything in exchange for a bribe. But I did not mention this to my mother. Like my father, she did not enjoy hearing about my trade.) What are you working on? I asked.

A belt for Moussa's daughter, she said.

Moussa had been our neighbor for many years—a cobbler by profession, but a gossip by vocation. He never moved from his stall at the street corner, but somehow he always saw the child stealing a loaf of bread, the woman sneaking out of her house, or the preacher buying a jug of wine. He heard about the quarrel between brothers, the bribe given to a judge, or the concubine kept in secret. And he caught a whiff of the cookfire on the days of Ramadan fast. When I was a young boy, prone to breaking my father's many rules, I had feared him, but now that I was a grown man I despised him.

She is getting married soon, my mother said.

Who? I asked.

I told you. Moussa's daughter. The belt is for her bridal gown. And you—when are you going to take a wife?

I had grabbed a fig from the plate and was biting into it when I noticed that my mother's eyes were watchful—probing, even. I was used to the warm glow of her glance, but now it was fixed upon me with a cold precision. Had she heard about my recent trip to the red house at the edge of town? No, that was impossible. I had gone only twice or thrice, at the urging of one of my suppliers, who had arrived from the province of ash-Shawiyya with excellent wheat and wanted to take advantage of all the entertainments that Azemmur had to offer. Unlike my father, I was not endowed with unbreakable willpower, so I had gone with the man. But at least I was discreet—unless, of course, someone, maybe even our neighbor Moussa, had seen me and reported me to my father. This would have been another severe blow to him from his wayward son. Suddenly I felt certain that I was the cause of my father's latest bout of melancholia, and the shame of it filled me with despair.

Mustafa, my mother said. She put down her embroidery. Answer me. When are you going to take a wife?

Someday soon, God willing.

But most men your age are already married. Why, I have heard from your father that the fqih's son is expecting another child . . .

A child?

Yes, a child. What is wrong with children, my son?

Nothing.

If you had still been studying, it would have made sense to wait before taking a wife. But you are working now, able to support a home and have children of your own.

Mother, I want to look after you and Father.

It is time you looked after yourself. Your father can make some inquiries.

No, Father has not been feeling well. Now is not a good time for him to be worrying about me. We can speak of such things when he is better.

My mother drew her breath to say something, but Yahya and Yusuf, having heard my voice, came running down the stairs—they were giggling, racing one another to the bottom step—and so interrupted our conversation. Mustafa! Mustafa! Look at the sword I made, Yahya said.

Oh, you made it? Yusuf said mockingly. And who made the handle?

Lower your voices, boys, I said. Father is still asleep.

I glanced at the double doors of his room; they were still closed. Nothing stirred inside. Let us go for a walk, I said to my brothers, and allow him to rest.

As Yahya and Yusuf ran to the door ahead of me, already arguing about something new, I thought about what I could do to brighten my father's mood. The idea came to me, as suddenly as if someone had thrown open a window to let in the light: I would buy my twin brothers new jellabas and take them to meet the fqih of our mosque. I had disappointed my father, but surely they would fulfill his dreams and become, like him, Men of the Book.

5.

THE STORY OF THE MARCH

While Señor Castillo went on his mission to the port of Pánuco, the governor continued his interrogations of the Indians about the precise location of the kingdom of Apalache. So for a long, miserable week, there was nothing to do in Santa María but wait. In the early mornings and in the late afternoons, when the summer heat was bearable, the soldiers came out of their huts and busied themselves however they could; they bartered some of their spoils or they played games of cards. Señor Cabeza de Vaca read his books of poetry. Señor Dorantes listened to the settlers playing the fiddle. But the young Diego went with Father Anselmo on long walks in the woods behind the village. The friar liked to collect the leaves of native plants, leaves he would later press between the pages of a notebook, above neatly written descriptions of their appearance. One afternoon, Diego and Father Anselmo came upon some concealed Indian traps, in which two odd birds with pink, wattling necks had been caught—one was a smallish hen and the other a very large tom, with dark brown and iridescent green feathers.

Where did you get this meat? Señor Dorantes asked when I served him one of the birds' roasted legs for lunch. He sat on a stool outside his hut and took the bowl from me, his long fingers wrapping greedily around it.

From your brother, Señor.

El Tigre killed this bird?

He took it from an Indian trap in the woods.

Ah, he said with a chuckle. Diego is not much of a hunter.

Poor Diego, I thought. Always trying, but somehow failing, to get his brother's approval. Why did my master not pay him any notice? Señor Dorantes looked much older than Diego, so perhaps they had not grown up together, but that alone could not have accounted for the strange distance between them. Oh, what I would not have given to be with my own brothers. They were seventeen years old now, young men already, though in my memory they remained the same little boys who used to run across the courtyard to greet me as soon as I stepped inside our home. Over the years, I had convinced myself that my sacrifice had been enough to spare them the life that was now mine, and sometimes I even dared to imagine that good fortune smiled on them. Had they made their way to the college of the Qarawiyin and fulfilled my father's dream? Or had they, instead, given up on the scholar's life and apprenticed with one of my uncles' friends? I could not know. But it was my desire to know and my yearning for them that dictated everything I did in those days, everything I saw, but chose not to notice or reflect upon.

Where is Diego now? Señor Dorantes asked me.

With the friar Anselmo.

Again?

They went to the river.

Did he at least save some of this meat for Castillo?

No, Señor. He said the meat should be distributed to all those present.

Tell him to check the traps again tomorrow.

Since our departure from Seville, I had seen Señor Dorantes treat Señor Castillo with brotherly care, which I rarely saw him display toward Diego, though Diego was his own flesh and blood. Once, when Señor Castillo had complained that his right glove had a hole in it, Señor Dorantes had reached into his saddlebag for his spare gloves, even as his brother watched, his bare hands resting on the pommel of his saddle.

I waited for Señor Dorantes to eat so that I could do the same. I had saved some scraps, enough to taste the native bird, but not so much that my master would ask me why I was helping myself to some of the meat. In the square, one of the soldiers was trying on a feather headdress from the temple and asking a friend to help him secure it around his head. Then, like an actor in a play, he walked down an imaginary road, his arms on his hips in an effeminate pose, while his comrades laughed and jeered. Across the way, a group of settlers were playing a game of baraja, excitedly calling out the points they scored. Patience, I thought, patience. Soon, we will leave this village for Apalache, where we will find the gold and where I can remind my master of my role in his good fortune.

SEÑOR CASTILLO AND HIS MEN finally emerged from the wilderness a few days later. How pitiful they looked! Their faces were gaunt, a result of the meager rations the governor had allowed for their mission, and their muddy clothes stuck to their bodies. In the hands of a young soldier, the flagpole leaned sideways, as if he no longer had the strength to hold it upright. Slowly, in small clusters, they made their way into the village square. Everyone came to watch them dismount. Did you find the port? the men asked. Did you come across signs of a city? Where is the hatchet you borrowed?

Señor Castillo raised his hand to quiet the hubbub. From the glum look on his face, it was clear he did not bring the good tidings for which he had hoped. Addressing himself only to his fellow captains, he said: We followed the Río Oscuro all the way to the ocean, but we found only a wide and shallow bay. The water never rose higher than our waists.

This news was greeted with silence. Then Señor Castillo took off his helmet and ran his hand through his hair.

What does this mean? Diego asked him finally.

It means we have no idea where the port is, Señor Castillo replied. It means we are lost.

Come now, Diego said. You are letting your emotions govern you.

It is true.

No, it is not, a voice said.

The crowd parted to let Señor Narváez through, and he came to stand in the clearing, in his blue doublet and impeccably clean breeches. The governor had a flair for dramatic announcements. This one was no different—it had the effect of quieting the whole company and shifting its attention to him. Now he looked around him with satisfaction and even a hint of amusement. Hombres, he said, my investigation has revealed that Apalache is not just the name of the kingdom, but also the name of its capital city. Think about it. When we Castilians speak of León, we can mean either the city or the province. Likewise, Apalache is both a kingdom and a capital. This was why the word Apalache caused some confusion in my interrogations. But the prisoners have confirmed for me everything that we already know about the kingdom of Apalache—that it is very rich with gold, that it has many fields, and many people who labor in them. At this moment, we are in the area of Apalache, but we have not yet reached the city of Apalache.

The governor always spoke to the soldiers in a familiar way. He laughed at the coarse jokes they made and, when the occasion presented itself, he was not above making one of his own. This was why the soldiers liked him, even if what he had to say was not what they wanted to hear. But Señor Castillo always sounded like a nobleman, with the full vowels and trilled consonants that would have been better suited for the royal court. Worse, he rarely addressed the soldiers directly, so he seemed aloof even if that was not his intention.

And look at this, Señor Narváez added, holding up a very large and heavy Indian necklace, of the kind that a person of high rank might wear. The necklace was made of white seashells, so small that they looked like beads, and at its center was a golden amulet shaped like an egg. My page found it in the bushes, a quarter of a league upriver.

The page tucked his thumbs in the loops of his belt and looked on with undisguisded pride. The men whistled and cheered and began to talk about conducting a thorough search along the riverbank.

But Señor Castillo interrupted them. So how far is the capital of Apalache?

Ten days, more or less, the governor said. It is impossible to get a precise answer from the savages because their idea of time is not the same as ours. In any case, we have tarried long enough in this village. It is time to resume the march.

And how will we return to the ships?

Exactly as I said before, Castillo. Once we secure Apalache, I will send a contingent to the coast, and from there to the port of Pánuco.

ALTHOUGH SEÑOR NARVÁEZ STILL LED the procession of horsemen, he rarely spoke to his captains, choosing instead to relay his orders to his page, who walked beside him on foot. He seemed annoyed with Señor Castillo for his insistence on a mission to return to the ships and disappointed that it had failed to quell the young hidalgo's doubts. Now the governor's gaze was always fixed on the horizon, as if he expected at any moment to catch a glimpse of Apalache; he did not want to miss it. The captains, too, withdrew into a thoughtful silence, all of them anxious now to reach the capital. As we marched deeper into the wilderness, the soldiers no longer sang, and few people spoke.

We were taking a break from the midday heat one day when I heard a distant melody. It sounded like a flute, or many flutes, and I suddenly recalled the words of an old Castilian official, a man who had spent some years in La Española and had been a frequent dinner guest in the captain's cabin during our trip across the Ocean of Fog and Darkness. The Indians in these parts, the official had said, do not have art. They make some music, but it is very primitive, of the sort that a child could make if he were given a drum. They have no painting, no drawing, no sculpture, no architecture of any sort, none of the things that we Castilians take for granted.

Yet now it seemed that the sound of music was getting closer and clearer. Señor, I said, as a wave of excitement rippled through me. I cupped my right hand around my ear and pointed with the other toward the trees at the edge of the clearing. My master's eyes widened and he turned toward the sound of the music. Abruptly the governor stood up. He had heard it, too. Others looked up from their food or stopped conversing with one another.

A group of flute players emerged from between the pine trees ahead of us. There must have been twenty of them, walking two by two, playing a beautiful melody on limb-sized instruments. The feeling behind the music seemed to be ancestral, the kind of music one might play at large gatherings or on special occasions rather than around the brazier or the campfire. All the musicians were quite tall, as tall as me, dressed differently than the Indians I had seen before, with elaborately painted deer hides stitched together to cover their private parts. When the last one of them came out from the woods, they lined themselves in a single row against the trees. They turned out to be the advance party of a chief, who arrived now, riding on a servant's shoulders. His long hair was pulled up in a very high knot that ended in bright red feathers and his body was entirely covered in blue tattoos. Behind him, a retinue of men and boys followed.

It seemed to me that we had come across this tribe of Indians by chance, but it was, of course, just as likely that they had spied us as we entered their territory and had come looking for us. I expected the governor to call upon the notary to speak on his behalf, as he had done with the

Indian army at the Río Oscuro, or even to ask for Pablo, his prisoner and chief interpreter, but instead he put his helmet on and advanced toward the cacique himself, his head slightly bowed in salute. An ostrich plume on his helmet had come loose and it drooped with his movement. The Indian leader dismounted and inclined his feathered head, in imitation of the governor.

Pánfilo de Narváez, the governor said. Then, pointing to his eight captains, he gave their names as well.

Dulchanchellin, the Indian chief said. And then he, too, named his deputies.

Señor Narváez reached into his pocket for a string of green glass beads, which he presented to the chief, again inclining his head with a humility this servant of God had not witnessed him display before. The tactic seemed to work: Dulchanchellin looked pleased with the shiny offering. He took off the painted deer hide he wore as a mantle and gave it to Señor Narváez. With these pleasantries out of the way, the governor told the chief, through a combination of gestures and a few words he had learned from Pablo, that he was looking for the capital of Apalache.

Apalache, Dulchanchellin repeated, as if he wanted to be quite sure before he replied. He looked beyond the governor, at the hundreds of Castilians who were assembled in the clearing. They were all standing, having abandoned their meals or their naps, and some had instinctively clutched their weapons, but the music had put them in a celebratory mood. In addition, the elaborate hairstyles and clothing of Dulchanchellin's retinue, and the formal way in which they had made their entrance, generated a mild curiosity among the Castilians, quite different from the hostility with which they had greeted the Indians of the Río Oscuro. After a moment, the cacique pointed to where the sun would set.

It is in that direction, Señor Narváez said triumphantly, as if he alone could understand the chief's gesture.

Dulchanchellin beckoned the governor to follow him.

He will take us there. Now the governor spoke directly to his captains for the first time. Gather your men. Tell them we are leaving.

We marched behind this cacique and his men for three leagues. The land around these parts was denser than before, with trees as tall as minarets, but the Indians led us through this wilderness the way one leads a blinkered donkey through a crowded market—carefully and with a great deal of patience. At length, we reached a river, so wide and so deep that new rafts would have to be built in order to cross it. The governor asked for his carpenters, but only Fernándes came forward, and it was to say that it was already the middle of the afternoon; the rafts would not be ready before nightfall.

That is not good enough, Fernándes, the governor said. You should recruit more men or build bigger rafts.

Don Pánfilo, this is not about the men. I cannot recruit more if I do not have enough tools to give them. I can build larger rafts, but as I said they will not be ready before the end of the day.

How long did it take you to build rafts at the Río Oscuro? Not more than three hours, as I recall.

Aye, three hours. But we are already losing light, Don Pánfilo.

Well, I think it can be done.

The governor was eager to cross the river, a sentiment that many of us shared; we were all impatient of the future that had been promised to us.

Dulchanchellin, who was watching these palavers from his seat under the shade of a tree, came to offer his canoes. But one of the horsemen, not having heard the offer or perhaps not believing it, decided to cross the river anyway. His name was Juan Velázquez. He was a jovial man, I remember, quite popular among the soldiers, whom he entertained with his songs and riddles. Now holding the reins with one hand and a long staff with the other, he nudged his horse into the river. It is not too deep, he cried.

The other horsemen lined along the riverbank to watch him. One of them said, See, we have no need for the savages' help. Yet he waited and watched.

Velázquez waded deeper. The water was gray, reflecting the fading afternoon light, but closer to the other bank, where cypress trees provided their shade, it was brown and green. Come, compadres, he called, his voice merging with that of the tumbling water below. Then the horse lost its footing and Velázquez dropped his staff and threw his arm out for balance. The horse raised its head out of the water, struggling to breathe, struggling with the weight of the rider on its back, but in a moment, just like that, the water surged around them and swept them downstream, as effortlessly as it carried twigs and leaves.

Velázquez, the soldiers cried as they ran down the riverbank. Velázquez!

Señor Narváez, who was still speaking to Dulchanchellin, heard the commotion and came to the riverbank. What happened? he asked. Find him.

A group of soldiers brought the body back sometime later, carrying it on their shoulders and hauling the dead horse as well. No one spoke. We all parted to let the procession through until it reached Señor Narváez. It was as though the soldiers were bringing a sacred offering to the governor, but he looked at them glumly and turned to his page. What are you waiting for? he asked. Have the men dig a grave.

IT WAS FATHER ANSELMO who delivered the graveside prayer, his voice trembling but unhurried. He spoke of Juan Velázquez as a simple man with simple concerns: a native of Cádiz, a devoted husband to his wife, and a father to three children. He was also a soldier, Father Anselmo said, a man who served his country faithfully in the battle of Pavia, who loved to sing and enjoyed his wine. Sometimes a bit too much. The soldiers nodded knowingly, repressing smiles. What I mean to say, the friar added, is that he was like all of us—an ordinary man caught in extraordinary circumstances.

The words of Father Anselmo, so different in tone from those of the commissary at the Río Oscuro, had a great effect upon the soldiers. Instead of accepting the death of one of their own as the inevitable price of conquest, they began to complain about the governor. Why had he not listened to the advice of the carpenter and waited until morning? He had been in too much of a rush to cross the river. If only he had given the order to wait, Velázquez would still be alive.

But, as I said, the governor knew how to handle the soldiers. Immediately after the funeral, he ordered the dead horse slaughtered and portions of meat served to every man in the company, including the porters and slaves. Until then, our rations had consisted of the corn looted from the last village, so everyone was exceedingly grateful for the meat, even as we hated the way in which it had come to be in our possession. And the governor announced that he had named this river in honor of the dead man: Río Velázquez. Thus the grumbling died out.

In the morning, Dulchanchellin's men shuttled all of us from one bank to the other in their handsomely painted dugouts, their oars dipping rhythmically against the current. The water ran fast and clear, but around the boulders that sat here and there in the riverbed, it turned white with foam. With the sun still in the east, the sky was a darker shade of blue, enclosed in all directions by the deep green of pine trees. When it was time for the governor to board, Dulchanchellin came forward and pointed to the ostrich feathers. Oh, the governor said. You want this? With a laugh, he plucked the loose feather off his helmet and handed it to the cacique, who stuck it among the other bright feathers in his headdress, like a king adding another jewel to his crown. At last, Dulchanchellin raised his hand to bid us farewell. He stood with his retinue, watching, until the very last one of us had departed from his kingdom.

We had gone only about a league in the direction of Apalache when two soldiers came to see the governor, dragging a young settler between them. He had been caught stealing a basketful of corn; the soldiers wanted him punished. The governor said that the sentence would be commensurate with this grave crime, but there was no time to apply it now. We can put him in irons, he said, when we reach Apalache.

Over the next ten days, this became a refrain among the men. When we reach Apalache, the thief will be punished. When we reach Apalache, the Indians will offer no resistance. When we reach Apalache, there will be plenty of food to eat and water to drink. When we reach Apalache, there will be time to rest. When we reach Apalache, we will build a settlement. When we reach Apalache, we will be made sergeants. When we reach Apalache, we will receive one bag of gold and two of silver. When we reach Apalache, my master will be rich. When we reach Apalache, I will be free.

6.

THE STORY OF THE SALE

The end of our happiness came in the year 928 of the Hegira. It was often said that the soil of Dukkala was so rich it could grow the hardy wheat as well as the fragile artichoke, but that year there was no rain at all and the harvests were poor. The elders clucked their tongues and said they had never seen a drought like this in their lifetimes. Men and women came to Azemmur from every part of the province, to borrow money, to look for work, or to sell the sheep and cows they could no longer feed. My uncles noticed that they had far fewer commissions than usual; they spent long afternoons sweeping floors and shooing flies. Before long, our streets filled with beggar children, their bellies distended and their hair the color of copper.

But our ill fortune did not afflict the Portuguese in our town: they still shipped gold and wool to Porto and still sent hanbals, kiswas, and other woven goods to Guinea. If anything, the drought and famine we were experiencing had only made their trade more profitable, because the price of wool had fallen so low that they could purchase larger quantities of it. That year, a strange thing happened. The farmers who had neither the funds to pay the Portuguese tax nor grain to sell at market had to give their children as payment. Girls of marriageable age were worth two arrobas of wheat; boys, twice that. A customs official of my acquaintance swore that he had seen three Portuguese caravels leave Azemmur, each carrying two hundred girls and women, who would be transported to Seville, where they would be sold as domestics and concubines. From that blighted time came the saying: when bellies speak, reason is lost.

There came a day when the sons of al-Dib let me go in order to hire one of their relatives, a young lad freshly arrived from the countryside, and I had to join the growing ranks of the idle in Azemmur. Just as I had taken excessive pride in my accomplishments, I found excessive shame in this failure. I did not tell my family about the loss of my employment. Instead, I spent my time going from merchant to merchant, hoping to interest them in my skills. My connections did little to help me, however, for many of my peers were in the same predicament.

To add to my worries, my father fell ill once again. He had trouble taking the stairs up to the roof, from where he liked to watch the ships in the harbor, and his legs often twitched uncontrollably. Sometimes, he had such terrible cramps that my mother had to hold his limbs down to calm his movements. I brought him two different doctors, but no one knew what was wrong with him. Soon, he stopped working altogether and the loss of his earnings, however meager, was cruelly felt at home. My mother went to Mawlay Abu Shuaib's tomb every week, to ask for the saint's intercession, but my father only regressed with each passing day. In just a few months he needed help to get in and out of bed or to use the water closet.

We all hoped that the following year would bring some mercy, but in the year 929 of the Hegira the drought persisted and the harvest was scant. This time, the elders clucked their tongues and said that the famine was a punishment for our failings. They complained about the greed of men, the looseness of women, the insolence of children, the inns that served wine. Just as God had punished Pharaoh and his people with starvation, they said, so too had He brought down this scourge upon us. In all the mosques of Azemmur, fiery sermons became a habit, each preacher finding a new sin where before there had been nothing but pleasure.

The imam warned about excessive adornment, I said to my mother as I walked in one day.

Every story needs a villain, she said grimly. She was stirring salt and cumin into a boiling pot of water and chicken bones; this would be our meal.

But surely you do not favor prideful adornment, I replied. I remembered how much she had enjoyed her work as a bridal attendant and how much my father had disapproved of it. My years of religious training had left their mark on me after all, for here I was, reproaching her about it while neglecting my own violations.

I favor not pointing fingers, she said, lest they point to me someday.

She ladled some soup into a bowl and walked past me, through the sunny courtyard, to my father's bedroom. He had started to refuse the scarce food we had, insisting that it should go to my young brothers, whose figures had grown dangerously gaunt over the summer. Every day my mother sat by his side holding his hand, cajoling him to eat or drink, but his lips remained shut.

The inevitable end came in Ramadan of that year. We washed him, carried his cloaked body to the mosque, read Surat Yasin over him, but it was not until the first shovelful of dry earth fell over my father's immaculate white shroud that the truth of his death tore into me like a dagger. My wails were so sudden and so loud that my uncles, perhaps fearing I might throw myself into the grave after him, restrained me. Be sensible, they said. Death is a part of life.

But I continued screaming and beating my chest until they took me home, carrying me through the creaky blue door of the house, the way they had when I was an infant. I felt as if my very life had been taken from me. I hardly left our house during the forty days of mourning; I read from the Holy Qur'an and I prayed for my father's soul. He had died without ever telling me what he thought of the choice I had made that fateful day in the courtyard of our house, surrounded by the remnants of our celebrations. About my conversion from scholar to merchant, he had offered neither reproach nor compliment, and I had been so pleased with myself that I had never sought his opinion about it. For years, I had resented his counsel, and now that he was gone I longed to hear it more than anything.

After the forty days of mourning were over, Zainab returned home with her daughter. Zainab's husband claimed he had divorced her because she did not bear him any sons, but my mother and I knew that he did it because he would not have to support her or her child any longer. My uncle Abdullah and my aunt Aisha went to live with their eldest daughter, the second wife of a wealthy customs official, leaving us alone to face our troubles. When my uncle Omar left town with one of his friends, our ruin was complete. Our family broke apart so swiftly after my father's death that I often wondered if he had been the fragile thread that held us together for so long.

In our house, there now lived five hungry, miserable souls, all of them under my charge. I could no longer keep the truth from my mother. But when I went to make my confession, she was not surprised, for our neighbor Moussa had already brought her the news of my deceit, just as, years ago, he had brought her the news of my visits to the red house at the edge of town. The disappointment I saw in her eyes was a painful blow. I felt as if I were the embodiment of every evil against which my father and my mother had warned: a trader of flesh and a traitor to my faith.

To atone for my sins, I tried to provide, in the only way I knew. I sold the rugs and the chests I had bought with such pride only years earlier. I helped my mother sell her gold bracelets and my sister the hanbal it had taken her two years to weave. Each time, the money lasted a few days, sometimes weeks, and then we went back to scouring our house for something I could sell or trade. I was so preoccupied by my transactions that news of the earthquake in Fes did not reach me until refugees appeared on the other side of the Umm er-Rbi' River, setting up their tents on the riverbank. They jostled for work, crowded our markets, and begged at our mosques.

I began to wander the alleys of the medina alone, as if the solution to my family's plight lay hidden somewhere, waiting to be found. The city was quiet—dogs and cats had long ago been caught and shamelessly eaten. Even vermin was a rare sight inside the city walls. I was on the lookout for anything: food I could eat, goods I could trade, rich people I could beg for mercy. Yet all I saw were people like me, their faces haggard, their bodies so distorted by hunger and disease that they looked like jinns. So great was my despair that I would have readily gone to the gates of hell if I knew it could save my family from starvation.

I MADE MY WAY through the crowds gathered on the quay. The Umm er-Rbi' was tranquil, the fading light of the day turning its water the color of shadows, and the sky was a mackerel gray. Soldiers watched from their posts as servants and slaves carried crates on or off the Portuguese ships. I held on to my twin brothers' hands, in fear that I might lose them in the flowing multitude of people. I felt as if I had already lost myself. My poor mother had spoken to me that morning with words that still rang in my ears. Mustafa, she had said. No. Not this.

But it was my fate to discard her advice, just as I had discarded my father's. Mother, I said, there is no other way.

There is a way, she said. There is always a way, if you will yourself to dream it.

May God forgive me, I thought she spoke soothing nonsense. My eyes must have betrayed my feelings, for she looked at me sadly and began to tell me the Story of My Birth. This time she told it to steel her own heart against the pain of losing me—it was easier to let go if she believed that my departure had been ordained. I listened patiently, the way I had always listened to her, but when she was finished I did not think about the story or its meaning. Instead, I thought about how I had broken my father's heart and how my sacrifice might redeem me, even if he was no longer there to see it. When I finally got up to leave, my mother stood in the doorway, silhouetted by the light from the courtyard. This is the image of her that I still carry with me, all these years later. She was still calling my name when I closed the blue door behind me.

On the dock, I saw a fidalgo I recognized—he had been a regular visitor to my uncles' workshop, buying chests or chairs or corner tables for his household in Lisbon. Senhor, I called. Senhor Affonso. He was a short man, with a prominent nose and a tight mouth. He wore a red vest and dark hose tucked inside freshly shined boots, and his right hand rested on the pommel of his sword. I knew exactly the price I could have fetched for each of these items of clothing, had they been mine to sell. The vest and hose were made of cotton—they would only interest a clerk or a notary— but the sword would have been worth at least twenty reais. When I realized what I had been doing, I wanted to turn around, but Affonso had already seen me. A hint of surprise lit his eyes. His gaze traveled from me to my twin brothers, and then back to me. I think he understood, without my saying a word, what it was I wanted from him. He did not ask me if I knew what life would be like once the ship crossed the river, once it had left Azemmur and traveled along the coast to the Land of the Christians. Instead he asked: Are you sure this is what you want?

I looked at my twin brothers. Their hair had started to turn orange and their cheekbones protruded under their frightened eyes. They looked at me uncomprehendingly. Yes, I said. I am sure.

Then come with me, Affonso said. We followed him across the quay to one of the merchant stations. A bald man, his head as smooth as an egg, stood up. The two Portuguese men shook hands, but the merchant kept his head slightly inclined in a gesture of respect to the captain. They spoke in hushed tones for a few moments, then they both turned to look at us. This one speaks Portuguese, Affonso said, pointing to me.

Isso é verdade? the bald man asked me.

Sim, I said. Eu trabalhei com os comerciantes português.

The merchant nodded at Affonso, as if to confirm that the good captain had not lied. With a long stick, he prodded the property he was
considering—it seemed the muscles were decent and the hands were
strong. The eyes appeared healthy. There were no missing teeth. He
offered a price: ten reais. The haggling took a while, because I wanted to
make sure I would get the best possible price. I agreed to the sale only
when it became clear to me that the merchant was on the verge of giving
up and that fifteen reais was indeed the most he was willing to pay.

A flickering candle illuminated the narrow office of the clerk who
recorded the sale. Our shadows danced across the wall behind him—
mine, tall and worried, and my two brothers', shorter and thinner than
their twelve years of age warranted, entirely unaware of the proceedings taking place before them. The clerk asked me my name. His missing
teeth gave his voice a perversely benevolent tone.

Mustafa ibn Muhammad ibn Abdussalam al-Zamori, I replied, naming
myself, my father, my grandfather, and my native town.

With deliberately slow movements, the clerk opened his register and
dipped his feather into black ink. Mustafa. Fifteen reais.

And thus it was done. Of all the contracts I had signed, this was perhaps the only one that my father could never have imagined me sign-
ing, for it traded what should never be traded. It delivered me into the
unknown and erased my father's name. I could not know that this was just
the first of many erasures.

I gave the money to my brothers. Take it, I said.

Yahya was the first to understand and his eyes widened with terror.
But Yusuf caught on soon enough and he cried out, No! He snatched the
money from my hands and tried to give it back to the Portuguese clerk,
but the clerk watched us with dispassionate eyes, eyes that had grown
used to such displays in his office. Yusuf, who had always been the more
sensitive one, started to cry. He pulled me by the sleeve of my tunic, told
me to go home with him.

I pulled both of my brothers into my arms. I will be back, I said, not
because I believed it at that moment, but because I did not know what
else to say. I would never hear their playful bickering in the bed next to
mine at night, I would never shake them awake for the morning prayer,
I would never sit beside them to eat from the same plate, I would never

watch them running toward me when I turned the corner of our street—all these things and more, I would miss. I entreated them to be faithful guardians to our mother and sister in my absence, to be good sons to our uncles, and to spend the money wisely. If it lasted until the next fall, my family might be saved.

I still remember how they cried, how their bony chests trembled against mine, how their warm breath felt against my cheeks. Looking back now, I wonder where I ever found the strength to let go of them and walk away, but that is what I did. Perhaps some things can never be truly explained.

I stepped onto the ship's plank, following the other slaves. Some of them had been captured in cavalgadas in Dukkala or in Singhana. Others had been bartered by their families to pay for the Portuguese levy. But a great many of them—one hundred and thirty on that ship alone—indentured themselves for no money, only the promise of a meal a day. In the end, whether we were abducted or traded, whether we were sold or sold ourselves, we all climbed onto that ship. A soldier led me to the lower deck, where I was shackled to other men, facing the row of women, with children in between us. On one end of the deck were animal stalls and on the other were crates full of goods. And everywhere, everywhere, hung the stench of bondage and death.

7

The Story of Apalache

During the march to the capital of Apalache, I distracted myself with daydreams. I conjured up images of a splendid entrance, not as glorious as that of Tariq ibn Ziyad in Toledo, no, nothing like that, because the signs we had seen since our landing on the coast had been more modest, but a splendid entrance nonetheless, a victory for my master and a chance for me. I did not always succeed in losing myself to the fantasy, and I remember that the beating of my heart would quicken at the slightest sign of a foreign presence—the sudden flutter of wings, the snap of a tree branch, or the call of an unknown animal in the distance—but I tried.

Oftentimes, arrows were shot at our company, startling us and forcing us to stop. These arrows were a wonder to behold: they were quite long, and so sharp that they could penetrate a pine tree by as much as a hand's span. The soldiers would run into the bushes to look for the archers, but the wilderness always closed behind them like a curtain, concealing them from our sight. The Indians never prevented our procession from going deeper into their territory, so it was unsettling to know that we were watched, without knowing who was watching us or how many of them there were.

One morning, the governor's scouts, two Indian prisoners and a Spanish soldier from Cuba, reported that they had sighted a very large town, larger than either Portillo or Santa María. They believed it was Apalache. Apalache! The news traveled down the procession, borne on the lips of soldiers and settlers and slaves, instantly reviving the ambitions, whether public or private, that we had nurtured since we had first heard about the gold. When Señor Narváez ordered us to take a break, the mood of the company turned to impatience. Why? the men asked. Now is not the time for breaks.

But once again, the governor assembled all his advisors. The commissary, the notary, the treasurer, and all the captains gathered around the governor, their backs turned to us, shielding him from our curious stares. My master had ordered me to feed and water Abejorro, so I could not hear what was said at the council this time. The sky was a magnificent blue, I remember, and a soft breeze softened the effect of the summer heat. All around us were sweet acacia trees, whose scent mercifully cloaked that of the soldiers and the horses. Unusually, I did not hear the men argue over a needed article, like a knife or a length of rope, or even a small luxury, like a wide-brimmed hat. I think everyone was simply anxious to get to the city now, and the governor's council seemed like an unnecessary delay.

Señor Dorantes returned after a few moments, accompanied, as he always was, by Señor Castillo. Fetch me something to drink, he said.

I brought him a flask of water—we had run out of wine a week before— and he drank from it in very careful sips, looking into the distance at the group of officers still talking to the governor. Beside me, Abejorro whinnied fearfully. I patted his neck and checked behind me for what might have scared him, but all I could see was an oak tree, its leathery leaves weighed down by the heat. Sshh, Abejorro, I said. Sshh.

Señor Dorantes chewed on his lower lip, which was burned by the sun, and licked the beads of blood that appeared. Why him? he asked. Why him? What skill or trait does he possess that I do not?

I followed my master's jealous gaze—it was fastened on Señor Cabeza de Vaca. Holding his helmet in the crook of one arm, the treasurer was pointing with the other at a crate filled with musket balls. Everything about him conveyed his earnestness: his sincere face, his calm voice, the zeal with which he carried out the governor's orders. It was this earnestness that made him less popular among the men, even though he never spoke roughly to them.

I fought for the king against the Comuneros, Señor Dorantes said, his thumb turned toward his chest.

So did he, Señor Castillo replied evenly.

But this is precisely what I mean. Why Cabeza de Mono and not me? I have just as much experience.

Abejorro whinnied again. There is nothing there, I whispered to him, rubbing his flank, but just to be sure I looked searchingly at the cluster of trees behind us.

And what about Capitán Pantoja? Señor Dorantes said. Everyone knows you could trust that man with your life. Or Peñaloza? Or even Tellez? Why him?

Until then, Señor Castillo had been indifferent, but now his voice became tainted by resentment. Amigo, it must be because Cabeza de Vaca agrees with the governor.

What about?

About continuing the march inland without securing the ships.

But Pantoja agreed with him, too. And he is not going on the mission either.

Señor Castillo ran his fingers through his brown hair. Maybe it is because he is the treasurer.

All the more reason he should stay behind. It is too dangerous for a man like him. He should guard the royal fifth, not fight for it.

Señor Castillo did not reply. He took off his gloves and slowly began to untie his boots. News of the planned raid on Apalache had already traveled around the camp, and the soldiers stood in animated throngs, waiting to see who would be chosen for the mission. When Señor Cabeza de Vaca asked for ten horsemen, twenty-five men, one elbowing the other, volunteered. For his foot soldiers, he chose forty men from among those who had come with him on his ship, and with whom he was already familiar. They departed before the almuerzo.

WHILE MY MASTER PLAYED CARDS with his friend, I retreated under the shade of a tree, my thoughts inevitably drifting to Apalache. What would it look like? Portillo and Santa María had simple huts covered with thatch, but this was the capital and its homes were bound to be larger and better. I wondered if it had the kind of fortified walls that Moctezuma was said to have built around his capital or if it was more modest, with only one or two lookout towers from which sentinels could warn about intruders. I was relieved that Señor Dorantes had not been chosen to lead the mission into the city because it meant that I did not have to go without armor or weapon into another bloody battle, but in a strange way I was also disappointed—his victory in battle would surely result in greater goodwill toward me.

I had settled myself for a long wait, but it was only the middle of the afternoon when a soldier sent by Señor Cabeza de Vaca galloped back into camp to announce that the city had been secured. There was no resistance, he said.

At these words, the company began its feverish preparations to enter Apalache. The governor put on his blue sash; the friars dusted off their robes; the soldiers grabbed their swords or muskets; the settlers tied their bundles; everyone lined up in a thick procession. All this was done swiftly and without complaint.

Even now, writing these lines many years later, it is hard for me to describe the anxiety and excitement I felt when we began that final march to Apalache. Although we had to walk only one and a half leagues, it seemed to me they were twenty. The trail was sandy and, in places where it was exposed to the sun, it was also hot against my sandaled feet, but I did not mind it. We passed by a small lake, over which there were fallen pine trees, and two open shelters that were likely used by the Indians when they were out on long hunts. At last, I heard a horn, announcing our entrance into the capital.

Apalache.

It had fifty houses.

I had expected that they would be opulent, but they turned out to be simple homes made of straw and brown thatch, with animal skins drawn across their doorways. They were arranged in neat little rows, under a canopy of tall trees, which provided respite from the sun as well as cover from the rain. Each one could accommodate perhaps a dozen people, making it suitable for one family. The air smelled of warm pumpkin, perhaps in a soup or a stew, but it puzzled me that there were no firepits anywhere—how had it been cooked?

Nor was there a well, which meant that water had to be drawn from some spring or river nearby and carried back to the homes or to a storage tub. Here and there were instruments of ordinary life: mortars and pestles for grinding corn, containers and cooking pots, simple looms made of wood and tendon, a few dolls and rattles. On the eastern side of the square were work stalls, where cut timber of various sizes was kept, along with some carpentry tools. And beyond the houses were cultivated fields, large swaths of yellow and orange and green.

As we proceeded toward the center of Apalache, we came upon an earth mound, shaped like a small pyramid, though its peak was flat. A wooden staircase led up the slope to a thatch-roof structure, which I took to be a temple. It was much grander than the temples in either of the villages through which we had passed. I remember there was a bracelet on the fifth or sixth step of the staircase, at eye-level, and that one of the soldiers picked it up to examine it.

Around the corner from the temple, armed soldiers from Señor Cabeza de Vaca's company were standing watch over a group of Apalache women, some eighty of them, who were huddled together. These were the first women we had seen anywhere since our landing in La Florida. They had been pulled away from whatever tasks they were completing that afternoon: some carried baskets filled with corn, others had brushes dipped in a red dye, and yet others held on to whimpering children. I noticed that all of the women had exceedingly long hair, either woven in braids or wound in thick knots high above their ears, and that on their chins they bore a single tattoo in the shape of a circle. The older among them wore blankets or painted deerskins, but the younger ones were uncovered, their breasts, arms, and legs completely bare. My heart filled with a sudden and fierce desire, a feeling for which I was unprepared, and I caught myself openly staring at their nakedness. It took all of my willpower and years of scholarly training to avert my eyes. Behind me, the men began to make obscene comments, comments that the women could not understand and that the captains did nothing to stop.

The governor cast only a brief look at the women before dismounting. Search the town, he said.

The captains, the soldiers, and most of the settlers fanned out through the city, but Señor Dorantes went straight to the temple. I followed him into the earth mound, my gaze traveling helplessly to the women as we passed them. The temple had very high walls and a coffered wood ceiling. It could easily have accommodated three hundred people, so it took a long while for us to walk the full perimeter. Along the eastern and western walls were short platforms, upon which sat magnificent red baskets, made from a woven fiber I did not recognize. On the northern wall were wood and stone idols, all of them adorned with feathers, beaks, and claws, giving them the lifelike appearance of birds of prey. I examined these idols most carefully. Whenever I lingered over a statue or a gilded weapon, my master would ask: Do you see anything, Estebanico?

But I had no luck. I found no gold or silver charms. No brass or copper. No precious stones.

The search of Apalache lasted until the sun completed its descent to the west. From every corner of the city, soldiers returned with their loot, although no one reported finding any gold. Instead, they spoke of granaries filled with corn, beans, squash, nuts, and sunflower seeds—the city's winter reserves—as well as fine woven blankets, tools for farming or cooking, and some weapons. Where was the gold the Indian prisoners had all spoken about? Even if it were mined far away, there should be traces of it somewhere here, in the capital. Drops of sweat trickled down my face and along my back. Mosquitoes swarmed around me and I swatted at them furiously for a while, as if I were the sole subject of their harassment, before giving up and turning my attention to the governor.

The captains had gathered around him now, and it appeared to fall upon Señor Cabeza de Vaca to deliver the results of the search, a task he did not relish. Don Pánfilo, he said softly. We found no gold.

Señor Narváez stood with his fists resting on his hips. He had not yet taken off his armor, and he looked piercingly at the royal treasurer. That is impossible, he said.

The soldiers looked everywhere. There is no gold.

No gold at all?

No. Not even copper.

But this is the town the cacique—what was his name?

Dulchanchellin.

Yes, him. This is the city he told us about.

Indeed it is.

The governor took off his gloves and looked beyond Señor Cabeza de Vaca at the city, darkening steadily now all around us. Apalache has gold, he said.

There is no gold, the treasurer repeated.

The governor slipped a finger under his black eyepatch and rubbed forcefully underneath it. The Indians saw us coming, he said. That is why all their men are gone. They went to hide the gold.

All around the city square, the settlers were lighting the evening torches. Slowly, the fading light of the day gave way to the yellow glow of the torch. In the trees, an owl began to hoot.

My son, the commissary said. He spoke kindly, as if he were about to invite a confession or comfort a gravely injured man. My son, I do not believe the Indians are hiding gold. If they did indeed have gold, their dwellings would not be made of straw and their women and children would not be naked.

Señor Narváez looked confused, as if the friar had spoken to him in a foreign language. The notary started to bite his nails—it was a nervous habit that seemed to have grown worse over the last few days, because the tips of his fingers looked raw. My master took off his helmet and handed it to me without looking back.

There is no gold, Señor Castillo said with finality.

Of course there is gold, the governor replied. Where else did the fisherfolk get the pebble that Dorantes found in Portillo? Or the charms that you yourself found in Santa María?

I noticed that the governor's tone was laced with a touch of blame. He sounded, or tried to sound, like an innocent man who had been misled by the traces of gold his officers had found. Señor Dorantes must have noticed this, too, because he put his right hand on his hip in a defensive stance. It was slowly dawning upon all of us that Apalache had no gold and there would be no glory. My fantasies of victory for my master and freedom for me had turned so completely awry that, for a moment, all my senses felt numb. I was rooted in my spot, unable to move, and my eyesight blurred. I thought about that night, long ago in Azemmur, when I had agreed to sell my life for a bit of gold. My father and my mother had both warned me about the danger of putting a price on everything, but I had not listened. Now, years later, I had convinced myself that, because I had been the first to find gold in La Florida, my life would be returned to me. But life should not be traded for gold—a simple lesson, which I had had to learn twice.

It was a long while before the voice of Señor Castillo reached me. The Indians did not get the gold from here, he said. This entire land is poor.

Señor Narváez looked at the young captain with disgust. How would you know what lies in this entire land? Since our arrival in this territory, you have pressed us to run back to the ships.

This is not about the ships, Señor Castillo countered. This is about the gold.

Señor Dorantes joined the quarrel. You told us that the prisoners mentioned gold, he said. As much gold as in México. Have they lied to you, Don Pánfilo? Or did you misunderstand what they said?

The elders teach us: when the cow is down, the knives come out.

But Señor Cabeza de Vaca intervened. There is no need to quarrel, he said. We should set up camp here for a few days. Then we can explore. We might yet find something valuable in the area around here.

Señor Narváez nodded, and the captains took this for their order to disperse. Señor Dorantes turned around and, as if suddenly noticing me, he said: What are you waiting for, Moro? Go water the horse.

I could feel the heat of his anger and disappointment. He had been pleased with me for finding the pebble of gold, but now he blamed me for its failure to deliver the kingdom. How foolish I had been to expect anything from him. I already knew about his fickle nature—on the ship that had brought us to La Florida, I had seen with my own eyes how quickly he formed friendships, especially when he needed something, and how easily his loyalties shifted when his needs changed—why did I think he would be different with me? Perhaps it was because, in those days, I fed my hopes of freedom in whichever way I could, without realizing that I was only hooking myself to different lures.

FROM A DWELLING he took for himself, Señor Narváez issued decrees throughout the rest of the evening. He declared that the soldier who was to be punished for stealing corn should be released instead, to celebrate our entrance into the city. He allowed the entire company double rations of beans for the next three days. All the woven blankets, animal hides, baskets—indeed, anything at all of any value in Apalache—had to be brought to him, and he divided the loot, most of it among his men. He assigned a large dwelling to the friars, one to the notary and the tax inspector, several to the captains, one as a prison, and thirty to the soldiers and settlers. The Indian women and children he quartered inside the earth mound.

In short, he attempted to govern.

But, as I discovered later that night, his orders did little to quell the captains' concerns. My master had been given an Indian dwelling, which he shared with Diego, Señor Castillo, and a friend of his named Pedro de Valdivieso. I had made a stew of beans and roasted some corn on the cookfire, which was built in the center of the lodge. Ventilation for the fire was provided by means of a hole in the roof, making it possible to prepare warm meals in any kind of weather. This was something I was particularly grateful for, as I did not want to be outside, exposed to the mosquitoes that traveled in thick clouds or, worse, to a sudden attack by the men of Apalache.

Señor Dorantes and his friends sat on fox furs while I ladled the stew and served it to them. I sat a few paces away from the Castilians, right by the entrance, and began to eat. Ordinarily, I ate alone, after my master had finished his meal, but the farther we went inland, the less these matters of decorum seemed to matter to him. Besides, if I had stayed outside and was injured by an Indian arrow, who would have prepared his meals? Who would have fed his horse or washed his clothes?

How long are we to remain here? Diego was asking. Did the governor say?

No, Señor Dorantes said. He wants to explore the area around the city, but I doubt he will find anything. We should be looking for the ships now, before it is too late.

It is not too late, Diego replied.

How can you say that, Chato? Have you any idea how precarious our situation is?

I just mean that you should have some faith.

Señor Dorantes shook his head. He looked as if he had used up all his faith, the way he had used up other luxuries like wine or cured meat. He said: When I tried to talk to the governor, he refused to acknowledge me. He told me he wanted to eat his dinner in peace.

But there was no peace to be had. We had just finished our meal and were still enjoying the feeling of being satiated, when we were all jolted out of it by a woman's horrifying screams. As I was nearest the doorway, I lifted a small portion of the deerskin and peeked outside. Some soldiers were dragging women out of the earth mound. The women clawed at the men's faces and pulled their beards, but the men easily restrained them. One of the Castilians lifted a girl off the ground and, slinging her over his shoulder like a sack of wheat, he ran to his lodge.

Señor, I said. Look.

My master pulled the deerskin wide open, so that all his kinsmen could see what was happening. It was dark outside, the only light coming from the torches that the men had placed to light the path to the necessary. We could see the shapes of the men as they pulled the women away, but we could not make out their faces.

Who are they? Diego asked.

They are not my men, Señor Dorantes said.

How can you tell? Whose men are they?

The governor's men.

Instinctively, we all looked toward the dwelling Señor Narváez had taken for himself. The fire inside was lit, the smoke rising out of it in a straight line. The page appeared in the doorway, and then disappeared back inside. Nothing else moved.

But how can you tell they are the governor's men and not yours? Diego asked.

Estebanico, my master said. Close the door.

I let go of the deerskin and returned to my seat. I covered my ears with my hands, but it was useless—I could still hear the women's screams. I closed my eyes, but the image that came to me was of Ramatullai under the weight of that vile Castilian, the pink soles of her feet, the look of shame in her eyes. The image tortured me, reminding me of my power-less rage. Here, halfway across the world, this servant of God was still just as alone, just as helpless. I tried to turn to happier memories, the sort that had sustained me during my journey to Seville and later to La Florida. I wanted the memories to help me escape from this wretched land, even if my exile's dreams were the only place I could go. But now I found it hard to conjure up images of the past on my own. It was as if I was no longer able to return to the times and places I chose, as if my past was no longer mine, as if it were receding from me. Worse yet: I could no longer escape to a future that involved my freedom. I had only the present, the dreadful present.

Eventually, the women's cries subsided, and a new silence fell on Apalache. I opened my eyes again. My master poked the fire with a stick and picked up the conversation where it had stopped. In the morning, he said, I mean to ask the governor—

A tremendous chorus of drums interrupted him. It came from the earth mound, where the women and children were held, and its sound rose so steadily that it now reached every part of the town. Then, over the sound of the drums, came the voices of the Indian women, mourning for their abused sisters. Their cries briefly rose to a high pitch, before extending into a low note, sustained and anguished. It was a communion of pain, and no one in the city could pretend not to have heard it. The women had made witnesses of us, even those of us who had chosen to close our eyes.

. . .

I WAS BRINGING IN LOGS for the morning fire when I heard the panicked cries of a settler. Indios, he shouted. Indios allá! A group of Apalache men, numbering at least a hundred and armed with bows, lances, and hatchets, were marching into the city. How they had gone past the sentinels that were posted at the entrance of the town, I never knew. (Perhaps the sentinels had been asleep. The long march through the wilderness in the heat of the summer had caused the soldiers, and indeed most of us, to suffer from fatigue, which the disappointment of not finding the gold had only worsened.) Now the Apalache warriors were flooding into the square, looking around them at all the signs of foreign presence—the horses tied to new posts, the crates of tools, and the strange white men who now appeared in doorways.

I dropped the wood and ran back into the lodge where Señor Dorantes lay asleep, stretched out between his kinsmen. Señor, I said, shaking him. The Indian men have returned. He shot to his feet—his hair was disheveled and his shirt wide open, but his eyes were alert. I helped him put on his armor. Of course, I had no such means to protect myself, not even a coat of quilted cotton, like those the settlers had made for themselves. Still, I went outside with him and the others. All around the little square, soldiers and settlers were coming out of their huts, weapons in hand. Finally, the governor appeared in his doorway, wearing his armor but not his helmet or blue sash. His eyepatch, hastily pulled on, rested on his head at a perilous angle.

As the governor came forward, two of the Apalaches detached themselves from the others. One wore a headdress of dyed animal hair and carried a long lance decorated with feathers. He had small, quick eyes and a scar that ran the length of his right arm. The other one was younger and had a bow slung across his chest. They took turns speaking, their voices urgent and threatening. Their arrival had been so sudden and unexpected that Pablo, the Indian interpreter, had not been brought forth from his cell. In any case, I thought, there was no need for an interpreter, because it was not difficult to guess what they wanted: their wives, their children, their homes.

Calmly the governor said, I am Pánfilo de Narváez.

The two Indians watched him unblinkingly; if the name of the governor caused them to be impressed or intimidated, their faces did not immediately betray them. The governor repeated his name, this time at a much slower pace: pán-fi-lo-de-nar-vá-ez. Then he pointed his forefinger at them. He was expecting the man who seemed to be their leader, the one with the crest of red animal hair on his head, to speak his name, too, the way Dulchanchellin had. But this cacique spoke at such length that it quickly became clear he was not simply stating his name. As he spoke, his left hand, the one holding the lance, moved in tempo with his words.

Have you any idea what he is saying? Señor Dorantes asked the governor.

I want him to say his name, the governor replied. But he does not understand me.

Maybe he said something else.

It is a simple enough question, Dorantes. The governor pointed his finger once again at the cacique. What is your name?

The Indian leader said something. One word—or at least it seemed it was one word, because it was short.

What did he say? Señor Dorantes asked.

Kamasha, said the governor, or Kaimasha? Komasha?

Señor Dorantes shrugged. Something like that, at any rate. So now what?

Now Kamasha raised his lance in the air. Its point, I noticed, was made of bone and fire-hardened wood. The soldiers reached for their swords and muskets, ready to fight at the first sign of confrontation, but Kamasha only brought his lance down to the ground with a great thud. That was when a swarm of butterflies, of a species I had seen neither in Barbary nor in Castile, appeared in the town square. These butterflies had large orange wings, which were laced with black veins and specked with white spots. I was amazed to see hundreds of them migrating across Apalache at such a moment. Their appearance, so soon after the cacique had hammered the ground with his lance, made it seem as if he had conjured them himself. For a moment, we were all of us stunned into silence.

But the governor soon returned to his questions. From his little finger, he pulled out a gold ring, which he held up to the cacique by way of asking where one might find such a metal in these parts. Kamasha and his deputy paid the ring no attention; they made great howling cries, which the warriors behind them echoed.

Return their women, I silently begged. Return their women.

Señor Dorantes turned toward me. What did you say, Moro?

I had not realized that I had spoken out loud, so for a moment I looked uncomprehendingly at my master's surprised face.

But Diego intervened. Don Pánfilo, he said. Return their women. That is what the cacique is asking you.

The governor pretended not to have heard. A butterfly had landed on his arm, just below the couter of his armor, but he paid it no attention. Instead, he held out the golden ring, lifting it up closer to Kamasha's face, as if the cacique were half-blind. This insolence infuriated the Apalaches, and one of them threw his lance into the open doorway of a hut.

He is threatening us, the page shouted.

The cry seemed to wake Señor Narváez. Like an actor who had suddenly remembered his lines, he lowered his arm and took a step back. It seemed he was about to say something—was it another one of his spectacular announcements?

Just then, the page fired his crossbow, striking Kamasha's deputy in the shoulder. This was met with a great rattling of lances and arrows, which forced those of us who were not in armor to duck to the ground. From my crouching position, I saw a chestnut mare fall to her side, moaning with pain; her eyes turned white, her nostrils flared. The other horses whinnied and shook their heads and pulled at their tethers, trying to set themselves free. Silently, the swarm of butterflies flew away from us and went to roost together on a pine tree.

Behind me, there was much scrambling and shouting. Some soldiers had been struck, others were running back, and yet others were loading up their muskets and arquebuses. What terrible power these modern weapons had! As soon as they were fired, a dozen Apalaches fell to the ground one after the other; those who had not been shot were so stunned that they ran away, dragging their wounded comrades. Within moments, the city square was empty again.

Señor Albaniz, the notary, rushed to the side of the fallen mare—his mare—and placed his hands on her neck, where the Indian arrow had landed. It was lodged very deep.

The governor turned angrily to his page. You should have waited for my orders.

But the savages were about to attack, the page replied.

You just cost us a horse.

I was only defending you.

Señor Albaniz looked up. His deep-set eyes usually gave him a gloomy look, but today they made him seem frantic. You just killed my horse, you fool.

I did not, the page replied. The savages did.

Albaniz, the governor said, you can have one of the packhorses.

But, like all the other horsemen, the notary was greatly attached to his animal and the offer did nothing to quell his anger. It was especially hard for him to hear the governor order that the dead mare be slaughtered for meat. Then, just as the governor turned around to offer some words of consolation to the notary, a fireball landed on the roof of a hut nearby. Others quickly followed, so that a dozen houses were ablaze before any of us had a chance to act.

Get water, the governor finally said. Hurry.

So unprepared were we for this attack that it took us a while to find buckets and to form lines going from the storage tub toward the different fires. Once water was thrown on the thatched roofs, however, the air filled up with thick, gray smoke, which stung our eyes and made it difficult to see anything. All around me, I could hear the coughing of exhausted men, the stomping of frightened horses, and the weeping of the women inside the temple.

Then came the cries of the warriors; they were breaking down the temple doors to release their women and children. Some of the soldiers left the water line to fight the Indians, but others remained, trying to save their food and supplies from the fires. So there was a great deal of confusion, especially as we could not hear the governor's orders, his voice being drowned out by all the screaming and crying. In the end, each man did what he thought was best. My master decided to fight. In spite of the smoke and the noise, he mounted Abejorro and managed to steer him toward the Indians, trampling as many of them as he could.

I hid in the nearest place I could find—the carpentry stall. The ground was littered with pieces of timber and various lengths of rope, signs of a project that had been abandoned after our expedition swept into town. Along the wall, hammers, saws, and hatchets hung in a neat row, reminding me of my uncles' workshop and at once making me feel safe. Perhaps it was this feeling that led me to peek over the wall, to try to get a view of the battle. Let them have the women, someone yelled. Get the cacique.

The order surprised me—had common sense finally pierced through the madness?—so I turned toward the voice and thus failed to see an Indian arrow darting through the air, aimed for me. It landed in my thigh. The pain flared through my leg, knocking the air out of me and dulling any other feeling. I had no time to think, because the man who had struck me was already loading his bow once more, I only had time to grab a hatchet and throw it at him. I was sprayed with something warm, something that I instantly knew was blood. The Indian slumped to the ground, dead.

I fell back into the stall, stunned by what I had done and by the agony I felt. Blood had begun to flow from my thigh, trickling down in several warm lines along my leg. There was nothing to do now but take out the arrow, which I did as swiftly as I could, pulling out bits of flesh and hair with it. Only then did I hear myself howl with pain, but also with the strange relief of being alive.

SEÑOR NARVÁEZ HAD CHOSEN to keep the cacique hostage in order to guarantee that the Apalaches would leave us alone, but in fact the Indians attacked us relentlessly over the next few days. When we went to fetch water at the river, they attacked; when we picked fresh corn from the field, they attacked; when we tried to gather firewood around the city, they attacked. The governor ordered us to use the wooden idols from inside the temple to feed our cookfires; he sent soldiers in chain mail to the river to fetch water or to the fields to pick corn; and he posted sentinels armed with muskets and arquebuses at all the entrances of Apalache.

As for me, I tried to recover from my leg wound. I washed it thoroughly and wrapped it in a clean cloth boiled in an infusion of oak bark, a remedy I had seen my aunt use whenever my uncles hurt themselves in their workshop. I gave great thanks to God that we remained in Apalache after I was injured, because in truth I could not have walked even a league on that leg, let alone the five or six leagues per day we usually covered in our march. I made myself a cane and hobbled around on it, attending to the cooking, cleaning, and mending.

Other men in the company had not been so lucky: nine had died in the battle against the Indians and three others later, of their wounds. They were buried, one after the other, in a small plot at the edge of the capital, their graveside prayers once again delegated to the young friar, Father Anselmo, who was becoming popular among the men. After the morning mass, after his brothers in brown robes retired to their huts, he would stay and play the fiddle. He played tunes from the old country, some mournful, others joyous, his long fingers moving gracefully on the instrument. The men—disappointed, fatigued, fearful, or sick—would listen and, for a few moments, they would forget about the lost gold, the long march, or the Indians waiting in the bushes.

But then, after the music had stopped and they had returned to their chores, the men would start to remember. Quarrels would erupt between them about little things, things that had not mattered when all they had to do was march and hope, but now seemed to matter a great deal: who received better quarters, who should be entitled to larger rations, who would inherit a dead man's armor or his boots. So the commissary spent much of his time adjudicating quarrels, trying to keep the peace as best as he could by means of difficult compromises.

Throughout all this, the governor was absent—he was busy with his interrogations of the cacique Kamasha and with the scouting missions he organized around the city. Then, one evening, he invited the commissary and the captains to meet him in the Indian temple. It was cool inside the hall—there had been two thunderstorms that day and the air felt new, with fewer flies and mosquitoes to torment us. A large cross of rough timber stood against the northern wall, where the wooden idols had once been, and the round baskets that had sat on the pedestals were gone, leaving behind only dark circles on the brown mats. The governor's candelabras had been lost in one of the swamps we crossed, so his servant had used wooden torches to light the bare table on which he served dinner—it was a good dinner, with roasted rabbit meat, cooked beans, and some fresh corn, although it was more modest than what was usually served for such councils. While the captains took their seats on benches, waiting for their leader to speak, I stood against the wall, waiting to refill my master's cup or clear his plate.

The governor stood up. He wore a gray doublet, but the edges of it were becoming yellow and there was a hole in his breeches, just above his left knee. Esteemed señores, he said. The cacique Kamasha has informed me that Apalache is a kingdom of many cities, but none is bigger or richer than this one, and that, on the contrary, the other cities are much poorer. However, about eight days' march south of here, he says, there is another city called Aute, which is very close to the ocean and has a great many quantities of corn, beans, and fish. My plan is to march to Aute, from where we can send a party to the Río de las Palmas. Since the city is on the coast, and since it has its own food reserves, we can stay there for as long as is necessary until we make contact with our ships. And of course, once we have the ships, we will sail along the coast until we find an area more suitable for settlement than this one.

The governor invited all the captains to give their opinions. It occurred to me that his insistence on seeking the counsel of others was his best quality, yet it was strangely coupled with an inability to take their advice. It was quiet in the temple for a long while, the only noise coming from the clattering of the officers' utensils, but as usual it was Señor Castillo who spoke first. I agree that we should leave this place, he said. But we rushed into Apalache without the proper precautions, so we must learn from our mistake and not rush out of the city without taking the proper precautions.

Rushing? We have been here three weeks, Castillo, the governor said.

How can we trust what the cacique is telling us? He wants us out of his capital, he will say anything to make us leave.

His deputy said the same thing. As well the servant who was caught alongside them. Do you think they all conferred on what to say before-hand? I will remind you that I had them questioned separately.

Señor Castillo looked around him for support. But, although many of the officers agreed with him, none dared to speak so plainly to the governor and all were quite content to let him argue their case and be reprimanded in their place. His voice rose to a higher register. We cannot take their agreement for proof, he said. Remember, all of the prisoners you questioned said that Apalache had great quantities of gold. And now we know this to be untrue. We should indeed return to the coast, but we should not follow the prisoners' advice on how to get there.

I have sent three scouting missions, the governor said, and none found a shorter trail to the ocean.

This is why I warned against letting the ships sail away while we went into the interior.

It is easy to criticize a plan when you do not have to make one. And may I add, Castillo, that your behavior since our landing in this territory has been so contrarian as to verge on the mutinous.

The word hung in the air like an accusation—you could almost see it in the way the captains shifted in their seats or looked away from Señor Castillo, as if they might be tainted by the allegation.

Señor Dorantes alone came to his friend's defense. Don Pánfilo, Castillo was merely offering his opinion, as you yourself asked.

Reluctantly, Señor Castillo said: Don Pánfilo, it was not my intention to dispute your authority. The decision is yours.

You would do well to remember it, the governor said.

With the charge of mutiny averted, the air shifted again. The commissary picked up a walnut from the bowl at the center of the table and used the handle of his knife to crack it open.

The safest thing to do, Señor Cabeza de Vaca said, is to return to Portillo and walk from there to the port. The chief pilot did say that it was no more than twenty leagues from that point.

But Señor Dorantes objected. No, he said. We do not have enough provisions for a return march.

The treasurer picked up a rabbit bone from his plate and held it up like a piece of evidence. We can hunt, he said. There are deer, rabbit, and fowl all about . . .

What if the hunt does not yield enough food for everyone in the company? Do you want to see three hundred men fight over the meat? If we want to return to the coast swiftly, we need to have enough rations for six weeks at the very least.

Then what do you suggest, Dorantes?

Find a shorter way to the coast.

The governor smiled. That is why I want to go to Aute, he said. It is only eight days from here. Arm yourselves with patience, I beg you. When we return to the ships, we will continue along the coast until we find an area more appropriate for settlement. And I shall not forget those who have served His Majesty loyally.

The governor looked pointedly at Señor Cabeza de Vaca, seeking his endorsement, but the treasurer kept his eyes on his plate and remained silent, as if he feared supporting this new proposal, only to be proven wrong later and be blamed for its failure. Although there was no great enthusiasm for the plan among the captains, I think they all knew that our situation in Apalache was intolerable: we simply could not stay in the city, surrounded by so many people who wanted it back. The Indians feared muskets and were powerless against them, but our reserves of ammunition were not limitless. What would happen when we ran out?

The governor closed the meeting by saying that he would hold another council in a day or two, once all the captains had had a chance to think about the plan. Yet early the next morning, when we were still eating the morning meal, the governor sent his page to inform all the captains that he had made his decision: we were to go to Aute. Once again, I marched behind my master into the unknown, led by a governor who, though he retained the use of one eye, was the blindest man I had ever met.

8.

THE STORY OF SEVILLE

All around me, voices rose and fell. Shackled slaves spoke in an overlapping multitude of languages, this one asking after an uncle, this other comforting a child, and yet these others arguing about a piece of moldy bread, their cries periodically interrupted by the bleating of goats from the animal stalls. But for a long time, I kept to my silence, wrapping myself in it like an old, comfortable cloak. I think I was still trying to apprehend the consequences of what I had done. For hours on end, I revisited the long sequence of events that had led me from the soft divans and rhythmic guenbris of my graduation feast to the timber bench and jangling chains of the caravel Jacinta, sailing with frightening speed toward the city of Seville. I had played my part in these events—I had made my decisions freely and independently at each juncture, and yet I was stunned by the turn my life had taken. The elders teach us: give glory to God, who can alter all fates. One day you could be selling slaves, the next you could be sold as a slave.

The hunger I had felt so keenly in Azemmur was tamed now, if not satisfied, by the hard bread the sailors distributed once a day, though it was quickly replaced by a renewed acquaintance with all of my body's other senses and needs. My head itched from the lice my neighbor, an old man with pockmarks dotting his face, had given me. My soiled clothes stuck to my skin, because I could not bring myself to use, on command and with little notice, the bucket that was passed up and down the gallery twice a day. My limbs grew stiff from sitting in damp and narrow quarters. My throat hurt, my feet swelled, my wrists bled. Above all, my heart ached with longing for my family.

My family. They had, all of them, learned to accept their fates. Without complaint my sister had spent her girlhood watching over our twin brothers, and without protest she had returned home after her divorce. My brothers went to school every day hoping to fulfill my father's dreams, dreams I had cruelly broken and then bequeathed to them. My mother had left her beloved people and her distinguished hometown in order to follow my father to Azemmur.

As for me, I had made a habit of defying my fate. Perhaps I could do that now and find a way back to my old life. I thought of the elder al-Dib, my employer in Azemmur, who had been born to a slavewoman, but had earned his freedom as a youth. Perhaps I could do the same. Perhaps my talent would be recognized by my master, who would let me purchase my freedom; or perhaps my misery would touch the heart of an Andalusian Muslim, who would free me from bondage in order to earn the favor of our Lord. To overcome my fear, I shackled myself with hope, its links heavier than any metal known to man.

Having convinced myself that my condition was temporary, I set about trying to survive it. I taught myself to ignore the stench of excretions, the moans of delirium, the sight of private parts. I learned to push back into my throat the rising taste of vomit. I tried to watch out for the rats. I slept only when my exhaustion overpowered my discomfort. And I passed the time by listening to the stories the women told their children, after the guards had left and the doors were locked for the night. In the darkness of the lower deck, the women brought to life a world entire, a world where sly girls outwitted hungry ghouls and where simple cobblers saved powerful sultans, so that at times it seemed to me I could see the ghouls' sharp teeth or the sultan's embroidered slippers.

Then, early one morning, the anchor was dropped, its tug faintly resonating through the varnished wood under my feet. I listened to the footsteps on the upper deck. Did the customs officer come aboard to greet the captain? Was that the stevedore inquiring about the merchandise? Then at last the deck door was flung wide open. A rush of cold air blasted into the lower deck, where it met with the suppressed heat and terrified silence of two hundred slaves. Row by row, we were unshackled and led up the stairs.

When I reached the upper deck, the blinding white light made me recoil in pain and I staggered like a drunkard, but after three weeks in closed quarters I was so hungry for the untainted smell of open air that I took my hands off my face. Seville reeked of fried fish, but its air was not briny, and there was a whiff of smoke coming from somewhere in the port. The morning chill gave me goose bumps and I put my arms around me, all the while steadying myself on my feet. Finally, I opened my eyes.

All around me were men whose faces were covered in brightly colored kerchiefs, with openings for the eyes. They carried long sticks, with which they prodded me to the way out. As I went down the ship's rope ladder, I saw that I was on a wide river. It ran fast, just like the Umm er-Rbi', and yet its sound, the particular melody it made as it rumbled beneath the ship, was different. Later, when I would learn that this river was called the Guadalquivir, the Arabic name would at once delight me with its familiarity and repulse me with its reminder of my personal humiliation. The city of Seville did not have a pier like the one in Azemmur, so we had to be taken by rowboat to the riverbank. The sky above was a tur-quoise blue, cut through by the black masts and white sails of the ships around us.

On the shore, a man whose face was hidden behind a yellow kerchief was separating the healthy from the lame, the sturdy from the weak, the young from the old. He jabbed me with a stick, and then pointed me to the first line. All around me, the port hummed with the sounds of sailors, officers, porters, and scribes, each hurriedly going about his busi-ness. Two men standing next to a tall stack of crates were having a loud argument, I remember, and one of them seized the other by his collar. Beyond the port, the city's white, square homes were slowly rising from their slumber. Carts creaked on the cobblestone. Horses clopped in the distance. Somewhere, I knew, a father was sitting down for a morning meal with his family. Somewhere, a child was receiving her bowl of milk. Somewhere, a brother was closing the door of his house behind him as he went to work. And I was here, at the port, ready to be sold once again.

A man with a red kerchief grouped a dozen of us together, the way farmers collect their eggs or bakers their loaves, tied our hands to one another with thick rope, and led us away from the port. It was a long and painful walk, because we were all weak from hunger and idleness. Periodically one of us fell and had to be helped up, but our wretched procession drew no stares of interest or curiosity from the many people we passed. Each one went about his business without the slightest pause.

At a bend in the road I caught the first glimpse of an imposing tower, which looked very much like the minarets at home. What is the name of that tower? I asked the man with the red kerchief. La Giralda, he said without turning. I had heard of La Giralda years earlier—it had been built by the Almohad sultans as a replica of the Kutubiya in Marrakesh—and I had even fantasized of seeing it someday, but never under these circumstances.

Around the corner from La Giralda, we stopped in front of a tall edifice, with large wooden doors and an imposing facade. As we ascended the marble steps, an older man in our group slipped and fell and we all tumbled in a pile over him. The slave merchant clicked his tongue at the delay we were causing him—his long day, already filled with labor, was made more difficult by our clumsiness. The fallen man stood up, his palm over his broken tooth and bloodied lips, even as the merchant pulled roughly on the rope and led us toward the entrance.

We were brought before an imam of the Christian faith, a man of freckled complexion and colorless eyes, who spoke an ancient tongue I did not understand. I could detect no pattern to the words that poured like a river out of his mouth, but I listened nonetheless, to distract myself from my thirst and my hunger. He wore a robe of immaculate white, with carefully embroidered edges. Behind him, a stained glass window colored the morning light in various shades of red, yellow, and blue. Though I had been taught to distrust pictures of the human form, I could not help staring at the white woman with a babe in arms and the brilliantly attired men gathered around her. They seemed removed from our untidy and disgraceful world, engaged in their own story, unconcerned about the scene unfolding beneath them.

Being the tallest man in my family, I was used to lowering my head when I passed through the doorway of our house and to seeing my knees stick out when I sat on my heels next to my uncles. Yet here, in this high-ceilinged church, I felt small and helpless. My hands were tied together and bound to the slaves on either side of me. If one of us moved his hands or feet in order to find a more comfortable stance, the slave merchant pulled on the rope to force the insurgent back in line. With a snap, the priest closed his book and laid it carefully on a table beside him. He nodded to the merchant, who nudged the first in our group forward, a woman with wide, protruding eyes. The priest's fingers traced a cross in the air, over her face and chest. I looked at him unblinkingly, all the while wondering what the action meant and why he repeated it with each one of us. It was not until much later that I understood the significance of the sign on our bodies. I had entered the church as the servant of God Mustafa ibn Muhammad ibn Abdussalam al-Zamori; I left it as Esteban. Just Esteban—converted and orphaned in one gesture.

The slave merchant led us out of the cathedral. He pulled his red kerchief back up over his nose to protect himself against the smell of his charges. Walking with the swiftness of a man determined to make the most of his day, he led us back to the port and to a holding pen guarded by dogs. In truth, there was no need for them since we were all so tired and hungry we would not have had the power to run far. The four women in our group went to huddle together on the far side of the holding pen. I had trouble speaking to them, on account of the fact that they spoke a different variety of Tamazight than I did, but by and by I gathered that they were the daughters of farmers who had suffered great hardship during the drought. Two of the men told me they were from Guinea and had been sold on the slave markets there, then transported to Azemmur, and from there to Seville. Just before nightfall, a man brought us bowls of cold soup. We called the name of God over our food, each in our own language and custom, and ate hungrily.

I lay down on the pallet that, by the following morning, would give me a terrible rash, and tried to go to sleep. But sleep eluded me. In the distance, I could hear the Guadalquivir, and my thoughts drifted to Yahya, who, despite my repeated efforts, had not learned how to swim. He had never been able to conquer his fear of water long enough to wade into the heart of the Umm er-Rbi'. How Yusuf would tease him! I tried to protect him from the taunts of the other boys as they swam in the river, but he always ended up in tears. Sometimes, during the mating season, a shad would fly out of the water, and I would try to catch it so that Yahya, seeing my feat, would finally want to leave the safety of the shore. But the fish were always too slippery for me and I was never able to pull off the trick. Would Yusuf teach him what I had not been able to?

Despite the faint sound of the river, this strange city filled me with dread. I tossed and turned for a long while before I realized why it felt so quiet and so empty—I had not heard the call for prayer. In Azemmur, I had heard it five times a day, every day of my life. The morning prayer woke me; the noon prayer told me that it was time to eat and rest; the afternoon prayer refreshed me after a long nap; the dusk prayer delivered me from my workday and to my family; and the evening prayer commended my soul to God. Now I was alone in the world. All I could do to contain the tears that welled in my eyes was to lie in the dark and call silently upon God until I fell asleep.

DAMAS Y CABALLEROS, this is a fine specimen. A negro from Azemmur, twenty to twenty-five years of age. Tall and broad-shouldered. A bit thin, but you can tell from his bearing that he is very strong. Good teeth. Do not be alarmed by his stained gums: the Moors clean their teeth with walnut root; it leaves behind an orange tint. What else? Let me see. The ledger says that he used to work for merchants. He is fluent in Portuguese, and can also manage some words in our idiom. A bargain at twenty-five ducats. Twenty-five ducats!

THAT I HAD ENDED UP on the auction block of my own volition did not lessen my fear. My breath quickened at the sight of the raised platform. The auctioneer's voice mixed with that of children laughing, dogs barking, and hammers beating, in a cacophony that had started long before my arrival and would continue long after my departure. Somewhere, a musician played the flute, but the cheerful tune failed to stand out from the other sounds or to distract me from my surroundings. The sun glinted off the metal platters of the silversmith across from me and I had to turn my face away. My eyes met those of a little boy in dark clothes who had been staring at me. He wanted to get a closer look, for he took off his short-brimmed hat. With a swift movement, his mother put it back on his head. Por Dios, she said in a voice ringing with annoyance.

Among the slaves waiting their turn, I noticed many who had two marks on their cheeks—one in the shape of a coiling snake and the other in the form of a cross. I ventured to ask an Andalusian woman, whom I had heard whisper some words in Arabic to her daughter, what the brand on her face meant. It means esclavo, she said, peering at me with curious eyes. Looking around me, I noticed that none of the black people in the marketplace had been marked with the brand. In Seville, the color of their skin—the color of my skin—was a sign in itself.

My group was led onto the platform and made to face the crowd. For a few moments, all of us, buyers and slaves, regarded one another appraisingly. The buyers looked for the slaves that were most likely to fulfill their needs: a domestic, a farm worker, a porter, a concubine. They all wanted a good bargain—the strongest, healthiest, or prettiest for the least amount of money. The slaves, too, looked at the buyers, trying to guess who among them seemed the least demanding, the least avaricious, or the least cruel, even though their guesses were of no import to the outcome.

The auctioneer's voice was as loud and strong as that of the town crier in Azemmur. I remembered all the times I had seen slaves in the marketplace of my hometown. I had never thought about these men and women, had never wondered how they had ended up in chains, had never worried about who they had left at home and who would miss them and pray for their return. I had passed them and gone about my business, delivering wax to a merchant or buying flour for the evening meal, without dwelling on the sight. Later, out of sheer greed for more gold, I had sold slaves myself. But now it was I on the auction block, while, in the distance, people went about their business without giving me a second look.

The first man in our group, the man who had tripped on the stairs of the cathedral, sold for less than ten ducats. He was swiftly taken off the platform by a grimy farmer, and in my mind's eye I saw the backbreaking work that awaited him, the leftovers he would be fed, the barn where he would sleep. I tried to suppress my fear. Perhaps I would be luckier. Perhaps I would end up with a better master.

Swatting flies, the auctioneer looked displeased with the price he had received. He called out for the first of the four women in our group. Without warning, he lifted her dress up. He held her breast in his palm and said she was young and healthy and could bear many children. In her shame, she could only stare at the ground as the boys in the crowd jeered and the girls muffled their giggles. At that moment, I gave many thanks to God that I was not born a woman and did not have to suffer her humiliation.

Next was a little girl who, moments earlier, had been digging in the dirt with a stick. The auctioneer said she could make a fine domestic, that she was young enough to be trained, but old enough not to need much care. As if realizing that she, too, could take part in the performance on the raised platform, she twirled around on one toe and smiled at the crowd. The auctioneer chuckled and called out a price, but he had to lower it twice before the woman with the hatted boy raised her hand.

Suddenly I remembered what my employers in Azemmur sometimes did when they received too large a shipment of cotton or glass. They quietly stored the goods in the warehouse to prevent prices from falling down in the face of so much supply. The less a customer paid for the goods he purchased, they said, the less he valued them. I am ashamed to say that, after watching the other slaves be taken away in such a manner, I stood tall and tried to look as healthy as I could.

It was my turn. The auctioneer's voice was getting hoarse from all the shouting. A fine specimen, he cried. The rope that tied my hands had cut through my skin, but I resisted the urge to chase flies away because I did not want to draw attention to them. Two buyers raised their forefingers. The auctioneer paced on the platform, pointing to my shoulders, my arms, my legs, and the price went up and up, and up again. The auction's winner, the man with whom I would spend the next four and a half years of my life, was a merchant by the name of Bernardo Rodriguez. When he took custody of me, Rodriguez asked the auctioneer to untie me. He might run away, the auctioneer warned.

This Moro? Look at him, Rodriguez said, he could not go far.

IN THE EYES OF his people, Bernardo Rodriguez was not an unkind man. He departed for work every day trailed by the perfumed blessings his wife, Dorotea, asked the good Lord to bestow upon him. When he was at the shop, he easily struck up a conversation with his customers, always remembering to ask after the health of an old aunt or the fortune of a traveling son. Sometimes, he played with his three children—Isabel, Sancho, and Martín—in the shaded patio of his house, and let them ride on his back as he went around the small fountain. At church, he sang with a clear voice and offered an unburdened Amen to the priest's prayer. Rodriguez had two unforgivable habits, however, and it was because of his unquenchable desire to satisfy both that he sold me. But I must not get ahead of myself.

Rodriguez was born and bred in Seville, and he knew many of its natives. For years, he had been a small merchant, eking a living out of a narrow shop much like those in the Qaisariya of Azemmur, with nothing but a few dozen rolls of poor-quality velvet to his name. But Rodriguez was also a dreamer. He liked to watch the arrival of ships from the Indies, a newly discovered land at the far reaches of the empire, and fantasize about the treasures in their holds. At the Torre del Oro, he had seen so much gold, silver, and precious stones coming from México that it had once taken three days to unload just one caravel. There were other goods, too, goods that anyone with enough funds could freely purchase: bales of cotton, woven cloth, rich tapestries, small ornaments, exotic edibles.

It so happened that, one day, as he was wistfully strolling along the Arenal, Rodriguez came face-to-face with Cristóbal Díaz, a friend of his he had not seen in almost a decade, when they were both young lads looking for cheap wine and cheaper women. While Rodriguez had dutifully apprenticed to a merchant, Díaz continued to visit taverns until he turned into a lout and eventually disappeared from the neighborhood. Yet now he was dressed in a fine doublet and good boots and had the worldly look of a soldier about him. Where have you been all these years? Rodriguez asked him.

New Spain, Díaz said. He began to relate his travels to La Española and Cuba, where he had taken part in the campaign on Camagüey and the capture of a native chief, who went by the name of Hatuey. But the gruesome crimes Díaz had witnessed in the Indies had caused him to have a change of heart—in fact, he was preparing to enter into the Franciscan Order. To atone for his sins, he wanted to relieve himself of a load of cotton he had acquired, which was why he had come to the Arenal. Rodriguez bought the load for ten thousand maravedis and sold it for five times that amount to a merchant from Toledo, the profit allowing him to finally enter the trade of Indian goods. This was in the year 926 of the Hegira. And now, just three years later, Rodriguez's business was large enough that he found himself in the position of purchasing a slave.

That slave was me.

I followed Rodriguez to his home in Triana, where he called on his wife to come see his new acquisition. Dorotea Rodriguez appeared at the door of the dining room, dressed in a severe black dress with gray trim. For a moment, she stood there watching me, her blue eyes wide with surprise. A long string of prayer beads dangled from her right hand. Pursing her lips, she crossed the courtyard and came to stand before me. At once her hand flew to her nose, shielding her from the smell of my soiled clothes. Bernardo, she said to her husband. Bernardo, what have you done?

What does it look like?

Are you sure you can afford it?

I only paid twenty-five ducats.

Oh, Bernardo.

I cannot take him back, if that is what you mean.

But it is another mouth to feed.

Worry not about that.

Has he been baptized at least?

Of course. His name is Esteban.

And you intend to keep him here?

Yes, where else?

How can we keep him here, with the children around?

I will lock him up at night if it makes you feel better.

I had averted my eyes when the lady of the house approached, but now I looked up. She brought her hands to her heart and rested her chin upon them. While she watched me, Rodriguez brought an old blanket and pointed me to a closet behind the kitchen.

He looks shifty, she said to him.

He looks hungry, rather.

Do not complain to me if he ends up cheating you of your money.

Rodriguez heaved a sigh and led me to the closet—this would serve as my room. The conversation that I had just witnessed would repeat itself in a different form nearly every day. In figure and temperament alike, my master and his wife were the opposite of one another. He was stout and short; she was thin and tall. He loved to take risks and try new things; she was very cautious and set in her ways. He was ambitious; she was content with her station in life. In short, they made an unlikely pair, but they had turned their mismatch into a source of banter and a kind of bond, all the stronger for its peculiarity.

TO GO FROM FREEDOM to slavery was a fate worse than death; it was a rebirth into an alien world, with its strange customs and unbearable rules. I had to learn all the things I was not permitted to do: to speak my language; to assemble with other slaves in an inn; to run in the streets; to carry a weapon; to look at a Castilian lady; to sleep after sunrise; to ride in a coach; to refuse an order; to make a joke; to complain or disagree—and the list grew longer each day.

In the morning, I followed Bernardo Rodriguez to the Torre del Oro or the Casa de Contratación, waiting quietly as he met with vendors and made his purchases. The work was familiar enough, and my instincts and training were useful: in my first week with him, I found a mistake in the ledger and caught two damaged crates before they were loaded onto the cart. Back at the store, he went over his inventory, decided on sale prices, and received buyers—merchants who came from as far north as Valencia. But I could not go home at an appointed hour, with the knowledge that my day's work was done and that my time was now mine, to use or waste as I wished. Like a horse or a mule, I had to keep working until I was pulled away from my task.

Time to stop, my master said one evening.

Sí, Señor, I replied. I began to sweep the floors.

Then a voice called out from the darkness of the wet street. Rodriguez.

Who is that? Step into the light so that I can see you.

A man of middle age, with thick blond hair and a large mole on his cheek, came inside the shop. A leather satchel was slung across his chest, just above his paunch. He smelled of horses. Herrera, my master said. How good it is to see you. When did you arrive?

Only this evening. We had many delays on the road because of the rain.

They inquired after each other and discussed their health and ailments for a while before Herrera asked what was new in the shop.

I have silk, linen, taffeta, Rodriguez said. Some serge of excellent quality. But I just bought this wonderful cotton from the Indies. See how soft it is?

How much do you want for it?

Twenty for each roll.

Outrageous.

You will sell it for twice that in Salamanca.

You have not been to Salamanca, have you? No one will pay that much.

Of course they will. This kind of cotton only comes from México. You will sell it all before Easter.

I doubt it, you crook. All the same, let me have a piece and I will call again tomorrow with my answer.

Esteban, what on earth are you doing cleaning up? Get Señor Herrera his sample.

Because Rodriguez had never owned a slave and I had never been one, our relationship was improvised. He decreed rules (Always check the purchase order), then changed them (Do not touch the purchase order). Sometimes, he asked for my opinion on the wares he bought, but if I offered it unbidden he told me to be quiet. He could be pleasant and undemanding one day, then exigent and cruel the next. I discovered that I could never take a small detour from one of my errands for the sake of watching the sunset over the Guadalquivir—any moment of contemplation or idleness earned me questions and reprimands.

I tried to seek comfort in prayer and to speak to my Maker in the only way I knew. Once, I was prostrated behind the counter in the shop, facing east toward Mecca for the 'asr prayer, begging the Lord to save me. Help me find a way home, I whispered. Help me, O merciful God. The sudden weight of a Spanish boot upon my neck silenced my voice, and the next moment my face, scraping against the brick floor of the shop, was smashed against a pot from Malaga. Stand up, Moro, Rodriguez said, even as he continued to press his heel on my neck. Blood rushed to my scalp and streamed down my cheeks. Stand up, he said, but I could not move for the throbbing in my head. A kick in the side made me double over and now I found myself on my knees, being yanked up by the collar of my shirt. The beatings repeated themselves with such a wearying frequency that I desisted from praying and retreated instead into silent communions with my Lord.

At night, when I walked in with Rodriguez and saw his children running up to greet him, I thought of my mother, who would always be there as soon as I closed the blue door of our house behind me. She would have water warming on the brazier for my prayer ablutions. Slower, I would sometimes say as she poured it over my hands. Or, the water is too hot today, Mother. It stunned me now that I could ever have complained about something so trivial. When I entered the closet behind the kitchen, no one was there to greet me. No one stood up to say that a neighbor had come calling for me, or to ask me why I had come home later than usual, or to quarrel with me for having yet again forgotten to bring home the bread from the neighborhood oven. No one held me and I had no one to hold.

After a while, even the trade lost its attraction. The act of buying or selling, which I had viewed as my calling only a few years earlier, and for the sake of which I had disobeyed my father, lost its appeal for me. And because I lost interest, I did not care about the goods my master purchased, did not feel excitement when we received a novelty item, and did not notice if the delivery count did not match the purchase order. My master took to calling me lazy, stupid, a disgraceful Moor with no sense of duty. He bought another slave, a man from Angola, and said he would put him up at the shop so he would not grow as soft and spoiled as I, who slept in the closet behind the kitchen.

My misery, or at least my solitude, was somewhat alleviated a year after my arrival in Seville, when my master brought Elena home. The price of slaves had fallen so much that spring that Rodriguez had decided to buy his wife her own bondswoman, someone who could help her with the housework and care for the children. He said that all the noblewomen of the city had slaves, whom they liked to dress up in finery and parade like thoroughbreds when they took their evening walks along the promenade. His wife ought to do the same. In this way, he said, she would meet and befriend ladies of the nobler classes.

And so Elena stood where I had once stood, three or four paces away from the lemon tree in the courtyard, submitting herself to the examination of Dorotea Rodriguez. Elena was small and finely built, with braided hair and high cheekbones. The tunic she wore did not disguise the beautiful shape of her hips or her graceful legs. But she seemed quite unaware of the world around her; she stared blankly ahead, lost in her thoughts, as though her entrance into the Rodriguez house were happening to someone else. Heavens, the mistress said, her face tightened into a scowl. Look at the filthy rag she wears.

I will bring you some serge from the store.

Serge? No, two or three varas of plain woolen cloth will do.

Very well.

And her nails are dirty.

She was at auction, Dorotea. What do you expect?

I hope she is not diseased.

She just needs a good scrub.

Good thing she is in Seville, then. Is she baptized?

Why do you ask questions to which you already know the answers?

Because if she is going to care for my children every day, I need to be certain. I will send her to Father Bartolomé for proper instruction this very week. I will not take any chances.

Will you also make sure to teach her how to cook? Or better yet, no. I have had quite enough of that dry roast you make.

Ordinarily, my mistress deposited my bowl of food, when she remembered it, on the red tiled floor outside the kitchen door, but once Elena joined the household and took over the cooking, my dinner appeared in its usual spot with comforting regularity. I fell into the habit of waiting by the door for it. One day, Elena motioned for me to come inside. We ate together on the sisal mat that served as her bed, under the high, barred windows of the kitchen. As she dipped her spoon into her bowl, I noticed on the back of her right hand a small tattoo in the shape of a comb, its teeth perfectly aligned.

We did not speak much at first, because our native tongues were barely intelligible to one another—she was from the land farther south than Mazghan, farther even than Mugadir, from a small town on the bank of the River of Gold, in Singhana—but eventually she learned enough Spanish to enable us to hold simple conversations, about an order that needed to be carried out or an errand that had to be done. One day, I asked her if Elena was her real name. No, she said. She seemed to hesitate, and then she whispered: It is Ramatullai.

I repeated the name out loud—Ramatullai, Ramatullai, Ramatullai—so surprised was I by the inflection the Arabic word had taken in her native language. What had sounded unfamiliar turned out to be familiar, and this discovery filled me with an unexpected and immense joy. My name is Mustafa, I said.

Like my father, she said. She smiled for the first time, revealing a set of perfectly aligned teeth. Her features moved with a grace I felt privileged to witness. And you work with him at the shop? she asked.

It was always like this when she spoke of our master—she said he or him, but she never said his name. If she happened to be in the patio when he came out in the morning, she would greet him with a proper Señor, but in her mouth the word seemed to suggest anything but deference.

I work for him, I said. Not with him.

Did you ever see a customer—like this? She stood up and walked the length of the kitchen with her shoulders hunched forward, her hand grasping an imaginary cane.

A hunchback?

Yes. With a hole here. She pointed to her chin.

A dimple, you mean. No, I have not seen him. (By then, as I said, I had lost interest in my master's trade and did not pay close attention to what happened in the shop.) Why do you ask?

My daughter Amna—she was sold to a man like that.

You have a daughter?

I have two.

I had been so taken with her that I had not paused to think that she might already belong to someone else, that she had had a life of her own before coming to the Rodriguez house. But, out of pride, I was unwilling to show that the revelation had disappointed me. Instead I asked, What happened to your other daughter?

I was sold and taken away before I could see what happened to her, she said.

For a moment, the vacant look I had seen on the first day returned to her eyes. She stood there, surrounded by pots and pans, with onions and garlic hanging in braids from the rafters, and it was as if she was not with me. Her soul had traveled up and out of the kitchen, flown across Triana, and now hovered somewhere over the marketplace, searching for a trace of her daughters. Was there a greater pain in the world, I wondered, than having your babies taken away from you?

At length, the spirit returned to her. Quietly, I asked: What about your husband?

They killed him, she said. He tried to fight one of the Portuguese.

I let out a breath—I had not realized I had been holding it—and leaned back against the tiled wall. If I see this hunchback at the shop, I said, I will tell you.

She looked at me with such gratitude that I felt as if the entire world were grateful to me. I resolved then and there to keep a close eye on all the merchants, in the hope that I might see her smile again.

I finished my bowl of lentils and was about to stand up when she took it from me. Sit. Sit a while longer.

While she washed our bowls I told her about my family—I felt fortunate that they had been spared the fate that had befallen me. At least I did not have to worry about them and wonder where they were. The next day, for the first time since my arrival in Seville, I did not dread my return to the closet behind the kitchen.

9

The Story of Aute

A settler—I never learned his name, I believe he was a butcher or a barber, someone unused to long marches in the damp heat—came down with a fever. A ride, he asked, going from horseman to horseman. Señor, please let me ride with you. But none of the officers allowed it; they were afraid of whatever afflicted him. It was only after he fell to his knees, unable to stop himself from soiling his clothes, that one of the captains ordered that he be carried on a packhorse. At the next river crossing, the settler asked to be lowered into the water, to clean himself or perhaps to cool down, but even so his fever did not break. Blood ran from his nose, trickling down on a shirt that had long ago lost its color to the dirt and the mud. He stared from unseeing eyes at those who came to bring him food, or pray with him, or just look at him, as if to reassure themselves about their good fortunes.

Perhaps those who came to console themselves by looking at the sick man were wrong; at least he, in his delirium, did not fear the Apalaches who had been following our procession ever since we began our march to Aute. The Apalaches were such skilled archers that their bows seemed to us like limbs, parts of their bodies they could use with unconscious ease. They could shoot arrows from a great distance with perfect aim and were familiar with the terrains we were traversing—the green, flat lands strewn with swamps, rivers, and fallen trees, and filled with strange animals.

Whenever we crossed a swamp, burdened by our loads and fearful of the lagartos, the Apalaches struck us, succeeding each time in inflicting some harm on our company. They killed a man in armor by aiming for his throat and forced a porter to leave behind one case of ammunition and two cases of tools as he ran for cover. They wounded a horse when it was wading through a swamp. They kidnapped one of the Indian captives the governor had brought from Portillo and, seeing the look of terror on the prisoner's face, I was not at all sure that his new jailers meant him well.

Then came the day when Gonzalo Ruíz broke down. Ruíz was a rough soldier, hard to impress and even harder to scare. During the journey across the Ocean of Fog and Darkness, he had been one of two men in charge of securing the lower deck of the Gracia de Dios. I remember that, about a month into our voyage, he accused the stable boy, a shy lad from the Gold Coast, of stealing a barrel of wine. A bitter fight between them had ensued, which Señor Dorantes had been forced to break up. The stable boy was put in irons for three days, a judgment that kindled in me a simmering aversion for Ruíz. But, aside from the usual grumbling of soldiers, Ruíz had not attracted anyone's notice again. Yet now he let out a terrifying howl that startled all of us. From his horse, Señor Dorantes turned to look. Ruíz, he said sharply, contain yourself.

Ruíz's eyes had the glint of madness about them. No, he said. I am not going to wait for the savages to hunt me down like a partridge. With his musket leveled before him, he left the procession and went looking for Indians deep in the bushes.

Ruíz, my master called. Return to the line immediately.

But the only reply was the rustling of leaves. Oak, cedar, and juniper trees stood tall in a sea of wild green grass. The smell of the sick man on the packhorse was all around us. Above us, the sky had lost its color, turning a bluish tinge of white. And the sun was so hot it made our ears ring.

We should send someone after him, Señor Castillo said.

He disobeyed my order, Señor Dorantes replied.

Each captain was responsible for his own contingent—usually, the men who had traveled with him from Seville—so the governor did not intervene. He nudged his horse forward on the trail, and we resumed the march. But only a moment later, a scream of pain cut through the air like a knife, and Ruíz reemerged from the bushes, without his weapon and with his hands covering his bloodied face. The Apalaches had thrown a rock at him with such precision that they had taken out his left eye, turning him into a younger, leaner version of the governor. His fellow soldiers gathered around Ruíz, but Señor Dorantes shook his head slowly, in a way that suggested Ruíz had been too foolish to merit a better fate.

• • •

SO WE LIVED IN FEAR. We feared the fever, the Indians, and our hunger. We feared the swamps, the water lizards, and the berries of unfamiliar bushes. We feared not finding Aute and we feared finding it. At least the sick man no longer had such varied and constant reasons to worry: he could lose himself to the disease and forget everything else. Perhaps it was this desire for the peace of delirium that led so many men in our company to succumb to the fever. By the fifth day of the march to Aute, the governor had to assign horses solely for the transport of the sick—nearly thirty men in all.

Sometimes, I thought of letting go, too. Sitting under the shade of a poplar tree as the company took its midday break, I wondered what would happen to me if I was infected with the fever and perished in this land. Who would wash my body for burial? Who would commend my soul to God? Who would mourn me? I whispered Ayat al-Kursi to myself, over and over, the way I had as a child, whenever I had been scared or troubled or worried, hoping it would grant me the same measure of peace it had back then. With the stick in my hand, I wrote the verse on the ground before me, each word, each stroke taking me back further to my days at the msid in Azemmur, to those days when my life was still my own. His throne doth extend over the heavens and the earth and He feeleth—

You can write? Señor Dorantes asked. He was looking over my shoulder at the line of characters in the dirt, his elbow resting against the trunk of the tree. I was startled by his silent appearance behind me and I rushed to stand up, but he put his hand on my shoulder, urging me to sit down. Where did you learn? he asked.

At home, Señor. In Azemmur.

My father's dearest friend is a converso—a jeweler from Cordoba. He still keeps his ledgers in Arabic, even though my father warned him that it might raise questions with the inquisitor. But I suppose it is hard to break old habits.

I ran my tongue on my lips, not sure what to say next. Experience had taught me that these kinds of conversations, with personal questions, friendly questions even, were dangerous, that they fed the master new ways of tormenting you later on, when you let down your guard. So I remained quiet, hoping the moment would pass. A soft breeze rustled the leaves of the poplar tree, shifting the dappled light on the ground. From the cluster of men behind us, someone called out for Father Anselmo to come hear a confession.

How did you end up in Seville, then? Señor Dorantes asked.

It is a long story, I said.

He slid against the trunk of the tree and sat down so close to me that I could smell his oily hair. (We had run out of soap a few days earlier.) What did he want from me? Was it not enough that he owned me and could dispose of me as he wished? Now he wanted that which had always been my own—my story.

Tell me, he said. I want to hear it.

Reader, the joy of a story is in its telling. My feet were throbbing with pain and my stomach was growling with hunger, so I could not resist the pleasure that a tale would bring me. I began with the Story of My Birth and continued until the Story of Ramatullai. Señor Dorantes listened to me with such curiosity and patience that I wondered if he would tell this chronicle to other people someday, to his wife, say, or to his children, so that it might continue to be told, even after my death. Telling a story is like sowing a seed—you always hope to see it become a beautiful tree, with firm roots and branches that soar up in the sky. But it is a peculiar sowing, for you will never know whether your seed sprouts or dies.

Later, when we resumed our march, and my exhaustion led me to hold on to his saddle for support, Señor Dorantes did not nudge Abejorro away.

IT WAS THE SMELL of smoke that reached us first, making our eyes water and our throats itch. As the day wore on, it covered the foul odor of unwashed men, the sweat of horses, the stench of corruption. The men coughed and covered their noses with rags; the horses whinnied and snorted and had to be whipped to compel them to continue. As we approached Aute, spires of black smoke appeared before us, each rising neatly into the gray sky like the towers of a city in Jehennam. Señor Narváez raised his right arm and we all stopped. Ahead of us, the world was made of shades of gray and black. No one spoke. When the governor pointed the way forward again, the gray metal of his armor seemed to disappear in the air around him.

By the time we reached Aute, the sun, barely visible in the smoke, was making its way to the edge of the horizon, taking with it the little light there was. What awaited us was a vision of hell, like something the men trembling with fever must have seen just before they closed their eyes. All of the houses in the village, some twenty of them, had been burnt to the ground, their beams broken and their thatched roofs reduced to mounds of ash. In the trees, the birds had deserted their nests. The only sound was the faint rustling of a river I could not see yet, somewhere farther ahead.

The smell of burning wood and singed fur sat heavy in my throat. In spite of the sandals I wore, I could feel the heat rising from the ground beneath my feet, and the smoke all around me made it painful to breathe. I was overcome with the desire to give up. Yet even in my exhaustion I felt something else, something like respect for the people of Aute, who would rather burn their village than let the Castilians take it. Perhaps if my people had done the same, the Portuguese would have left Azemmur for good and I would not have sold myself into bondage. A useless thought now. A tormenting thought. I leaned against Señor Dorantes's horse; I felt I had endured all I could. I could not know that this was just the beginning.

Quietly, without waiting for an order, the soldiers spread out through the village. With their walking sticks, they poked at the ruins to see if anything of value could be rescued. One of them returned shortly to report that he had found large reserves of beans in an underground hut and that there were fields of corn and squash, most of it ripe and ready to be picked, but the governor paid no mind to the statement. Instead, he cantered about the village on his white stallion, his gaze fixed on some point far in the distance, as if he were chasing after something that only he could see. The captains watched him with dismay, until at last Señor Cabeza de Vaca rode up beside him and whispered something to him. Then the treasurer announced that it was not safe to stay in Aute and we would continue to the river farther ahead.

So we marched to the river. Like condemned men, we were now in a state of fear and denial—fear of the plague that was spreading through our company, and denial that the burning of Aute was a harbinger of worse things to come. It was dark by the time we began to set up camp and, although none of us could stand the smell of smoke any longer, we had to light torches to do our work. We were completely covered with ash, which turned yellow in the glow of the fires, making us look like strange creatures from another world. Even the Apalaches, who had pursued us relentlessly for ten days, stayed away from us that night. The friars began to attend to the men suffering from fever, the soldiers lined up to receive their rations of corn, and in hushed tones the captains debated what to do next.

The governor's white tent had been set up for him, with his bedding and worktable visible through the open flaps. His standard hung limply from the pole outside and a pit was ready for his evening fire. When he dismounted, all the captains gathered around him, each ready to ask a question or offer an opinion, but Señor Narváez raised his hand to stop them from speaking. At first light, he said, we will go look for the port.

Don Pánfilo, the commissary said pleadingly. The fever is spreading. Some of the men will not be able to walk.

The governor uncorked the water flask his page had handed him and drank in big, noisy gulps. He looked beyond the captains at the men spread out in clusters beneath the trees. How many are sick?

Forty-two, the commissary replied.

If this continues, Señor Dorantes said, we will not have enough horses to carry the sick.

The governor's eye glazed in the yellow light. I need only take a few men for a reconnaissance mission. Each of you should pick the healthiest men you have. He interrupted himself to wipe his nose, then stared with confusion at the streak of blood that appeared on the back of his hand.

Don Pánfilo, the commissary said, do you have the fever?

Señor Narváez put his hand to his forehead, then let it drop quickly.

Are you afflicted?

It is nothing, Señor Narváez said. Just a cold. Dorantes, Castillo, Cabeza de Vaca: I want the three of you to take thirty men and go look for the port. The rest of us will wait here by the river.

For once, his orders were greeted with no quarrel, just silent agreement. Señor Castillo had always insisted, alone at first and then with the support of Señor Dorantes, that the armada should not have been split; no two men in the company would have been more eager to find the ships now and return as saviors. Señor Cabeza de Vaca had stood by Señor Narváez and argued the opposite, but he was just as eager to find the ships, if only to prove that leaving them behind was not a foolish gamble but a measured risk. This was what made the governor's choice so clever. If the mission succeeded, our struggles would be forgotten when the history of La Florida was told; if the mission failed, he would not be alone to bear the responsibility for its failure.

We departed at first light, with dew still dripping from the petals of magnolia flowers, leaving behind us men wrapped in their blankets, dreaming of food and relief. The horses bore their riders obediently, but their pace was slow and their breath heavy. As we advanced into the wilderness, their hooves kicked up the gray ash that had settled overnight on the ground, so that we were soon covered with it again. Fortunately, when we had gone about two leagues away from the camp, the wind picked up and the air became freer of dust and ash. Before long, the captains began to chat amiably with one another. Once we return to the ships, Señor Cabeza de Vaca said, I want to pick up a charm my wife gave me for good luck. I left it behind on the day we disembarked. I hope it was not stolen.

Señor Dorantes sniffed. How strange that you forgot this charm, and yet remembered your books of poetry.

For some time, there had been a muted antagonism between Señor Cabeza de Vaca and Señor Dorantes, but now, away from the camp and from the governor, they were finally free to take a jab at each other.

It was an innocent oversight, the treasurer replied. You make too much of it.

I did nothing of the sort, my master said. I merely expressed my surprise at the strange work of memory.

My wife gave me that charm when we married, six years ago. I kept it in a silk pouch, which I packed inside my writing case. But the governor discouraged me from bringing the case; he said that the notary had all the writing implements I might need and that I could borrow them if I needed them. That was how I left it behind.

I did not know the governor took such interest in your luggage.

Friendship. Loyalty. You should try them sometime.

A blinkered horse is loyal, too, Álvar.

The sun had reached its zenith now and there was a great stillness in the air. The ground was dry and cracked under our feet. One of the horses moaned, shaking his head against the sweat that rolled down his sides. Farther ahead, the sky slowly melted into the green horizon.

In any case, Señor Cabeza de Vaca said suddenly, we will find the ships.

Is that a promise or a prayer? Señor Dorantes asked.

Neither, said the treasurer. But at least I never blame other people for honest mistakes.

Señor Castillo had not taken a side in this quarrel, but now that the two men had at last fallen silent, he tried to diffuse the tension. Everyone makes mistakes, he said, I make them all the time.

Señor Dorantes did not reply, and neither did Señor Cabeza de Vaca, but their bitter argument had cleared the air between them and for the rest of the day they seemed much more cordial to each other, like two men who now knew exactly what to expect from one another. They began to talk about the most efficient way to transport the sick men, while also limiting the risk of contamination.

At sunset, we reached a very large bay. It was as calm as a lake, with few waves disrupting the surface. Here and there, oyster beds of various shapes jutted out from the water. These oysters were a welcome change from the corn and beans we had consumed for so long. We ate them straight from the grill; the men who owned small knives pried the shells open for those who did not, so that the warm, slippery food was passed from hand to hand regardless of rank.

The meal greatly revived our spirits and we set out early the next morning to explore the areas around the bay. The first trail we took led us inland—the air grew drier, with no scent of salt in it, and the trees were taller and leafier—so we retreated, for fear of coming across any Indians who dwelled in these parts. From our starting point, we took a second trail, and a third, but each one led us to a small and shallow inlet, where the water rose no higher than a man's knee. Our search went on like this for two days. Whenever we returned to our camp in the bay, we looked hopefully at the horizon, but there was no sign of the ships.

SO OUR MOOD WAS somber when we returned to Aute. None of us felt at ease with himself; any private jealousies or ambitions had disappeared from our minds as we pondered the full extent of our joint predicament. I think, too, that we were filled with doubt that we had missed some clue along the way, something that could have led us to where the ships were waiting for us. When we reached the edge of the camp, we found one of the friars standing by himself in a clearing, his head bowed in prayer, the bottom of his robe soiled with mud. A dozen graves surmounted by wooden crosses lay at his feet. Hearing our approach, the friar turned toward us, raising his hand to shade his eyes from the sun. It was Father Anselmo. Capitán, he said. His gaze drifted from Señor Dorantes to Diego and back again. Welcome back.

What happened here, Father? Señor Dorantes asked.

The fever, Father Anselmo replied. Some of the sick men did not have the strength to eat or drink, he explained, and they had begun to die on the day we left.

Who died?

We lost fourteen Christians. And, pointing to each grave, the friar gave the full name of the man who had died, his voice slow and solemn.

We all grew quiet as we contemplated the mounds. It was one thing to lose men to a swamp, a river, or a battle with the Indians, and quite another to lose them to the fever. An accident could be easily dismissed as a rare occurrence, a stroke of bad luck. As for combat, we had each conceived a reason why we had been spared: we had fought valiantly or had better weapons or had found a good place to hide. But disease did not discriminate—it could strike the rich as well as the poor, the brave as well as the coward, the wise as well as the fool. Disease leveled all the differences between us and united us in a single abiding fear.

We walked in a slow procession toward the camp. A guard with wild eyes, eyes like a jinn's, sat in the dirt, his musket trained on five soldiers whose hands had been tied behind their backs. As we passed by, Señor Cabeza de Vaca recognized two of his own men and asked the guard what it was they had done. Deserters, the guard spat. We caught them trying to leave with their horses in the middle of the night.

My first thought upon hearing this was: leave to go where? We did not know how to get to the ships, so this desertion was nothing more than the last rebellion of the doomed, like the lambs that stagger back on their feet after their throats have been cut.

In the camp, the men were huddled in small groups along the river, talking or praying or napping under the shade of poplar and cedar trees. The soldiers in our company recounted the story of our failure to those who had stayed, and the news spread quickly from group to group. Their disappointment made the men critical: How well did you look? they asked. Did you take every trail? Was there not one you missed?

Faced with so many questions, those of us who had gone on the mission were tormented by even greater doubt. So when the three captains went to the governor's tent to give their report, they spoke with urgent voices. Don Pánfilo, Señor Dorantes called. We are back.

The governor did not come out of his tent to greet the captains. Instead, he threw open the flap and spoke to them through this opening. He had traded his formal doublet for a simple cotton shirt and plain breeches, with no embellishments of any kind.

We found only a shallow harbor, Señor Dorantes said, but nothing resembling a port.

A port, the governor said, sounding like an echo from an empty well.

We will have to send a second mission, Señor Dorantes said.

A smaller group of men, this time, Señor Cabeza de Vaca added, all of them on horses, so that we can cover greater distances.

There was no response from the governor.

Don Pánfilo? Señor Cabeza de Vaca asked.

When the governor's voice finally came, it was very low. Five of the horsemen tried to desert me, he said.

Yes, we saw them on our way here, Señor Dorantes said.

And do you know that the Indians attacked us while you were gone?

No. The friar did not speak of it.

They killed one of the horses. We cannot stay by the river any longer. We will go with you to the bay you found.

Señor Dorantes exchanged a thoughtful look with Señor Cabeza de Vaca. The Bay of Oysters would provide safer camping ground than the river, and missions could more easily be mounted from there. For the first time, their bitter rivalry had given way to agreement.

WITH THE ORDER PASSED DOWN, the captains retired, and I was left alone. I took off my clothes and went into the river, as naked as the day I was born. Had I been asked what I was doing, I would have said that I was going for a swim, but no one in the camp asked. No one cared—each man was worrying about his own ability to survive the fever. The water was very cold; I felt a shudder running through me, numbing all the pain in my body. The current carried me away from the bank, and I did not resist it. Soon, the voices of the soldiers faded, and the only sound I could hear was that of my own breathing, as calm as in times when my life had been free of the troubles of conquest.

I had put my life in the hands of others and now here I was, at the edge of the known world, lost and afraid. All along, I had told myself that I did not have a choice, that I had been the one to put myself into bondage and I had to accept this fate. Somehow I had also convinced myself that my redemption could only come from some force outside of me—that if I were useful to others, they would save me. What a terrible thing to believe. I had to stop playing a part in my own misery. I had to save my own life. Time passed, and a feeling of tranquility settled inside me, as if some old, nagging question had at last been answered. The hair on my chest uncoiled, the goose bumps faded. I rubbed one foot against the other, feeling the hardened edge of the heels and the soft surface of the blisters that had formed under my toes.

At length, I felt the water pulling me with greater force downriver. I stood up and saw that I had drifted well apart from the others, so that I could no longer see the camp. I could walk straight into the green wilderness and disappear forever, a free man once again. But I would have to go alone into the unknown. Where should I go? East toward the rising sun or west toward the bay? Neither alternative seemed safe to me, as I had no provisions and no weapon with which to hunt or defend myself. Here, in the Land of the Indians, I was as much of an intruder as the Castilians were—and I would be treated the same. Even if I survived, naked and alone, in the wilderness, I would never be able to return to my family, my people, and my hometown. So I made my way back to the camp. There had to be another way. There was always another way.

EARLY THE NEXT MORNING, we marched toward the Bay of Oysters. Their misery had silenced the men afflicted with fever, but the healthy among us were quiet out of a renewed awareness of all the dangers we faced. Thus the noise of the wilderness grew in our ears: the chirping of birds, the buzzing of mosquitoes flying in thick clouds, the rattling of snakes in the bushes, the melancholy calls of strange creatures, even the fluttering of a grasshopper on a leaf—all of these added to an unbearable cacophony that was a torment to us all. But in spite of the heat, our pace was good and when the ground turned sandy we looked at the horizon, hoping to see the ships in that shallow bay. It was a wild hope, yet strangely our disappointment was all the more intense.

The beach was quite large. It was possible now to separate the sick from the healthy in order to limit the spread of the disease. There was a decent supply of food: oysters from the reefs, of course, but also crabs, seaweed, and waterfowl. And, past the line of bushes that bordered the beach on the west side, there was wild grass for the horses.

Narváez waited until the men had eaten their dinner before he stood up to address them. Amigos y compañeros, he said. From the beginning of this enterprise, your bravery and your patience have been a credit to Castile. We have had a few setbacks because of the heat and the terrain, but mostly because of the deceitful nature of the Indians. They have misled me. Their minds are as devoid of honor as their bodies are devoid of clothes. I know that this expedition has been difficult. Some of you are sick. Some are tired. Some may even wish you had not decided to join.

From the back came the voices of the men. Aye, they said. Aye.

But remember: the conquest of New Spain was not accomplished in two months. It took two years. Two years! Imagine if those soldiers had given in to despair—México would not be under Christian rule and they would not be the richest men in the empire today. But they did not give up and nor will you. La Florida is a large territory. Once we regain the ships, and we have had time to resupply ourselves with all that we need, we will find a better place to land. Remember that those who risk the most, but remain steadfast in the face of hardship, will gain the most in the end.

But how will we get to the ships?

This question exercised the men for the greater part of the evening. Some wanted to remain in the bay until the ships came looking for us. But, even with the addition of oysters and crabs to our rations, our reserves of food were limited. What would we eat if the ships did not come for weeks or even months? Others proposed that we march past the bay, keeping the ocean in our sight, until we reached the port of Pánuco. But this, too, seemed perilous because too many of the men were afflicted with fever and would not be able to march for such a long distance.

After a while, everyone fell silent, pondering the fact that either of the alternatives offered was impossible. The beach, which had seemed to us such a welcome sight, now felt like nothing more than the little corner of the new world where we would all die. Yet we were sitting under a canopy of stars, so bright and so close that it seemed to us we could reach out and touch them.

There is another way, I said. We can build rafts.

All eyes fixed themselves upon me. So accustomed were the Castilians to my silence—one or two of the lieutenants might even have thought me deaf and dumb—that only shock greeted my pronouncement. But my idea had already been spoken. It could not be unheard.

We cannot build rafts, Cabeza de Vaca said after a moment. It would be too—

Dorantes interrupted him. No. Estebanico is right. This might be the only way we have of leaving the bay. Miruelo said that we were only fifteen leagues by sea from the port. If we sail westward, we cannot fail to reach it. We have carpenters, do we not?

Nárvaez called upon Fernándes, the man whose hammer he had borrowed to torture the Indians, and put the question to him. Fernándes replied that he could indeed build rafts large enough and sturdy enough to carry all of us into the ocean, and that there was plenty of wood nearby, but that such an undertaking was impossible because he would need tools the porters had lost in a swamp, when they were attacked by the Apalaches.

We can make the tools, I said.

Suppose you have the tools, Dorantes said to Fernándes, how long would it take you to build the rafts?

It depends on how many men we commit to it.

Por Dios, Narváez said. All of the men. All the healthy ones. How long, then?

Three weeks. Maybe.

But what about the horses? Cabeza de Vaca asked.

We cannot take them, Dorantes said. The horses are too heavy for the rafts and too weak to endure another sea voyage.

It is not fair to ask the horsemen to give up their horses, Cabeza de Vaca said. The horses are all they have.

Is it fair that five of them tried to desert me? Narváez replied sharply.

The treasurer, whose contingent had been home to two of the deserters, lowered his gaze and did not reply.

If we are going to reach Pánuco, Narváez said, everyone has to make sacrifices. We can eat the horses for sustenance.

He was right, I thought. We were too weak to work the long hours it would require to build the rafts and we needed to be fed somehow. We all loved horses and could not have conceived of slaughtering healthy ones for the sake of food. But this was another disgrace we were willing to take upon ourselves in order to escape from the bay.

THE PLAN WAS AMBITIOUS, complicated, dangerous—but it was a plan. And for two days, there was no word from Narváez about it. He prayed with the commissary in his tent, ate his meals alone, and took long walks along the beach, followed at a respectable distance by his page and three of his men. He seemed always to be in deep thought, weighing the possibilities that had been presented to him: stay in the bay and hope that the ships dare to come in its shallow waters; venture on land yet again, looking for the port; or build rafts and try to reach the ocean, from which we could either sail to Pánuco or be seen by some passing ship or other. But perhaps I was wrong; perhaps he was not considering the proposals at all but was instead contemplating the failure of his expedition. Was he thinking about Cortés—the lucky, cunning Cortés—who had found unbelievable riches and become famous?

At last, Narváez issued the order: we would build rafts and go to Pánuco. It gladdened my heart to hear him agree to the plan and I began to feel a kind of purpose I had not experienced in a long time. It seemed to me, too, that Dorantes had had enough of his adventures under the command of Narváez, and that, when he reached Pánuco, he would make his way back to Seville. I swore to myself that, once in Seville, I would find a way of returning to my people; I would make in reverse the journey I had made five years earlier. This was how I went from the complete despair of uncertainty to the feverish dream of a new beginning.

In our company was a blacksmith from Bilbao, a man by the name of Echeverría, who said he could make all the tools we needed if we helped him build a forge and provided him with a pair of bellows. For an entire morning, Echeverría searched the beach around the Bay of Oysters for the most suitable spot, and, having finally found it, he had us gather stones to build the forge. We had no leather with which to make the bellows, but Gonzalo Ruíz, the soldier who had lost an eye to his confrontation with the Indians, had the idea of using horse skin.

With the forge ready, Narváez ordered the soldiers to turn in whatever metal they had. One by one, they took off their helmets, untied their breastplates, stripped off their chain mail, tossed their stirrups and spurs onto the pile. Dorantes even threw into the fire the marked scales he had brought to weigh gold.

If one of the soldiers was reluctant to part with his protection, the commissary spoke to him. You are here at the service of His Majesty and His Holiness, he would say. It would be a grave sin to disobey their delegate in this province. Besides, you can still keep your sword.

Inevitably, the soldier would remove his armor and add it onto the pile. The sound of steel against steel startled the seagulls and sandpipers that had been foraging along the shore and they departed in a great flutter of wings.

Echeverría fashioned a dozen crude axes and saws for our company. Meanwhile, Fernándes, the carpenter, took a group of men inland to look for raft wood. He selected pines and cedars, which were light enough to float but heavy enough to carry our weight, marking each tree he wanted with a cross, carved at eye level, on its trunk. As soon as the first axes came out of the forge, the men began to cut down the trees, stripping them of their branches and carrying them to the beach, where Fernándes trimmed them to equal lengths. The logs were added to one of five piles. (Narváez had decided that Fernándes should build five rafts, each carrying the same people who had come off the five ships.)

In order to tie the logs together, we needed more rope than the lengths we still had; Cabeza de Vaca suggested that we use horsehair. Every time a horse was slaughtered, its mane and tail was washed, brushed, and braided in long pieces. Much to my surprise, the horsehair rope turned out to be quite sturdy. The oars were made of cypress wood, which we procured from trees half a league inland. As for oakum, a Greek settler collected the pitch of some pine trees and mixed it with ground tree leaves into a thick paste, which he spread between the logs.

Because I had worked with fabric in Seville, I offered to cut and sew pieces of cloth together to make the sails. I walked around the camp, collecting flags, sheets, shirts, vestments—all the extraneous fabric I could find, even handkerchiefs. The result was a great jumble of colors, textures, and shapes. When I unfurled the first sail and it caught the wind, I stood back to admire it. No sailcloth I had seen before looked quite like it, yet my heart filled with boundless pride.

During the five weeks it took to build the rafts, we fed on the oysters from the bay and on horsemeat, but every few days, Narváez and his men went on a raid to Aute, in order to pick the ripened corn from the field behind the village. Much of the corn he brought back was saved, because we needed to build stocks of food for the journey to the ocean. It was difficult to know exactly how long the journey to Pánuco would take, but Narváez managed to collect enough corn for a week.

The first horse to be slaughtered belonged to one of the deserters—this was a direct order from Narváez, and though the soldier was brought to tears by the idea, he had to surrender the reins. Then the captains' horses were taken one by one behind the big boulders, where they were butchered. And so there came the dreadful day when poor Abejorro's turn came. Dorantes took him for a long walk on the beach, and then I gave him some of the fruit he liked and took him to the river for a drink and cooed to him and rubbed his nose and his neck, but no matter how long I delayed it the moment came anyway. The butcher took the reins from me and disappeared behind the rocks. Then there was the long, dreadful sound of Abejorro's last breath. And the stream of blood that ran toward the ocean swelled once again.

We finished building the five rafts just as the fall season began. The winds were strong and it had not yet begun to rain. The first boat, under the command of Narváez, was for him and the men closest to him. Having ridden horses and received better rations for the last few months, they were some of the strongest and healthiest among us. They also had the best sails, for these were made with the governor's standards and tent, which were the largest pieces of canvas to be found. (Gentle reader, if I point out these details, it is not because I was jealous or resentful, but simply because I wish to be as precise as I can about the conditions under which we left La Florida.)

The second boat Narváez put under the command of the comptroller, Alonso Enríquez, and the commissary; they were to be accompanied by fifty-three other men. The third boat was given to Capitán Téllez and his deputy, Peñaloza, with forty-nine others. On the fourth boat, the governor put Cabeza de Vaca and Albaniz the notary, with fifty-one men. On the fifth and last boat, Narváez put Dorantes, Castillo, and the rest of their original company, including this servant of God, Mustafa ibn Muhammad.

We had arrived in La Florida men of different nations and stations, but now the differences between us were not so stark. Many of us were half-naked, having given up our clothes to make the sails. We were all thin and tired and eager to leave. The prolonged strain of our ordeal had reduced our greed to the simplest one of all: survival. So we carried the rafts into the bay and climbed on.

To the best of my recollection, we sailed out on the first of Muharram in the year 935 of the Hegira. I stood at the fore of our raft, eager to make my way to Pánuco, to Cuba, to a rescue ship, to anywhere but here. As Dorantes gave out the order to unfurl the sail, I turned to look at him and saw my own desires reflected in his eyes: let us leave this land, where we have met nothing but ill luck and misery, and which resembles nothing so much as a great test of our faith and a punishment for our sins.

10

THE STORY OF RAMATULLAI

She looks like you.

Ramatullai kept repeating these words like an incantation that could break any curse. Her comportment was less reserved than usual, I noticed; she touched my arm and leaned in close to me as she told me about her day. And she was distracted, too. The smell of saffron rice rose in the kitchen, but she did not stir the bubbling pot. Wallahi, she said, I heard the laundress clearly. She looks like you.

That morning, our mistress had decided to go to the bathhouse in San Juan de la Palma. It was not in her habit to visit public baths, but after a week of particularly bitter quarreling with her husband, she said she sorely needed it. In the steam of the entrance hall, she shed her gray dress and dour mood, and asked for a treatment with perfumed oil. On one of the wooden benches in the hall, Ramatullai sat waiting for her, with a pitcher of cold water and a bowl of fresh oranges. She passed the time by tracing the stars on the tiled wall with her fingers. That was when the laundress noticed the blue tattoo on the back of Ramatullai's hand; she had seen a little girl who had the same mark.

A tattoo like this? Ramatullai asked her. With seven teeth?

The laundress was a pudgy woman with thick eyebrows and a high bun. Standing with her hip against the counter, she was folding towels, lining up the edges of them quickly and expertly. Seven or eight or nine, how should I know? she said. But it was a comb.

When was she here?

Last week.

With her mistress?

Of course with her mistress. Did you imagine she could come into this bathhouse by herself?

Ramatullai had stayed quiet, but as soon as I came in that night she told me the story, repeating the laundress's words to me again and again: She looks like you.

After that, on every errand Ramatullai was sent, whether to the butcher or the baker, the tailor or the cobbler, she asked the slaves or servants she came across about Amna—she was convinced it was Amna at the bathhouse that day, even though the tattoo could have appeared on any other girl from her tribe. Then, just after the Christian feast of the Nativity, the neighbors' servant said he had seen the tattoo on a girl at the Hospital of Santa Ana; she was carrying a basket of victuals for an old woman. It is her, said Ramatullai. I know it. It is her.

Then send her a message, I said.

I cannot write, Mustafa. Nor can she read.

I can write the letter for you, and she can find someone to read it to her.

Someone who reads Arabic? Here, in Seville?

Yes, I said. Someone like me.

So I wrote the letter in my best penmanship, on a piece of paper stolen from the master, dipping the feather tip in a bowl of indigo dye. Looking over my shoulder, Ramatullai dictated: Dear Amna, this letter is from your mother. I live in a house in the barrio of Triana. The master's name is Bernardo Rodriguez. He is well known and his house is not hard to find if you ask at the market. I am in good health, praise be to God. I pray that you are as well. Write to me and tell me where you are.

Under her direction, I signed the letter: Your loving mother.

Ramatullai blew on the ink until it was dry, then slid the tiny piece of paper inside her corset. She sat close to me on the sisal mat; I could smell lavender on her dress. I allowed myself to put my right hand over her left and she did not withdraw it. We sat like this, hand over hand, for a long time. It had never occurred to me to send a letter to my own brothers. But why? Perhaps, I thought, it was because I was too ashamed to tell them about the life that was now mine: the conversion, the beatings, the kitchen closet. Perhaps I did not want to deepen their sorrow at my absence. Or perhaps it was because this keeping up of familial bonds was something that women, more than men, never forgot how to do.

. . .

I WAS DRIFTING INTO SLEEP one night when I heard the clattering of the copper pots that hung on a rail in the kitchen. Had a thief slipped inside the house? In that hazy moment between sleep and consciousness, I remained where I was on my pallet until my thoughts drifted to Ramatullai and I bolted upright, suddenly awake. I crept out of my closet, armed with nothing but my blanket twisted into a rope, hoping to surprise the thief in the middle of his crime. I walked out into the darkened patio, all my senses watchful for any accomplices that might lurk behind one of the pillars. From the kitchen came the rattling of metal. The thief seemed to pay no mind to the amount of noise he was making. Gingerly, I pushed the door open with my foot.

The long legs of Ramatullai were thrashing in the darkness, under the weight of Bernardo Rodriguez. I could see the pink soles of her feet as they went up and down, up and down, up and down. Though the pots rattled and the master heaved, Ramatullai heard the door creak open. She turned her face toward me. We stared at one another over the back of our master. The silent gaze between us spoke of our disbelief. Every slave knew this could happen, but no slave believed it would, until it did. Pain, anger, and rebellion bubbled inside us. But in the end fear won out; she turned her face away and I lowered my eyes and returned to my closet.

Ramatullai did not speak of the violations she endured, and I did not bring them up, but the image tortured me that night and many nights to come. When I came into the kitchen, and saw the curve of Ramatullai's hips, I tried not to think of my master's stubby fingers curling around them. I tried not to think of his lips on her neck. And I tried, especially, not to think of his knee parting hers on the same mat upon which we sat every night. Whenever these thoughts came to me, I shuffled them like a deck of cards with less painful memories, hoping, somehow, to lose them forever.

Although we did not speak of the master's violations, we began to look for ways to strike back at him: Ramatullai by tainting his food and drink, or I by dropping a crate of merchandise on my way back from the port. Small, discreet measures of vengeance, as reprisals by the weak tend to be. They managed to irritate him, but they did not always give us the satisfaction we expected from them. Sometimes, they had the reverse effect: he would punish us for the smallest of infractions.

Ramatullai lived up to her name; she was a blessing from God, for she was the only friend I had in that household, the only one I could speak to, the only one who shared the pain of exile and servitude with me. When the master whipped me for breaking a pot, she rubbed butter over my lash marks; when the mistress abruptly cut off all of Ramatullai's hair, I said she looked better without it. Our friendship grew, strengthened not only by our common ordeal, but also by a sense that we had no one else with whom to share it. Increasingly, the words we exchanged after dinner in the kitchen sounded like the conversations of old friends, people who had lived long enough together to have their own, private language.

We talked about the letter often—we thought it had reached Amna, but that she had not found someone to read it for her yet; or that she had found someone to read it, but no one willing to write a response; or that the letter had been intercepted by her mistress before it could be sent out. But all of this was conjecture. Like watching a clear sky and trying to guess when it would rain.

Still, at the store, I kept an eye out for the hunchback.

A YEAR PASSED, THEN ANOTHER. My master's business thrived. The ships coming in from the Indies brought surprise cargo each time—parrot feathers in flamboyant red and yellow, which Spanish noblewomen found fashionable; an edible root called batata, which had a strange, starchy taste; tapestries of uncommonly fine detail—and all these novelties sold well in Seville. Still, Rodriguez complained incessantly about the taxes that the Casa de Contratación charged on everything he imported. How can a decent and honest man, he asked, his fingers bunched together in a gesture of supplication, run a business under the tangle of all the rules and conditions that the Crown imposed? Upon hearing this question, his friends, most of them involved in one form or another in the same trade, rarely answered him. They did not share his frustrations or, if they did, they did not complain as much about them.

Señor Rodriguez's success at business was a result of his gift of persuasion. And, not unrelatedly, he had an extraordinary ability to adapt. He could speak to a merchant, a sailor, a royal official, or a hidalgo and somehow manage to modulate his manner and his speech to each one of them. They all responded favorably, although the hidalgos were often amused and occasionally irritated at the sight of a simple merchant daring to speak to them as though he were one of their own. Señor Rodriguez even managed to get invitations to their card games, at which large amounts of money were gambled. One evening, he returned drunk from one of these gatherings to tell his wife that she needed to make herself new dresses from silk or taffeta, or else the woolen mantles she insisted on wearing would always betray her as the daughter of a butcher from Cádiz. They quarreled; she fell on her knees in prayer and he went back out to the tavern.

The next day, my master brought his wife a silver bracelet and, kissing her hand, slipped it over her wrist. He gave her some silk and an oil portrait of a religious figure, in which she seemed to take particular delight. In Seville, Señor Rodriguez was not the only merchant who was finding new ways to spend his new money. Once, as he and I were walking to the public bath, a coach stopped next to us, and the face of his friend Mateo poked out of the window. My master was so surprised he took a step back and had trouble answering his friend's courteous greeting. As we continued on our way, I knew that he was already thinking about how he needed to buy himself a coach, too. The workers Bernardo Rodriguez employed and the slaves he now owned made his continual presence at the shop less necessary, leaving me in charge of opening and closing. He began to spend more time with his friends at the tavern. His gambling turned into a habit.

IT WAS A HOT summer night, I remember. From the street came the sound of the syrup seller's cart creaking on the cobblestone. Pink and white roses wilted in the heat of the courtyard, their scent as heavy as the heat. And in my closet the air was still and the walls were damp. I had taken off my shirt and was lying on my pallet in my breeches when Ramatullai appeared at my door. In her hands were bowls of the leftover bean soup that was to be our dinner.

I can come to the kitchen, I said, getting up and quickly slipping on my shirt.

No, the kitchen is even hotter, she replied. Her eyes had what I thought was the special glint they did whenever she wanted to share a particularly scandalous bit of gossip with me.

We sat down together on the pallet. It was made from scraps of fabric I had rescued from my master's store and sewn, one over the other, to make a sort of bed. Hanging from a nail on the wall were the only other garments I owned, a woolen shirt and dark breeches that the mistress of the house had purchased and insisted I wear on Sundays.

He has quarreled with his wife again, Ramatullai said.

What about? I asked.

His gambling.

Fourth time this week, I said. The more his business prospered, the more my master seemed to find ways to waste his money, a fact that his wife, with the unimpeachable common sense of a butcher's daughter, found profoundly distasteful.

He does not have the money to pay back his debts, Ramatullai said.

Nonsense. He has the money.

No, he needs to pay his creditors by next week, before they sail for the Indies.

I shrugged and took a bite of bread. None of this, I thought, was any of our concern. I did not know why Ramatullai insisted on following the conversation at the masters' dinner table. I myself found it too painful to hear about the drudgery of their daily lives, for it only reminded me of my loved ones and how much I missed them. I had failed to notice the tone in Ramatullai's voice, but now, in the half-light of the closet, I finally saw the sadness in her eyes, the hardness around her mouth. I stopped eating and waited.

Eventually Ramatullai spoke up again, though her voice was merely a whisper: His wife told him he needed to sell one of his slaves to pay back his debt.

Not this, I thought. Not this. For many months now, the mistress had been looking for ways to rid herself of Ramatullai, but it had never occurred to me that the master himself would give her a pretext. Now, to pay for his gambling debt, he would sell the only friend I had in Seville and I would never see her again. The prospect of that pain seemed almost unendurable to me and, sensing this, Ramatullai drew near and put her arm around my shoulders. The light from the candle went out.

THAT DAY STARTED OUT like any other. Bernardo Rodriguez and I departed for work at the usual time, stopping once along the way so he could buy boiled chickpeas from a cart—a habit he thought was beneath his station, but which he found hard to break. At the store, we went over the inventory: I counted the rolls of linen and he checked his ledger, while the other workers cleaned the storage room. A customer came in, about mid-morning, to ask for merchandise on credit; the master said no. There was a quarrel between some delivery boys outside and we all stood briefly in the doorway to look. But there was nothing, however small or insignificant, that separated this day from any other. Then, without warning, my master stood up from his desk and told me to follow him.

Instead of walking toward the Arenal, we took the road to the residential quarter. The streets were clean; no vegetable peels or animal droppings were in sight. Elegantly dressed gentlemen passed by us, conversing in moderate, unhurried voices. We stopped at a white house with wide arches—I was later to learn that it belonged to a count by the name of Luis de Prado. We were there to see one of Don Luis's guests, a certain Andrés Dorantes de Carranza, who had recently arrived in Seville. The butler sniffed and directed us to a side door, from which we entered an empty hallway. We stood there a while, admiring the plaster ceiling and the vine scroll pattern on the rug, before the butler returned to lead us into a parlor.

A man was standing at the window, looking out into the street. It was not until Bernardo Rodriguez cleared his throat for the second time that Andrés Dorantes detached himself from whatever he was watching and turned to face us. He was a well-built man, with blond hair and blue eyes. I noticed a long scar on his right cheek and I wondered what could have caused it. (I would learn later that he had sustained it fighting for his king in the Comunero rebellion.) He crossed the room in quick steps and stared at us with the candid arrogance of a nobleman toward his servants. This is the slave, then?

Sí, Señor, my master said.

He does not appear to be worth the money you owe me.

This was my first inkling of the business we had come here to conduct. I had thought my master would honor his wife's wishes and sell Ramatullai, but now it seemed he was selling me instead. Why had Rodriguez not told me about this? One moment I was in the store, tying up rolls of cotton, and the next I was in this house, waiting to be sold to someone else. I had not even said farewell to Ramatullai. And why sell a slave at all, I wondered. If he needed money so desperately, why did he not sell the new coach he had bought?

Esteban is worth more than that, Señor. He is a very good slave.

What makes him so good?

He is quiet and honest—two qualities that are hard to join in a slave.

Where is he from?

A town on the Moorish coast. He is hardy, he can handle a sea journey.

A journey from the Moorish coast is not the same as a journey to the Indies.

No, no, of course. But I am confident he will serve you well there.

I was stunned by this characterization of me. The slightest delay in my deliveries had regularly earned me accusations of being a lazy Moor; the most innocent of my questions had been met with orders to be quiet. But now that Rodriguez wanted to sell me, I had become a model slave. Give glory to God, who can alter all fates.

If you say so, Señor Dorantes said. But this slave will not cover the two hundred ducats you owe me. So take him back and bring me my money.

I let out a shallow breath. Perhaps I would be safe after all.

But Rodriguez pulled out an embroidered handkerchief from his pocket and wiped his face down. Señor, he said, two hundred ducats may seem like a lot of money, but here you have a good and faithful worker. The price of such a man is not so high in Seville. I know you can get a decent slave these days for as little as forty ducats, but in the Indies, where so few of the savages speak our language or are capable of following directions, he will fetch six or seven times this amount. You could sell him in your first port of call for that much. The plantations in La Española are in desperate need of slaves.

Señor Dorantes cocked his head to the side. Six times? he said mockingly.

Easily.

But why should I go through the trouble of transporting your slave to La Española in order to collect my money?

You would collect more than what I owe you.

It is simpler if you pay me now.

Simpler, Señor, it would be. But not more lucrative. Besides, you would enjoy the services of the slave for the duration of the journey.

This is not a pleasure trip, you know.

No, there is risk and danger. But a slave can be used to lessen both.

Señor Dorantes pressed his forefinger into my arm—the appraising touch of a man considering property. It was not the first time I had been handled in this way, but it seemed to me I would never get used to it or to what it meant.

And as a token of my good wishes to you, Rodriguez said, his voice more confident now, I present to you this golden earring from the Yucatán.

Señor Dorantes took the earring in his hand and examined it with great curiosity. How odd, he said. They put wild beasts on their jewelry. Do you suppose the Indians of La Florida do the same?

I would not know, Rodriguez said. I am just a merchant, not a brave sea captain.

Very well, Rodriguez, Señor Dorantes replied. He put the earring in his pocket and said: But do yourself a favor and give up the game of cards. It is too risky for a man like you.

He laughed at his own joke, and Rodriguez joined him with relief. Then Rodriguez produced a contract, and each man put his signature to the document that transferred the legal ownership of me from one to the other.

IT WAS EARLY in the morning, but already the Casa de Contratación was humming with noise. I had often come to this building with Bernardo Rodriguez, but this time I followed Señor Dorantes down a different set of corridors, past the stately hall where a painting of the king hung on the wall, past the balcony where two officials argued over a map, to a small, dusty office where merchandise bound for the Indies had to be reported. From the high windows on the far wall, a gray light fell onto a brass crucifix, a book-lined shelf, and a lamp with a damask shade, before coming to rest on the clerk. He was a hunchback, with a dimple on his chin.

I found him, I wanted to cry. Ramatullai, I found him!

It seemed to me that Fate liked to mock me. For three years, I had searched for the hunchback—at the store, on the streets, along the Arenal—and now that I had finally found him, I could not tell Ramatullai about him. Even if I could somehow secure a piece of paper and some ink, I had no one to whom I could entrust a private message. She would never know that her daughter's master was so close. I stared at the hunchback, as if my intent gaze could wordlessly communicate his presence to Ramatullai.

Señor Dorantes said he needed to record his slave, here present, who would be traveling with him to the Indies in a few weeks.

Certainly, the clerk replied. He opened a leather-bound register and, licking his index finger, turned to the right page. He asked a series of questions and, as he recorded the answers to them, I learned that Señor Dorantes was from a town called Béjar del Castañar, in the province of Gibraleón, that he was thirty-two years old, that he intended to sail as a ship captain on the Gracia de Dios, and that the expedition he was to join was led by Señor Narváez.

Pánfilo de Narváez? the clerk asked, his ink-dipped feather poised in the air.

Yes, he himself.

Do you know how Narváez lost his eye? the clerk asked.

No, Señor Dorantes replied. Why does it matter?

The clerk ignored Dorantes's question and instead answered the one he had posed. Nine years ago, Diego Velázquez, the governor of Cuba, heard from a group of sailors who had drifted off their course that they had found a new land southwest of his island. Judging from the gold and silver the sailors had bartered to the Indians for beads, this land seemed to be rich. Diego Velázquez wanted to send his secretary, a certain Hernán Cortés, to explore and conquer it. But he was not entirely sure if Cortés could be trusted. So Velázquez dithered and delayed, while Cortés bought ships and provisions for the journey. When Velázquez finally made up his mind to relieve Cortés of his command, it was too late: Cortés had left Cuba, without even taking formal leave of his commander. Once Cortés arrived in New Spain, he established a settlement at Veracruz and began to make alliances with some of the native chiefs, who were vassals of the emperor Moctezuma. This Moctezuma, as you know, was rich beyond all imagination, and Cortés was determined to lead a march onto his capital. But the soldiers were often quarrelsome and even doubtful about the mission. So Cortés had all the ships destroyed, leaving the men no choice but to march.

What does this story have to do with Narváez?

Well, in order to stop Cortés from claiming this new province for himself alone, Velázquez sent an old friend of his in pursuit: it was Pánfilo de Narváez. Narváez arrived in New Spain with an army that was four times larger and better equipped than that of Cortés. He set up his camp in a native town on the coast and sent messages to the emperor Moctezuma that he was the true representative of the Crown. But Cortés found out about these messages through his spies and native allies. He returned to the coast, bribed Narváez's sentinels, and swept into the camp at night. In the battle that followed, not only did Narváez lose his right eye, some of his own soldiers deserted to join Cortés. And in the end it was Cortés who took México for His Majesty.

Old man, Señor Dorantes said, this mission has nothing to do with Cortés. Narváez has a license from His Majesty to claim La Florida for the Crown. No one else has such a license.

The clerk's story had been spoken in a tone of warning, but I do not believe that Señor Dorantes noticed it. He was in too much of a hurry to complete these tedious proceedings and return to Don Luis's house.

My master registered me in that book under the name he used with me ever since. I had entered the Casa de Contratación as Esteban, but I left it as Estebanico. Just Estebanico—converted, orphaned, and now dismissed with a boy's nickname.

THREE DAYS LATER, I found myself on the deck of the caravel Gracia de Dios. I could feel, under my sandaled feet, the movements of the animals in the stalls of the lower deck and, underneath them still, the gentle tug of the Guadalquivir, its waters running fast and deep. I was standing behind Capitán Dorantes when a man clad in an elegant black doublet and breeches boarded the ship and approached my new master in quick steps. Albaniz, Señor Dorantes said. Welcome aboard.

Señor Albaniz retrieved a document from his leather satchel and unscrolled it, his movements slow and deferential. The Gracia de Dios was the last ship on his rounds; he had already visited the other four ships in the armada.

Everything is in order? Señor Dorantes asked as he received an ink-dipped plume. Without waiting for the notary's answer, he turned toward me, his eyes not seeing me, his blond eyebrows knotted in concentration. Wordlessly, I offered him my back and he, laying the page against it, signed his name. There, he said. This is signed. Now we are ready. Estebanico, ring the bell.

As I pulled on the knotted rope, I looked at the city before me. During my time in Seville, I had tried my best not to grow attached to anything— not to the tools that dangled from my belt when I worked in the store, nor to the lentils in my bowl at night; not to the sound of the water fountain in the patio when I woke, nor to the soft glow of the afternoon sun on the Alcázar. Above all, I had tried my best not to love. I knew it was the sensible thing to do if I wanted to survive my bondage. But I had not been able to keep myself from loving Ramatullai and so, once again, I was forced to drink from the bitter cup of separation. The little joy I had managed to wring from my bondage, the joy she gave me, was gone from my life. I wondered now whether she, too, was thinking of me, whether she knew I was sailing to La Florida, the property of Andrés Dorantes, distinguished nobleman, war hero, and ship captain.

11

The Story of the Rafts

With experienced sailors, lateen sails, and favorable winds, a caravel like the Gracia de Dios can travel at the startling speed of four knots. Its lower deck provides respite from the elements and privacy for the use of the chamber pot, while its upper deck offers ample room for exercise. But the rafts—flat, plain, crudely made—had none of these conveniences. Even when the winds were strong, our progress remained modest because our sails were made of motley pieces of fabric, which were unevenly cut and roughly sewn together, allowing the air to whistle its way through. For an hour or two in the morning, and then again in the afternoon, the sails gave us some shade, but otherwise we were exposed to the sun and the heat.

The rules and formalities that had existed on land could not be maintained on the rafts—a nobleman had to sleep beside a blacksmith; a royal official was forced to share a cup of water with a carpenter. Worse: our ablutions were no longer private. A man who has had to relieve himself in full view of others finds it harder to assert his superiority over them. For Dorantes, especially, it was a humbling experience. But for one like me, who had already known these humiliations, it was a reminder that all fates, including my master's, could turn upside down. And I would do whatever it took in order to right mine.

Having seen it only from the perspective of our camp on the beach, none of us had known quite how large the Bay of Oysters was. It was immense—steering the five rafts out of it took up an entire week. In all that time, the water never rose higher than a man's waist and often it was so shallow that the rafts were only a few qibadh above the seafloor. While we waited for the wind to take us to the open ocean, we passed the time however we could. Some of us told stories; others recited poems; yet others played games in which they gambled whatever remained of their possessions.

And what are you reading, Father? Dorantes asked the friar.

Father Anselmo held up a printed page, dog-eared and torn in several places. This? he asked. My book of prayers. The spine came apart. Now all the pages are like this, you see.

Father Anselmo regarded Dorantes with benevolence and curiosity, waiting for further questions about the book, but when none came he returned to his reading. He was sitting back-to-back with Diego, who was carving a piece of cedar wood into a sparrow. Diego had already chiseled the bird's crest and bill, and now he was engraving the feathers. At the edge of the raft, Ruíz stared with his good eye at the seafloor, his hands hovering over the surface of the water, ready to catch any fish that passed underneath.

So when did you become a friar? Dorantes asked.

It was five years ago, Father Anselmo replied.

What happened? Did you just decide one day that you wanted to be a friar?

Everything must be decided one day.

But why? Dorantes asked again.

Diego turned around to look at his brother, leaving Father Anselmo with no back support. The friar caught himself just in time; he sat up and fixed his green eyes again upon Dorantes.

You are young, Dorantes continued. You look about the same age as Diego here. Seventeen or eighteen, maybe?

I am about twenty.

Did you not think of all the good things you could never have if you joined the order?

It is a calling, Capitán.

You felt called to become a friar? And you do not miss . . . Here, Dorantes said a dreadful word, which propriety prevents this servant of God from committing to paper.

There is g-g-great j-j-joy in the s-s-service of the Lord, the friar said. His face turned the color of carnations, as always happened when someone pressed him with questions. His stuttering made some of the men smile and they turned to watch, united in their desire for a good spectacle, something that could distract them from their predicament.

Well, Lord knows I could not do it, Dorantes said, casting a quick look toward Castillo. As if on cue, Castillo let out a mischievous laugh. You could not do it, could you? Dorantes asked him.

No, Castillo said. Never.

Dorantes looked around him, seeking further confirmation of his opinion on the natural lust of ordinary men. His eyes glided over me, then settled on his brother. And what about you, Tigre? Could you do it?

Just then there was a huge splash and we all turned to look. Ruíz had grabbed for something in the water—and caught it. He held it up in triumph; it was a speckled fish, its silvery body glinting in the sunlight. I have it, he said, I have it. But somehow the fish fought its way out of his hands and fell back into the bay. Ruíz let out a string of colorful curses, words so shocking that the friar looked on with mouth open.

Then the moment passed and Dorantes turned again on his brother. Well, could you do it?

Diego gave his brother a piercing look. Not everyone is compelled by the same instincts as you, he said.

With his nail, Dorantes scratched at a rusty spot on his sword, peeling the orange flakes that had settled on it during our stay at the Bay of Oysters. Everyone was accustomed to his mean retorts, so we expected him to say something, but Diego's answer seemed to have shamed him into silence.

It was almost lunchtime now and Father Anselmo got up to distribute our morning rations. The task had been delegated to him because he was a man of the cloth, but also because his popularity meant fewer complaints about the size of our portions. To each man, he handed out two raw ears of corn and a handful of nuts, which were eagerly accepted and quickly consumed. Father Anselmo was passing out the cups of water when Diego complained about the taste. The friar took a sip of the water himself and licked his lips thoughtfully. It tastes fine, he said.

Holding out a cup, Castillo said: Let me try it. Then, with finality: It tastes rotten.

Are you sure? Dorantes asked, taking the cup. The look on his face confirmed Castillo's judgment.

At the Bay of Oysters, we had stripped the skin from the horses' legs, dried it, and made water containers with it. But we had had no means to seal these pouches and now they had begun to turn rancid. So it was that, after only five days at sea, we found ourselves without drinking water. We cooled ourselves with rags dipped in seawater, we sucked on each kernel of corn in our rations before swallowing it, we tied our shirts over our heads to protect ourselves from the rays of the sun—we tried everything we could think of to distract ourselves from the thirst, but sleeping was the simplest remedy, even if the first sensation that came to us upon waking was of our tongues, swollen and pressing against our teeth. In the end, the only respite we could find was in the bottom of the rotten containers. We drank the fetid water we had at first refused and, when it ran out, began to quarrel over the juiciest ears of corn.

ON THE EVE of the seventh day, a large swath of hazy green and yellow appeared in the horizon. Land! one of the soldiers cried, standing up. Land! We were so excited at the prospect of drinking fresh water that, using our paddles, we raced the other rafts to the island. As we approached, we saw that the island was not far from the continent, forming a kind of strait that would finally lead us to the open ocean. Curious pelicans came to hover over our rafts and then returned to the seashore. From behind the bushes that bordered the beach, plumes of white smoke appeared—fires that had been hastily put out with water. Five painted canoes were moored on the rocks.

What a sight we must have made for whoever lived on this island: two hundred and sixty strange men of different ages and colors walking or hobbling to the beach, already scouring the world around us for anything to eat or drink. Our clothes, or what remained of them, hung absurdly on our bodies. Our faces were burnt, our lips were blistered, our limbs covered with sun rash. We were a plague in human form. But Narváez still managed to look better than the rest of us. On his head was his feather-adorned helmet—while the officers had all sacrificed their morions to the forge, he had decreed that his position entitled him to keep his—and he still had his doublet and breeches. In addition, his recent weight reduction made him look like a younger man.

Presently, he began to issue orders: this island would be called San Miguel, after the Christian saint whose feast day it was; Albaniz and Cabeza de Vaca were to look for the nearest river; Dorantes and Castillo would go to the Indian village to bring whatever supplies they could find; the friars would report on the health of the company; and Fernándes was to check the rafts for any needed repairs.

Dorantes did not relish the chance of intruding upon the Indians, even with the help of ten armed men, but being the one in charge of getting the supplies would give him the first choice of them, so he agreed without protest or complaint. I went with him, tucking under my belt one of the axes we had fashioned at the Bay of Oysters. The sandy path that led from the beach to the Indian village was covered with fresh footprints, and it seemed to us that we were watched from the bushes, but to our relief no Indians came forward to confront us and no arrows were shot at us.

The village was small: eight thatched-roof dwellings, arranged in two neat rows. A pyramid of firewood sat under a cluster of palm trees; some baskets made out of palm fronds were stacked beside it; and a large fish-net was laid out for repair. But behind each row of huts we found tall wooden racks, on which dozens of mullet fish were drying. What a gift this was for hungry men! The mullet tasted dry and salty and chewy and it was the most delicious thing we had eaten in a long time. We collected all of it, as well as some mullet roe, filling up several baskets.

Then we searched the huts. I was fortunate; in the first one I entered, I found a covered jar filled to the brim with cold water. I dropped on my knees, tipped the container, and drank and drank and drank until my stomach began to ache. It was the same kind of pain I used to get when I broke the fast on the first night of Ramadan, a feeling of being at once satiated and yet still thirsty. An odd feeling, but not altogether unfamiliar, and it made me dizzy. I fell down on the pelts to rest, allowing myself at last to look around me properly.

In one corner were two children's rattles, made of bone and wood. A thick garment of animal skin lay in a heap by the entrance, as if discarded in a hurry, next to a woman's comb. I ran my finger on its even teeth and was reminded of the tattoo on Ramatullai's right hand. The shame of my theft settled upon me all at once. How low I had sunk as a man. But once again I told myself that I had no other choice: I was trying to flee from La Florida and in order to do that, I needed food and water. It was necessity, rather than greed, that had driven me to this.

When I came out, I saw that Dorantes had already raided the village storehouse. Having run out of baskets, he and Castillo were using the edges of their shirts to carry corn and fruit out of the hut. Beneath their round burdens, their white waists and thin legs were exposed, making them look like half-stuffed rag dolls. We need clean containers for water, I said, lifting up the jar in my hand to show them. As I went into the next hut to look for another one, I heard Dorantes call out to his brother. Diego. Diego, leave that. Help Estebanico round up all the pots. Hurry!

We carried our loot back to the beach, where we found Narváez's men destroying the painted dugouts with their axes. What are you doing? Dorantes asked, unfurling his shirt and letting all the fruit inside roll to the ground.

Oh, good, you brought some food, Narváez said. Set it aside, I will divide it. His brows were furrowed as he watched the men work.

What are you doing? Dorantes repeated.

Breaking up these canoes. We can use the wood as gunwales.

You should not have done that. It is one thing to take food from them and another to destroy their property. They will come after us now.

How? They will have no canoes with which to pursue us.

What if there are others who do?

We will be gone by then.

You should have consulted with us before taking such a drastic measure.

Castillo stepped forward, eager to support Dorantes in his complaint. You have endangered all of us, he said.

Narváez regarded Dorantes and Castillo wearily. Their doubts no longer angered or saddened him; he was now resigned to them. We are about to reach the ocean, he said, and we need to ensure that the rafts remain dry. Do you have a better idea?

A brown sandpiper had walked up from the shoreline and was eyeing the fruit that was on the ground. I shooed the bird away before it got too close.

Dorantes's reply, when it finally came, was quiet and grudging. No, he said.

By the time all the rafts were fitted with gunwales and the containers filled with water from the river, it was late afternoon. The men wanted to spend the night on the island—to be able to stretch out on the sand and sleep alone, without having to smell another man's bad breath or dirty feet, seemed like a wonderful luxury. But Narváez's decision meant that we could not take that risk; we had to leave San Miguel Island right away if we wanted to avoid retribution for breaking up the canoes. We departed under a darkened sky, eager to reach Pánuco—a word that, for every one of us now, was synonymous with salvation.

IN THE MORNING, WE passed the strait and reached the open sea. We sailed westward under skies the color of mackerel, with patches here and there of darker gray. The oppressive heat of the past two weeks had finally broken, but that was little comfort to two men on our raft, a cobbler from Segovia and a crossbowman from Sicily, who were burning with fever. They had been well at the Bay of Oysters, but the journey on the raft had weakened them; they lay indolently at the far edge of the boat, sometimes using the pot and sometimes helplessly soiling themselves. It was a horrible sight and a cruel reminder that the sickness had followed us out of La Florida.

Dorantes sat at the other end of the raft, far from the sick men, and he took frequent naps, but Diego stayed up all day, carving up his little birds. It surprised me that a nobleman like him should be so skilled with his hands. Where did you learn how to do that? I asked him.

The whittling knife stopped midair. Diego looked up. I taught myself, he said.

You have already made two birds, I said. Why are you making another one?

This one is the older brother of those two, he replied with a little smile.

I took the little sparrows in the palms of my hands. How expertly he had shaped their beaks and tail feathers. And look how alive their eyes seemed. Diego could have been an artist if he had not been a nobleman. I have twin brothers, I said, more to myself than to Diego. A memory, buried away in a corner of my mind, surfaced now: we were walking by the side of the Umm er-Rbi' River, returning home from a trip to the shrine, where we had given prayers for my father's health. Yahya had grown tired; he threw up his little hands, wanting me to carry him on my back. Right away, Yusuf proclaimed himself the more tired of the two. I lifted them both up and carried them home. I could still remember the weight of their bodies against mine.

You will see them again someday, Diego said.

My longing for Yusuf and Yahya was so plain that Diego had seen it. And rather than ignore it, the way Dorantes would have, he had tried to soothe it. Ojalá, I replied. A word of hope in his native language, borrowed from a word of prayer in mine—Insha'llah.

Once again, Father Anselmo stood up to distribute the rations. The water and mullet we brought from the island had lasted only a few days, after which we returned to eating corn. We did not mind the small rations so much; it was the thirst that was unbearable. We were weak with it. It gave us headaches and made us dangerously lazy, so that when the rafts drifted away from their course, we did not have the strength to use our paddles and depended increasingly on our sails. So you can imagine, gentle reader, how relieved we were to find another island.

THE BEACH WAS NARROW and ended in a small dune that was covered with bright green palmetto, hiding whatever lay on the other side. No Indian trail was visible, nor any dugouts. We would have to walk over the dune to look for water. The argument about the gunwales had deepened Narváez's dislike for Dorantes and Castillo, so he chose two different captains for this mission: Tellez and Peñaloza. Everyone else was to remain on the shore.

I gathered some firewood to toast the last of the corn and walked the shoreline looking for crabs or oysters, but could not find any. The men had scattered into smaller groups on the beach, quietly waiting for the captains to return. The only sound came from the rattling of the rafts on the waves; even the herons and egrets we had grown used to seeing in these parts were gone. It was the middle of the afternoon and the sky was darkening steadily by the time Tellez returned. He was a slight man, with narrow shoulders and a handsome face. When he spoke, he kept his eyes on the ground, as if embarrassed by the sound of his own voice. Don Pánfilo, he said, I did not find a river.

Nothing?

No, not even a spring.

Narváez pursed his lips in a way that suggested he had once again been disappointed by one of his lieutenants. But Peñaloza came back from the other side of the beach soon after, bearing the same news. No river.

The panic that gripped our company was so sudden and so strong I felt as if I could touch it. How would we survive without water? The ration master, unable to bear the thirst any longer, filled up his flask with seawater and, despite warnings from the more experienced soldiers, drank all of it at once. With a sigh of relief, he lay on the beach and closed his eyes. Not an hour later, while the commissary was taking the confession of a dying man, the ration master began to convulse. His arms and legs seemed to acquire a life of their own, kicking up the sand in all directions. There was no expression in his eyes and his mouth was white with foam. The friars tried to comfort him by holding down his limbs, but this did nothing to stop his seizures. He looked for all the world like a man possessed by a demon. Peace came to him only when his soul left his body.

When we carried the ration master to the shallow grave that had been dug for him, I noticed that he still had, hanging from his belt, the native hatchet he had bartered me for some water. Now the ration master was gone, and so was the poor horse the barter had helped. The elders teach us: we all belong to God, and to Him we return. I knew that I was not supposed to rebel against the will of God. Yet the death of the ration master, so sudden and so brutal, stoked my anger. Had I built a raft and sailed this far away from La Florida only to die on a barren island? Had I been forsaken?

Then, quite suddenly, the gray clouds that had followed us all day rumbled with the sound of thunder and the wind picked up, blowing through the beach at furious speed. A good wind could not be wasted—it was a chance to travel a greater distance toward the port—so we ran to the rafts and hoisted the anchors. The air was thick with the smell of our fear. As we moved away from the shore, flashes of thunder interrupted the eternity of darkness around us. We turned our faces up to the heavens and when at last it began to rain, we opened our mouths to catch the raindrops. Like beggars, we held up every jar, every bucket, every cooking pot we had toward the skies. We had waited so long for this mercy.

WE SAILED FOR ANOTHER WEEK, keeping the continent in our sight as best as we could manage, but seeing no sign of a river. If we could not be certain to find water, we dared not risk another landing, even though our supplies were dwindling. But early one morning, a dozen Indian fishermen in painted dugouts, much like those Narváez had broken up, approached us. They rowed in a wide circle around our rafts, taking stock of our pitiful condition and our meager possessions. We could see no food or water in their canoes, but in our state of utter exhaustion the Indians seemed to us more like guardian angels than men of flesh and blood. We followed them to the continent.

Upon landing, Narváez produced two necklaces made with blue

beads, handing each one slowly and ceremoniously to the fishermen. The Indians were surprised by the gift and delighted by the clattering sound the beads made when the necklaces were slung together. His gift earned Narváez an invitation to the Indians' village, but since some of the men were too sick to walk and others unwilling to trust the Indians, only a small party of healthy men—no more than fifty or sixty of us—went with him.

We marched behind Narváez down a narrow path that cut straight through the green wilderness like a fresh scar. It led to a village of a dozen dwellings, arranged around an earthen mound of the kind we had seen in Apalache. Three boys were racing each other on stilts while their friends urged them to go faster, faster, faster; some women were spreading red paint over a deerskin stretched upon a triangular frame; and two young girls were taking turns pounding something in a mortar. The air smelled of fish and smoke, a combination that, in our state of deprivation, was a particular torment. As we proceeded to the village square, the women and children stopped what they were doing and watched us. The cacique, an old man with heavy-lidded eyes and droopy earlobes, was waiting for us, his sentinels having given him advance notice of our arrival. He wore a cloak of marten and ermine skin, whose front ends he held in his hands, so that they would not drag on the ground. Armed with plumed lances, his deputies appraised us from where they stood.

Head bowed, Narváez offered the cacique some bells and a long string of yellow beads. The chief accepted the items with a nod, then took off his magnificent fur cloak and gave it to Narváez, who immediately wrapped himself in it. The village, so still and quiet for a moment, returned to life. The children resumed their play, the women went back to grinding corn, the men invited us to sit. Up in the trees, turtledoves cooed to one another. Pablo, Narváez's prisoner and interpreter, was asked to come forward. From him, we learned that this cacique's name was Echogan and that he ruled over this village and two others some distance away along the coast. In reply, Narváez told Echogan that he was the emissary of a powerful king, more powerful than anyone here could imagine. He had come to this land as a friend, he said, to teach the Indians all that he and his Christian brothers knew, but for now he was looking for his comrades, from whom he had been separated. Have you seen men who look like us in these parts? he asked.

No, Echogan replied. Have you lost some of your brothers?

They are waiting for us on our ships. Perhaps you have seen their ships sail nearby?

No. The cacique was quiet for a while. Then, his eyes darting from Narváez to the lieutenants standing behind, he asked: And your powerful king, will he come to your aid?

To admit that his powerful king had no idea where he was would have made Narváez look insignificant, so he chose to lie. Surely, he said. As soon as he hears from us.

Narváez then asked the cacique about any rivers nearby; Echogan told him that a few leagues west of the village was a wide river, which in his language was called the Great River. This news was a great comfort to all of us, for what other great river could there be in these parts but the Río de las Palmas? We were finally in the vicinity of Pánuco.

The cacique offered us great quantities of fish and squash, and a drink made from fermented fruit. To the men who had remained on the beach, he sent baskets of victuals. In all ways, he was a generous host, honoring us with his presence until sundown, when visitors from a nearby tribe arrived to see him and together they retired into their temple for the rest of the evening.

Now that we were left alone, we broke up into smaller groups, warming up by the side of the campfires. The thought that we would soon reach the port made the men fantasize about everything they would do once we arrived there. Diego said he wanted to take a hot bath. Imagine the sensation of soap against your skin, he said. Cabeza de Vaca said he would settle for some paper and ink, so that he could write to his wife. But Dorantes wanted to hear good music. All the fiddles in our company, including the friar's, had been stripped of their strings, which had been used to tie the sails. He missed music the most, he said. Castillo was about to say something too, when a rock landed on his hand.

Before I could turn to look for the source of the projectile, another one landed on my head. The pain was so sharp that it took the air out of my lungs and numbed any other feeling; I fell on my knees and covered my head with my hands. A third rock landed on our campfire, sending bright sparks high up in the air. As I shot to my legs to look for cover, the notary leveled his musket and fired. One of our Indian hosts fell to the ground, clutching his leg and screaming. Stunned by the sound and the smoke, the others retreated.

Narváez came out of the lodge the Indian chief had given him for the night. What happened? he asked. The Indians turned against him now, hurling rocks at him. To the rafts, he screamed.

We ran back to the shore under a shower of stones. Our sudden return alarmed those who had remained on the beach and they quickly set up a line of defense, but we were in very poor shape. The horses, which had given us such an advantage at the Battle of the Río Oscuro, were gone now and there was little ammunition left for the five muskets we still had. Many of us suffered injuries: Narváez was bleeding from the forehead, Cabeza de Vaca was nursing a sprained elbow, one of the carpenters had a broken leg, and I could feel a large lump throbbing on my head. To make matters worse, several men were missing, including two from the Dorantes contingent. The Indians returned twice that night, to hurl rocks or shoot arrows at us and the musketeers and crossbowmen held them back as best they could. All night long, we waited for the missing men, but they did not return.

We were forced to leave at first light, rowing away from the coast as fast as we could. The fate of our missing companions, the guilt we felt at leaving them behind, and the prospect of dying on the rafts weighed heavily on all of us, putting us in a quarreling mood. The men wanted to know why Echogan and his tribe, who had been so generous to us at first, had turned so suddenly and so inexplicably against us.

Perhaps we offended them, Father Anselmo said.

How, Father? Dorantes said. We did not set foot in their temple.

Do you think we did something to them? Ruíz said. No one did anything. That is just how the heathens are. Look what they did to me. He pointed to the dark socket where his left eye had been, oblivious to the role he had played in his own predicament.

Looking back on these events now, and having given them much thought and gained the perspective that can only be given by the passing of time, I have come to believe that this tribe of fishermen attacked us because they had been warned about our wickedness. The visitors we had seen at sundown must have told them what we had done on San Miguel Island: the dugouts we had destroyed, the containers we had stolen, the food we had taken. It may seem a far-fetched idea, but not as far-fetched as generous hosts turning against their guests for no reason. God, may He be glorified and exalted, tells us: God will not deal unjustly with man in aught; it is man that wrongs his own soul. Now we were back in the ocean, drifting like tree leaves in the wind, and we dared not land anywhere for fear of encountering more Indians.

TWO DAYS LATER, we sailed into the mouth of a mighty river, the largest I had seen in all my life. Its flow was so powerful that we were able to drink freshwater directly from our rafts and to refill every one of our containers. Thank God, I thought. Now that the port was near, so was our salvation. But some of the men among us, perhaps having grown used to our misfortune, insisted that this river was not the Río de las Palmas and that we had been led astray. Do you see any sign of Castilian presence on the shore? they asked. But others, and this servant of God among them, insisted that there was only one way to know whether this was the right river: we would have to go upstream to look for the port.

The Indians had good reason to call this the Great River. At the point where it met the ocean, its current was still strong enough that it would be very difficult to maneuver our rafts, whose oakum had washed away and whose floors were so damaged that we could see the water in between each pair of logs. And there was, too, the risk that the five vessels would be separated or lost. This was why Dorantes called out to Narváez: Don Pánfilo, we ought to throw lines to one another.

It was a good suggestion. No matter what happened, at least the rafts would remain together. But Narváez did not reply. The sun was setting and a strong wind blew from the east, growing more intense as the light faded.

I do not believe he heard you, I said.

Dorantes cupped his small hands around his mouth, so that his voice would carry farther. Don Pánfilo!

Still, there was no reply. Cabeza de Vaca, whose raft was nearest ours, took up the request in his own way. Don Pánfilo, he said, how should we proceed across the river? What are your orders?

Narváez's eye patch gleamed in the half-light. The time for orders is past, he said at last. Each raft should try to save itself. That is what I intend to do.

There was a moment of stunned silence, then the questions and complaints started. How can you say this?

Are you forsaking us?

Traitor.

Reason with him, Father.

How are we going to cross with only these tattered sails?

Grab one of his oars!

Stop! I will have you shot.

Then there was the sound of thunder. The skies opened up and the rain fell fast, hitting us at an angle and blinding us. The wind pushed us across the mouth of the Great River and the noise of the storm, terrifying in its intensity, quickly drowned out the sound of our quarrels. Our raft would capsize, we would all die, no one would know what happened to us—such thoughts flitted through our minds even as we tied our sails and tried to keep the raft level. I can say in all honesty that each one of us wrestled with his fate that night. We prepared ourselves to die, praying to God that He forgive us our sins and grant us eternal life in heaven.

12.

The Story of the Island of Misfortune

The wind carried us well past the mouth of the Great River. By morning, we found ourselves in the open sea again. From horizon to horizon, we could see only water, glazed white by the sun. The other rafts had disappeared, as if charmed away by night sirens or swallowed up by sea monsters. Lord Almighty, the men said, where have they all gone? The loss of so many of our companions, especially after the hardships we had endured together, was intolerable. And yet we could not help feeling grateful that our own lives had been spared. Still, as the day wore on and clouds began to fill the sky again, we realized just how desperate our situation was: we had neither food nor water; the horse rope that tied the logs together was rotting; and the mast was leaning dangerously against the wind.

With daylight fading, the water turned glossy black and a grim peace fell upon us—we were but condemned men waiting for their executioner. I could not escape the thought that I had brought all of this upon myself, first by engaging in greedy trade, later by selling myself into bondage, and later yet by stealing from the Indians. And it seemed to me that the others, too, were confronting their own sins in that misty, moonless night. Father, one of the men asked, will you hear my confession? The friar clambered over the bodies of his neighbors, this one prone, the other curled up, and slowly made his way to the supplicant. He listened to whispered admissions of theft, lies, envy, or adultery, all of which he absolved. The Christians' outlook toward sin and salvation was a mystery that even six long years of life among them did not entirely elucidate for me. I had been raised to expect judgment for my actions. Perhaps, I thought, this was what was being meted out to us now.

The warmth of the morning sun brought with it the smell of disease and death. My breath grew shallow and I felt myself helplessly drifting into the final slumber when one of my companions called out that he could see land. Land? The word revived my spirits to such an extent that I lifted myself up on one elbow to look at the horizon. An island with leafy trees danced in the hazy distance, but I was too weak to gaze at it for long and had to lie back down. The heartiest among the men had already grabbed their paddles. Whether it was the rocky shore or their feeble paddling I could not guess, but by the time they threw the anchor down our gunwales were gone, one log had detached itself from the raft, and pieces of fabric hung loosely from our sails like so many flags of surrender.

I crawled unsteadily out of the boat, like a child learning how to walk, and lay on the wet sand, the waves lapping my feet as if to call me back to the ocean. Oh, what relief it was to be on land! I closed my eyes and let darkness embrace me. I dreamed that I had returned to Azemmur on a ship filled with other voyagers from the province of Dukkala. No sooner had I disembarked than I ran down the winding streets of the city to our old house. I pushed its creaky blue door open and came upon my mother, my sister, and my brothers, sitting around the brazier having their soup. My mother dropped her spoon; my sister cried out; my brothers got up. They were all staring at me as though I were an intruder. Mother, I cried, Mother. Do you not recognize me? But she looked confused and I realized then that I had spoken to her in a foreign tongue, though it was not any tongue I had heard or known before.

The sound of chatter woke me up. Ruíz had found a clear spring nearby and brought water for everyone in the company. A few sips of it and I felt as if I were hoisted from the abyss in which I had fallen. I sat up and took the raw oyster that was being offered to me—out of caution, the men had not built a campfire—and I returned to sleep.

I woke with a start, my face wet with the drizzle of early morning. All around me, the others were taking stock of what was left on the raft, which had been pulled all the way to the safety of the shore: two muskets and five swords; two sets of axes, saws, and hammers; some bowls, jars, and cooking pots; animal skins of different sizes; the cloak of marten and ermine skin that Narváez had left behind; beads and trinkets; some bibles and rosaries. But no food; no ammunition; no rope or twine; no fishing poles or nets; no tents or bedding; nothing that could help us survive on the island. The raft looked pitiful; I dared not ask the others whether they thought they could repair it because I feared I already knew the answer.

Dejected, I went to the spring to get water, but as I refilled my flask I noticed footprints leading away from it onto a native trail. I followed the path for a while, and then prudently climbed up a tree to survey the area from above. The island was quite narrow, only half a league wide, but lengthwise it stretched several leagues. In the distance, the continent was outlined between gray clouds and a sea of dull green. If we could somehow cross this stretch of ocean to the continent, we could continue on foot toward the port. From my perch, I could see that the native trail led to a village of perhaps a dozen huts, of the kind that can be struck easily and moved to a different site. Tiny figures moved about in the square, occupied with their chores and unaware of being watched. Running among them were what looked like dogs, white and fawn in color. I had not seen dogs in the new world before and, although I took their presence as a good sign, I decided to retreat for fear that they would smell me. Returning to the beach, where the men were still working out what to do with the supplies, I reported what I had seen.

The island is not that far from the continent, I said, but this raft won't carry us there in its present state. Perhaps we can go to the Indian village for help.

With his good eye, the soldier Ruíz gave me a vicious look. No, we cannot.

There was an authority to his tone that I resented immediately. We must, I countered. We have no other choice.

Did you forget what happened to us the last time we went to an Indian village? Ruíz asked. Echogan's men turned against us. And that was when there were two hundred of us. Now there are thirty-nine of us left, and not ten can bear to walk, let alone fight. El Moro says he saw a dozen huts—how many Indians does that make?

At least a hundred, Dorantes conceded. Maybe more.

See? We cannot go.

We cannot stay either, I said. We have to find food and shelter.

What if the savages sacrifice us to their idols and eat us? Ruíz asked.

These words had a great effect upon the men, already rattled by our dangerous journey on the raft. Echeverría, a blacksmith whose brother-in-law had accompanied Cortés in the conquest of México, began to tell stories about midnight sacrifices to idols with evil faces and enormous tongues. The victims were carried up the steps of the great Temple of Huichilobos and put upon an altar, where their still beating hearts were torn out of their chests, and their arms and legs cut off to feed caged lions, tigers, and snakes. Dozens—nay, hundreds—of Castilian prisoners of war had been sacrificed in this gruesome way. By the time Echeverría stopped speaking, few of the men wanted to go anywhere near the Indian village.

So we remained on the beach for another night, not daring to build fires, or to stray too far from each other. Those who were afflicted with fever could do nothing for themselves and their condition only worsened after it rained. By the next morning, we were all drenched and shivering with cold. Still, Ruíz and the others refused to venture inland. I stood up, brushing the sand off my clothes. I will go alone, I said.

No, Dorantes replied.

If we stay here, we will die, I said. I will go.

You will not, he said.

I was almost startled by his order. Did he think he could still impose his will upon me? I had already lost everyone and everything that mattered to me. All I had left now was my life, which I had sworn never again to put in the hands of others. I would not break my promise to myself. So I walked away, feeling his eyes upon my back. I half-expected him to run after me or even to try to hit me, but he did neither. From where they stood on the beach, the men watched and waited.

Estebanico, Dorantes called after me. If you find any food, bring it. His tone suggested that it was his idea to send me to the Indian village.

Diego stood up and fastened his sword belt. Wait. I will come with you.

Where are you going? Dorantes asked him.

Where do you think?

It is too dangerous, Tigre.

No one is asking you to come.

In the end, four of us went: Diego, Father Anselmo, Fernándes the carpenter, although he was looking rather sickly, and this servant of God, Mustafa ibn Muhammad. Diego had his sword, but the rest of us carried, tucked into our belts, axes we had made at the Bay of Oysters. Scalloped clouds hung low on the trail, where the trees were still shedding drops from that morning's rain. From the soft earth beneath our feet, worms crawled out, unconscious of the rapacious beaks awaiting them. The brisk wind penetrated our clothes, making them flap around our bodies.

As we came into view of the village, barking dogs signaled our presence, with the result that two Indian youths came with them to investigate. The dogs encircled us, snarling at us and baring their fangs. I was alarmed, but Father Anselmo, who had a natural ease with animals, cooed to one of the dogs and it came to sniff his hands. The barking died out.

The two Indian youths were exceedingly tall, taller than even the friar or me, and had the broad chests typical of good archers. A reed as long as a hand's breadth perforated each of their nipples, and another, short reed cut through their lower lips. One of them had a scar on his chin and the other had a squarish jaw, which made him look older than he likely was. For all this, their manner was completely gentle, as if they knew, without needing to be told, what great hardship we had endured. They seemed especially taken by the differences in our hair—the friar's was red; Diego's was blond; Fernándes's was brown and straight; and mine was black and curly. Everything about us seemed exotic to them: our colors, our beards, our clothes, our weapons.

With my hand on my chest, I said: Mustafa. My name is Mustafa.

Kwachi, said the youth with the scar.

Elenson, said the other.

This was the easy part. Now I nudged Diego; he offered them several strings of yellow beads. In return, Kwachi gave Diego an arrow from his quiver. The exchange of gifts appeared to convince them of our good intentions and they invited us to their village, which was much larger than I had thought. I counted twenty dwellings, made with wooden poles and covered with tree branches and animal skins. The Capoques, for that is the name of this tribe, numbered at least two hundred souls, most of them now congregating in the square to stare at us. The women were nearly as tall as the men, though they were more modestly attired, with deerskins trimmed with white seashells covering parts of their bodies. The children took great delight in our beards and two or three of them came up to pull them. The adults shooed them away, but we smiled and offered them another string of beads.

Kwachi and Elenson invited us to sit by the fire, which was a great comfort to us in our damp clothes. We were offered bowls of a warm, dark drink, made from a leaf I had not seen before, and which revived us greatly. The color returned to poor Fernándes's face. Later on, the cacique—he turned out to be Kwachi's father, an elderly man by the name of Delenchavan—joined us for a meal. In those early days, the entire Indian vocabulary I had at my disposal consisted of ten or twenty words, overheard when Narváez or his interpreter spoke to the caciques or prisoners, words about gold and silver, land and rivers, time and distance, and which would be of limited use to me now in my attempt to get help with finding shelter from the rain and repairing the raft. I had much to learn. The Capoques asked me where we had come from and somehow I managed to communicate that we were travelers heading to the continent on the other side of this island and that we were stranded on the beach—not a lie, but not the complete truth either.

YOU BROUGHT THEM HERE? Ruíz asked when I returned to the beach. His fingers were already wrapped around the handle of his hatchet. You brought them to us?

I was bewildered. I thought he would have been relieved to see the baskets of food—fresh rabbit, dried fish, edible roots—we had brought back from the Capoques' village, but his only concern seemed to be that our benefactors had followed us to the beach. This is their island, I said. I cannot stop them from going wherever they please.

Without waiting for an answer, I began to divide the victuals. The men fell on their shares and the quarrel stopped.

The two Indian youths, Kwachi and Elenson, sat on their haunches to watch us eat, their gaze traveling from our beached raft to our strange weapons, and from the bible the soldiers had been reading to the cross they had set up for mass. Kwachi and Elenson did not need to speak Spanish to notice the bitter argument their appearance had caused, so after only a short while, they stood up to take their leave.

We lit a bonfire and sat huddled around it to discuss our plans. In order to reach Pánuco, we would have to repair the raft and ply the coast until we saw a sign of the port, but the past month had exhausted the men and most of them were weary of getting back on the water so soon, especially under the rain. Someone suggested that we stay on the island until the spring, which would give the sick a chance to recover and the healthy some time to repair the raft and build up food reserves. But once again, Ruíz objected. We cannot set up camp here, he said. The Indians already know about our location. What if they return in the middle of the night and kill us all? We should set up camp on the other side of the island, away from them.

But the raft is here, Dorantes said. And we have to stay close to where we know there is food and water.

Suit yourself, Ruíz replied. But I am not staying. I did not come half-way across the world to be eaten by these savages.

Most of the men were afraid of setting up camp in an unknown part of the island, so they all agreed that we should remain near the beach. But four men, all of them soldiers, sided with Ruíz. They left the very next morning, taking with them their weapons and some of the tools we still had and said they would return to the beach in the spring so that we could all leave the island on the same raft. Dorantes tried to reason with the soldiers: they would be safer with us, since our group was larger in number; they would have better access to food and water; they could receive confession if they wished. When they refused to listen to his pleas, Dorantes became angry. As your captain, he said, assigned to this office by His Majesty the King, I order you to remain with us.

Ruíz's reply was swift and scornful. If the king wants me to remain with you, he can come and tell me himself.

IN A CLEARING just behind the beach, we set up three simple huts, modeled after the Capoques' dwellings and covered with tree branches. One look inside showed you that we had tried our best to make it into proper quarters: in one corner were the water jars we had taken from San Miguel Island; in another corner were the tools and weapons we still had; and laid out in the center was the cloak of marten and ermine skin, which Dorantes had salvaged, and which served as bedding for the hut he shared with Diego, Father Anselmo, Castillo, and me. The hut kept out the worst of the cold, but the rain leaked through the openings between the branches and more than once during the night we were drenched with rainwater.

Three days later, I went to the Capoques' camp to return their baskets. Dorantes and Castillo decided to come with me, in the hope that they could convince the Indians to give us some meat to supplement the oysters and seaweed we had been collecting. As we approached their site, the dogs began to howl and a group of children ran out to greet us. Excitedly, they led us by the hand toward the square, where a small crowd was gathered, noisily trading comments and questions, but it was only after the Indians parted that I saw a white man. He turned around—it was Cabeza de Vaca.

What a shock it was to see him. We had given him up for dead and now he was standing there in the flesh. He hugged Dorantes and Castillo mightily, saying Gracias a Dios and Increíble, but only glanced in my direction. As we sat around the Capoques' campfire, he told us his story, which I record here for the reader, as best as I can remember it.

Amigos, Cabeza de Vaca said, this is what happened. As the governor did not see fit to throw me a line, I endeavored to remain close to the raft nearest mine, which was that of Capitán Peñaloza. We sailed together for two days and two nights, but were separated by a storm. At dawn on the third day, I heard the sound of breakers, though I could not be sure if it were a dream or not. With my men too weak to row, it was left to the skipper and me to land the raft. I sent one of my men to reconnoiter the area and he found some Indians returning from a fishing trip. They gave us their catch and later brought us some roots and nuts. All of this was a great succor to us. But as I could not be completely sure of their intentions toward us, I had my men repair the raft and we set it back on the water the next day. We had gone only a crossbow shot from the shore when a wave hit us and we lost our oars and some of our tools. The next one overturned the raft entirely, forcing us to swim back to the beach with only the clothes on our backs. But poor Solís refused to let go of the boat, and he and two others drowned underneath it.

The tax inspector is dead? Dorantes asked.

Yes. He and two others drowned.

God have mercy.

Lord hear our prayer. I also lost three other men to the fever. The Indians, who are from a tribe that calls itself the Han, returned with more food later that day and, when they learned what happened to us, they entreated us to go with them to their camp. We told them we were too weak to endure the walk, but they built bonfires along the path from the beach and carried us all the way to their encampment, where they held a feast in our honor, with much singing and dancing. That was when I noticed on one of the dancers some yellow beads of the kind we brought from Castile, and I asked him where he had obtained them. From a nearby tribe, he said, where some white men like me had visited. So I told him to bring me here, that I might find out who these white men were.

Now that Cabeza de Vaca had finished his story, Dorantes informed him of Ruíz's desertion, which he said he had been unable to stop. Cabeza de Vaca replied that he had had desertions among his ranks, too: four soldiers and one criado—strong and healthy all of them—had decided to try swimming to the mainland. Once on the continent, they planned to walk along the coast to Pánuco, where they would report news of our shipwreck. It is too far to swim, Dorantes said, but perhaps they will be lucky.

Do you still have your raft? Cabeza de Vaca asked.

Yes. But I doubt it is navigable in this weather. It is best to wait for spring.

Then bring your men to my camp. We can remain there together.

Why not bring your men to my camp?

The argument between Dorantes and Cabeza de Vaca was not about survival. It was about who would dictate what camp we stayed in, and who would be the leader. Leaning against my walking staff, I said: The Capoques have given us food, water, and even animal skins for the cold. If we leave to go with their neighbors across the island, they might take it as an insult.

It would be smart to join together, Cabeza de Vaca said.

Smart, but not wise, I said. The Capoques saved our lives. We would do well, I said, to try to be good guests to our hosts, since we depend on them to show us the best places to fish and forage. The storms that led us to this island are not over yet and it would be dangerous to leave now, with no reserves of food. In the spring, God willing, we can join forces, repair our raft, and leave the island.

And you, Dorantes, do you agree with this? Cabeza de Vaca asked.

My men are in no condition to go anywhere, Dorantes replied. We have to wait for spring.

So it was that Cabeza de Vaca and his men returned to the Han village, while we remained with the Capoques.

MY MEMORIES OF THE WINTER we spent on the island are colored now by sorrow and guilt: sorrow at what we had to endure and guilt at the calamity that befell the Capoques. But in the late fall of the year 935 of the Hegira, as we settled ourselves for the rainy season, we had some reason to be optimistic. The dwellings we had built for ourselves and the abundance of drinking water curbed the spread of disease in our ranks. We picked oysters and seaweed or looked for bird nests and edible fruit in the wilderness behind our camp. The terrible hunger and constant uncertainty we had felt on the rafts began to recede.

But now we craved hardier fare, especially on evenings when it rained and we lay in our huts shivering with cold. We asked the Capoques for meat and they gave us freely of whatever they had—fish, fowl, squirrel, rabbit—but very quickly we turned into a tribe of beggars, constantly pleading with them for more. Delenchavan, the cacique, put a stop to all of this. He decreed that we were to work for the meat his hunters were giving us: we had to collect firewood or fetch water or grind nuts for it. A fair judgment, but one that, I noticed, several among the Castilians appeared to resent—they considered it beneath them to work for the Indians.

One day, Kwachi and Elenson invited us to go hunting with them. Dorantes and Castillo said they could not use Indian weapons, so only Diego and I went. We departed at dawn, creeping into the woods behind a dozen young lads from the village. The bows that had been lent to us were so large that they slipped off our shoulders, but resolutely we kept up pace with the others. An owl flew low overhead, silently swooping down on a squirrel before I had a chance to even reach for my bow. Diego mistook crackling branches for the footsteps of a beast and shot arrows into the bushes. Neither one of us caught anything. For men raised in the city, even for those who, like us, had marched through the wilderness for so long, the trackless fields of green still retained much mystery. Disconsolately, we watched as Elenson skinned a rabbit, cutting around the legs and the neck to pull the fur off. The animal's pink skin was revealed, its heat turning into steam in the cold morning air.

We thought we might do better at fishing, but the Capoques catch their fish by spearing it, a task that requires a great deal of patience and precision. A long day spent in the bay yielded us only two sea trout, which we shared with the others in our hut, under an unspoken agreement that each man must share his food with his hut companions. In this way, we were able to partake of the fruit that Father Anselmo collected during his foraging trips, and the oysters that Castillo and Dorantes picked.

But our poor hunting skills caused the other Indians to tease Kwachi about his new friends, until he tired of it. One day he said: Go pick roots with the women. He scratched the scar on his chin, his eyes avoiding us in embarrassment. It is easy work, he said.

Reader, it was not. The roots came from tall plants with thorny stems that grew in a marsh half a league from the village. By then, the oyster beds near our camp were almost entirely depleted, so Dorantes and Castillo joined us in the bog. The water was cold and murky and the long leaves of the plant tangled around our feet. We had to burrow deep into the mud with our hands and when we managed to pull out the roots it was often at the expense of deep cuts on our hands and arms.

The Capoque women were amused by our slow progress, but they taught us how to pull the plants without getting hurt and how to clean up the roots before roasting them. Sometimes, when they took a break under the shade of the trees, they shared their meals with us. They sang and gossiped and giggled and nursed their babies and strapped them to their backs before going back to the marsh.

It was while listening to the women that I began to learn their language. At first, I found it difficult to pronounce the strange and guttural sounds of the Capoque tongue. Words like Teshedalj or Hamdoloq, so different from any names I knew for Bone or Feather, taunted me, appearing when I least expected them. I was puzzled by the order of words in Capoque, by the fact that the doer and the done-to were spoken of before the deed itself. When I said, Bawuus ni kwiamoja, one of the women inevitably corrected me, Ni bawuus kwiamoja. But every day, as a child does, I learned new words.

Eventually I was able to carry on longer conversations with my new friends. How did you get the scar on your chin? I once asked Kwachi.

We were sitting outside his hut, with the last of the day's sun on our faces. I was helping him make a new arrow. My task was to hold the sharp end in place while he fastened it with deer sinew to the wooden shaft.

Kwachi cocked his head toward Elenson, who stood a few paces away, showing a group of boys the proper way to hold a bow. My brother gave it to me, he said. We were racing in the woods, tugging at each other. Then he pulled me a little too hard and I fell against a tree trunk.

Though Kwachi called Elenson his brother, the two were not kin. Kwachi had lost his mother as an infant and would have died if Elenson's mother had not nursed him. So the two of them were very close, and one was rarely seen without the other. Perhaps that was why I thought of them as a pair, an indistinguishable twosome. But as the weeks passed and I grew more familiar with them, I discovered that Kwachi was more generous with us castaways, more tolerant of our mores, and more sympathetic to our plight. He would have continued to give us of his game, even over the objections of the cacique, had Elenson not insisted that he cease.

ONE DAY IN WINTER, the blacksmith Echeverría complained of stomach cramps. His companions counseled him to keep the fast and say his Hail Marys, but despite this, his moans of pain did not abate. He threw up even in his sleep. Father Anselmo was bringing water from the spring one morning when he found him curled up under a tree, his right hand still clasped tightly around a pinecone. We carried Echeverría to a little clearing south of the river and as we were about to put him in his grave, Fernándes, the carpenter, called for us to stop. He wanted Echeverría's belt.

No, Father Anselmo said.

But he will not need it, Fernándes protested. What is the harm? He stripped Echeverría of his belt and took it to the village, where he exchanged it for food.

The shame of this trade was added to all the others we had known, and had come to accept, and then taught ourselves to forget. Before long, the men began to trade all the small luxuries that belonged to the dead— hats, boots, rosaries—reasoning that, if some of us had to die of the bowel disease, the others should at least try to survive however they could. And when the dead had no more to trade, the living took up the habit. Dorantes gave up his sword; Castillo his gloves; Diego his collection of birds; and I my precious sandals.

With frightful speed, the bowel disease spread among the Capoques. In one week alone, I remember, they buried ten of their people. One day, a woman who had lost two of her children accused us of willfully making them sick. She had no trouble getting the rest of the tribe to turn against us, because the sickness had already ravaged them—men were too sick to hunt, women too sick to nurse their babies, and those children not sick with fever already weak with hunger and deprivation. Some of the Capoques wanted to kill us, which would not have been hard for them, or even unfair, but the cacique Delenchavan told them that, had we been powerful enough to kill, we would have been powerful enough to save our own men from the bowel disease.

WE WERE FEEDING THE FIRE for our dinner one night when Ruíz returned. He appeared quietly out of the wilderness, his black beard so bushy that his eye, small and yellowish, seemed to disappear in his face. The dirt and the rain had turned his clothes a greenish shade of brown. So insistent had he been about wanting to stay away from the Capoques that we were stunned to see him venture into our camp, where he could run into the Indians at any moment. Ruíz! one of us said. Is that really you? Where are the others?

They did not come with me.

Why?

They did not want to.

Are they coming in the spring?

How should I know? I did not ask them.

What have you been eating in your camp?

Oysters.

But the oyster beds are mostly empty now.

We ate fish.

Fish? Where did you get a fishing pole?

We made spears.

We did not know you could fish with spears. Why did you not return earlier?

Why are you asking me so many questions?

We just want to know. We want some fish, too.

Do you think I am lying?

You need not be so prickly. Where are the others?

They have the fever.

But you said they did not want to come. Which is it?

I know not.

Ruíz, where are the others?

I ate them! There, I said it, is this what you wanted to hear?

Gasps of horror greeted this admission. The men stopped their bantering to stare at Ruíz. It seemed hardly possible that the great evil he had just confessed had not resulted in some sort of physical transformation.

His skin looked ruddy and his beard was flecked with mud, but otherwise he looked much the same as before, which is to say like an ordinary member of our expedition.

In a low voice, he continued: After we went away, Palacios became sick with the bowel disease and died. We were going to bury him, but then Lopes said we should just eat his flesh. We had not had anything to eat in five or six days. I said no. I swear to God Almighty, I said no. But Lopes did it anyway. And I was so hungry. So hungry. And then Lopes killed Sierra. And Corral after him.

Ruíz was the last to partake of human flesh and, having no other means to feed himself, he had decided to return to our camp.

We ought to kill this cannibal, said the carpenter.

We cannot kill a man, Father Anselmo said. That would be murder.

He killed the others, the carpenter said. And ate them. He cannot be trusted with the living.

In the end, we could only banish Ruíz from our camp. We told him that if he were to try to rejoin us we would surely kill him before he had a chance to kill one of us. Ruíz was a soldier from Galicia and he had not, to my knowledge, ever given an inclination toward cannibalism, but such was the wretchedness that the Narváez expedition forced upon him. It was after learning of this unforgivable sin that we took to calling the island on which we had landed the Island of Misfortune.

How the Capoques found out about what Ruíz had done, I never knew. It seems to me now that, just as I had learned the Capoque tongue through my exposure to it, the Capoques, too, had learned the Spanish language by listening to it. I seem to remember that Kwachi and Elenson had been with us on the night Ruíz returned and confessed his crime. They must have heard him. So great was their horror at the sacrifice of human flesh that, for weeks afterward, they refused to have anything to do with us and would not let us even enter their village. Diego and I waited for Kwachi by the river, where we begged him to plead with the tribe on our behalf.

Tell them we are not all like Ruíz, Diego said.

We are not cannibals, I said, we do not eat each other. Tell them that.

But Kwachi called to his dog and returned whence he came. We were never able to convince him to bring us back to the village.

The bowel disease combined with constant deprivation to decimate our ranks. By the end of that cold winter, twenty-three Castilians, one Angolan, and three Portuguese lay buried in the clearing south of the river, their long journey to conquer this terra firma having at last come to an end. Only twelve men survived: Andrés Dorantes, Diego Dorantes, Alonso del Castillo, Pedro de Valdivieso, Ricardo Gutiérrez, the friar Anselmo de Asturias, Álvaro Fernándes, Felipe Benítez, Jorge Chaves, Pedro Estrada, Diego de Huelva, and this servant of God, Mustafa ibn Muhammad. But more than one hundred and twenty Capoques perished during that same interval, and were buried in ceremonies whose terrible noise carried all the way to our camp, reminding us of the evil we had brought with us to the island and which we would yet carry with us when we left.

ON THE RARE OCCASIONS when Dorantes or Castillo had gone to visit Cabeza de Vaca in the Han village, I had stayed behind. I was not fond of the treasurer. He displayed an unflagging disregard for men of lower station—not unusual among noblemen, of course, but in his case the disregard was particularly pronounced. And there was, too, his support of every one of Narváez's foolish decisions, which, given our present condition, I could neither overlook nor forget. But now spring was here, and in order to make plans for our joint departure from the Island of Misfortune, I agreed to go with Dorantes and Castillo to the Han village.

The huts were similar to those of the Capoques, but they were much smaller and squarer, which gave them the appearance of little squat boxes. A Han youngster, wearing an officer's boots, had cut the head of a sea turtle and now was hanging it to bleed. A few paces away, a woman was repairing the roof of her home with the help of her children. A brown dog slept in a patch of sunlight, flies hovering above him. I could not hear a river, and wondered briefly where the Han procured their drinking water; the location of their camp did not seem to be as advantageous as that of the Capoques, who had established themselves near several sources of water. The entire camp was quiet, as if its people were away on a hunting expedition. A pestilential smell hung over the place.

We found Cabeza de Vaca at the far end of the square, sitting on his haunches, so occupied with skinning a squirrel that he did not hear us. He held the brown head in his left hand and with his right slowly ran the knife between the meat and the fur, with the careful, deliberate movements of a man who had not been born to such a task, but enjoyed doing it well. When he finally noticed us, he poured water over his hands and, wiping them on a loincloth cut from his own doublet, stood up to greet us. I could have counted his ribs had I been inclined to, so thin had he become. His eyes sunk inside his face and his thin yellow beard pointed like an arrow down his chest.

Presently Cabeza de Vaca handed the animal to a handsome woman, who smiled when she noticed us. He shook hands with Dorantes and Castillo, but only raised his chin in my direction. Dorantes reported the most recent deaths in our group, and the names of the twelve who were still alive. The bowel disease had spread much faster in Cabeza de Vaca's group, however, and only three of his men remained: the notary Jerónimo de Albaniz, a settler by the name of Lope de Oviedo, and Cabeza de Vaca himself.

Castillo said he would be forced to trade the last of his possessions for dried meat we could take on the journey to Pánuco, but because the Capoques were no longer excited by the novelty of Castilian items, the amount of meat he hoped to receive in exchange for them would likely not last our party more than a day or two. How much food do you think you can bring for the journey? Castillo asked.

I am not going with you, Cabeza de Vaca replied.

What?

I am not going.

I mean—why. Why are you not coming with us?

We have not had any rain in three weeks, Dorantes added. We need not wait any longer.

It is not the weather.

Then what is it?

I have a wife now. I cannot leave her behind.

My gaze drifted to the handsome woman standing behind him. Her hair was glossy in the sunlight and her face had that rare pairing of grit and grace. She wore a necklace made of white seashells interspersed with red doublet buttons, a simple yet appealing jewel. Though Cabeza de Vaca had his back to her, the bond between the two of them was obvious. I thought of what the elders teach us: love is like a camel's hump, for it cannot be disguised.

You already have a wife, Castillo said. In Jerez.

Not like her.

But your wife is a lady! Have you thought of her at all?

Castillo, you know nothing about the lady in Jerez. Leave her out of this.

You would desert your own kind for this Indian? Dorantes asked, casting a disbelieving glance at the woman.

Cabeza de Vaca shot his friends a dark look. I will not leave her.

Then bring her if you must, Dorantes said. But come with us.

I already told you, I am not going. We do not know how far Pánuco is. Do you believe we will survive another long journey through this land? We will die in the wilderness, and no one will ever know what happened to us.

This woman has poisoned your mind.

On the contrary. She has taken the poison out.

I leaned on my walking staff. Beside me, Castillo and Dorantes had fallen into an uncomprehending silence, but I could see that Cabeza de Vaca loved this woman and that his heart was filled with yearning for her. I knew only too well what that felt like, and so I was drawn to him as I might to a fellow sufferer, a sentiment that surprised and befuddled me.

What about Albaniz and Oviedo? Dorantes asked. Do they have Indian wives, too?

There is something wrong with Albaniz, Cabeza de Vaca replied. But you can try talking to him if you like. And Oviedo is still recovering from the bowel disease. If they wish to go, I will not stop them.

We found Albaniz wandering through the village, trailed by two scrawny dogs, faithful in the way of mangy animals. His beard had grown bushy and he was thinner now, but otherwise he looked much the same as before. He wore a blue cotton doublet and black breeches. In his right hand was a short stick, which he used as a cane. Slung across his chest was his leather satchel, filled with the requisitions, contracts, and petitions he had been entrusted with when the armada left Seville, but also with the names the governor had given to the places, people, and animals of the new world—Portillo and Santa María, Pablo and Kamasha, lagartos and castores.

Albaniz, Dorantes called. The notary smiled when his name was called. With a wave of the hand, he invited us to sit with him on Indian benches that had been placed under an oak tree. He leaned forward on his cane and rested his chin on his hands. We are crossing to the mainland, Dorantes explained. We are going to Pánuco. Come with us.

Albaniz smiled, baring teeth that had turned mossy green. Adios, he said.

No, Mochuelo, Dorantes said. He stabbed his forefinger in Albaniz's chest and then turned it back against himself. You come with us.

Adios.

Are you deaf? Castillo said. We want you to come with us.

Albaniz smiled heartily, as though the words Castillo had spoken were some great joke, to which only he was privy. With his cane, he scribbled something in the dirt—words in a language I could not read, though the Castilians later said that it was no language at all, just gibberish.

Oh, Lord, Dorantes said. The man is mad. He ran his hand on his forehead, as if he were having trouble keeping up with the thoughts inside. Let us find Oviedo.

Oviedo was in the woods behind the village. He sat with an old, toothless woman, weaving what looked like a basket. Although he smelled terrible and his clothes were filthy, something about the way he sat suggested that he was in fine health and would be able to walk. But when Dorantes explained our plan, Oviedo refused to come. He said that our fate on the mainland might not be better than here on this island and could very well be worse, and that in any case he was finished risking life on a journey to someplace we were not certain we could find.

Why was it that Cabeza de Vaca's men agreed so readily with each other, while those of us from the Dorantes group agreed on the opposite? It was as though we belonged to different tribes now and could think no differently than the clan we called our own. In the winter, when the men all around us were dying of the bowel disease, I had heard Dorantes wonder aloud, around the campfire, why it was that this land refused us, why it would not grant us a reprieve. Our sins cannot be washed away so easily here, someone had replied, we have to go back to Castile. I felt much the same. My heart ached with the desire to return home to the country where I belonged, where everything would once again make sense. But maybe Cabeza de Vaca and the others believed the opposite. Maybe they believed that if they became people of this land, living alongside its natives, they could find some semblance of peace.

In the end, Castillo had to give up his beloved game of chess, Dorantes his marten and ermine cloak, and I my scissors, in exchange for passage to the mainland on a canoe. I sat at the fore of the dugout, so eager was I to begin the journey out of the island. When we reached the other shore, I was the first man to step off, and turned around to help Dorantes; he looked up at me gratefully, his eyes shielded from the sun by my shadow. As the twelve of us gathered on the shore of the mainland, I realized with a start that, although no rope tied our hands and feet together, I was as bound to these Castilians as I had been to the Barbary slaves under the colorful glass windows of a church in Seville, all those years ago.

13.

THE STORY OF THE THREE RIVERS

Across the sky, groups of geese flew north in formation. We walked in twos and threes, with our shadows in front of us made soft and shapeless by the passing clouds. The oak trees all around us were heavy with spring leaves. Bees hummed among the wild flowers. The wilderness that had once seemed so alien to us had grown familiar and the calls of animals in the distance no longer alarmed us. When we came upon a river, none of the Castilians thought to give it a name, I noticed; they had stopped thinking of themselves as unchallenged lords of this world, whose duty it was to put it into words. Later, much later, whenever we spoke of this first river, we called it the Primero Río—not Río Primero, but simply the Primero Río, in order to distinguish it from the other rivers we would yet cross.

Because the Primero Río was too deep to cross on foot, we all agreed to build two small rafts—each one would carry about half of our number. With only one ax, the work was slow, but no one complained. This changed once Fernándes the carpenter started tying the logs together. You are using too much horsehair, we said. What if we come across another river tomorrow?

I am using just enough, Fernándes replied. I have done this before, you know.

And why are you making only two paddles for each raft?

Am I the carpenter or are you? Fernándes said testily. His ax was raised, its iron blade catching the light.

Father Anselmo had to intervene. Let Fernándes do his work, he told us. He knows what is best.

Once the first raft was ready, we set it onto the water. The oak logs were rough and splintery, barely held together by precious strands of horsehair. Diego and I sat on either end of the vessel, with the paddles in our hands, while Dorantes, Castillo, and Father Anselmo sat in the middle. A cold wind blew from the east, making their shirts flap violently against their bodies.

We should stand against the wind, Castillo cried.

It was an ingenious idea: the bodies of those who were standing arm in arm became a kind of sail, so that the wind propelled the raft forward. The water was fast, but murky. It could easily conceal a dangerous boulder or a fallen tree trunk. With fear and excitement coursing in equal measure through our veins, we paddled in the direction of the current, and to our great relief we made it to the other bank.

From there, we beckoned the others to cross. Oddly, both of the paddlers on the second raft sat at the fore of the vessel, which made it difficult for them to maintain a good balance. And, although they must have seen how Castillo had used the wind to our favor, they did not imitate us. They paddled more vigorously than they needed and their raft quickly acquired speed. Standing on the riverbank, we were as tense as captives—we could watch them, but could do nothing to help them. They were going downriver at a frightful pace. As soon as they passed within earshot, Dorantes called out to his friend Valdivieso: Jump, amigo! Jump, you can swim the rest of the way.

Valdivieso threw himself in the river, gasping as his body hit the cold water. His raftmates were left in a panic. The vessel was very plain; it was a squarish structure with no sweeps to control speed or direction. Now, with Valdivieso gone, it became lighter and even faster than before. The current carried it about like a dry twig. After a moment, several others jumped into the water, too, but Estrada and Chaves, who did not know how to swim, stayed on. We never saw either of them again.

To lose two of our number when we had been away from the Island of Misfortune for only one day was a terrible blow to us. It was hard to escape the feeling that our journey was doomed. Sitting on the riverbank afterward, my limbs trembling despite the crackling fire, I began to wonder whose turn would come next. And when would mine be? In two days? Three? A week? And yet, at the same time, I tried to tell myself that no, this was it—this had to be—the final test. I had gone through enough.

I would be found innocent of whatever evil we were all being punished for, I would reach Pánuco soon, I would return home. I would be saved.

We continued along the trail all of the next day, eating nothing but blueberries and meadow grass. Our beards had already grown long and bushy, but now, with our teeth stained blue and our stomachs bulging with undigested grass, we began to look like figures from some ancient story, told by generation after generation to warn young children about the dangers that lurked far away from home. At length, we came to a beautiful green lagoon, where a man was floating peacefully. It was the flash of yellow hair and white skin in the glinting waters that made the friar call out to him. The man swam to the shore in quick, smooth strokes, emerging as naked as the day he was born.

It was Francisco de León, a settler from Cabeza de Vaca's company, a cobbler who had proven himself useful to the captain during our long journey through La Florida. (On a long march, nothing was more precious than shoes and no one more vital than a shoe mender.) Tall and broad-shouldered, he had a scar on his cheek, just beneath his right eye. We had not seen him since our crossing of the Great River and had thought him dead long ago, but León explained that, after landing at the Island of Misfortune, he and two others had walked to a beach nearby, where they had found an abandoned Indian canoe. They had taken it here, to the continent, but had failed to moor it properly and now it was lost. We were all stunned into silence, imagining what we could have done with a canoe if only we had known about it.

But why did you not tell Cabeza de Vaca about the canoe? Dorantes asked, his voice made shrill with indignation.

The dugout would have been too small to carry all of us, León replied.

You could have taken turns.

Cabeza de Vaca had let the Indians come to our beach. And he wanted us to go with them to their camp.

So you chose not to tell him about the canoe? You fool! He could have used it to shuttle all of his men to the continent and maybe my men, too. They would not have needed to spend the winter on the island. Do you know how many of them have died? Their deaths are your fault.

How are they my fault? The captain did not ask me what I thought about going with the savages to their camp. Why should I ask him what to do about the canoe?

This response so angered Dorantes that he turned away from León and faced the lagoon. His authority had been challenged nearly every day since our departure from the Bay of Oysters, and he did not know how to respond as his power frittered away.

It was Castillo who tried to fill the awkward silence. What happened to the others who went with you? he asked.

They died of the fever, León replied.

What about you? What did you eat all winter?

Oysters. Seaweed. Grass. Bird eggs. Lizards. Whatever I could find.

Once again, Father Anselmo tried to diffuse any friction. He placed his arm around León's shoulders and, squeezing him affectionately in spite of his terrible revelation, he said: We lost two Christians yesterday, but now the Lord has delivered you to us and us to you. He whispered a long prayer, thanking God for the blessing of a new companion and asking for our safe return to Pánuco. Gratefully, León kissed the friar's hand. Then, with the ease of a squirrel, he climbed up a nearby tree, from which he retrieved his clothes, a knife, and a pair of gloves that looked too large for him. He was the first addition to our party, which had known nothing but loss for the last year. In spite of everything, we tried to take this as a good sign. We needed one.

SOME DAYS LATER, we came upon an immense forest of oak trees, a landscape of deep green cut through by sharp, brown lines. As we made our way through the woods, yellow warblers congregated on the branches above us, though their sweet melodies were eventually muffled by the sound of a mighty river. This was the Segundo Río. On its gray and rocky bank, half in and half out of the water, the wind whistling through the logs, was one of the rafts we had made at the Bay of Oysters. A white vestment stitched to the sails—I had sewn it there myself—helped me identify it as the raft captained by the comptroller. It had also carried the commissary and forty-seven other men. How did it arrive here?

We looked for clues of the men's whereabouts, but there was no sign of them anywhere. No remnants of a campfire, no traces of food, no tracks leading away from the raft into the wilderness. It was as if Enríquez and all his men had simply vanished into thin air, leaving their raft behind. Silently, and with eyes cast down, Fernándes the carpenter began to undo the horsehair rope from the part of the raft that sat above the water.

Dorantes tore the sails from the masts; they could be used for bedding. As for the logs, they were rotten; they broke easily and fed our fire that evening.

All around us, frogs croaked, crickets sang, and twigs snapped under the feet of some nocturnal beast or other, but we ate in complete silence, all of us in a mood of barely suppressed panic. If the comptroller and his men had managed to sail this far away from La Florida, two hundred and fifty leagues away by one reckoning, only to disappear without leaving a trace, what did this mean for the rest of us? I was tormented by visions of death, which I tried to push to the back of my mind.

To break the mood, Diego began to sing an old ballad from Castile, a cheerful ditty about a lady who acts by turns brash and bashful, tormenting her lover. Diego had a beautiful voice and we all listened to him with pleasure. His older brother began to reminisce about a dinner they had both attended in Seville, where a young lady of their acquaintance had signaled her interest in him in a most brazen way. Do you remember her? Dorantes asked.

Yes, Diego said. But she was married.

I know, Dorantes replied with a rueful smile. That did not stop her.

Stop her from what?

What do you think, Chato? Her husband was in Italy—he had been there for two years, I think—and he almost never answered her letters. You saw her, did you not? She was beautiful. And she was getting lonely.

Dorantes seemed to take no notice of the horrified look on Diego's face; instead he delighted in the smiles of admiration from the others and in their questions about his affair with the lady. After a while, however, silence fell on our company again. This time, Dorantes tried something different. Estebanico, he said. Can you tell fortunes?

Fortunes? I said. Me?

Your people are known to be great fortune-tellers.

Remember, Castillo said, the Moorish woman on the Gracia de Dios?

Yes, Dorantes replied. I was thinking of her just now, which was why I asked Estebanico.

What did she say? I asked.

I do not believe—Father Anselmo began.

Come now, Father, Dorantes said. We are just trying to pass the time.

It is harmless fun, Castillo agreed.

But do you not think—the friar said.

La Mora, Castillo interrupted, was from the town of Hornachos. I do not know if any of you remember her. She was one of the women on the Gracia de Dios.

What was her name?

Her name? I know not. But she was a shrew with dark eyes that made you feel as if she could see right into your soul. When we were still at port, one of the sailors called her a bad name, and she flew into a fury and said she was leaving the expedition. You know how women are, especially the Moorish ones. But before leaving the ship, she told the other women that their husbands, and indeed all the men in the armada, were going to die in the new world. The women should look for new husbands, La Mora said, for they were, all of them, widows already, even if they did not know it yet. Naturally, this prophecy upset the husbands, and they tossed her out onto the dock with all her belongings. Don Pánfilo had to speak to the passengers in order to quell the commotion. He said that although some of us might perish in La Florida, those who fought valiantly would receive such riches they would look upon their rewards as miracles.

Dorantes laughed bitterly. Such riches we have received. Miracles!

The flames crackled and a log broke, shooting up sparks.

Perhaps the miracle is that we are alive at all, Father Anselmo said.

Dorantes turned to me. Well, can you tell fortunes or not?

Give me your hand, I said. He offered me his left palm. Red calluses dotted the line from his index to his little finger and a new scar crossed his wrist, likely the result of his work with Fernándes on the raft some days earlier. You have a secret, I said. Something you have hidden from everyone.

Everyone has secrets, Dorantes replied.

But this, I said, this is something else entirely. Let me see. I turned his palm toward the light of the flames. It is something you have hidden from everyone, even your own brother.

Dorantes yanked his hand away.

Everyone has secrets, I thought, but no one wants to hear one's private shame turned into a public fame. I had not expected to be right; I was only teasing him, but his reaction suggested I had uncovered something. What was he hiding, I wondered with a smile.

What do you know? Dorantes said. You are just a Moor.

A Moor whose prophecy you seek, said I.

. . .

THE TERCERO RÍO WAS fast, wide, and very dark, as if it carried the soil of all the earth toward the ocean. The seagulls and pelicans that hovered above the riverbank suggested that we were close to the river's mouth, though the birds' calls were drowned out by the noise of the current. As usual, we had to build a raft in order to cross, but Fernándes was lagging behind, along with his friend Benítez, a night watchman from Toledo. The two of them had been eating great quantities of meadow grass, with the result that their stomachs had swelled, making it more difficult for them to walk. Their pace had grown increasingly slow and when they finally caught up to the rest of us, they slumped on their knees, exhausted.

We were standing on the riverbank, trying to decide what to do, when two Indians appeared in a red dugout canoe. Like the Capoques, they wore reeds in their nipples and lower lips, though their tribal tattoos looked different. Still, they looked to be allies of the Capoques and we hoped that they would be as generous to us. We did not have any beads or trinkets left, but the friar agreed to part with his rosary, which we presented to the two Indians, in exchange for a ride across the river. Afterward, they told us to wait for them on the rocky shore; they were going to bring one of our brothers for us.

Who could it be? someone asked.

Should we wait?

No, we should continue without delay.

But look at Fernándes. He cannot walk much farther.

Benítez is running a fever.

We were still arguing in this way when we saw the Indians return with a Castilian, a short, thin man with a patchy beard. His name was Martín. He was one of the five deserters Cabeza de Vaca had told us about, the ones who had swum all the way from the Island of Misfortune to the mainland. He and León embraced, but the rest of us were more eager to find out what had happened. Are the others with you? we asked.

No, they are all dead, he replied. Two drowned during the crossing. One made it to the continent with me, but he died of the fever about a month ago.

What about the servant? I asked. Cabeza de Vaca mentioned that a criado had gone with you.

He is dead, too. Fever.

A bitter taste invaded my mouth. I had to sit down against a tree, with my arms around my knees, and wait for the moment to pass. Above me, a woodpecker drummed on the trunk, pausing and starting, again and again. Meanwhile, Dorantes was telling Martín about our winter on the Island of Misfortune and about the raft we had found on the river the day before.

I know what happened to it, Martín said. I heard the story from the only survivor from that raft. After the storm, the comptroller's raft was marooned not far from this area, at the mouth of the river. The men walked a short distance to the bay, in order to feed on oysters and crabs, but once there they found the Narváez raft. So many men had died during the storm that both crews could have fit on one raft, but the governor refused to take the stranded men aboard. On the contrary, he ordered his own men to disembark and said that, henceforth, both crews would travel by land while he and his page would follow in the water along the coast. If they came upon a river, he promised, he would ferry the land crew across.

The comptroller rebelled, of course. And with an order like that, who could blame him? Once again, he complained, the governor was dividing the men into land and sea contingents. Had he learned nothing from his experience? Narváez immediately relieved the comptroller of his command and put one of his own men in charge of the land crew, a brute by the name of Sotomayor. So everyone was forced to walk along the shore, while Narváez sailed close by. The next night, while they were camped on a beach, Narváez slept on his raft, with his page and helmsman by his side. But the wind picked up in the middle of the night, and the raft was swept to sea. The rest of the survivors walked along the shore for several days, hoping to reach Pánuco on foot. When one of them died of disease, they ate his flesh. Before long, they began to kill and eat one another. The last man alive was Esquivel the welder, who was still feeding on Sotomayor when these Indians you see here found him.

The m-m-men t-t-turned into c-c-cannibals?

Yes, Father.

A-a-all of them?

That is the story Esquivel the welder told me.

No, the friar replied. No, no, no. He must have had the fever and was delirious. Or he made up the story just to frighten you. I knew Esquivel. He could not have done what he told you he did.

Father, who would lie about something like that?

No one, I thought. No one would lie about having become a cannibal. Esquivel must have been telling the truth. What a terrible story. It was the sort of story that would be told and retold, getting worse with each repetition. Between Esquivel and Ruíz, all of the Indians in these parts were probably convinced by now that the white aliens who had come to their territory were flesh-eating monsters. And where did that leave me, a black man among these white men? From my seat under the tree, I asked: How far do you think Pánuco is?

Very far, I would wager, Martín said.

The Indians with whom he lived, he explained, did not know of a Spanish port anywhere near this area. It had to be much farther away and he could not guess whether it was a march of two weeks or twenty. This was why he had made up his mind to live with them for good.

The news he had brought silenced us for a while and we all sat on the riverbank, suddenly weary of the long march that still lay ahead of us. We must have looked quite pitiful, because the two Indians offered to give us some food for the night. Martín and the friar went with them to fetch the baskets, but an hour later only Martín returned with dried meat and nuts.

Where is Father Anselmo? Diego asked, standing up.

He did not want to come back, Martín replied.

What are you saying?

He does not want to look for Pánuco any longer.

Liar, Diego said. Tears had already welled in his eyes, and he blinked them away forcefully. Anselmo would not say that. He would never give up.

He did not want to come back, Martín repeated.

What have you done with him? Where is he? Diego was about to strike Martín when Dorantes held him back.

I am telling you the truth, Martín said with a shrug. The friar said that he wanted to settle with this tribe, just as I have, and that you should not try to go back for him or convince him otherwise.

It was one thing to lose men to the river or disease, and another to have the friar choose to remove himself from us. He always saw the better natures in each one of us. Who would do that now? I mourned his sudden absence the way I would have mourned the absence of any good man with whom I had lived for many months, but for the Castilians, and especially for Diego, his departure felt, I think, like a cruel abandonment.

Diego refused to eat the rabbit meat that Martín had brought for us and retreated into silence for the rest of the evening.

WORSE WAS YET TO come. In the morning, we could not wake either Fernándes or Benítez; they had died in their sleep. It was not in my character to give in to superstition, but now I began to wonder about the prophecy of the Moorish woman from Hornachos. Perhaps she had been right—the armada was cursed and we would all die here in this strange land. I might as well hang myself from a tree now rather than wait for death to come for me in its own cruel time. Such was the depth of my despair that this ungodly thought did not arouse in me the immediate rebellion that it would ordinarily have caused.

Dorantes stood over the bodies of the dead men, his face a pure expression of defeat. Quietly, he said: We have to leave them.

No, Diego replied. We have to give them a proper Christian burial.

How? We have no shovels.

We can dig with our hands.

None of us is strong enough for the task, and even if we did manage it, the graves would be so shallow that wild animals would get to them by nightfall.

But we cannot just leave them here.

We have to. We have our own lives to worry about now.

Diego looked as if he might cry. The death of these two men, the loss of the friar, the realization that we were still very far from Pánuco—all this had added up to an unbearable burden and now he bit his lip and turned his face away from us.

From where I sat under a tree, I noticed that the limbs of the two dead men had swelled and that their faces had turned an unnatural shade of pink. Even in the final slumber, they looked tormented. And yet, I thought, what would these two men not give to be in my place? I was alive. The warmth of the sun was on my face and hands. Heavy against my hip was a flask filled with fresh water. Beside me, a beetle was trying to carry a crumb back to its nest, working slowly and patiently, undaunted by how far it was from its goal. The longer I watched it, the more my despair receded. I had to survive, I told myself, if not for me, then for the sake of all those I had left at home. Diego, I called, standing up. Help me carry them to the river. They can at least have a water burial.

14.

THE STORY OF THE CARANCAHUAS

It was late in the morning, I remember, and we were lying in the wild green grass, eating the blueberries we had picked during our march. Our meager meal combined with the damp heat to lull us into a kind of indolence. Dorantes lay on his belly, his head resting on his folded arms, while Castillo curled up on his side and drifted to sleep, his breathing a faint whistle. I heard the soft flutter of insect wings, and a grasshopper landed on my chest. It tilted its head sideways as it gazed upon me, a stranger in its world. Then there was the sudden crunching of twigs underfoot. I barely had time to sit up before the Indians appeared. There were ten of them, hunters all, armed with lances and bows. One of them carried on his back a beautiful doe, its hind legs dragging on the ground and its eyes still fixed, in surprise, on something in the distance. Slung over their shoulders, the others had smaller game, most of it hare. We scrambled to our feet and introduced ourselves to them, enunciating our names slowly.

Mustafa.

Dorantes.

Cas—

I know who you are, one of them said. His body glistened with grease, a common recipe for warding off mosquitoes, though it also had the effect of making him look intimidating. A neat braid, threaded with bright parrot feathers, hung down each side of his face. His gaze was direct, but indifferent. And when he spoke, his voice commanded the attention of every ear. I heard about you from a Capoque shell trader, he said.

But what had he heard? Was it only the surprising news of our shipwreck on the Island of Misfortune a few months earlier? Or was it a bitter complaint that we had brought with us a disease that had killed most of the Han and the Capoques over the course of one short winter? Perhaps he had heard a tale that combined all of these details, and maybe even exaggerated them. Whatever it was, I hoped it was not an account of the cannibals among us—disease could always be excused, but eating human flesh would never be forgiven. The elders teach us: let my friends remember me; let all others forget about me.

And we have heard of your great people, I blurted in response. My flattery had no effect on the hunter who had spoken, and the others seemed to be taking their cue from him. To fill the silence, I asked: What is your name?

Balsehekona, he said.

He was a Carancahua. Like the other tribes in this area, the Carancahuas were hunters and fishermen who moved their camp with the seasons. In the winter, they picked oysters, fished for trout and perch, or waded into the bays to pull out the edible roots that grew in them. In the summer, they ate nuts and berries, and hunted deer, hare, and other game. Now, the warm months had started; they had just set up their camp not far from where we had been resting in the meadow, unaware of their presence.

Having had nothing to eat but blueberries for the past three days, the sight of the doe awakened our hunger, but we had nothing to trade for it. I had resigned myself to picking more berries when I noticed Dorantes's eyes darting around. After what seemed like a costly inner debate, he reached into the pocket of his breeches—and out came the Yucatán earring that had been given to him by Bernardo Rodriguez in Seville, as an incentive to purchase me. I had not seen the golden earring since that day, almost two years earlier, when I had stood in Luis de Prado's living room and prayed to God that Dorantes would refuse it. That sudden memory—the memory of a nervous Rodriguez standing in an opulent room, with oil portraits watching from the walls—intruded now on the present, on the image of Dorantes standing in the green meadow, pressing the golden bauble into Balsehekona's hands, with all of us silent witnesses. I could not imagine how Dorantes had kept that earring hidden throughout our ordeals and desperate barters.

Balsehekona looked at the gold with mild curiosity, and then returned it.

Take it, Dorantes cried, holding it up. Take it. It is gold. Take it and give us some of that meat. He pointed to the doe.

The earring had been put in Balsehekona's hand, and eventually he stopped resisting. Without further comment, he and the other Carancahuas picked up their weapons and began to walk. We followed them. Their camp consisted of ten movable huts set up against mulberry trees. Tools and utensils were stacked neatly beside each hut. Two young girls worked the mortar and pestle, while their mother painted a deer hide a vivid hue of red. An elderly man was testing a flute he had just made, playing notes and adjusting the holes on the instrument. For some reason our arrival did not arouse as much curiosity as we had grown to expect. Dogs barked, children ran up to us, and women paused whatever they were doing to look, but within moments, the entire camp had returned to its usual tasks. So we gathered firewood, set up a campfire, and waited. At dusk, Balsehekona brought us an entire shank of deer, its meat soft and faintly ribboned with fat. We nearly wept with joy as we took it from him. He looked upon us the way one looks upon a persistent beggar—with indifference or compassion now; later, it would be with irritation.

OUR PLAN HAD BEEN to depart early the next day, but the smell of a soup the women had made for the morning meal was so tempting that we all agreed to wait. We would eat some of it and, having rested and regained some of our strength, we would resume our walk along the coast. But the following day, the hare roasting on spits smelled so heavenly that it made us lose our resolve. I do not believe that any of us had intended to stay with the Carancahuas, but the drowning of Estrada and Chaves, the desertion of Father Anselmo, and the deaths of Fernándes and Benítez had rattled us and made us fear venturing into the wilderness. The Carancahuas were intimately familiar with this coastal territory: its waterways; its hunting grounds; which plants you could eat and which could poison you. Relying on them was the surest way to survive.

At the end of our first week with the tribe, we received a visit from the cacique Okmantsul. The sun had risen an hour earlier, but a few among us were still asleep, curled up around the remnants of the evening fire. Others were eating scraps given to them by one of the women. Okmantsul looked at our modest site, taking stock of what we had and what we were doing. Over his shoulders, he wore a cloak of animal skin, decorated with white beads and feathers. Though he was short of stature and thin of build, he was blessed with a natural authority; it would not have crossed anyone's mind to defy him. Now he spoke softly, almost in whispers.

From this day hence, he said, you will work for the meat that is given to you. And you must go on the hunt.

All of us nodded and politely averted our gaze, but once the cacique was out of earshot, Dorantes complained that he could not use the native weapons. The Carancahua bows were about seventy pulgadas long—the length of a grown man—and were strung with tendons. I cannot use a bow like that, Dorantes said.

I can, Diego said.

You, Tigre?

Yes, me.

You will hurt yourself.

You heard what the cacique said. One of us has to go on the hunt.

For a long moment, the two brothers stared defiantly at one another. Then Dorantes walked away, shaking his head.

I will go with you, I said. I remembered how Diego had walked with me to the Capoques' camp when no one else would, and I wanted to return his act of kindness.

And I as well, Castillo added.

This came as a surprise to me. Castillo's frequent disagreements with the governor had given me the impression that he was a smart and stubborn man, but he had not struck me as a hardy or able worker. All that was disappearing in the face of our repeated hardships. After all, a clever retort does not feed you or keep you warm at night. Now the young nobleman had begun to let his heart, rather than his mind, guide him.

IT WAS THE HOUR when the owls swooped down to feed. Quietly, we followed the Carancahuas out of the camp, accepting offers of sips from a flask filled with an infusion that sharpened our senses. Every crackle in the bushes, every flutter in the trees seemed as loud as a cannon shot. Beside me, Balsehekona threw his lance at what seemed to me nothing but dry thickets, and yet he caught his prey, invisible though it had been to me. At length, the trail dropped down toward a creek, its shallow waters swirling slowly in a circle, forming a kind of pool before flowing toward the river. A frog leapt out of the bushes into the basin, where a hare dipped its tongue.

I motioned to Castillo to circle the creek on the left, while I went right. Diego had the borrowed bow. Gingerly, we stepped forward, but when

Diego took the shot, his arrow only grazed the hare. It limped away, with Castillo and I running after it, each from his side. I fell upon it, but it propelled itself on its hind legs with such vigor that it slipped halfway out of my arms. Then Castillo hit it with a stone, smashing its skull. Blood ran from it, dying the hare's brown fur a dark shade of red.

When they saw the mess we had made of the hare, the Carancahuas had great fun at our expense. I could hear them telling stories about us to the rest of their tribe when we returned, but at least we had meat that night, which we shared with the others in our group. The meat was soft and tasty and came easily off the bone. I tried my best to eat slowly in order to make the moment last, but I could not help myself—I ate avidly.

The sound of drums from the camp square made us turn to look; the Carancahuas were celebrating something.

One of them is taking a wife, León explained.

How do you know?

This morning I saw them bathe and adorn the maiden.

You saw her naked?

As naked as the day she was born.

What did she look like?

Very pretty. For an Indian.

Are you married, León?

Aye.

You must miss your wife.

Obviously, you have never met her or you would not be saying that.

We all laughed. León joined us, too. We did not know him well; he had been a part of Cabeza de Vaca's company and now he seemed encouraged by our merriment. I could see him smiling in the firelight.

Have any of you taken one of them to bed? he asked.

Of course not, Dorantes replied. Though he loved talking about his romantic conquests, he looked insulted by the question.

I have, León said. His tone was unembarrassed, even boastful.

You have, have you? And when was that?

In Apalache.

That was you?

Abruptly the memory of what I had witnessed in Apalache came back to me: in my mind's eye, I could see the women kicking the soldiers and in my ear I could hear their howling cries of pain. Was León telling the truth or was he making up a vicious tale to entertain his fellow Castilians? With the back of my hand, I wiped the grease off my lips. I scrutinized León's face—his small eyes looked untroubled and he chewed on his meat with evident joy.

Aye, that was me, he said. And Martín. And Eugenio. There were a few of us that day in Apalache.

The flames flared up when drops of fat from the roasting hare fell into the fire. In the distance, the drums stopped and started again, this time at a faster pace.

She was young, León said. Twelve or thirteen, maybe, with small breasts and wide hips. I took her into the storage hut, where they kept the nuts and the oil. In the beginning, she put up a fight. They all do, you know. She bit me here and here. He pointed to his shoulder and arm. But she stopped fighting after a while. I think she liked it. And then there was another girl, from—

I was upon him before he knew what happened to him. We tumbled on the ground and I put my hands around his neck and did not let go. He gasped for air. Under his flared lips, I could see bits of meat stuck between his crooked teeth. The look of surprise on his face quickly gave way to anger. He tried to push me back, but I had him pinned down. I would have strangled him had Diego not pulled me off. Come now, he said. Estebanico, come. What good would it do now?

The others helped León to his feet. He tried to lunge at me, but they restrained him. Having joined our band so late, he had no natural allies among us. So he said something between his teeth—something I could not hear—and sat down again. The drums had drowned out the sound of our quarrel, and the Carancahuas had been too busy dancing to notice our fight. But the animosity between León and me was born that night.

ON DAYS WHEN we did not take part in the hunt, we worked for our food in other ways. We fetched water from the river, washed animal skins, or gathered huge heaps of firewood that we carried, strapped with rope, on our bare backs. In the beginning, we did these tasks voluntarily, hoping they would earn us a meal at the end of the day. But before long a pattern was set. The Carancahuas began to issue orders—and if one of us was inclined to disagree, they would withhold food from him or beat him with a stick. And there were other rules. Our campfire had to be set a good distance from the center of the camp; we could not go into certain huts; we could not touch implements they used in their ceremonies; and we were forbidden from speaking to the maidens.

The children were the only ones who were unafraid and unworried. They seemed particularly curious about me because my skin color was so different from that of my companions. Often, the children came to watch me work, and it was from them that I gained fluency in the Carancahua language—until then I had had to rely on what I knew of the Capoque tongue, but now I could expand my vocabulary and grammar. The price for my new knowledge was that, sometimes, the boys, and even one or two of the little girls, pulled my beard for fun, or rode on my back, or tied me up just to watch me fight with the knots. I was their entertainment. It was harmless fun to them, but to me it quickly grew tiresome.

Though my fluency in Carancahua was a great advantage, it also cost me dearly, for I became, without my having chosen this profession, an interpreter. One afternoon at the end of spring, Balsehekona came to say that dried mullet from the tribe's reserves had been disappearing. It was inconceivable that one of the Carancahuas would have defied their rules, so the thief, Balsehekona said, had to be one of the aliens. My companions and I were bewildered by the accusation—we had taken nothing. The cacique Okmantsul joined us where we stood, near the heap of deer carcasses at the edge of the camp. In his typically soft voice he said to me: Tell your people to surrender the thief.

I translated his words faithfully, speaking slowly to make sure I did not corrupt their meaning or lose some of their intent.

Did any of you take the meat? Dorantes asked the others.

All the Castilians shook their heads.

Tell your people, Okmantsul said, that if they do not surrender the thief, all of you will be punished.

Once more, I translated the cacique's orders.

But this is unfair, Dorantes said. How can he punish all of us for the crime of the thief? I was asleep when it happened. Tell him that. Tell him it is not fair.

As he heard my translation, Okmantsul curled his lips in disgust, though his voice remained level. Is it fair that you come to our camp, he asked, and eat our food? Or use our firewood? Or cover with our pelts and skins?

We should surrender the thief, Dorantes said, facing his country-men. He no longer sounded surprised or irritated; his tone had shifted to urgency. As for me, I stood in the space between the Castilians and the Carancahuas, waiting to translate.

But we do not know who the thief is, someone said.

Maybe it was one of their own.

And they want to blame us instead.

This is just another one of their elaborate tricks.

What trick? Food was stolen, the thief has to be found.

They just want to kill one of us.

León interrupted the Castilians' quarreling when he grabbed me by the elbow. It was you, he said. You did it.

I freed myself from his grip. I did not steal anything, I said.

You are the only slave here. You must be the one.

I am no more a slave than you.

He raised his hand to slap me, but I caught it and twisted his arm behind his back. If you try this again, I said, I—

Stop your quarrel, Dorantes said. The Indians are looking at you. They will think one of you did it.

Okmantsul asked me to report on what my Castilian companions were saying. I hesitated, because I did not wish to incriminate myself when I had done nothing wrong. But León pushed me toward the Carancahuas and by means of simple gestures and mangled local words, he told the cacique that I was the man they were looking for.

Did you steal from us? Okmantsul asked me.

No, I said.

León stabbed me with his finger. The slave did it.

Stop this at once, Dorantes told León.

Yet León continued to point his accusing finger at me. It is him.

In a flash, I found myself on my knees, surrounded by the Caranca-huas. Two of them began to beat me with balled fists and a third used his lance wherever he found an opening. I fell on my side, my head in my arms, taking the hits but not daring to protest, for I feared it would only invite more blows. Then they tired of me and, kicking me like a discarded toy, they went about their business as if nothing had happened.

The world around me was a blur of shapes and colors. I felt myself being lifted up by the Dorantes brothers; they carried me to our side of the camp and Diego brought me a drink of water. Dorantes knelt beside me, inspecting my left arm. You are losing a lot of blood, he said.

The ringing in my ears began to recede, replaced by a sharp pain. I had a gash just above the elbow; a long stream of blood flowed freely from it onto my hand.

You should tie it, Diego said.

It is not as bad as it looks, I said, I just need some oak bark for it. (I was trying to sound braver than I really was; I did not want to give León the satisfaction of looking weak.)

I will get you some, Diego said, standing up.

I lay down and closed my eyes again. Of all the humiliations I had endured in the Land of Indians, this was the hardest one for me, because I had been entirely innocent of the charge and because the word León had used—slave—had revived a pain that I had been trying to bury. My heart was consumed with anger and, while nursing the injuries the Carancahuas had inflicted upon me, I spent my days thinking up ways to revenge myself on León.

LIFE WENT ON LIKE THIS, my time filled with menial tasks, with rest-less sleep, and with meals that were eaten hurriedly, in fear that they were my last. One day, as I was walking back from the river, carrying jars of water on my back, I spied León hiding in the bushes, eating some-thing. Again, I said to myself. He has stolen food again. My anger burned through me like a brushfire and, without considering the consequences of my actions, I signaled to three passing Carancahua boys and pointed them to León's hiding place. They found him eating nuts from the winter stores and dragged him before Okmantsul. There was no lengthy ques-tioning this time—the evidence was clear. I felt mighty satisfied to see my accuser get caught in his lies, but my moment of vindication was short. The Carancahuas began to beat León and, when he raised his fist to strike back at one of them, they stuck a lance right through his chest, killing him. Fear and horror quickly settled inside my vengeful heart.

WE WERE GRINDING NUTS in a mortar, Diego and I, when Balse-hekona pulled him from this task, taking him to the center of the camp. It was a cold morning in autumn. The trees were bare and the ground was covered with shriveled red and yellow leaves. A large puddle reflected the gray sky above. Diego and I had been talking about how we measured the passage of time, the differences between the Julian calendar, which relied on the sun, and the Hegira calendar, which relied on the moon. Out here, separated from our lands and our peoples, neither one of us could be entirely certain of the date—we did our best to estimate it.

But now Balsehekona had Diego by the hair. The poor lad's feet dragged on the ground, leaving wet tracks behind him; his hands thrashed in his attempt to find his balance and get back on his feet. What is it? I cried, running after both of them.

When they noticed the commotion, Dorantes and Castillo left the washing they had been ordered to do. We all followed Balsehekona to the camp square, where his pregnant wife stood, her hands resting on the mound of her belly. Her face was wet with tears. One of her sisters stood beside her, with an arm wrapped around her shoulder. The other women watched from outside their huts. Again I asked: What did Diego do? Why are you holding him?

He visited her dream, Balsehekona said.

A dream?

What is he saying? Dorantes asked.

A dream, I replied. Then I turned to Balsehekona, What dream?

He stole her child and killed it, Balsehekona said.

What do you mean? I asked.

Is that him? Balsehekona asked his wife.

She nodded.

Are you sure you did not mistake him for one of the others? Balsehekona asked, pointing to Dorantes, Castillo, and me.

But what did he do? Dorantes asked. He stood beside Diego, his hand on the lad's elbow, as if to free him from Balsehekona's grip, though he did not dare pull him away. What is wrong? he asked again.

Diego had not done anything to the woman or to her baby—his only crime, as far as I could tell, was that he had appeared to her in a vision, in which he had harmed her and her baby. But the Carancahuas gave great meaning to their dreams, believing them to be omens of things to come.

Balsehekona's wife shook her head. With the end of her shirt, she wiped the tears from her eyes. No, she said. It is this one.

Without further ceremony, Balsehekona ran his knife across Diego's throat. The blood sprayed out like a fine mist. Warm speckles hit my arms and hands, but most of it landed directly on Dorantes and he closed his eyes against it. In an instant, his face turned into a mask of blood. When he opened his eyes again, he looked like a stranger. Then Diego slumped to the ground before us, bleeding like a lamb on the day of Eid. Dorantes fell on his knees and cradled his brother's head in his hands. Diego, he called. Diego, my brother. My brother.

Diego's eyes flickered. He tried to say something, but the bubbling of the blood that had pooled inside his mouth made it impossible to understand him. He brought his trembling hand to his neck.

I tore my loincloth from my waist and bunched it around the wound; the fabric soaked the blood greedily, but the bleeding did not stop. Diego's gentle soul left his body within moments, right before our eyes.

Oh, Lord, Castillo said. He muffled a cry with one hand and put the other on Dorantes's shoulder.

But Dorantes pushed him away. With great tenderness, he lifted his brother up and carried him past the watching crowd to our side of the camp. We buried Diego in the wilderness that night, the only sound the hooting of a watchful owl.

Looking back on these events now, I realize that something changed when Diego was killed. Dorantes became a different man. He rarely spoke anymore and whenever Castillo tried to engage him in conversation, regardless of its subject, Dorantes rebuffed him. It was as if all of the love and friendship he had spent on Castillo haunted him now that his brother was gone for good; he no longer wanted to have anything to do with Castillo. At night, Dorantes tried to muffle his sobs, but I could hear him just the same, even when he turned on his side, with his face buried in his furs.

After Diego's death, the Carancahuas tired of our presence overnight. The tasks that, a few weeks earlier, would have guaranteed us a good meal now seemed to assure us only that we would not be kicked or beaten. We gave them the last things we owned—what remained of our clothes, the ax, León's gloves—in the hope that they would treat us better. We played with their children. We even tried to join in one of their dances. But it did not seem to change their minds about our thieving, our lack of honor, or our uselessness. Not a month later, Gutiérrez, Huelva, and Valdivieso had the misfortune of going into a tent that the Carancahuas had forbidden them to enter. They were put to death that evening. Before the spring season was over, there remained only three of us—Dorantes, Castillo, and this servant of God, Mustafa ibn Muhammad.

Our life with the Carancahuas was filled with misery—I know that my Castilian companions have testified to the Audiencia at length about this, but my reasons for mentioning this are different—I say, our life with the Carancahuas was filled with misery because what started out as indifference developed into such intense hostility and violence that we did not dare disobey them. We began talking about escaping but, having witnessed so many of us killed for the slightest infraction, we were afraid of being caught. And even if we managed to escape, we did not know if we could survive for very long in the wilderness, without Indians who were familiar with the area, and its sources of food and water. In the evening, when we sat like pariahs on the side of the camp where we were allowed to sleep, I watched the faces of Castillo and Dorantes, lit by the flickering light of the fire, fill with despair. These faces were, I knew, reflections of my own.

I AWOKE EARLY ONE MORNING to find the space beside me empty—only the impression of Dorantes's body remained on the bedding. Instantly, I knew something was wrong, because he never left the hut before me. We were both under the same orders to gather firewood at first light, but Dorantes had developed the habit of staying in bed just a moment longer than I, waiting for me to stand up and leave the hut before he did the same. It was his way of maintaining the illusion that, though we both served the Carancahuas, he had once been my master and I his slave. No lies are more seductive than the ones we use to console ourselves.

I reached across the empty space and shook Castillo awake. Quietly, we went around the camp looking for Dorantes, but could not find him. The Carancahua women, early risers like us, took notice of his absence, too. Over the morning meal, they told their menfolk, who immediately turned on us. Where did your brother go? the cacique asked.

It was common for the Carancahuas to refer to us as brothers, a custom I had not minded or paid much attention to, but today the word carried an implication that frightened me.

He did not tell me, I replied. I know nothing of this.

Balsehekona took a long sip from his flask. He ran away, he said.

After all we have done for him, the cacique said.

He must have stolen something.

Like his brother before him.

And he was lazy, Balsehekona said.

In the eyes of a Carancahua, there was no greater shame in the world than idleness. Now, with the wood side of his lance, Balsehekona caned the back of my legs. The next blow was for Castillo; it caught him on the shoulders and he fell on his knees. We ran away to do our tasks before Balsehekona became angrier.

As I gathered firewood that day, and scraped and washed deerskins, I felt a multifarious anger well up within me. Dorantes had brought me to the Land of the Indians, where I had known nothing but misery; he was the reason for the beating I had endured; and he had left just when I had begun to let myself believe that the bond between us had evolved into one of fellowship. In my own attempts at consolation, I had been lying to myself, too.

When we were finally alone in our tent that night, Castillo asked me: Why do you think he left?

He did not want to do the work they wanted him to do.

But why did he not wait for us?

Because, I thought, this was Dorantes—he cared only about himself. But just as I was about to say as much, I wondered if he had left simply because he could no longer bear to be anywhere near the young Castillo, who reminded him of the brother he had lost. So I said nothing.

I cannot believe he left us, Castillo said. Just like that.

I was thirty-three years of age by then and had seen my fair share of misfortune. But Castillo was much younger than me—he looked about twenty years old, more or less—and his shock at being betrayed awoke in me a protective feeling, not unlike what I had felt when I witnessed his grief at being separated from the doctor's daughter. (Have I mentioned her yet? She had been a passenger on the Gracia de Dios. Castillo used to spend hours on the upper deck, pretending to be busy with something or other, until she made her appearance. She looked a little older than him, and rumor had it that she had already been promised to a settler, but Castillo would try to talk to her anyway. In the end, Narváez's decision to split the armada had forced the lady to remain on the ship.)

How did you become friends with Dorantes? I asked Castillo.

He fought alongside my older brother, Miguel, in the Comunero rebellion, Castillo said. They became very close. After my brother died of consumption, Dorantes suggested I come with him to the Indies. He said that I would become very rich or at the very least I could be made a mayor of a new town. But my father did not want me to go. He had already lost a son to disease and he did not want to lose the other to conquest.

But you would not listen, I said, recognizing in his story my own tale of disobedience and stubbornness.

No, Castillo said. I was too eager to follow in Miguel's footsteps, so I sold a piece of land that had come to me from a maternal uncle in Salamanca and joined the expedition. And now . . .

Now, we are here, I said. In the bushes, the crickets were singing, suddenly interrupted by the wailing of a baby. It was a hungry wail and, after a moment, the baby was cradled to its mother's breast and the crying subsided. We will find a way out of this land, I said. You will see. I think I was trying to reassure him as much as myself.

As it happened, I did not have to wait long. One of the Carancahua boys, for whom I had made a reed flute and to whom I was teaching an old Zamori tune, told me that Dorantes had gone to live with a tribe called the Yguaces, a nomadic band that sometimes traded with the Carancahuas. Castillo wanted to leave right away; he was sure the Carancahuas would kill us, as they had killed the others, and that it was simply a matter of time. I tempered his excitement. Not for another week, I said. In a week's time, the moon would be new—and the wilderness dark enough to conceal us. And a week would give me enough time to find out the best way to reach the Yguaces' camp.

All right, Castillo said. And then: Gracias.

It was a word I had never heard another Castilian say to me.

15

THE STORY OF THE YGUACES

Along the winding path, drops of dew sat like diamonds on blades of grass. Sparrows watched us with curiosity from the high branches of poplar trees. Under our feet, fallen leaves lay deep. Then the trail dropped toward a river, where a woman was cleaning an animal skin, scraping with such zeal that she did not hear us approach until Castillo and I came near her. She turned—and I saw that she was really a he, a man whose slender body and seashell-trimmed dress had fooled my senses. A streak of white ran from the center of his part through his black hair, though he was still young. From his right ear hung a bone earring, of the kind worn by the Yguaces. He had small, graceful features and a genial look about him that immediately put me at ease. I had not seen anyone like him before: a man who dressed as a woman, did a woman's chores, and took another man to his bed, but was in all other respects an ordinary member of the tribe. I did my best to hide my surprise at his attire. He expressed no astonishment at our appearance either, for he had already heard about us, both from Dorantes and from traders who passed through the encampment of the Yguaces.

His name was Chaubekwan and, in addition to his household duties, he was a healer. As he rinsed a deerskin, he asked us about our winter with the Capoques on the Island of Misfortune. A great many of them died of a bowel disease, he said, but not you. How did you cure it?

I crouched beside him, taking one end of the deerskin and helping him wring out the water. I cannot claim to have cured anything, I said.

But why were you spared when so many others perished?

I thought about this for a moment. I had noticed that those of us who drank an infusion of oak leaves for the morning meal had not been afflicted, so I told Chaubekwan about it.

Oak leaves for the bowels? Chaubekwan asked. He tilted his head to the side, pondering this for a moment. As a healer, he was naturally curious about diseases and always on the lookout for new remedies. He was so intrigued by the mention of our infusion that he invited us to the Yguaces' camp.

It was a modest site. A dozen tents that could be easily struck were arranged around a larger one that was used for religious ceremonies. Months with the redoubtable Carancahuas had taught me to bow before the cacique, to avert my eyes when maidens passed by, to let children reach for my beard without recoiling in anticipation of the pain, so as I proceeded into the encampment I had a good notion of the behavior that was required of me. But the Yguaces seemed to pay no attention to my overt deference; they went about their tasks and expected me to do the same.

It was our great luck to have met Chaubekwan. We were his guests now, and the cacique Oñase had no objection to our joining his band, provided that we worked for our food and followed their laws and customs. Except for bits of fabric and tattered animal skins, we had no possessions to speak of, but we spread these out in a shaded area of the camp, under the curious gaze of a handful of bright-eyed boys who had stopped their games to come watch us. At sunset, Dorantes finally appeared, bent under a huge load of firewood. A woman came to help him unstrap the bundle from his back and he made his way over to us, unhurriedly and without any display of emotion. You came, he said a little dully.

You forsook us, Castillo began. His voice was high, and its nasal tone made him sound childish, an effect he was aware of but was powerless to stop.

I did nothing of the sort. I ran away from the Carancahuas.

What about us? Did you not care what happened to us?

You were not in any danger. They killed my brother. They would have killed me next if I had not run away.

But they could have killed us because of you. Did you think about us at all?

I left you with Estebanico, who speaks their language and understands their mores. I knew he would find a way out of their camp. And you made it here safely, did you not?

That is not what troubles me, and you know it.

I have heard quite enough of your accusations, Castillo. Besides, this tribe is not much better.

Now Dorantes turned to me and began to list his complaints, counting them on the fingers of his right hand: the Yguaces made him carry enormous quantities of firewood, which left deep cuts on his skin and gave him unendurable pain in his lower back; they had taken him on a deer hunt that had lasted all day, leaving him so exhausted that he fell asleep before the evening meal was even cooked; they drank a mixture that left them intoxicated well into the night, dancing and singing so loudly that he could never get a proper night's rest; they accepted and even celebrated sodomites, when they should have cast them out. This is why I intend to leave the Yguaces as well, he said.

How thoughtful of you to give us advance notice, Castillo replied.

You cannot say that you were not warned, Dorantes shot back.

Castillo shook his head slowly, in a way that suggested that Dorantes was either too proud or too foolish to acknowledge a legitimate grievance. I listened to my companions quarrel, but all the while I wondered whether the Yguaces were really as harsh as Dorantes had made them sound. Having just completed one frightful escape, I felt unprepared for another one. What would happen if the Yguaces treated us as poorly? What if I had to run away again? Was I meant to go from tribe to tribe, fearing for my life at every moment? The prospect of an endless exile weighed so heavily on me at that moment that I would have given anything not to feel adrift.

But when the Yguaces took us on a hunt the next day, I discovered that unlike other tribes with whom I had lived they ran after the deer for great distances, sometimes for as long as three or four hours, before attempting to spear them. If it was arduous work, at least it did not require as much skill with a bow and arrow. Castillo and I managed to hit a young stag and the taste of its meat over the fire that evening made up for the labor it had cost. As for Dorantes's other complaint, the mosquitoes in these parts were so numerous and so vicious that the only way to keep them away was to burn damp wood; the smoke chased them off, although it also made our eyes water. We had to take turns feeding the fire at night, but even that was not an impossible task.

And yet, Dorantes persisted in his intention to go live with another tribe, one that would not make him work as much as the Yguaces. As soon as the spring rains ceased, he began to make preparations to leave. He had fashioned himself a small satchel from scraps of deerskin, and this he filled with nuts, dried strips of meat, and other provisions for the road.

Dorantes, I said. Stay with us. Traveling alone is too dangerous.

I will manage, he replied.

Castillo intervened. What if you come across a hostile tribe? The Carancahuas journey through these parts as well.

You need not concern yourself with my safety, Dorantes replied. His voice had taken a sharp edge. He was still grieving for his dead brother and rebuffed any signs of friendship from Castillo.

The next morning, when Dorantes left, I did not join him and neither did Castillo. The Yguaces had treated us fairly and, although the work was not always easy, we had learned how to do it properly. Why leave them now?

In the summer, the Yguaces struck their camp and moved southward to the bank of a long and winding river, which in their language is called the River of Nuts. All along its slopes were leafy trees that yield a fruit much like the walnut, although the shell is smoother in appearance and the seed sweeter in taste. The Yguaces fed on these nuts for the entire summer and harvested more for the cold months. They also hunted deer and fowl, and traded with neighboring tribes whose peregrinations brought them to this river as well. Whenever I think back about that summer, what I remember most is how the sound of cracking nutshells filled the entire valley. Other sounds added to that cacophony: new arrivals pitching their tents, neighbors calling out to one another, children playing hide-and-seek, the wind rustling through the leaves of the trees, the fires crackling in the night, the singing and dancing that accompanied the many betrothals and weddings that took place over the summer.

The music often started out slowly, with only two or three drummers sitting in line on their knees. Once the camp had begun to quiet down, a flute player would join in with a melody, and another, and another. Then the dancers would step forward, in twos or threes, their seashell anklets echoing every movement of their feet. In many ways, the dancing reminded me of the great feasts we had on market days in Azemmur—everyone coming out to enjoy the cool evening, singing and dancing and gossiping until the early hours of the morning. One night, spellbound by the music, I joined the Yguace dancers, at first imitating their movements and later letting the rhythm guide me as I moved about the field with the other dancers.

As the days passed, I began to look upon my fate with new eyes. I often lamented the wicked turns my life had taken, but I rarely considered how much I had to be thankful for, how I had survived so long where so many others had perished, how I had seen wonders that no other Zamori had. Had even Ibn Battuta witnessed the things, both terrible and wondrous, that I had seen? I had been so intent on counting all the miseries and humiliations I had endured that I had neglected to thank the Almighty for the blessings he had bestowed upon me: saving me from disease, from the treacherous seas and rivers, and from the Carancahuas.

LITTLE BY LITTLE, the Land of the Indians, which I had viewed first as a place of fantasy and later as a temporary destination, became more real to me, and I began to take greater notice of its beauty. Often, I took a break from my work just to sit under the lilting branches of a magnolia tree and smell its fragrant flowers. Or I would watch the dance of dragonflies and the flitting of hummingbirds all around me, and, for a while at least, I would stop worrying about the fate of the world or the end of my exile. At night, when everyone settled down to sleep, I watched the peerless evening skies or listened to the crickets singing to their mates. In this way, I taught myself to savor what joy was within my reach. The world was not what I wished it to be, but I was alive. I was alive. I set my mind to surviving my trials, which would end soon enough, delivering me only to the eternity of death.

Even my appearance began to change. Since I had bartered my scissors for food on the Island of Misfortune, I usually trimmed my hair by borrowing a comb and a blade from one of the women. But now I allowed my hair to grow and began to braid it in tight plaits along my scalp. I made myself a deerskin vest and a pair of slippers, in the style worn by people of the tribe. These alterations, however modest, made it easier to live and work with the Yguaces.

My days followed a comforting pattern. In the morning, I attended to my duties, usually in the company of Castillo. Life among the Indians had tempered both his candid belief that he was right all the time and his constant need to have the approval of others. Now, free of those pressures, his true nature blossomed; I discovered he had a good sense of humor and a great resilience, qualities that were most helpful in our new environment. We worked side by side, taking turns with the more unpleasant tasks: curing animal hides or removing the entrails from the game the hunters caught. Whenever I trace back the history of my friendship with Castillo, I always return to that summer we spent with the Yguaces and to the work we did together. I still cannot smell cured deerskin without thinking of him.

In the afternoon, I sat with Chaubekwan to help him with whatever chore he was completing. Some years before, he had adopted a boy whose father had been killed in battle and he would spend long hours sewing winter garments for the child. Other times, I helped Chaubekwan prepare his concoctions or stitch up the elaborate costumes he wore when he performed his cures. Once, I asked him: Why do you take as much care of one as the other? Is the cure not more important than the dress? It was a question he found strange and I had to rephrase it two or three times before my meaning became clear to him.

This is like asking why an ibis has a curved bill, he replied, or why a heron has long legs, he said. Because they need to.

Chaubekwan taught me that, just as unfounded gossip can turn into sanctioned history if it falls in the hands of the right storyteller, an untested cure could become effective if the right shaman administered it. From him, I learned how to grind roots without destroying their power, how to store medicinal plants, how to prepare various poultices, but also how to wear a costume and entice a patient to drink a bitter potion.

In the evening, everyone gathered around the campfire, to eat a meal, report what they had seen, or trade news about neighboring tribes. This was how I heard that the Mariames, the tribe with whom Dorantes had gone to live, had recently arrived in the valley. They were a smaller band, known for the artistry of their bone ornaments, which they traded for animal furs and other necessities during the summer, when their travels brought them to the River of Nuts. The Mariames had friendly relations with the Yguaces, so Castillo and I traveled to their camp one night, after the day's labor was done. All along the riverbank, bonfires lit our way, though they did not entirely keep out the flies and mosquitoes that flew in thick, fearless clouds. A swift breeze brought us the smell of roasting meat and singed fur, the cries of children, and the croaking of frogs.

Dorantes looked healthier than when we had last seen him, with a good color on his face and a little thickness around his waist. Still, when we asked him how he was getting on with the Mariames, he began, as usual, with a string of complaints: like the Yguaces, the Mariames went on day-long hunts; they, too, struck their camp every few weeks; they, too, made him carry huge quantities of firewood on his back. And yet, just as Castillo and I had grown accustomed to our tribe, so, too, in the end, had Dorantes.

Nowadays he had the good fortune, he said, of working for a family that did not require him to go on hunts, but instead gave him more mundane and therefore more manageable tasks: he cooked their meals, washed their clothes, set up their tent, and struck it when it was time to move. The reason he did this was because all of them—grandfather, father, mother, and three boys—were blind.

All of them? I asked. How can that be?

It was the pox that made them blind.

Heavens, Castillo said. Are you not afraid you will catch it from them?

The marks on their faces and arms are already healed.

But how did they get the pox?

I suspect it was from someone who traded in New Spain.

Do you think—does that mean we are close to Pánuco?

There is no way to know for certain. These tribes move their camps so often and cover such great distances . . .

Then one of the women called out to Dorantes that he was needed with the cooking, and Castillo and I had to take our leave. As we walked back to the Yguaces' camp, it occurred to me that Pánuco rarely intruded on our conversations these days. And now that it had, it was in connection with a disease we all feared. There were moments when it seemed to me that Pánuco was not a city, but merely a myth we had dreamed up or been told about by others.

We were swimming in the river the next day when Dorantes came to find us, waving his arms like a madman. His face was alight with the fire of excitement. There is another Castilian upriver, he said. It must be one of our men.

It was hard to resist his enthusiasm—we wondered who this man could be and what news he may have for us. Hurriedly, we made our way to the camp, about a quarter of a league upriver, where the white man was said to be. It was the camp of the Charrucos, who had arrived at the River of Nuts just the day before. We asked a young boy about the stranger living with them, and he pointed us to a simple hut, beside which a white man was sitting on his haunches, grinding something in a mortar. The man turned around when he heard us approach. It was Cabeza de Vaca.

Dorantes and Castillo spoke in one voice: You?

The three Castilians hugged each other mightily, for it had been almost three years since they had last seen each other. I leaned against my walking staff, watching them. Then Cabeza de Vaca turned to me and embraced me, too. In my surprise, I dropped my staff and stepped back, but he was not deterred. He hugged me like a brother, squeezing the breath out of me.

How did you end up here? I asked. What happened to you?

Cabeza de Vaca sat down to recount his tale for us, a tale I have committed to memory and which I repeat here for my gentle reader. Amigos, he said, I stayed with the Han on the Island of Misfortune until the end of the fishing season, after which I moved with them to the mainland. The cacique had died of the bowel disease by then, as had many of the tribe's elders, so there was always great disagreement among them about matters small and large: which routes to take, or when to set up camp, or whose son was ready to have his nipple pierced. The cacique's daughter—my wife, Kakunlopa, whom you have met—urged her people to stay together and to follow the same traditions their ancestors had used. But there was constant quarreling.

In the middle of the spring, when we had migrated farther inland for the season of the blackberries, my wife gave birth to a baby boy. Amigos, I am nearly forty years old. I had always longed for a son, but I had not before been blessed with one, so you can imagine my joy at this birth. I named him Pedro, after my grandfather Pedro de Vera Mendoza, of whom you may have heard, if you enjoy stories of chivalry and adventure. I could already see myself in this little boy, in the tuft of curly hair that sprouted from his head, the way his smile dimpled his face. But by the end of the season, he caught a fever, which did not break no matter what remedy I tried.

After we buried Pedro, I told my wife that we should join another tribe along the coast, like the Charrucos or maybe the Quevenes. The reason for my proposal was that her people had thinned to no more than forty souls, many of them women, and it seemed to me they would not be able to survive another winter on the Island of Misfortune without their hunters and fishermen. But my wife refused to leave her tribe. She said she had a sister and an uncle left, not to mention the rest of her people, and that they needed her. So I had to take her back to the island, while I returned to the mainland to trade with the tribes along the coast.

I brought with me seashells, deer hides, ocher, and pigments, and traded them for dried meat, ground corn, and other useful things. Whenever I went back to the island to bring back provisions, I would try to talk some sense into Kakunlopa, but she refused to leave the island. Then, last winter, while I was trading on the mainland, she came down with the fever, too. She died before I could see her.

Cabeza de Vaca's voice grew hoarse and he averted his eyes for a moment. I have been traveling from tribe to tribe along the coast ever since.

What about Oviedo and Albaniz? Dorantes asked.

Oviedo is dead. Albaniz I could never convince to go anywhere with me.

Cabeza de Vaca asked us about our own journey through the coastal lands. So I told him the story of our travels, the fate of the comptroller's raft and the governor's raft, our stay with the Carancahuas, the murder of Diego, how Dorantes had fled, and how Castillo and I had come to live with the Yguaces. Cabeza de Vaca listened with great attention, neither interrupting nor hurrying me to reach the end of my tale. Here was a man, I felt, who knew how to tell stories and how to listen to them, who appreciated their purpose and their value. A kindred spirit, a fellow storyteller.

Come live with me, Dorantes said to Cabeza de Vaca.

At least this way, Cabeza de Vaca would once again have the companionship of another Castilian, and together they would provide some solace to one another. So it was that, when our stay at the River of Nuts ended, Cabeza de Vaca joined Dorantes with the Mariames, while Castillo and I left with the Yguaces.

THE NEXT STOP in the peregrinations of the Yguaces was the River of Prickly Pears. I had never seen so much of the fruit in one place before—the valley was an ocean of green, dotted everywhere with red and orange.

All the Indians from the coast gathered here for the month, feeding on the fruit and little else. Here they traded feathers or beads or tools. Here they came to find a match for a son or to buy a new wife. Here they exchanged news about births or deaths. Here they heard about wars with hostile tribes, here they told about their dreams, here they repeated rumors of alien invasions—and here they came to get a closer look at the bearded men.

Harvesting prickly pears was not an easy task; spikes would inevitably lodge themselves on my fingertips, no matter how careful I was. After a long day of working in the bushes, I went with Castillo to soak in the river. I sat in the cool water, with my fingers raking against the current. It was so soothing I let out a long sigh of relief. The mosquitoes buzzed in the air around us, but mercifully the flies hovered around the mountain of fresh peels by the camp and left us alone.

Castillo asked: What is it like, being with a woman?

I was startled by his question. Why do you ask?

He fell silent, then looked away. I followed his gaze—it settled on a group of three maidens, who were sitting some distance away by the riverbank. They had lifted their tunics above their knees and dipped their feet in the water. That woman on the ship, I said, Doctor Galiano's daughter . . .

Before I could formulate a question, he replied: She was promised to one of the settlers, but she said she did not want to marry him. That she wanted me. Then Narváez decided to split the expedition, and she had to remain behind.

Is that why you did not want Narváez to leave the ships? I asked.

Castillo shrugged. It matters not why, he said. In the end, it was a mistake to leave them behind.

Do you still think about her?

From time to time. But she must be married; she might even have a child by now.

He lay back against the water and started floating, his long black hair pooling in a circle around him. I did the same and the river carried us both. We passed under a canopy of trees and the sky, a perfect summer blue, was momentarily hidden from view. Some among the Yguaces were looking for brides and it was difficult for me not to look at the maidens without dreaming of having one for a wife. What I felt was not lust, not exactly. It was more than lust, it was a desire for love and companionship and the warmth of another body against mine.

That night, when we returned to the camp, we learned that Dorantes and Cabeza de Vaca, who had just arrived with the Mariames at the River of Prickly Pears, had been reprimanded for witlessly interfering with Indian rituals. They wanted to leave the Mariames now, before their relationship with the tribe deteriorated any further. They suggested that the four of us reunite and travel together again.

But it so happened that one of the Mariames made an offer to marry a woman from another tribe. The bride price was agreed upon, the girl was made ready, and the feast was prepared, when her father asked for an additional set of bow-and-arrows. A great fight broke out, which was compounded when the cacique of the Mariames brought up old grudges against the other tribe. They came to blows over it, and the next day the Mariames struck their camp and moved farther along the banks of the river, taking Dorantes and Cabeza de Vaca with them. If we wanted to leave together, we had to wait until the following season.

It was a full year before our travels brought us back to the River of Prickly Pears, where we were reunited with Dorantes and Cabeza de Vaca. Their disagreements with the Mariames had worsened, so that we had to leave under the cover of night, following the river as it curved out of the green valley. In the morning, we came across a band of Anegados, who warned us that the entire area to the south was peopled with Indians who hated Castilians so much that they would kill them without hesitation. For the last few years, Castilian soldiers had been traveling all the way from México and forcibly removing Indians to enslave them. They had done this to such an extent that all the southern tribes had learned to always flee or fight them, and to never trust them. Hoping to circumvent the area where the hostile tribes lived, my three companions and I went west.

16.

THE STORY OF THE AVAVARES

Hunger began to torment us almost as soon as we left the valley. Along the trail, there were many prickly pear bushes, but their fruit had already been picked by the Indian tribes who migrated through the area. All that remained were the peels, rotting in small heaps under the bushes, their smell an irresistible call to flies and gnats. It was true that we had learned how to hunt deer and hare, where to find roots, grasses, and fruits, which of these were edible and which were poisonous, but we had no spears or bows and arrows of our own and, if we continued marching farther west, we might go for days without coming across a river or a spring. To survive, we had to find a tribe—and soon.

But God, who is the best planner of all, willed that on the afternoon of the fourth day we came across a little boy who was playing by himself in the wilderness. He ran away in great fright when he saw us. Our thick beards and unusual colors must have scared him, or perhaps he had heard the stories that had been spreading for a while now, stories that grew more terrifying with each telling, of sharp-toothed and bloodthirsty aliens who snatched away children that strayed too far from their homes.

I ran after the boy. Wait, I cried. Wait.

He turned around to size me up. He had almond-shaped eyes and two new front teeth that poked out of his pink gums—he must have been seven or eight, though he was quite short for his age. From the tattoo on his chin, blue dots in the shape of a triangle, I guessed that he was an Avavare. This was a relief; I was somewhat familiar with the Avavares, having met them before at the River of Prickly Pears, where they traded animal skins and parrot feathers with the Yguaces. We are but poor travelers in the land, I said. Can you take us with you?

The boy glanced past me at my white companions, who were now catching up to us. To protect himself from the sun, Cabeza de Vaca had tied a strip of painted deerskin around his head and parts of it fell down to his cheeks, flapping as he ran toward us. Dorantes was carrying his walking staff so he could move faster, and its end dragged on the ground behind him. Having caught up to us, my companions stopped to take their breath. Castillo pressed his thumb on the sore that had been growing under his heel; clear pus drained from it. So pitiful was our condition that the Avavare boy made up his mind quickly. Come along, he said.

THE CACIQUE OF THE AVAVARES, an older man by the name of Tahacha, came out to greet us in person. He had a kindly face and a weak chin that disappeared into the folds of his neck. Behind him, in the open hut, his wife was nursing a baby, singing and cooing to it, but all the while she gazed curiously in our direction. A little boy sat beside her, too absorbed by his game of marbles to bother looking up. Before we had even asked, Tahacha offered us shelter for the night and some water to quench our thirst. Later, when we joined him for a meal of roasted fowl, he asked us about the land whence we came. I pointed behind me, in the direction of the sunrise. We come from lands far away, I said.

How far?

On the other side of the ocean.

Tahacha exchanged a surprised glance with his shaman, a lanky old man with an impressive array of tattoos. I had the feeling that this conversation was the first entertainment they had had in a long while, for they listened eagerly to everything I said, leaning in whenever the crackling of the fire or an animal's cry in the distance interrupted the sound of my voice. All of you come from that far? Tahacha asked.

My three companions are from one tribe, I replied. And I from another.

Tahacha considered this for a moment. Is that why you look different?

Yes.

But how did you get here?

On boats, I said. And then, skipping forward in my story, I added: But a storm destroyed our boats and our people with them. The four of us are the only survivors. We have been living with different tribes ever since.

And what brought you here?

This was a question that had been asked of one or another of us many times since we had lived with the Indians, but we had learned that it was impossible to answer it completely truthfully. I glanced at my companions, hoping they could help me give Tahacha a suitable response, but Dorantes and Cabeza de Vaca stared glumly at the campfire. It was Castillo who answered: Our cacique was looking for something.

Did he find it?

No. On the contrary, we lost everything.

You blame this cacique?

Yes, Castillo said. Yes.

It is easy to blame the cacique, Tahacha said. But he is only a man; he derives his power from other men, who will follow him for only as long as they believe in him.

It seemed to me that Tahacha spoke from experience. His words struck me with the force of a revelation. Everyone in the expedition had believed Narváez's story about the kingdom of gold and had eagerly followed him there. Of course, there had been doubts about his decision to leave the ships behind and about his handling of the march, but never about the story he had told us, the lie that had started everything. Why had so many of us believed it?

So what did your cacique promise you? Tahacha asked.

He had directed the question to me, since I was the more fluent speaker. It was, of course, a difficult question. If I told him the truth, he would know that these Castilians sitting by my side had come to these lands as conquerors; that they had wanted to make him a vassal of their king, to whom he would have to pay a tribute; and that they had planned to destroy his idols and turn him into a Christian. The truth, in this case, would have been a death warrant for my companions and me. So I had to improvise. He told us there was much gold in this land, I said.

Gold? Tahacha's chin retreated farther into the folds of his neck. In this country, gold was not held in much esteem; macaw feathers, turquoises, and some animal skins held greater value and were much preferred in trade. Where is he now, your cacique?

Dead, I said. And dead, too, I thought, was his dream of conquest—for the Castilians were the ones who had been vanquished; they were the ones who lived as servants in this land; and they were the ones who dared not practice their faith openly out of fear that they would incur the Indians' wrath. As for me, an interloper among the Castilians, I had shared their fate. Now, years later, I was no longer a slave, but my freedom had come at the price of being an interloper among the Indians. Give glory to God, who can alter all fates.

Tell me about the tribes you have lived with, Tahacha said. He was already familiar with the customs of his neighbors the Yguaces and the Mariames, but he was curious about the tribes that lived farther away, so I related for him our life with the Capoques and later with the Carancahuas. Whenever I told stories around the campfire, I sensed that Cabeza de Vaca was anxious to rival them with his own, for he was a gifted storyteller. This time was no different; he spoke at length about his life with the Han and later with the Charrucos and the Quevenes. He described the game they hunted, the foods they ate, the tattoos they bore, and the crimson red pigment they made by grinding an insect that lived on cactus plants. The tales of our travels delighted Tahacha, and he offered us some furs to protect ourselves from the night chill. For the first time, the story of our adventures, supplemented by neither labor nor begging, had earned us not just a meal, but gifts of blankets.

I WAS WOKEN EARLY the next morning by moans of pain. Beside me, Dorantes was writhing about, his arms tightly folded over his belly. Our experience on the Island of Misfortune had bred in him the habit of eating gluttonously whenever meat was plentiful, so I suspected that the large amounts of fowl he had eaten for dinner were the cause of his discomfort. I left Castillo to attend to the cookfire and went into the fields behind the camp to look for some zaatar, which I used to make an infusion. Drink this, I said, kneeling beside Dorantes.

He took a sip, then spat it out. It is too bitter, he said.

Castillo chuckled and shook his head slowly. You never learn, do you?

I am fine, Dorantes said. He ran his hand on his forehead, wiping away his sweat, and stood up. See, I am fine, he said, just before a bout of nausea seized him and he bent down again.

Come now, I said. Drink.

Although he fought me about it, he eventually drank the zaatar—he had tried it before and knew it would work. When I looked up, I noticed that the Avavares' shaman was observing us. His name was Behewibri. He was a morose-looking man, with a narrow face and suspicious eyes. The night before, at dinner, he had sat beside the cacique and listened attentively to all our stories without offering comments or questions. But now he asked me: What did you give your brother?

I showed Behewibri the zaatar.

Ah, he said. He called it by its Avavare name and pressed the leaves of the plant between his fingers, releasing its aroma into the air. He wanted to know how I had prepared it, how much of it I had used, and whether it was safe to give to a child as well as to a man. I told him what I knew: it was a simple remedy my mother used whenever I complained of a stomachache, and it was safe to use on anyone.

I thought nothing more of the incident. The Avavares struck their camp later that morning and we followed them to their next site, a small valley where they would be picking blueberries for a few weeks. But it so happened that a young boy complained of an unbearable headache that night. Behewibri had already attended to him, breathing deeply and blowing air on his forehead, yet the boy had not shown any sign of improvement. Do your people get headaches? Behewibri asked me.

Yes, I replied.

We are just like you, Castillo added. We get headaches, too.

Do you know how to cure them?

No, I said.

Behewibri looked incredulous. You say you come from wondrous lands in the sunrise, with massive villages and many peoples, but you cannot help this boy?

It was true that I had helped Dorantes with his indigestion, but I knew nothing about cures and I had never pretended to be a doctor. It is just a headache, I said. It will pass.

Behewibri narrowed his eyes at me; the suspicion that had filled them the night before returned. Now I worried that any failure on my part to heal this boy would endanger our stay with the Avavares. Helplessly, I turned to Castillo. Your father is a doctor.

But I am not.

Surely you must have learned some things from watching him? When you took care of the friar on the Island of Misfortune, his fever broke.

All I did was put cold compresses on him, Castillo said. I know nothing of cures.

Behewibri was still watching us. Would he say something against us to Tahacha? I wondered. Would we be cast out to fend for ourselves in the wilderness again? I had to try something. The boy lay in his hut, sleeping on his side, his face turned away from the entrance. With Behewibri looking over my shoulder, I knelt on the fur bedding. Does it hurt here? I asked, as I placed my fingertips on the boy's temples. Or here? I said, touching the nape of his neck. The boy considered my question. The pain was in his temple, he decided. I pressed my fingertips on his temple, making small circles. And now? I asked.

Better, he said reluctantly.

I massaged his temple for a long while and then declared that he would feel better by the morning. At least, I had bought myself some time. I told my companions that we should be ready to leave at first light, but by the great mercy of God, the boy improved the next day and was even better the day after that. The Avavares thanked me by giving me a small piece of turquoise, which I threaded and wore around my neck. My relief was such that, when they began to dance at night, I joined them, under the amused glance of the shaman.

IT WAS AN EARLY FALL that year, the trees quickly shedding their red and yellow leaves, as if in a hurry to stand, unadorned, in God's rain. Soon, it would be time for the Avavares to strike their camp and move again. I was returning from the river with a jar of water when I came across Behewibri's daughter, Oyomasot. She had long, dark hair, which she wore in elaborately wound knots on either side of her head, and she always stood very straight and tall, like a sultan's daughter contemplating her dominion. Since our arrival, she had not said a word to any of us—this was not unusual, of course, since we were nothing more than alien drifters who worked menial tasks—but in her case the silence was accompanied by a mocking stare, as if she knew something about us that the others did not.

I found Oyomasot struggling with a length of palm-frond rope, trying to pull it down from the mulberry tree on which it was stuck. I put down my jar of water and rushed to help her. Taking the rope from her hands, I whisked it away from the tree branch and handed it to her. She fixed her beautiful eyes upon me; they were filled with surprise.

There, I said with a smile.

Gentle reader, I had hoped to impress her. Instead, she became angry with me. What have you done? she asked.

I pulled the rope down for you.

I was trying to hang it, not pull it down. Furrowing her brow, she looked up at the branch, where a small piece of rope had remained. Now you broke it.

I am sorry, I said. I was only trying to help.

I did not need help.

I can see that now, I said. I was rattled by her fiery replies and, fearing I might say something harsh in return, I picked up my water jar and walked away.

Wait, she said. She stood there, under the dappled light of the mulberry tree, watching me. One of the knots in her hair had come loose in our tussle over the rope and the strap that held her tunic had slipped, uncovering her shoulder. My throat felt suddenly dry; I wanted a sip of water, but had forgotten all about the jar in my hand. You could at least help me hang this, she said. She pointed to a wide drum that had been set against the tree trunk. White seashell bracelets were strapped upon her tiny wrists. What graceful arms she had.

Well? Are you going to hang the rope or not? she asked.

Yes, I said. My voice was hoarse and sounded as if it came from far away. I put down my jar again and, taking the rope from her, I climbed up the mulberry tree. The first branch bent dangerously under my weight, but I continued to the next one and the one after that.

Be careful, Oyomasot called. I looked down; the irritation that had colored her face had disappeared, replaced with what looked like genuine concern.

Is this high enough? I said.

Yes, she said, her manner changed now. Just tie it and come down.

As I did so, I felt her worried gaze upon me. The image of Ramatullai, waiting for me every night in that Sevillian kitchen, came to me unbidden. She was standing just so, with the light from the candle behind her, leaning against the counter where our dinner bowls sat side by side. Bouquets of lavender hung from the wall beside her, filling the room with their scent. I had not seen Ramatullai in many years, but I knew she had waited for me on the day I had been sold to Dorantes. She had been the only one who cared whether I lived or died.

After I climbed down from the tree, I was disoriented, more because of the image that had been in my mind's eye than because of the descent itself. But Oyomasot asked: Are you well?

Yes, I said. The wind rustled the leaves of the tree above me. A blue jay landed on the nearest branch and regarded me with curiosity. I was trying to think of some way I could prolong the encounter, so I lifted the drum and handed it to her. Her fingers brushed ever so slightly against mine—was I imagining it or did she do it on purpose? You made this drum? I asked.

It is nothing.

It is beautiful.

Every maiden is expected to make drums, she said. It sounded as if the expectation itself took away any pleasure she might have found in making the instrument. She hung the drum from the rope and, by the time she turned around again, her expression was once again distant. Without another word, she walked back toward the camp.

FROM THE START, what struck me about Oyomasot was that she did not care what anyone thought. She did not care that the other Avavare maidens thought her strange because she preferred going on walks in the woods to sitting by the riverbank with them. She did not care that her father and mother disapproved of her wandering off alone. It was true that she did all her tasks uncomplainingly, whether it was collecting mountains of firewood or washing smelly animal skins, but I cannot say that she did them zealously or expertly. Once her chores were completed, however, she would go set up traps for wild fowl, or she would play a popular game of sticks, but she would often be rebuked, since these were not proper pastimes for a girl. It was on such days that she would wander off in the woods until it was nearly dark. She seemed to be nursing a resentment that could not be healed.

It was raining one day when I saw her coming back home. The weather had turned abruptly: the sky had been clear one moment and the next it had opened up and poured like a river over the entire camp. We had carried everything inside and huddled in our huts, waiting out the storm. The light was low, but I saw Oyomasot's face clearly—it was the face of someone who was preparing herself for a burden. As she came into the camp square, her mother stepped out of their hut. Where have you been? she asked. She stood with her legs apart and her hands resting on her hips. I could see that Oyomasot had the same eyes—large and slightly upturned—but that was where the similarities ended, for the mother's mouth was set in a contemptuous turn and her voice was grating. You left your brother's furs hanging on their racks, she said.

Why did he not bring them in from the rain? Oyomasot asked. She said this in a level tone, but that only made her mother angrier.

That was your duty, not his.

He would rather they get wet than bring them in himself?

They must be ruined by now. And it is your fault.

It was quiet in the camp; everyone was in their huts, listening to the quarrel outside. The rain grew heavier now and Oyomasot had to raise her voice in order to be heard. Everything is always my fault, she said. How powerful I must be to command the whole world.

Her mother grumbled something about her uselessness, before drawing the deerskin closed across the doorway. For a long moment, Oyomasot stood in the rain, considering what her mother had said about her. Her tunic was wet and clung to her, and her feet were sinking in the mud. Then with a sigh she walked to the edge of the camp to get the furs.

I do not know why I fell in love with Oyomasot. Who can explain such things? Perhaps it was because I saw in her someone who, like me, chafed under the rules that were imposed upon her. Perhaps it was because, though she lived at home, she did not seem fully at home—an outsider of a sort, another interloper. Or perhaps it was because, despite her fiery disposition, she was the one to whom children flocked when they needed someone to watch them race or to sort out their quarrels. But I can say when I fell in love; it was that day, when she stood in the rain, her feet sinking in the mud, but her back straight.

WE HAD BEEN at the fall camp for only a month when we received word that the cacique of the Susolas had fallen ill. They were a neighboring tribe, camped some two or three leagues south of us, where they would remain for the season. They had heard about my helping with the Avavare boy's headache and, since their medicine man had been unable to cure the cacique, he wanted me to come visit him. I could not turn down the invitation because I was afraid of causing some offense that might complicate our stay with the Avavares, but neither could I accept it, for how could I help this man?

For a while, I tried to delay. I told Tahacha that it was better to give the Susolas' shaman more time to find a cure. I said I was too busy with my chores. I even complained that I could not walk all the way to the Susolas' camp. But all my excuses were uncovered for what they were. And, to my amazement, the shaman Behewibri encouraged me to go, even though he had not been asked himself. Was he hoping that I would fail and be thrown out of the tribe? I really could not guess. But I had no recourse, especially if I wanted to keep the peace with my hosts.

I asked my Castilian companions to come with me, but Dorantes and Cabeza de Vaca both refused. The rivalry that had existed between them when the expedition first landed in La Florida had disappeared, replaced by a friendship that had grown more steadfast during the year they spent together as servants of the Mariames. Conversely, the friendship that had existed between Dorantes and Castillo had all but faded away after Diego's gruesome death. So I was not entirely surprised when only Castillo offered to go with me.

By the time we arrived in the Susolas' camp, three days after the invitation had been sent, we found the cacique bedridden and nearly delirious with back pain. I fell into a panic. Obviously, I could do nothing to help this man and now I was certain that I would be blamed if I failed. But with the clarity of mind that comes at such fraught moments, I remembered how, years before, in the market of Azemmur, my father had gone to the hijama tent, complaining of similar pains. I had seen a cupping cure performed on him that day and, although I had no experience with it myself, I felt I had no choice but to try it.

Calling the name of God upon the patient before me, I asked for a cup and, heating it over a fire, I placed it on the cacique's back, causing the skin under it to lift and stay trapped. After a few minutes, I released the skin gently and started the process again. All the while, I told a story, to distract the Susola chief from the pain and also to entertain his kin, who sat all around us in the hut. Years ago, I said, taking some liberties with my tale for the sake of my audience, my father suffered from the same predicament. He was a formidable chief who was known throughout the town for his fairness. But once he was afflicted with these spells of back pain, he took to his bed. He could no longer work. My mother and brothers grew hungry. One of my uncles, taking pity on my father, brought him a medicine man, an old man in black clothes. This medicine man had been forced out of his land and had only recently settled in our town, so no one was sure whether he could be trusted. But he used this cure you see today. The cup traps the illness and then releases it into the air. Not only did my father get better, but he returned to work and became stronger than he ever was.

Sitting beside me, Castillo whispered that he had once seen his own father use a cupping cure in Salamanca. He asked for a cup and began to help me. To my great and lasting relief, the cacique was able to sit up and eat the next day, and by the third day he was able to stand.

IF I HAD HOPED to be rid of the vocation that had been thrust upon me, the welcome I received when I returned to the Avavare camp cleared away all of my illusions. The entire tribe came out to greet me and I was hugged like a long-lost brother. Over the next few days, the recovery of the Susola elder became the subject of tales among the Indians in the area and, with each new telling, my healing powers seemed to acquire greater force. In one version of the tale, the Susola chief had been on the verge of death and his people were already in mourning—until I had brought him back to life. No matter how many times I explained that this was a simple cure that had been used in my hometown, people did not believe me; they thought I was being humble. And because I had succeeded where the Susola shaman had failed, my alienness became connected in people's minds with my healing power.

Soon, the Avavares began to receive visits from their allies the Maliacones and the Cultalchulches, and other bands that call themselves the Coayos and the Atayos. These tribes brought their sick with them and I could not attend to all of them by myself, so my companions had to join me in honoring people's requests as best as they could. Castillo relied on memories of his father's practice in Salamanca. Dorantes and Cabeza de Vaca used soldiers' remedies they had learned when they fought in their king's wars. As for me, I used what I had learned growing up in Azemmur. I gave infusions of wild garlic for pain in the joints; I cleaned wounds with the ground bark of young oak trees; I treated constipation with verbena; for a sore throat, I suggested gargling with salted water.

If I was confronted with an illness I did not recognize, I listened to the sick man or woman and offered consolation in the guise of a long story. After all, what the sufferers needed most of all was an assurance that someone understood their pain and that, if not a full cure, at least some respite from it lay further ahead. This, too, was something I had learned in the markets of Azemmur: a good story can heal.

I had feared that Behewibri would resent our success, but, as it turned out, he welcomed it: the tribes that visited us always brought many gifts with them, gifts that were shared among all the Avavares, particularly the cacique and the shaman. And Behewibri taught me many things, too. From him, I learned how to use hot stones on the body, how to cut the skin around a wound and draw blood from it, how to blow warm air on an afflicted limb. Of course, not every cure was effective, but it is a fortunate law of human nature that our greatest accomplishments are more easily remembered than our occasional failures. The stories of successful cures seemed to be the only ones that were told over and over in the neighboring camps, heightening people's interest in us, while our failures were quickly dismissed or forgiven.

By the end of the winter, the Avavares began to treat us as honored members of the tribe rather than drifters who had to be tolerated. No longer did they ask us to collect firewood or fetch water or wash animal skins. Nor did they ask us to take part in hunts, since we received so much deer and hare meat in payment for our cures. And as the Avavares' treatment of us changed, so, too, did our behavior toward them. We never refused to attend to a patient, whether his complaints were serious or trivial. We listened carefully to the stories the Avavares told around the campfire, about their ancestors, their neighbors good and bad, the spirits that populate their world, but also stories about their origins, the dangers they had faced, and the murderous white aliens who were now snatching them away.

When the Castilians heard about the abductions, they always insisted that not all aliens were the same. Indeed you are not, Behewibri replied. You come from the direction of sunrise whereas those people come from the sunset. You speak our tongue and that of our neighbors, whereas they speak an alien language. You do not carry weapons, whereas they are armed and ride upon animals. You helped us heal our people, whereas they snatch or kill them.

The cures we performed may not have healed everyone we attended, but I can vouch that they saved at least four lives: our own. We were finally able to walk the land without fear for our safety; we had food, shelter, and companionship; and everywhere we went, we were treated with kindness and respect. One night, as I took my seat next to Behewibri, I noticed that the disdain in his daughter's eye was gone, replaced by a glint of curiosity.

·   ·   ·

I HAD THOUGHT that my condition of poor exile would forever doom me to a life of loneliness, but as my position changed, so, too, did my prospects. The Avavares had already begun to treat me as one of their own, but after Dorantes and I helped set a young boy's broken leg, Tahacha decreed that we would all marry maidens from his tribe. Cabeza de Vaca, who was still in mourning over his wife and child, declined the offer, but the rest of us accepted. Dorantes married the cacique's daughter, Tekotsen. She was a plain girl, with a narrow face and thin lips, who had been taken with Dorantes almost from the moment she saw him. Every cure he performed, she declared a miracle. Every fawn he caught, she proclaimed a stag. In her, Dorantes found not only a devoted wife, but a relentless advocate.

Castillo married Kewaan, the youngest daughter of Tahacha's deputy. Kewaan was a great beauty, and her sudden marriage caused some grumbling, for there were two youths among the Susolas who had wanted her for a wife. She was also known for her crafts, particularly her basket designs and the bracelets and anklets she fashioned out of deerskin.

But I was the luckiest one of all, for I married Behewibri's daughter, Oyomasot. My experience with women was limited and, since my arrival in the Land of the Indians, I had had few interactions with them. After our encounter by the mulberry tree, I had dared speak to Oyomasot only once or twice—when I had sat beside her father for the evening meal and when I brought some wild mint for one of his cures. But perhaps Oyomasot had seen some merit in me, for she did not object to the proposal. Her eyes shone with a fierce intelligence that had intimidated me. Now that she was my wife it made me proud, though I had no part in it.

With trembling fingers, I undid the shoulder knot on the tunic Oyomasot wore on our wedding night. She stood before me, unembarrassed of her glorious nakedness. For a moment I feared I would not be able to move; my heart was pounding in my chest. But she put her hand on my cheek and traced the outline of my face with her fingers. Her touch was light and gentle, unlike any I had known before, and I heard myself call out her name. Then her fingers found the scar on the back of my neck. How did you get this? she asked.

I had grown so accustomed to leaving out details of my life story in order to survive that, for a moment, I considered making up some reason for the scar. But her gaze swept away all of my reservations. I had to tell her the truth, the whole of it. As I spoke, she slipped her hand in mine and pulled me down to sit beside her. Propriety prevents this servant of God from describing that night any further, but I wanted to record it in this relation, because it marked the beginning of a new time in my life, a time when I was no longer alone and bereft. (I know that none of the Castilians have mentioned their wives in their Joint Report, but I feel bound by honor to reveal everything that came to pass, without leaving anything out.)

This was how I began to fashion a new life for myself in the Land of the Indians. When I had sold myself into bondage, or trudged behind Narváez in the wilderness, or embarked on that crude raft with patchy sails, my keenest desire had been to go back to my old life in Azemmur, where I could start my days with my mother's blessings and end them by contemplating the rustling river from the solid safety of our rooftop. Instead, I had been pushed further and further into a fate from which no escape or reprieve seemed possible. And so there came a moment when I stopped struggling, when I decided that I would cease making any more plans to return to the old days. I made up my mind to look upon the present as exactly what it was: it was all I had. To add to my sense that my curse had turned into a blessing, not only was I free—I was no longer alone.

17.

The Story of the Land of Corn

In the spring, just as the Avavares were preparing to strike their camp and move east, an emissary of the Arbadaos arrived, bearing many gifts and an invitation. I was not familiar with his tribe, because they lived well outside the areas we visited in our seasonal travels and, even though I was busy with packing provisions, I offered him the pipe and asked what ailments afflicted his people that they should have come so far in search of healers. What the emissary described—a skin rash, a knife cut, a spider bite—sounded neither urgent nor out of the ordinary and, when he spoke, his voice had a flat tone that seemed, to my ears, a little too imperative. So I was inclined to reject his invitation.

But, that evening, when I told Oyomasot about it, she stopped sharpening the spearhead she had been hunched over when I came into the hut. She was a good spearwoman, who could hit a target from as far away as ten qasab with unerring aim, but the tribe's traditions precluded her from taking part in a hunt. What was more, she was not supposed to make or carry a weapon. In another girl, such violations would have been severely punished, but in Oyomasot, they were tolerated the way one tolerates the peculiarities of misfits, mystics, and madmen.

Did you already send him away? she asked me.

Not yet, I replied. We were sitting on a black bear pelt that had been given to me by a Maliacone elder, after I had relieved his neck pain with an infusion of ground willow leaves. But the night was unseasonably hot and Oyomasot had pulled up her tunic well above her knees. I took one of her feet in my hands and ran my thumb on the soft part of her sole. You have such tiny feet, I teased.

You should not send him away, she said.

Why not? Gently, I tugged at her foot so that she would come sit a little closer to me.

Because his people need you.

But the Arbadaos are at least four days' walk from here. If I go visit them, and you move eastward with your family, it might be weeks before I catch up to you. I cannot be away from you for so long.

I can come with you.

Your mother will not like that.

What if she doesn't? Oyomasot asked with a smile. Her eyes challenged me. Besides, she said, the cacique of the Arbadaos is very powerful. It would make little sense to refuse him.

How vast this country was, I remember thinking, and how complicated the alliances between its tribes. If I refused the invitation of the Arbadaos, I could cause friction with the Avavares. I still had much to learn. Oyomasot set aside her spearhead and sharpening tools, carefully covering them with a rabbit fur. What do your brothers think? she asked.

Dorantes and Cabeza de Vaca want to go, I said. But Castillo refuses.

Then talk to him.

He has already made up his mind.

Did you not tell me once that you could convince a dove it was a hawk?

Reader, beware: the things you say to impress a beautiful woman have an odd way of being repeated to you when you least expect them. I was embarrassed by my boasting, but, in my defense, I had said those things many months earlier, when I was starting out with the Avavares and I was still trying to attract Oyomasot's notice.

Besides, she added, Kewaan would welcome the chance to travel.

Very well, I said. I will talk to Castillo.

At last, she leaned closer to me.

SO IT WAS that we ventured westward, across a trackless wilderness filled with yucca, wild grass, and prickly pear bushes. The march was long and arduous, and we all felt a little lost, but the emissary behaved as if he were simply taking a trip down a cobblestone road in any city of Barbary. In the middle of what looked like nothing but an empty stretch of land, he would stop, examine a green thicket for a moment, and suddenly change course. At length, we came within view of the Arbadaos' encampment. It was set in a wide expanse of dry land, without the usual protection provided by a canopy of tall trees. It gave me the impression of a fearless people.

Living so far from the coast, the Arbadaos did not fish at all. Instead, they hunted deer and fowl, as well as a hoofed beast that looked like a cow, though it had horns. The skins of all these animals they used in their homes or traded to their allies, but the Arbadaos were just as often involved in wars against their neighbors. At such times, they were known to be merciless in battle—this was another reason why Oyomasot had warned me against rebuffing their invitation.

On the night of our arrival, the cacique Beaset gave an extravagant banquet for us, with many different varieties of game skewered on wooden spits before us. Eat! Eat! he said cheerfully. He sat cross-legged, periodically cocking his head to the side to hear whatever one of his deputies whispered into his ear, and then he would smile, displaying a set of perfectly aligned teeth. All over his body, he had scars of different sizes and shapes—far more than would have been caused by a hunting injury or a fall in the wilderness. I found it hard to enjoy the lavish food or even the music and dancing, because I was not sure what he expected from us.

A special tent was set up for us the next morning, wide enough to accommodate all the patients who wanted to consult with us. Although the Arbadaos' language was intelligible to us, it was distinct enough from the languages we spoke that we needed an interpreter to conduct proper examinations. Right away, Dorantes's brother-in-law, a young Avavare by the name of Satosol, declared himself the man for the task. It occurs to me now that he acted as more than just a translator—he was also an usher, an aide, and a eulogizer, with an instinctive flair for spectacle.

I asked the Arbadaos' shaman to sit beside me when I received the day's patients, in order that I might share any success with him, and mitigate any failures. The stream of patients started early and continued for the rest of the day: an old man complained of swollen feet; I advised soaking them in salted water. A teenage girl said she had a cough; I offered her some of the nut oil we had brought, telling her she should take a few drops of it after every meal. A mother brought a child covered with bug bites; I suggested some wild marjoram. Throughout the day, Satosol translated my advice. And then Oyomasot began to render it in rhyme, a skill I had not known her to possess: If your sleep is troubled and your mood is sour, old auntie, drink a brew of passionflower. Or: Little boy with a stuffy nose, a tea of gumweed cures your woes. Or: For the baby with loose bowels, I made a drink of cactus flowers.

These rhymes made it easier for our patients to remember our cures, though it seemed to me that, coupled with Satosol's introductions and eulogizing, they also turned our session into a kind of theater. The memory of the traveling healer in the souq of Azemmur returned to me all of a sudden. Every market day, he set up his large, black tent, where he told stories and healed the sick, providing spectacle and service all at once. Though I had traveled far from Barbary, I had come across a similar tradition in the Land of Corn. And I found comfort in it.

Halfway through our assembly, Beaset sent his shaman away and took the vacant seat beside me. I want to try, he said. His smile confused me—I could not tell if it was friendly or mocking—and when he abruptly put his foot in my lap, I almost jumped. On his toes were a dozen warts, all of them hard to the touch and very brown. Can you make them go away? he asked me.

None of my mother's herbal treatments would have worked on warts, but when I was living with the Yguaces, I had seen the healer Chaubekwan cure a similarly afflicted child. Now, in imitation of Chaubekwan, I tied strings of yucca fiber on each toe and in my most confident voice I told the man that the warts would fall off on their own.

And it worked—the warts fell off in just three days. This time, I was not so surprised, because I had seen how a good cure, combined with just the right story and a little showmanship, could restore anyone's spirits. In payment for my services, Beaset gave me a very handsome satchel made out of a painted deer hide, a turquoise necklace, and three bone bracelets, all of them of very fine quality. These gifts I shared with my companions, just as they shared whatever they received with me. From the beginning, that had been our agreement: we would share all of our earnings.

IN THE MORNING, as my companions and I were packing up our belongings to return home, Beaset came to tell us that the Coachos had sent for us. I had already rolled up my black bear pelt and was trying to fit it into my leather satchel while, beside me, Oyomasot was tying up the bundle that contained our cooking pots and utensils. Kewaan and Tekotsen were folding the animal skins we used as bedclothes. A warm wind blew, rattling the feather-and-bone vestment that had been used in a dancing ceremony the night before and that still hung on a pole nearby. And who are the Coachos? I asked.

Allies of mine, Beaset replied. Their cacique is married to my sister. It would be an honor for me if you visited them as well.

He put his hand on my shoulder, as though we were old friends. At the base of his neck was a small scar, which pulsated now with the beating of the blood in his jugular vein. I could not help wondering how Beaset had sustained this injury and, considering its position, how he had survived it. I know not where the Coachos live, I said.

These women can guide you, Beaset replied with a smile. He pointed at three women, who were sitting on their haunches some distance away, watching us.

There is no need for guides, I replied. I was so unsettled whenever I was near Beaset that I was eager to be away from him and his servants. I think, too, that I was irritated to be forced into another long visit away from home. We can find the Coachos' camp on our own, I said.

Dorantes and Cabeza de Vaca did not mind this change in our plans, but Castillo reproached me. You should have consulted with me, he said.

Did you see the look on Beaset's face? I asked. How could I say no to him? If I acted quickly, it was only because I had no other choice.

The argument distracted all of us and after only two hours on the road, we realized that we had lost the trail. We found ourselves in a sandy stretch of land, as near a desert as we had seen in the new world, and we had no idea how to find a source of water. We wandered around for the rest of the day, all of us getting increasingly thirsty and nervous, until we noticed a hawk in the sky—we walked in the direction of its flight until we came across a spring.

There, we found the three Arbadao women, sitting on their haunches, as if they had been miraculously transported from their camp to this watering place. One of them, a large woman with a tattooed chin, began to refill our flasks for us, clicking her tongue at us as she did so. You should have waited for us, she said. You are not familiar with these parts and you will get lost. She continued scolding us for a while, telling us that she and her friends could have saved us a great deal of time and hapless searching. By then, everyone in our party was so tired that we all agreed to let the three Arbadao women guide us.

The Coachos lived in a village of nearly one hundred thatched-roof dwellings, set against a chain of mountains. The village was on the other side of a wide river, which the three guides insisted on crossing ahead of us, in order to announce our arrival to the Coachos and to tell them about the cures we could perform. Their recommendations must have been strong because, by the time we shuttled across the river, a large crowd was already waiting for us. It seemed as if the entire village of the Coachos, sick and healthy, young and old, had come out to get a proper look at the exotic healers. We walked to the square under a cacophony of overlapping joy cries and hooting calls, and another banquet was given in our honor that night.

The shamans among the Coachos carried rattles—dried calabashes filled with pebbles—that they used in all their healing ceremonies. I had not seen calabashes since I had left Azemmur and, not having come across any fields in this area, I asked these shamans where they had obtained them. They said the gourds come to them from the gods: once every year, when the great river floods, the gourds travel downstream and wash out on the banks. By now, I knew better than to tell the medicine men that these gourds must have fallen from their vines and been carried down the water, for it would have seemed to them a great sacrilege and, in any case, these fruits, like their vines, and the river, and everything else around it, came from God. So I accepted the gift of a rattle, and added it to the growing array of medicinal herbs, dressings, and tools that I carried everywhere. Little by little, my cures were becoming more elaborate and, perhaps not unrelatedly, more convincing.

Because the Coacho village was larger than others we had visited as healers, there were more than eighty people waiting to see us. Dorantes began to complain about the amount of work there was to do, especially since some of the Indians were not ill at all; they only wanted to get a closer look at the foreign shamans, or to receive a blessing, or to ask a question. All I hear is their endless talk, Dorantes said. Can they just tell me what they want and save me all the chatter?

These complaints were discreet, spoken in Castilian, and only when the four of us were alone, for fear that our hosts might overhear them and doubt our talents. Our shared experiences made fellows and allies out of us. We always consulted with each other and never openly disagreed about cures, because we knew that our comfort—nay, our freedom—depended on our success. I came to feel that Dorantes, Castillo, and Cabeza de Vaca were men I could trust and that they trusted me in return.

. . .

WITH OUR VISIT to the Coachos drawing to an end, we began, at long last, to make preparations to return to our homes with the Avavares. We stood side by side on the riverbank, trying to decide how many canoes we would need to carry us and the many gifts we had received across the river. Its water was dark and fast and, as I turned to say something, I noticed Cabeza de Vaca staring at it with a wistful look on his face. What troubles you? I asked him.

The Coachos told me that their neighbors want us to visit them, he replied.

We have to return home.

Why do we have to?

We cannot stay on the road forever. We live with the Avavares. That is our home now. We have wives and—

I have no wife.

Are you saying you want to travel from tribe to tribe like this?

It would not be a bad life, Cabeza de Vaca said. We would no longer need to worry about providing for ourselves, or fear for our safety among Indians, or be the subject of suspicious jokes or vicious taunts. If it involves traveling from tribe to tribe every few weeks, then that is a small price to pay for it.

Farther upriver, three women were washing animal skins. One of them raised up and wiped the sweat from her forehead with the back of her arm. Behind her, on the bank, a group of small children played in the dirt, rattles and marbles and scraps of deerskin scattered around them.

Dorantes had overheard my exchange with Cabeza de Vaca and now he came to stand between us. If we return to the Avavares, he said, we will have to return to our tasks sooner or later. Do you miss hunting? Do you miss picking prickly pears?

These things I did not miss, it was true, but I was surprised that both Dorantes and Cabeza de Vaca had come upon the same idea all at once. Neither of them had been keen on the tasks that the Avavares imposed upon them, but it could not have been sheer coincidence that they both wanted to become itinerant healers. How long have you two been talking about this? I asked, suspicion burrowing into my mind. I signaled to Castillo to get closer. Listen to this, I said. I repeated what Cabeza de Vaca had suggested, expecting Castillo to share my disagreement, but he only cocked his head to the side.

Well, Castillo said, regardless of which tribe we live with, we will have to move camp every few weeks. If we go back to the Avavares, who is to say that they will not tire of us as the others have tired of us before? So it seems to me that the better course is to work as traveling healers with different tribes.

I could feel my resolve weakening in the face of their arguments. Our wives had noticed our council and, when they found out what we had been discussing, they offered their opinions. Both Tekotsen and Kewaan sided with their husbands; they wanted to travel on to the next tribe. The more experienced we became, they said, the more gifts we would receive, and the more our reputation would grow. Satosol agreed with them, too.

But do you not wish to return to your home? I asked.

Satosol looked beyond me at the Coachos' village. Hunters were returning to the camp, carrying deer and fowl, and a group of young girls were setting up the fires for the farewell banquet and dance that was being planned for us that night. Look, he said, opening his arm wide, in a gesture that took in the entire scene before us. You can have this every night.

It was a good life—there was no denying that. We were providing comfort and service to people who needed it; we all enjoyed the many gifts that were bestowed upon us; and everywhere we were treated with respect. Though Oyomasot had refrained from taking sides, I knew that she had especially loved the time we had spent away from home—out here, she did not have to listen to her mother's complaints about her many idiosyncracies. And as for me, having tasted the heady sweetness of fame, I found it hard to forget it. Greed, that dreadful monster, ate what remained of my resolve.

When it was finally time for us to leave their village, the Coachos gave the Arbadao women gifts of deerskins, and they returned home content, but now the Coachos, too, wanted to have their own guides escort us to the next village. This custom seemed to develop almost overnight and without our realizing it. It was at once a relief and a burden—a relief because we no longer needed to worry about finding a good spring or a place to camp while we traveled, but also a burden because the guides always expected gifts from the tribe to which they had brought us.

As we moved from tribe to tribe over the next few weeks, we tried to put a stop to this custom, by telling our guides that we did not need their services. Once, I remember, we even left in the middle of the night, alerting only our families of our plans, but the guides caught up with us less than half a league away from where we had been camped. I think now that Satosol was encouraging the guides, for he thought that this way of traveling the land assured us an increasing fame—and increasingly large gifts. Dorantes tried to send Satosol back several times, but his wife, Tekotsen, would intervene and unfailingly prevail upon him to keep her brother with us. So we were powerless to put a stop to this custom.

BUT ONE RESULT of this new habit was that we received a warm welcome everywhere we went because the guides always preceded us, boasting of our talents. They began to call us the Children of the Sun, by which they meant that we were strangers from the east. The Children of the Sun had treated warts, sewn up wounds, or delivered a child whose mother had previously been cursed with stillborn babies. Over time, the name itself lent us greater power; it made us seem different from the local healers, more special, more successful. And the guides made our feats seem greater than they were: the Children of the Sun had raised a man from the dead or had returned to a lame woman the use of her hands. It was difficult to escape these elaborate tales, even though they were tales we had, unwittingly, helped start.

Over the next year, so many people wanted to join our traveling band that our numbers swelled from just twelve souls to twelve hundred. There came a moment when I realized that these new additions were no longer scouts or guides, but something else entirely—disciples and followers— and I grew worried. This will not turn out well, I said to Oyomasot one morning. All these people following us.

She had just come in from the river; her hair and face were still dripping with water. I pulled one of the blankets from the pile by the doorway and, standing up, wrapped it over her shoulders. You worry too much, she said, shaking her head. From her ears dangled new turquoise earrings.

Why should I not worry? This is dangerous, I said.

On the contrary, it is much safer to have so many people with us.

But can you not see that they all expect something? What will happen when I cannot deliver what they expect from me?

She slipped on a new garment, a dress with a fringed hemline that had been given to her as a gift, and began to wring what remained of the water out of her hair. You always manage to give them what they want, she said.

What do I give them? Tell me.

When you listen to people talk about their ailments, you always give them hope that they will get better.

It had not troubled me that I was offering hope to the people. But now it came to me that I was wrong. It was one thing to console a dying man or a barren woman, but another to offer them hope against things that could not be healed. Hope was what disciples wanted. But I was not a prophet and I had no need for disciples. Yet the look of admiration in my wife's eyes silenced my worry. How long will this last, I wondered.

As it happened, it lasted a long while—almost a year.

THAT SUMMER, we made our way across a range of mountains covered with iron slag and arrived at a river on whose banks grew thick pine and nut trees. On the other side of the water was something we had not seen in our years of wandering in this part of the continent: homes made of mud bricks, arranged in rows, and surrounded by large, cultivated fields. The sun gave the town walls a warm orange color, which contrasted against the wide green fields and the turquoise blue sky. It was as near a picture of my hometown as I could have drawn. My heart filled with longing, mixed with a simultaneous and contradictory feeling of belonging.

The town we had reached was that of a tribe who call themselves the Jumanos. They wore clothes made of dyed cotton and shoes fashioned out of animal hides. Their dwellings were large and sturdy, with mud-plastered walls and handsome doors. They cultivated corn, beans, and squash, and also hunted the horned cow, deer, and other game. Our stay with the Jumanos lasted only a few weeks, but it was among the happiest we had in this country. Sleeping in firm dwellings seemed to us an uncommon luxury. This, added to the Jumanos' treatment of us, made us, I believe, particularly conceited. Every request we made was granted immediately and uncomplainingly and, before long, we had gathered so many valuable things—skins, amulets, feathers, copper bells—that we needed porters to carry them for us when we set out again.

In early fall, we came to another large range of mountains. The guides who were with us now were well acquainted with the passes, however, and advised us that the best way to cross was to go in a southwestern direction. The valley that stretched out on the other side was a sea of green. Square fields of corn and beans pushed up against one another and, in the hazy distance, mud houses dotted the horizon. These were permanent dwellings, built with bricks, and some even had two or three levels, connected from the outside by means of tall wooden ladders.

For several months, we traveled through this valley, stopping for a few days in each village to perform our treatments and cures. The gifts we received became increasingly extravagant. One cacique, I remember, gave us three bags of beads and corral, two of turquoises, and so many animal hides that we had to leave some behind. When I protested that this was too much, he said that I should be grateful for the gifts I received, and that he himself would receive something when he took us to the next village. I felt as though my three companions and I were building a beautiful yet fragile tower from which we might tumble down at any moment.

In one of the villages we passed, a young boy who had been watching for our arrival was run down by the stampeding crowd, and broke both his right arm and right leg. Broken bones were Dorantes's specialty—he had seen enough of them in the trenches of his king's wars—and he set to work right away. Afterward, the boy hobbled around on his good leg, shadowing Dorantes and running errands for him. When it was time to leave, the boy's father, a trader by profession, gifted Dorantes five hundred hearts of deer. They were all perfectly carved, so that the holes from which the deer's arteries would have sprung were clean and neatly cut. They had been dried in the sun and now they were reduced to small dark things that made great rattling sounds in the bags the porters carried. This was why, when he spoke of that village later, Dorantes called it Corazones. Only later did it occur to me that my Castilian companion had returned to the habit of giving new names to old places.

18.

THE STORY OF CULIACÁN

It was midday and, although the sky was clear, it was very cold. Cabeza de Vaca and I were with a group of half a dozen of our followers, gathering plants and tree bark for our cures. I was trailing behind the others when a glint caught my eye. I should have looked away the moment I saw it: a shard of glass, nearly hidden from view by a thicket of cactus. I still do not know what compelled me to speak of it. I imagine it was my surprise at seeing glass in the middle of the wilderness. But maybe it was only my insensibility, my fateful insensibility, which my beloved father had tried in vain to wring out of me all those years ago. The word came out before I could consider its consequences. Look, I said.

Cabeza de Vaca dropped to his knees and retrieved the shard from under the cactus. Sunlight filtered through it, breaking up into many vibrant colors, but when he turned it around in his fingers, the rainbow effect disappeared. This is Castilian glass, he said.

It could have been left behind by Indian traders, I said. We had come across signs of Castilian presence before, but they had always been barterable things—beads that were used to adorn garments of animal skin or belt buckles that served as necklace charms.

Perhaps, he said. But just then, he spotted some bootprints and started walking, as if pulled away by some invisible string. The footprints disappeared for a while, and then reappeared again around a little green hill. I went with Cabeza de Vaca, though I was unconvinced about his search, and our companions followed behind, curious about this diversion.

It was already the afternoon when a column of five horsemen appeared before us, outlined against the darkening horizon. I watched their inexorable approach, their features growing clearer while my own feelings about them became more muddled. I was excited and nervous, curious and afraid, relieved and worried all at once, as if my heart could not settle on what it wanted to feel. At the head of the column was a man in a helmet, breastplate, and boots; the other four wore long-sleeved shirts, dirty breeches, and leather sandals. They sat their horses a short distance away but did not greet us. Mouths agape, they stared.

And why not, for we were quite a sight. Cabeza de Vaca and I wore thick furs on our shoulders and knee-length tunics made of deerskins. My braids hung down to my chest, my ears were adorned with turquoise earrings, and my walking staff was painted red and decorated with scarlet macaw feathers. As for Cabeza de Vaca, his hair fell in a yellow mass all around him, his beard reached his navel, and he carried, slung across his chest, a satchel filled with the herbs we had been collecting. Around us were six of our guides, clad in similar ways.

It was Cabeza de Vaca who broke the silence. What is your name? he asked of the horseman who seemed to be the leader.

Patricio Torres, the man said. From his accent, I could not tell what city in Castile he called home, though it seemed from his tone that he was a man accustomed to taking orders.

And what day is it? Cabeza de Vaca asked.

The fifth of January.

I mean, what year is it?

Fifteen thirty-six.

That makes it eight years, Cabeza de Vaca said to me.

After our shipwreck on the Island of Misfortune, we had kept track of time by counting the full moons, but many of the tribes with whom we had lived told the time by noticing the changes that seasons brought to their livelihoods—the ripening of roots, say, or the appearance of fruits and the migration of river fish—and we had fallen into a similar pattern. So we could never be entirely certain how much time had passed since our landing in La Florida.

Eight years, I said. Can it be that we have been here that long?

But this man Torres had confirmed it. I felt like one of the People of the Cave, awakening after many years of slumber into another world, a world they no longer knew. Where were we now? Had we finally reached the province of Pánuco or were we somewhere else? What had happened in the world during our absence? What news was there of all those we had left behind? So many questions pressed themselves against my lips that I did not know where to begin.

But who are you? Torres asked us.

Cabeza de Vaca turned back to him. My name, he replied, is Álvar Núñez Cabeza de Vaca. I was the treasurer of the Narváez expedition, which landed in Florida in 1528.

Torres opened his mouth to say something, but nothing came out.

Are you here with others? Cabeza de Vaca asked.

We are camped half a league this way, Torres said. He pointed south.

Take me there.

Sí, Señor. Torres held out his arm to Cabeza de Vaca and lifted him onto his horse, while I followed on foot with the rest of our party. The Indian guides asked me where we were going and I told them what I knew—we were going to meet some Castilians. My own emotions were too muddled now to make me of much use to them as anything but a translator. The smell of horses, to which I was no longer accustomed, was overpowering me. It brought back memories of the long march through the wilderness of La Florida, times and places I had thought were firmly in the past, behind me. As we walked, our shadows, six mounted and seven on foot, grew long and melted into each other.

It was almost dusk when we reached a river, on whose banks a dozen Castilians were gathered. They all stood up to get a look at our strange procession. After a moment, one of them detached himself from the others and came forward. What happened? he asked Torres. And then, without waiting for an answer, he turned to the fur-covered white man sitting on the horse and asked: Who are you?

Cabeza de Vaca replied: I am the royal treasurer of the Narváez expedition, appointed to this office by His Holy Imperial Majesty.

The mention of the king had the effect that Cabeza de Vaca seemed to have intended for it. The man briefly cast his eyes down, as if the monarch had traveled the depth of the ocean and the length of the continent to extract a proper acknowledgment. The Castilian officer had thick hair, thick eyebrows, and a thick blond beard, which he began stroking, in a gesture that looked more like a recent affectation than a nervous tic. And what is your name? Cabeza de Vaca asked him.

Diego de Alcaraz, at your service.

Cabeza de Vaca climbed down from the horse and came to stand next to me. It is getting late, I said. We have to set up camp here.

And who is el negro? Alcaraz asked.

This is Estebanico, one of the survivors of the expedition. The others are Capitán Andrés Dorantes and Capitán Alonso del Castillo.

Just then, one of the Indian guides asked me what the white men were saying to one another. When I replied in his language, the Castilian soldiers regarded me with the same look of wonder I had seen on their countrymen's faces eight years earlier, whenever they encountered the strange creatures of the new world. Nothing in their gaze suggested that I was a man like them rather than some exotic beast or other. It was only decorum that prevented them from reaching out to touch me, to see if I was real.

That night, Alcaraz offered us hardtack for dinner. With each bite of it, I tasted a little more of the past, its bitterness and sweetness both, startling flavors that transported me thousands of leagues away, first to Seville and then to Azemmur. Oh, Azemmur. I had dreamed of making contact with the old world, had waited years for this moment, had prayed for it many times, and just as I had given up and begun to make a life for myself in the new world, the Castilian soldiers had appeared, like jinns springing up from a lamp.

Now Cabeza de Vaca began telling the story of our arrival in La Florida and everything else that had happened to us on the continent since. We had all of us told this story dozens of times to our Indian hosts, but that day Cabeza de Vaca gave it another guise. In this account, he was no longer a conqueror who had fallen for lies about a kingdom of gold; instead he was the second-in-command of a fierce but unlucky expedition to La Florida. He had played no part in the decision to split the armada into two; now the villain was Narváez only. He had not taken on an Indian wife; now he had simply chosen to trade among the Quevenes and Charrucos for three years. He had not depended on his companions for his survival; now he cast himself as our leader, the man who had followed the footprints that led from the shard of clear glass to the Castilians' camp.

Although it was difficult, I tried my best not to resent Cabeza de Vaca's account of our adventure. I told myself that he had altered some of its details because he was the one who told the story—he wanted to be its hero—and also because he was mindful that his audience was made up of soldiers. These men knew well what it was like to receive orders you found foolish and yet had to obey, even at the cost of your life. They worried about how their faith might be tested in the new world, and loved to hear that a man could remain steadfast in the face of temptation. They saw themselves in the brave treasurer who had survived where others had died and now had led his men to salvation. So they offered the storyteller praise and prayers, and they refilled his cup with wine.

Then Cabeza de Vaca asked Alcaraz: Do you know what might have happened to the ships we left behind in La Florida?

No, Alcaraz replied. This is the first I have heard of your expedition. He himself had sailed to New Spain only three years earlier, he said, and was not familiar with people who might have journeyed to this continent before him, much less those who had been shipwrecked and lost so long ago. Now he asked: And your companions—the other hidalgos you mentioned—are they safe where they are?

Perfectly safe, Cabeza de Vaca replied. They are with a group of Indians very much like those you see here.

Alcaraz sipped from his metal cup. I must tell you, we have not seen any Indians at all in these parts for at least three weeks. In fact, we were preparing to return to Culiacán in the morning.

There are thousands of Indians here, Cabeza de Vaca said. But they have run away or hidden in the mountains.

Because they heard terrible stories about the soldiers, I added.

Alcaraz gave me a strange look. I know not what you may have heard from them, he said, but I would wager that it is nothing more than a string of lies and fabrications. He turned back to Cabeza de Vaca. Your friends, the two señores, you say they are safe with the Indians, but we will send for them.

Cabeza de Vaca and I glanced at each other; the stories we had heard about the Indians' enslavement were numerous, but they were too consistent to have been untrue. Still, he did not seem to think it wise or worthwhile to argue with his host just then, for he remained quiet.

LATE THE NEXT DAY, I returned to the Indian village where we had been staying, flanked by my Indian followers on one side and Patricio Torres and his men on the other. (Alcaraz had cajoled Cabeza de Vaca into staying behind, telling him that they still had much to discuss with one another.) The sky was gray and a fine, persistent drizzle had made its way through the fur and the deerskin I wore; I was shivering with cold by the time I made it to the village square. My appearance with bearded white men caused an immediate commotion—dozens of men, women, and children came out to greet me and to ask questions.

Who are these strangers?

Where is your brother?

Did you bring me oak bark?

Why were you gone for so long?

Oyomasot made her way through the small crowd. When I saw her, the kindness and intelligence in her eyes, I knew that everything would be fine. She put her hands in mine; they were so warm that they were an instant comfort to me.

I was worried about you, she said.

It was unlike her to speak so plainly of her feelings in front of others. I drew her closer. All I wanted now was to be alone with her. We ran into these soldiers, I said, nodding at the dusty Castilians.

Now Dorantes and Castillo came running through the square. Hombres! they said, and Gracias a Dios! and Míralos! There was much hugging and crying.

The soldiers looked relieved to see their countrymen in this Indian town and one of them finally stopped pointing his musket and instead slung it across his chest. Names were exchanged; inquiries were made about hometowns; details were traded. It was another hour or two before I had the soldiers settled in their own quarters and was finally able to speak to Dorantes and Castillo alone.

Imagine being found after all these years, Castillo said. I wonder if my mother is still alive.

We can all go home now, Dorantes said. If only my poor Diego had lived long enough to share our deliverance.

The memory of Diego's last day returned to me, the weight of his body in our arms as he bled to death in the Carancahuas' camp. His death had marked the beginning of our exile in the Land of the Indians. Now that our exile was ending, it was as if he were with us again in spirit. He was a good man, I said.

That he was, Dorantes said, blinking. When he spoke again his voice was hoarse: But you will be able to see your brothers, just as he foretold it.

I still remembered that morning on the raft, when Diego had comforted me by telling me that I would return to Azemmur someday.

Dorantes had remained quiet then, but over the last eight years, he and I had shared so much danger and so many hardships that our relationship had been transformed. A feeling of fellowship, which could not have existed between us on that raft bound us together now. We both wanted the same thing: to make our entire journey in reverse, return home to what remained of our families, and try to forget about Narváez and his expedition.

THAT NIGHT, I COULD NOT SLEEP. I lay on my pelts, listening to the crickets and the wind outside. I kept thinking about the trip back to New Spain, then to Seville, then to Barbary, and then, finally, to Azemmur. Thirteen years had passed since I had closed the blue door behind me one last time, with my name still on my mother's lips. The image of her in my mind had not dulled with the years; I could still see her in her house-dress, standing in the arched doorway, silhouetted by the light. Now I felt I was on the threshold of a new possibility—that I would fulfill a dream I had had for many years.

I turned to Oyomasot, and found her quietly watching me. She was on her side, her long hair undone, her shoulders bare under the blankets. I ran my fingers along her arm, all the way to the beauty mark at the base of her neck. When we get to New Spain, I said, I will get you a new—

We?

I smiled. Of course, we. You did not think I was leaving without you?

You did not ask what I wanted.

My heart skipped a beat. Do you not wish to go with me?

You misunderstand. I said you never asked.

I brushed her hair away from her shoulders. I am sorry. I should have asked.

She was quiet for a moment. You miss Azemmur, she said.

Yes, I said. And I have grown so used to the pain of missing it that sometimes I feel as though I have learnt to walk after an amputation. But now, Oyomasot, it is as if I can sense that severed limb again. Barbary is a country unlike any other. Its people are famous for their kindness to travelers and exiles—you would like them, I am certain of it. They form many tribes, speak different languages, worship in different ways. The soil is so rich that you could never count the varieties of fruit it produces. Cherries, figs, pears, pomegrenates . . .

Which one is the one you press into oil?

Olive. You can also eat it raw or pickled.

Oyomasot had always had an adventurous spirit—after all, she had agreed to this wandering life in the first place—and this new journey would mean that she would see a part of the world she had not seen before. I think, too, that she was curious about my family and my home-town, the people and places I had told her about, and which I longed to see once again. I imagined her standing on the rooftop of our home, watching the sunset over the Umm er-Rbi' River. It was a picture I had never conjured up in my mind before and its newness filled me with delight. I could take her on a walk along the crenelated walls of Azemmur all the way to the port, or maybe she would like to go to the souq, to watch acrobats, musicians, apothecaries, and storytellers. How would she get along with my mother? It would take them some time to get acquainted with one another, but they could grow to be friends.

I will go with you, she said.

But by the morning, there were already complications. Somehow the entire village had heard of our intention to leave, and our followers said they wanted to come with us. We spoke to them in their language, urging them return to their homes now, as we would be returning to ours. And some of them did. But most of them refused; they insisted that they had to follow the custom of taking us to the next settlement. Around the square, Alcaraz's soldiers were watching us, their hands resting on their weapons. We gave in, telling ourselves that, once our followers had reached Alcaraz's camp, and saw that there was no one there to reward them with gifts and banquets, they would return to their homes on their own. It was a mistake we—or at least I—would live to regret.

THE SHEER SIZE of our party made our journey slow. The elderly and the children required frequent rest stops, and a woman gave birth along the way, so that it took us nearly a week to reach the Castilians' camp. Our numbers impressed Alcaraz and he climbed on a boulder to survey the large camp that was being set up around him. Men were digging poles in the soft earth, calling for a hammer, spreading deerskins over the skeletons of their huts, laughing as they worked, but also, in the way of men the world over, keeping an eye on their neighbors to see who would be done first. Women were collecting firewood, filling their jars with water from the river, washing the old uncle who soiled himself along the way, grinding corn for the evening meal, running their fingers over the gum of a teething child, while keeping an eye on the other two. Children were digging in the dirt, running after each other, swimming in the river, splashing each other with water and then running to their mothers to complain about one another.

At last, Alcaraz came down from the boulder to greet Dorantes and Castillo properly. The breastplate he had worn a few days earlier had been replaced with a simple white shirt, which was tucked neatly in his breeches, and his belt buckle glimmered in the afternoon light. He asked for the names of the hidalgos, though he already knew them, and nodded politely as he heard their answers. Then he said: Cabeza de Vaca told me there were hundreds of Indians with you, but I confess I had a hard time believing him. I see now that I was wrong. He smiled, looked beyond us at the camp for a long moment, then cast his eyes once more on Dorantes and Castillo. Why do they follow you? he asked.

But I have already explained, Cabeza de Vaca replied. They think of us as doctors. They—

I know, Alcaraz said, interrupting him. But I want to hear from your friends here. What hold do you have over the Indians? Why do they run from us but not from you? They seem to be following you like—like devotees.

Castillo opened his mouth to speak, but Dorantes took hold of his elbow to silence him. In a cautious voice, Dorantes said: Any power we have over the Indians is granted by God our Lord. We make the sign of the cross upon them and pray for their health. That is all we do, and nothing more. They follow us of their own free will, because we do not seek to harm them in any way.

Alcaraz shot a dark look at Dorantes, as if he suspected that this answer had been rehearsed and he was not being given the whole story. He pursed his lips. We had not counted on staying in the wilderness so long, he said. We ran out of hardtack yesterday and we have at least ninety leagues to go to reach Culiacán.

You need not worry about food, Dorantes said. The Indians have their own and whatever else they need, be it meat or fruit, they can provide for themselves.

In any case, I said, the Indians will not be coming back with us to Culiacán.

Why not? Alcaraz asked. They followed you here. They will follow you there.

But what do you intend to do with them? I asked.

Bring them to the city, of course, Alcaraz said. That is my mandate.

Cabeza de Vaca intervened. I have tried to impress upon the captain that our Indians are kind and friendly, and that they can be convinced to join the Christian faith and the empire without enslaving them.

It seems to me, Alcaraz replied, that perhaps you have lived among the savages for too long. Your judgment of their abilities has been impaired.

Capitán Alcaraz, Castillo said. The nasal tone in his voice was deeper than usual. I agree with Cabeza de Vaca here. These Indians have followed us because they believe we will not harm them. We cannot force them to go anywhere.

Who is forcing them? They are following you of their own free will, are they not?

But we have given them our word that no harm would come to them, Castillo said. They are following us only to the next Indian settlement and then they will return home. He turned to Cabeza de Vaca and, in a voice filled with impatience, he asked: Did you not explain all this to him?

Cabeza de Vaca nodded wearily. He looked beyond us at the camp that was being set up.

But Castillo continued arguing with Alcaraz. We cannot take them to Culiacán, he insisted. We promised them they would not be enslaved.

Alcaraz chuckled. Well, Capitán, you should not have made promises you were not legally permitted to make.

This back-and-forth went on for a while, and then Cabeza de Vaca tried to appeal to Alcaraz's self-interest. He told the captain that this entire area had become barren because the Indians were fleeing the soldiers and that taking a few hundred more would only make it more difficult for future missions to find Indians. It would be better to let these people go and thereby to establish a feeling of trust between the empire and the Indians. But Alcaraz replied that he had already roamed these parts for too long in search of slaves, that he did not intend to let so much wealth go just when he had it in his hands, and that, whatever the merits of the gentlemen's arguments, he was merely complying with the law. By way of closing the discussion, Alcaraz added: And if you try to take these Indians away, I will report you to the alcalde.

Do you realize, Cabeza de Vaca said, that you are nothing more than a troop leader, while I am a royal treasurer? I outrank you.

Not out here, Alcaraz said. He put his hand on the pommel of his sword, a gesture at once imitated by two of his deputies. The others quietly leveled their muskets and arquebuses. Tell your Indians that we are leaving in the morning, he said.

Dorantes spoke for the first time. Please put down your weapons, he said. We are all hidalgos here. Surely we can come to an understanding.

The only understanding I have is this, Alcaraz said. I lost my brother to the Indians two years ago, I have been roaming the wilderness for nearly a month, and I am not going back without the slaves.

Very well, Cabeza de Vaca said. We will go with you. But I wish to inform you that once we reach Culiacán I will speak to the alcalde mayor myself and I will make sure that you are demoted.

We left Alcaraz where he stood and walked through the Indian encampment, intending to speak to our followers, but the soldiers followed us, making it impossible to hold a proper gathering. So we split our numbers and, each in our own way, we instructed our guides to tell the Indians that Alcaraz could not be trusted. We told them that we could not guarantee their safety and that they should all go back to their lands, where no harm would come to them.

But almost all the Indians said that they would not leave us, that we were the Children of the Sun, after all, and that they trusted us to protect them. We had lived with them for so long, and had given them so little reason to doubt us, that even when we told them not to follow us, they insisted on keeping the custom they had set for themselves.

We set out for San Miguel de Culiacán the next day. After marching southward for ninety leagues, we came upon a wide river, on whose bank a large party of armed soldiers, some forty or fifty of them, were waiting for us. They escorted us to the town. It was an outpost at the border of the empire, nothing more than a dusty garrison and half a dozen hastily built houses that faced each other across a wide road. It had been built next to a small Indian settlement, of the kind we had seen everywhere in the Land of Corn.

All the inhabitants of Culiacán had come out to get a good look at the four castaways who were rumored to have bewitched hundreds of Indians into following them. The alcalde mayor, Melchor Díaz, was waiting for us at the end of the road, dressed in his finest cotton and brocade. He had white hair and a broad face that would have been forgettable were it not for his extravagantly long mustache, whose ends curled upward toward his eyes. In the name of the Gobernador of Nueva Galicia, he said, it is my deep pleasure and privilege to welcome you to San Miguel de Culiacán. My men and I, and indeed everyone else in Culiacán, are at your service.

With these niceties out of the way, Díaz asked us who was our leader. Cabeza de Vaca stepped forward and said he was the surviving member with the highest rank. In the flowery language he knew so well, he thanked the alcalde for his warm welcome and for extending his hospitality to us. Then he offered gratitude to God for having led him to this outpost of the empire, where he could once again speak his native language and enjoy the companionship of civilized men, and where he might yet again serve His Holy Imperial Majesty. And now, he said, I would like to ask for your assistance in the matter of the Indians who accompany us.

As he listened to Cabeza de Vaca's relation of our dispute, Díaz stroked the ends of his mustache, twisting them in thick half-moons. Then he shook his head sadly. I must apologize for the behavior of Alcaraz, he said. I have told the settlers that the province of Nueva Galicia is losing all its Indians and that we cannot survive as a town if they keep selling slaves to the capital. We need our Indians here to till the land. But as you can see, we are here at the farther reaches of the empire, and it seems some of the men have trouble retaining the logic that is the privilege of their race, as well as the good manners our society requires of them. You must not trouble yourself with this matter any longer; I will have it taken care of presently.

Alcaraz stepped forward, but Díaz held up his palm as if to say he would hear nothing more about the matter. Then he ordered one of his deputies to take us to our quarters, where servants would be waiting for us.

I knew it, Cabeza de Vaca said as soon as we rounded the corner; I knew that the alcalde would understand.

But as we reached the bend in the road, we noticed that the soldiers had put all of our Indian followers in what looked like a horse run across from the garrison; the tents were being set up. This is probably the only place where they can accommodate them, Cabeza de Vaca said out loud, in answer to a question no one had asked, but all of us had thought.

We continued past the horse run to Culiacán's Indian settlement, where several dwellings had been assigned to us. I found Oyomasot unpacking our bundles and preparing our bedding, thick blankets that we used for winter nights. No sooner was I alone with her than I reported to her all the arguments with Díaz about our followers. Silently, she closed the door of our lodge and leaned back against it, as if she could not trust it to remain shut. Listen, she said, her voice barely above a whisper. I do not trust this chief. We should warn the people to leave.

I shook my head. I warned them already and yet they want to follow. We should never have allowed this custom to develop. I told you about this last year. I said that no good would come from having so many followers. There was a tone of blame in my voice that I was powerless to stop. My guilt, which had been bubbling inside me for a while, erupted now, its hot embers burning the person closest to me, the woman dearer to me than myself.

From somewhere far away came the sound of a trumpet, announcing dinner at the garrison. A horse clopped in the distance, then came to a sudden stop. Dogs barked.

Calmly, Oyomasot said: The people refuse to leave because you have never given them reason to fear. But perhaps they will heed your warning if I speak to them instead. I will tell them to leave the city.

But how will you speak to them without attracting the soldiers' notice?

She put her hand on my arm. I will speak to the women and they will pass the story on to all the others.

Be careful.

It was without hesitation that she left the house and disappeared into the night, charged with a mission in which I had already failed.

IN THE MORNING, Dorantes, Castillo, Cabeza de Vaca, and I were called to the alcalde's office. On our way there, we stopped by the horse run to visit the Indians. They told us that, having heeded Oyomasot's warning, two families had tried to leave a little before sunrise, but they had been caught by one of the soldiers and returned to the horse run. This had caused a great commotion among the people. But Cabeza de Vaca repeated all the assurances that the alcalde mayor had given him and promised to ask why the soldiers had prevented the Indians from leaving.

We went straight to the alcalde's office. Díaz greeted my three companions as if they were old friends, getting up from his desk and embracing them, and then nodding in my direction. I have just received a message from Nuño de Guzmán, he said. The governor of the province, I mean. He is very eager to meet you and to hear your amazing story for himself. Are you well rested? When might you be able to undertake the journey to the capital?

Soon, Cabeza de Vaca said. First, I must ask about the Indians. A dozen of them wanted to leave this morning. Why did your soldiers prevent them?

I know not, Señor Cabeza de Vaca. I will have to investigate.

But your soldiers stopped them from leaving.

I will have to hear from the soldiers first. I am sure you agree that we cannot know what truly happened until we have talked to the soldiers? Or do you now take the Indians at their word and discount what your countrymen have to say?

Cabeza de Vaca looked at the alcalde with great frustration, but in the end he nodded his agreement. Yes, he said. Yes, of course. Please talk to the soldiers.

The alcalde frowned. Are you still worried about the Indians being turned into slaves? He looked at all of us, seemingly wounded by our lack of faith. I apologize, señores. I forget that you have been gone for eight years. You have not heard that His Majesty, after conferring with His Eminence, has forbidden the enslavement of the Indians in New Spain. So, you see, you have nothing to worry about. It would be against the law. In fact, if I may share a little gossip with you. Here, he paused and lowered his voice to a whisper. Our governor, Nuño de Guzmán, who made a name for himself out here in the frontier, is said to be in great disfavor at the moment, precisely because of his vile treatment of the natives. We are entering a new era, señores. A new era for the empire. He sat back in his chair and stroked the ends of his mustache with evident satisfaction.

ON OUR WAY BACK to our quarters, an idea occurred to me. We should offer to buy the Indians from Díaz, I said. If Díaz could be compensated, surely he would agree to let the Indians go. (Now that I had returned to the old world, it seemed I had also set aside what I had learned in the new: that gold and freedom could not be traded.)

But the others agreed with my suggestion. So the four of us pooled all of our valuables together: five emeralds shaped into arrows, ten leather pouches of the finest quality, a small bag of oyster pearls, and other things that had been given to us as gifts. Cabeza de Vaca took them to Díaz the next day, but the alcalde said that the value of the gifts was far below that of the Indians, and that in any case there was no need for gifts because the Indians were not slaves and did not need to be freed. Conversations with Díaz always had a hint of the absurd about them.

The Indians in the horse run began to run out of corn and meat and, increasingly, they depended for their meals on whatever the soldiers gave them. Many of them were becoming sick with colds and even the fever. In all ways, they looked pitiful, but Díaz remained implacable. Cabeza de Vaca's arguments with him continued for two months, but they always ended with the same assurances that the Indians would be well treated and that they were not slaves. Then he sent us word that we could not tarry any longer in Culiacán—the governor of Nueva Galicia was expecting us.

19

THE STORY OF COMPOSTELA

Compostela was not the sprawling capital of Melchor Díaz's gossip: it had a church, a prison, a bathhouse, soldiers' barracks, and only forty dwellings, not all of which were completed. Still, its sidewalks were swept clean, and horse-drawn carts and carriages traveled along its main thoroughfare, testifying to its nascent farming and trade. The ten horsemen who had escorted us to the city led us directly to the town hall, where a sergeant and several deputies, standing under the tall wooden cross of its facade, were waiting for us. In spite of the warm spring sun, the sergeant wore a plumed cap, a long-sleeved doublet, and hose of immaculate white. Bienvenidos, he said.

The sergeant informed us that the governor, Nuño de Guzmán, had been called away on urgent business but that he would be delighted to have our company for dinner that very night. The governor had also ordered that comfortable lodgings be arranged for us: Dorantes, Castillo, and Cabeza de Vaca would stay at the hacienda of a certain Capitán Flores; Satosol, Kewaan, Tekotsen, and Oyomasot would be quartered together at the military barracks; and I would board in the sergeant's own home.

I followed the sergeant down the main road of the town, to a simple but elegant little house, with whitewashed walls and a red-tiled roof. The inner courtyard had a gurgling water fountain, much like the one Bernardo Rodriguez had built for himself in Seville all those years ago. I could almost hear the squeals of Isabel as she chased Sancho and Martín around it, trying to catch the edge of their shirts, then shrieking that she had won and that it was her turn to be chased. The memory made me uncomfortable, a feeling that was exacerbated by the stifling heat in the room that had been assigned to me. I tried to open the windows, but after wrestling with them for a while, I realized that the knob had long ago rusted in place. I lay down on the bed; the mattress was too soft, I decided, and I would have to spend the night on the tiled floor. As for the pillow, it was a luxury I had forgotten existed and I wondered what it would feel like under my neck once again.

After a few moments, I left the sergeant's house to go see Oyomasot at the military barracks. The sentinel raised his musket when I approached, but immediately lowered it again when he saw that it was I. The women's quarters turned out to be nothing but a large pantry, from which the clanging of the pots and pans in the kitchen could be heard. There were no beds or windows, but uncomplainingly each of the women had set her things in one of the corners. Satosol was not so accommodating. Before I had even had a chance to greet him, he asked me, Why am I quartered here?

We are guests, I said. We have to take whatever lodgings are offered to us.

He sniffed, then looked through the open door at the other side of the barracks, where some Indians, dressed in deerskin shirts and cotton breeches, were chatting amiably with the guards. By then, the sun had begun its afternoon descent to the west, and on the grounds the watchtowers cast long, dark shadows.

I turned my attention to Oyomasot. How are you?

Tired, she said.

It was not in her nature to complain, and I searched her face for signs of illness, but saw only exhaustion and worry. I wished we could be alone, so that the others would not hear our conversation. I wanted to tell her that the journey would be long and that there would be moments when it would seem arduous, but that it would come to an end before long and in the end we would be home. I can make you an infusion, I offered. A bit of rosemary might restore your spirits.

Why can I not stay with you? she asked.

Guzmán forbade it. He forbade all of us from having our wives in our lodgings. The customs are different here.

She looked down at the coverlets she had been folding, and which had been given to us by the Indians of the Land of Corn. They were blankets

of fine cotton, decorated with vibrant patterns that told their makers' stories, whether real or imagined. Ancestors had crossed the Shadow Waters
and settled into this continent; some of them had tethered themselves to
the land, while others had freely followed its rhythms wherever they led.
After a moment, she said: Maybe this new chief will accept the gifts the
first one refused.

We intend to make him the same offer.

Is he not more powerful?

Yes, Guzmán is much more powerful than Díaz. He governs the whole
of the province.

So he can free the people we left behind?

He can, I said. But I know not if he will.

Why would he not listen to you?

My voice grew soft. Things are different here, I said.

Oyomasot looked at me with dismay. For nearly as long as she had
known me, I had had the power that came with healing: when I spoke,
people listened. But here, in New Spain, my words did not hold the same
value, and neither, it seemed, did those of my companions, for none of
them had yet been able to secure the Indians' freedom. We were no
longer healers. We were merely petitioners, and we were as likely to be
indulged as we were to be rebuffed by the governor.

We will talk to Guzmán, I promised. We will not give up.

A moment later, my three companions arrived. The house where they
were staying was not far from the barracks, which meant that Dorantes
and Castillo would be able to come see their wives whenever they wished.
Leaning against the doorjamb, Cabeza de Vaca added that Guzmán would
be sending food for the women, but that the four of us were expected for
dinner at the hour of vespers. And, he said with a wry smile, he wants us
to take baths.

IN THE BATHHOUSE, servants were already waiting for us, with tubs
filled and braziers lit. We discarded our loincloths, earrings, necklaces,
anklets, and amulets, and stepped inside the baths. What a miracle an
iron basin was! Warm water embraced me and, within moments, I felt
lulled into indolence. I closed my eyes, but the first image that came to
me was of the Indians in their hundreds, penned in the horse run at Culiacán, like lambs for the slaughter of Eid. If I had not said anything about

the shard of glass in the wilderness, perhaps those Indians would still be free. Was I, however obliquely, responsible for their fate? Would I ever be able to stir a finger without bringing harm to somebody? And what about me in all of this? No bondsman would have been given a room in the sergeant's own home, I knew, and yet no free man would have been separated from other free men, either. So who was I in New Spain?

I opened my eyes. In the dimly lit bathhouse, with the steam from our tubs rising in the air, the faces of my Castilian companions were barely discernible. Next to me, Dorantes splashed water around like a child and cried out, My God, it feels so good. As I began to scrub myself with Castilian soap, I kept my eyes trained on him, the way I used to when we were on the ship that brought us across the Ocean of Fog and Darkness. I was trying to divine his intentions—a foolish exercise, but one for which I now had ample time. We had had to depend on one another so often during the last eight years that it seemed to me we could never go back to the way things had been. But would he make legal and official in New Spain what was tacit and obvious out there, in the Land of the Indians?

Wrapped in a towel, I drank the juice of oranges grown in a Spanish orchard here in Compostela, their tangy taste lingering on my tongue long after I had finished my cup. A barber was waiting, one hand holding short-bladed scissors and the other resting on the back of a high chair. As Dorantes sat in it, I watched him transform into a new man, his braids cut off, his beard trimmed, his hair perfumed with special oil. Except for the color of his skin, a light almond, he looked like all the other Spaniards in the city now.

Then it was my turn. Large tufts of hair fell to the ground under the barber's scissors, yet an unaccountable heaviness settled upon my heart. It is hard to describe it, but the nearest I can come is that it was like coming up for air and finding yourself in a fog. Dorantes held up a mirror for me. In it, I saw a stranger—an older version of me, without the reserve that I had worn like a garment for many years.

Our clothes were brought in: undershirts, breeches, doublets, capes, shoes, handkerchiefs. The servant said they came from Guzmán's personal wardrobe. The pilled fabric made my skin itch and my trousers were hopelessly constricting, so that I walked around the bathhouse with a strange, uneasy gait.

The shirt is too tight around the chest, Dorantes complained, before taking it off altogether.

But the servant cleared his throat. Señores, the governor's instructions were quite specific. You cannot be seen naked on the streets of Compostela.

THE GOVERNOR'S DINING ROOM was musty and dark, lit only by a pair of candelabras that sat on either end of a long table, but he moved about the room with great ease, pointing to each of the pictures on the wall and telling a little anecdote about it.

This is a painting of the Nativity, he said, done in the Italian style. I so love the artist's contrast between light and dark. And here is a portrait of the king—I was once his bodyguard, you know, but this was years ago when I was a young lad. This tapestry here is from the México campaign; it once hung in Moctezuma's palace. But sit, señores, sit.

Then Guzmán nodded to his servants and the food was brought forth— vegetable mixes, roasted chicken, and bread that tasted almost exotic to us after so many years without wheat. He raised his glass in honor of us, the four survivors of the Narváez expedition, giving great thanks to God for our miraculous rescue, and welcoming us once again to the province of Nueva Galicia. Tell me, he said, is it true that the Indians follow you wherever you go?

Don Nuño, it is more complicated than that, Cabeza de Vaca said. We have lived with them for so long, dressing as they do, eating as they do, and speaking as they do, that they have come to trust us. We were able, thanks to the great favor of God our Lord, to be of some service to them in ordinary matters, but which the Indians came to think of as extraordinary. For this reason, each tribe escorted us along the way to the next tribe. We lived among them in peace. It is my belief, Don Nuño, that these people can join the empire through peaceful means.

Is that right? And what are these tribes called? ·

There are so many. We lived the longest with the Avavares—they are a tribe of great fishermen, who migrate during the seasons of nuts and prickly pear. Then we visited the Maliacones, the Susolas and the Coayos, and others that call themselves the Arbadaos and the Cultalchulches. These are nomadic tribes, but once we crossed the mountains, we began to see tribes like the Cuchendados and the Jumanos, who live in permanent settlements. All of the Indians, without exception, are skilled with their bows and arrows, though of course none of them could offer much resistance to even the smallest of our troops. Which is why I want to reiterate that it is possible to establish imperial settlements through peaceful means.

Castillo's face was already flushed from the effect of the wine and, when he spoke, his voice was high. I agree, he said. The tribes we visited live in sophisticated towns and decide their affairs by consultation. I think Cabeza de Vaca makes a good point about the use of force.

My companions wanted to convince the governor that peaceful conquest was possible, but my experience suggested otherwise. Azemmur had already witnessed a bloodless conquest, and the outcome had been just as bleak as if the cannons had been fired. So I felt I had to speak. The Indians, I said, are like people everywhere else in the world. They are born and die, and in between they live lives according to their own laws and customs: they worship God in their own way, find joy in raising their children, and when the moment comes they mourn their dead. They do not seek war, but they will not retreat from it if it is brought to them. All they wish is to carry out their own lives in peace.

Yes, yes, Guzmán said, but do they have metals of any kind?

It was Dorantes who answered the governor. The Jumanos have copper bells, he said. Beautiful little things, etched to look just like a human face.

But those do not count, Castillo said quickly. They are likely from the south. The truth is that we did not see any metals. The Indians of the north have no mines, no gold, no silver that we could see. Most of the tribes we lived with were quite poor.

I see. And would you be able to draw me a map of the area?

Silence fell on the table.

The governor looked around him in astonishment. Have I spoken out of turn? he asked. Why is everyone quiet all of a sudden?

Cabeza de Vaca asked: Why do you need a map?

I am the governor of Nueva Galicia. It is my charge to be familiar with the lands I am administering for the empire.

Don Nuño, Cabeza de Vaca said. Nueva Galicia ends where the mountains begin. The tribes live on the other side of that range.

The governor smiled. All of this terra firma is part of the empire. I am the representative of the Crown here. My duty is to pacify any savages that could pose a threat to us.

But that is what I have been explaining all this time, Cabeza de Vaca said. The Indians are no threat at all. They can be convinced to join our faith without any intervention. They are a kind and peaceable people.

Cabeza de Vaca's hands were gripping the arms of his chair and his knuckles had turned white. I remembered suddenly how, years earlier, he had chosen to bring his books of poetry on the long march to Apalache; he seemed to believe that it was always possible to appeal to the nobleness of men.

You will find, esteemed señor, Guzmán replied, that even those who are most biased in favor of the Indians will not deny that they kill their own infants, treat their women like beasts, practice sodomy, and worship stones. If you wish to defend them, for whatever mysterious reasons of your own, then by all means do, but I do not think that convincing us that they are a kind and peaceable people is a winning proposition. Then he stood up from the table and asked if we would join him in the parlor.

We had hoped to bring up the question of the Indians who had been left behind in Culiacán, rather than the subject of the Indian tribes in the north, but now it became painfully clear that there would be no point in doing that with someone like Guzmán. There was something coarse and obdurate about him, something that could never be moved by the power of words.

I was forced to report this conversation to Oyomasot later that night, when I went to visit her in the barracks pantry. We spoke to Guzmán about the people, I said. The words came out with difficulty, punctuated by false starts and long pauses. And as I spoke, the expectation on her face slowly turned into disappointment and shame.

The men and women who had put their faith in us, who had put their lives in our hands, would be left in Culiacán for good. The awe that once colored my wife's eyes whenever she gazed at me began to disappear. Slowly, I was returning to what I had always been: a man. Not a shaman, but only a man.

OVER THE TWO WEEKS THAT FOLLOWED, Guzmán met with each of us in turn, in long sessions about which we later gossiped well into the night. Cabeza de Vaca, Dorantes, and Castillo were forthcoming about the strange mores they had witnessed while living with the Indians, but Guzmán was not the least bit interested in customs or habits; his sessions always ended with his request that they draw him a map. Having heard of Guzmán's taste for lucre—and mindful, too, of the true value of such knowledge—each one of them gave a different reason for why he could not draw a map. Cabeza de Vaca said that, being the royal treasurer, he was bound by duty to report anything he knew to the highest authorities in New Spain, before he could share it with anyone. Dorantes said that he had spent much of his time as a captive, and that his thoughts had been focused on escaping these lands, rather than taking notes for any future reports or maps. Castillo took the stance that he was the third-ranked survivor of the expedition and could not go against the wishes of the other two. I was the last to be questioned.

Guzmán rose from his desk to shake my hand and offer me a seat, then poured me a cup of something dark and hot. Chocolatl, he said. It is popular down in México.

I had never tasted anything like it—it was strong and bitter—and for a moment I felt out of sorts.

They tell me you are a native of Barbary, Guzmán said.

That is true.

You know, I went there once. I was on a ship that docked in the port of Arzilah for two days. A beautiful town.

I would imagine so, I said, though I have never seen it.

Dorantes must be a good master. You look very healthy and well. He told me that you were quite the scout. That you spoke to all the caciques, that you translated for them, that you found food and shelter whenever they needed to be found.

Señor Dorantes flatters me, I said.

And modest, too! Dorantes is fortunate. I have never been so fortunate with slaves myself, for whatever reason. In any case, since you are by all accounts an exceptional member of your kind, I want to see if you can draw me a map.

On the desk between us, he unscrolled a fragile piece of paper, upon which was drawn in thin, trembling lines, the shape of a continent. The southern part of the territory was covered with names for cities, rivers, mountains, and plains; the northern part was an unmarked, narrow mass. With his forefinger, he tapped the blank area. Here, he said.

I looked up from the map. Don Nuño, as you yourself said, I am merely a slave. Whoever heard of a slave who can read or write, much less draw maps?

Guzmán heaved a sigh. Come now. I know you cannot read or write, but I am sure you know more than you are letting on. Here is a map of the province. These are the mountains, see? Imagine that you are standing in front of these mountains. Can you point to the best place to cross them?

Don Nuño, I do not know how to read a map.

Let us try this another way, he said. His speech slowed down now, so that each word was spoken very carefully. How far past the mountains is the first Indian town? Five days? Seven? Fourteen?

I am not sure, I said. I did not pay attention to time.

Guzmán stared at me for a long time. Then he put down his cup. You are following your master's lead, I see. Very well, he said. Return to your quarters. To the guard who stood by the door he said: Bring me the Indian.

The Indian Guzmán wanted to question was Satosol, Dorantes's brother-in-law. How they managed to communicate with each other, I never knew. Guzmán did not ask me to translate for him, so I imagine he must have had his own interpreters. When Satosol finally emerged, he did not go back to the women's quarters, where we were waiting for him, but to a different room, on the second floor of the barracks. Good for him, Dorantes said. At least he got the old man to give him separate accommodations.

WE WERE SITTING on a blue blanket, outside the women's quarters, the next morning. Plates of bread, olive oil, and dried squash lay between us. The sun had not yet reached this part of the barracks courtyard and we buttoned up our doublets and cloaks. Then a young soldier with a patchy beard arrived with a message from Guzmán: we were to leave Compostela the next day because the viceroy was expecting us in México. Even after delivering his message, the recruit stood there, watching us with curiosity. Cabeza de Vaca grew irritated. What are you waiting for? he asked. The soldier clicked his heels and ran off without another word.

Satosol chose this moment to announce that he would not be going with us to México. I have gone far enough from home, he said.

Dorantes laughed. Since when did you care about straying away from the tribe?

I never wanted to come here, Satosol said. You were the ones who wanted to come to this city.

It is Guzmán, Cabeza de Vaca said. He convinced him to be a guide.

Can you not see that he is only using you? Dorantes asked. He wants you to show him the way to the Indian settlements in the Land of Corn.

Why do you care? Satosol said.

What did he give you? Dorantes asked. Turquoises, is that it?

What if he did?

He is going to make slaves of your people.

You left people behind in Culiacán. What did you think would happen to them?

That is not the same. The alcalde left us no choice.

You had a choice. You chose to leave.

All morning, we tried to get Satosol to change his mind, but neither plea nor reason worked, nor even threats. I had not brought up the subject of my legal bondage with Dorantes but I felt unsettled enough by Satosol's cold observations that I needed some assurances. Dorantes, I said, as we left the barracks. When we get to the capital, we should speak to a notary.

What do you mean?

I will need a letter from you so that I can travel home unhindered.

Estebanico, Dorantes said, putting his arm around my shoulders, I do not even have the bill of sale any longer. It was on the ship. You are one of us, you know that. It is a long way to México, but once we make it there, I will find a notary to draft a document declaring you a free man.

WITH THIS PROMISE I left Compostela for México. Our first stop on the long march south was Guadalajara, a small town that was established by Nuño de Guzmán and that, like Compostela, he had named after a city in Spain. I could not understand this habit of naming settlements after Spanish cities even when, as in the case of Guadalajara, that city had received its name from those who had conquered it. In Arabic, the name Guadalajara evoked a valley of stones, a valley my ancestors had settled more than eight hundred years earlier. They had carried the disease of empire to Spain, the Spaniards had brought it to the new continent, and someday the people of the new continent would plant it elsewhere. That was the way of the world. Perhaps it was foolish to wish that it were different. But as for me, I could not continue to be involved with conquest. I would go to México and there I would get a contract that made legal the freedom that God had bestowed on me at birth.

20.

THE STORY OF MÉXICO-TENOCHTITLÁN

Tenochtitlán was a new beginning. This was the city where I could at last secure passage on a ship bound for the old world. In a few weeks, I would travel across the Ocean of Fog and Darkness, return to Azemmur, and begin to repair the thread of my life where it had been broken. Thoughts of this future filled me with delight, which became intertwined for me with the pleasures of the magnificent city of the Aztecs. Even now, if I close my eyes, I can recall the heat of the sun that first day in Tenochtitlán, the blue of Lake Tezcuco, the rise of the pyramids, and the promise of home.

On the morning after our arrival, my companions and I were brought to the back door of the cathedral, where a thin priest was waiting for us. He had stiff blond hair that was parted down the middle, and wet eyes that seemed to take great offense at everything they beheld. He led us into a small office, where he ordered us to take off the Spanish clothes we had received in Compostela and to put on the loincloths and deerskins he had brought for us. But why, we asked. Bishop's orders, he replied. He leaned against a bookshelf and did not avert his eyes while we changed. Then he handed us necklaces, earrings, and amulets. Where he had procured them, I did not know. They were not from any of the tribes with whom we had lived.

Once he was satisfied with our costumes, the priest marched us down the long hallway of the cathedral. Cabeza de Vaca was to enter the great hall first, he said, followed by Dorantes and Castillo; this servant of God, Mustafa ibn Muhammad, was to enter last. From behind the doors at the end of the hallway, I could hear the low murmur of a large audience, occasionally interrupted by the sudden burst of a laugh, the wail of a child, or the tentative notes of an organ. The priest gave us a final, appraising look, readjusting a crooked feather on Dorantes and tightening the snakeskin belt on Castillo. At last, there came the sound of a ceremonial tune on the organ. This is our signal, the priest said. When the music stopped, he opened the doors for us and stepped aside.

We entered the cathedral under the curious eyes of four hundred men and women, some of them standing on their toes to catch a glimpse of the survivors they had heard so much about. But since reality can never compete with imagination, their murmurs were soon replaced by a surprised silence. Here and there, I noticed, a brown or black visage disrupted the firmament of white faces, though everyone, regardless of color, was dressed in formal Castilian clothes. The light in the hall came from high windows, only a few of which had been fitted with stained glass; the others were still covered with drapes. And the murals of the church were not completed yet, so that a few of the figures looked like the half-formed shapes of a dream.

The bishop stood at the end of the aisle, watching us with all the benevolence his title of Protector of the Indians required. Juan de Zumárraga had arrived in New Spain ten years earlier, a simple friar who had not even received consecration as bishop, but he had managed to outwit all his rivals and formally receive his title from the king. With his left hand, he pointed to where we should be seated: in the front row, next to the viceroy himself.

That day was the feast of Yaaqub ben-Zebdi, whom the Spaniards call Santiago de Apóstol, so the service was particularly long and elaborate. My thoughts wandered back to that old cathedral in Seville, where I had received the name the Castilians called me. Back then, the priest had made the sign of the cross upon me and swiftly dispatched me into a life of bondage. What did Obispo Zumárraga intend to do? Much to my surprise, he began his sermon by telling the story of our journey across the continent.

My brothers and sisters, he said, the four men you see here today are the only survivors of the Narváez expedition. For eight years, they were deprived of all worldly comforts and material wealth. They were poor, hungry, and alone, but selflessly they served the Indians and tended to their ailments. I cannot help but think of Saint Francis. Consider: just as Saint Francis was taken away from his companions in Perugia, so, too, were these four Christians separated from their people in Florida. Just as he nursed the lepers in Assisi, so, too, did they attend to the Indians and pray for their souls. Like him, they walked barefoot in the wilderness, wearing only the animal skins you see on them today, preaching the word of God where it had never been heard before.

Zumárraga was a stout man with sparse brown hair, and close-set eyes that darted around the hall as he spoke to the congregation. He had the tone, half-weary and half-indignant, of a man who had long been in possession of a great truth, even if others were too blind to recognize it. There was no room, in his weariness, for four heroes who were guilty of thefts and, through their silence, accomplices to pillaging, beatings, and rapes. Nor was there room, in his indignation, for Indians who did not wish to be ruled by outsiders. Listening to him, I began to understand why he had dressed us in loincloths and why he was making us sound so pure. He, too, wanted to tell the story of our adventure in his own way.

Praise God, Zumárraga said. His voice grew louder now, reaching high above the altar and bouncing back down from it into the great hall. Praise God, for there is a lesson here for those who heed it. A few people in New Spain, though their hearts are devoted to the Lord, treat the Indians in ways too horrible to recount. This is painfully true of those at the outer reaches of the empire, who live so far away from the counsel of the Church. But these four Christians you see here today have been sent to remind us of the right path. We should preach the gospel of peace to the Indians. We should treat them with kindness. We should teach them the values of hard work and forbearance. And they will flock to us, just as the multitudes in Italy flocked to Saint Francis.

So the bishop wanted us to be instruments of a greater mission: converting the Indians to Christianity without the threat of soldiers' muskets. But I was struck by the irony of his using me as a model for such a mission. What would he think of what I had really done? I had taken the Indians' medicine and made it my own. I had adopted their ways of dress, spoken their languages, and married one of their women. I was as far removed from the bishop's idea of a proper Christian as any Indian was. Standing in that half-finished church, surrounded by statues of prophets and saints, I wondered why God created so many varieties of faiths in the world if He intended all of us to worship Him in the same fashion. This thought had never occurred to me when I was a young boy memorizing the Holy Qur'an, but as I spent time with the Indians I came to see how limiting the notion of one true faith really was. Was the diversity in our beliefs, not their unity, the lesson God wanted to impart? Surely it would have been in His power to make us of one faith if that had been His wish. Now the idea that there was only one set of stories for all of mankind seemed strange to me.

Let us pray, Zumárraga ordered. For a moment, the cathedral was plunged into silence. The air had steadily grown hotter and now the smell of burning candles made it stifling. I tried to resist the temptation, but I could not: I sneezed. Again. And again. Three times. My eyes filled with tears from the force of the emissions. Cabeza de Vaca leaned forward in his seat and frowned in my direction, but I was powerless to stop myself. My head fell back of its own volition and the sneeze came out with even greater force. A few people around me coughed. In different parts of the hall, pews and kneelers creaked, but the sneezing continued. I felt as if the entire congregation's eyes were on me.

Finally, the Amen came and the doors were opened. People filed outside, although many of them huddled at the entrance, waiting to get a closer look at the four survivors of the Narváez expedition. I was desperate for fresh air. I tried to make my way to an opening on the right, but my foot hit something—no, it was someone: an old Indian man with a branded face and a missing arm, who was shaking coins in a bowl, waiting for alms. I almost fell over him, but was pulled back just in time by Castillo.

Then a trumpet was sounded and the entrance slowly cleared of all the devout and the curious. My companions and I advanced toward the front steps. No city square I had ever seen was quite as large as the one in Tenochtitlán, no streets leading to it were so wide and so perfectly aligned, no buildings surrounding it so majestic. That day, it was filled with crowds of people waiting for the festival of Santiago de Apóstol to start. Stages had been set at the four corners, each presenting a different play, and in the center of the square two teams of men, some dressed as Moors and others as Christians, held on to their lances as they prepared to joust. The viceroy raised his arm to signal the start of the festivities, and the city erupted with joyful noise.

Beyond the square lay the famous pyramids, their brown peaks grazing against the blue sky. I thought of the Egyptians, the Sumerians, the Babylonians, of all those who had built empires and left behind an imposing trace of their passage in the world. To be present in a place where one empire was ending and another was rising made of me a privileged witness. Yet I did not try to keep a record of the moment. All I wanted was to return to the city I called home.

BEHIND HIS PALACE, the viceroy had built a guesthouse, a small edifice hidden from the street by a row of leafy trees. It was in that little house that Oyomasot and I stayed while we were in the capital of México. Our bedroom had whitewashed walls, blue-curtained windows, and a four-post bed that remained untouched because neither of us felt comfortable sleeping so high above the floor. That morning, our third in the capital, Oyomasot tried on the Spanish dress that had been left for her inside the walnut chest at the foot of the bed. The dress was made of green cotton, with puffed upper sleeves and a tasseled girdle. Smoothing the skirt down with her hands, she asked: How does it look?

You have to close the back, I said. I had been watching her from the armchair; now I stood up to tie the girdle around her small waist and button up the dress. I had never seen her wear green, but the color suited her well. Still, when I drew her close to me, she resisted. I glanced over her shoulder at her reflection in the windowpane and was met by a look of sheer panic.

I cannot breathe, she said.

I loosened the tassel over the girdle. Better? I asked.

No, it hurts, she said. It hurts.

That is how the dress is worn.

But how do their women breathe?

It was not a question I had ever asked myself. I was a thirty-eight-year-old man, so I had had plenty of time to consider the world through the eyes of someone else; yet that someone had rarely been a woman. What was it like to wear a girdle for the first time? To feel your chest crushed under metal boning? To walk with your feet tangled in the hems of your dress? I felt keenly aware of the sacrifices my wife was making for my sake, and keenly grateful. I checked the girdle, but I could not loosen it any further. It is only for a short time, I said by way of apology. You will not have to wear these clothes for very long.

There was a knock on the door, and an Aztec servant came in to inform us that Señor Dorantes and the friar had arrived. Oyomasot took small, careful steps toward the door, as if she were not sure she could trust herself, and together we walked down the corridor. The living room was large, with a peaked ceiling and tall windows, but the spaciousness they conveyed was counteracted by dark brown walls and damask-covered armchairs.

Dorantes and the friar were standing together in the middle of the room, admiring the oil portrait that hung above the fireplace. The painting was a likeness of King Carlos, the son of Felipe el Hermoso and Juana la Loca, a long-faced man with small eyes and a receding hairline. He was the emperor of parts of the old world and most of the new, and a defender of the Catholic faith besides. His subjects, one charged with conquering and the other with converting, looked on him with appropriate awe. I cleared my throat. Ah, Estebanico, Dorantes said. There you are. The viceroy invited us to dinner.

Today?

No, next week. A formal celebration of our return.

Where are the others?

Cabeza de Vaca is still in his quarters at the palace, writing letters. Castillo was coming with me, but one of his neighbors from Salamanca called in on him—here, at the other end of the world! Can you believe it?

The door opened again, and Dorantes's and Castillo's wives walked in, both of them wearing ill-fitting gray dresses. Their glossy hair was pinned low on their necks and covered with black lace. Kewaan had a surly look about her, but Tekotsen smiled brightly at her husband. Good morning, she said in the Avavare tongue.

Good morning, Dorantes replied. Then he averted his eyes and switched to Spanish. This is Father Herminio, the teacher.

A pleasure to meet you, Father Herminio said with a nod. He was very tall, well built, and carried himself with confidence. Were it not for the dark red stain on his right cheek, he would have been handsome. Now he sat down on the sofa and, with a wave of the hand, he invited all the wives to sit around him.

Oyomasot can manage some Spanish, Dorantes informed him.

Very well, Father Herminio said. You can leave us now.

The friar's abrupt dismissal of us made Dorantes want to say something sharp, but he seemed to think better of it. Together we stepped out, through the glass doors, into the courtyard. The long terrace lay before us, hot and white with sunlight. Lavender hedges grew along the right wall, their pale purple flowers humming with bees. Along the far wall was a shaded gallery, whose railings were covered with white bougainvillea. There is even an orange tree here, Dorantes said, pointing to the fruit tree by the left wall.

It looks just like a Sevillian home, I said.

We were quiet for a moment, both of us suddenly reminded of distant days in Castile, long before either of us had journeyed through the Land of the Indians. Dorantes had been a young nobleman in possession of a good fortune, which he had risked in order to find gold and return home covered in glory. Now he was a penniless man, freshly arrived in a strange city where he knew no one and where he was not sure whom to trust. As for me, I had been the slave of a fabric merchant, traded in payment for a gambling debt, and I had lost far more than a good fortune. But, I thought, all of that was in the past now.

How much will we need for the passage to Seville? I asked.

Fifteen thousand for each of us, I should think. The emerald arrowheads will not cover everything.

We have the turquoises.

True. But we also have to pay for our transport to the port of Veracruz.

Again, we fell into a long silence. We were both thinking of the treasures we had brought with us from the Land of the Indians—not just the emeralds and turquoises, but also the furs, pelts, parrot feathers, leather purses, seashell necklaces, bone ornaments, and even deer hearts. These treasures had seemed to us incomparable when we lived in the Land of Corn, but they paled next to the elaborate jewels all around us in Tenochtitlán. Still, in the public squares of the city, there were markets for every kind of merchandise and I told Dorantes that I would make inquiries about the value of our wares. I will go this afternoon, I said.

And I will see if I can get a better price for the emeralds, he said.

A turtledove landed on a branch in the orange tree and began to preen its tail. Two dragonflies chased each other along the hedges. The courtyard felt peaceful in the stifling heat.

There is something else I want to ask you, I said. I felt Dorantes tense beside me. But when he spoke again, his voice was light.

I know what you are going to ask, he said. I will give you your papers soon.

When?

We just got here three days ago, Estebanico. I have not had a chance to find a notary. But you will get your papers. I am a man of my word.

He spoke in a way that made me feel I had caused him great offense and that I ought never to have asked him. Of course, I said. It is just that—

Besides, he said, I have had other things on my mind. He chewed on his lower lip, drawing beads of blood. It was an old, nervous habit that had returned now that we were in the city. She is pregnant, he said.

Your wife? I asked.

We were never married in a church. She is not my wife.

The sun was so bright and so hot that we both turned away from the courtyard to face the living room. Inside, Oyomasot sat on a narrow brown chair, her eyes fastened upon the friar who had been personally sent by the viceroy to teach her about the Bible. Tekotsen and Kewaan were seated on either side of her, making up a half-circle around their young teacher.

Could you not marry her again, in a church? I asked.

It is not that simple, Dorantes replied.

I wanted to ask him why, but I did not wish to press him and thus turn him against me, so I kept silent. Years ago, silence had been my refuge, and now I sought its shelter again. I listened as Dorantes told me about the viceroy's banquet and all the distinguished guests who were eager to meet us. He said it would be appropriate to give some turquoises as gifts to the viceroy, by way of thanking him for his hospitality and for all the elegant clothes he had given us.

We will have to ask the others, I said. Everything we had brought back from the Land of the Indians was shared property and we would have to come to an agreement about what could be sold and what could be given away.

Of course, Dorantes said. But I think Castillo and Cabeza de Vaca will agree with me. Then he opened the glass door to ask if the friar was done with his lesson.

Yes, Capitán, Father Herminio said, standing up. His voice was calm, but it did not disguise his irritation. I am done for today, but there is much to be done. They must practice.

I will tell them, Dorantes said.

The women stood up as well. Tekotsen smiled at her husband and asked if he would like to eat something. But Oyomasot walked out behind the friar, her hands already reaching behind her to the small of her back, unfastening the girdle.

21

The Story of the Palace

Much had happened in the old world during our absence and, in the week that followed our arrival in México, we finally heard some of it. The king of England had wrested himself from the authority of the Church and married a courtesan named Anne Boleyn. A new pope was installed in Rome, from where he issued a proclamation that Indians were beings endowed with reason. In Barbary, Sultan Muhammad al-Burtuqali died, leaving a throne and a squabbling country to his brother, Ahmad al-Wattasi. The Ottomans took Baghdad from the Persians. High up in the Andes Mountains, Pizarro tied the Inca emperor to a garrote and strangled him, in full view of his subjects.

And here, in the beautiful city of Tenochtitlán, Antonio de Mendoza became the viceroy of New Spain. This was a new title, designed by the king to make Mendoza the most powerful man in the territory. But it was not easy to wield this power while Hernán Cortés, the peerless and popular hero of the conquest, watched and waited. Though I had been in the city only a week, I had already heard about the rivalry between the two men, and of Mendoza's ambition to quickly make his mark.

Mendoza's mansion, as I discovered on my first visit, was a fitting tribute to his position. Built with the stones of Moctezuma's palace, it was an imposing white building that stretched the length of the square. Guards lined up along the path that led to the entrance, nodding their heads as my companions and I passed. When I walked into the main hall with Dorantes, light from a dozen chandeliers dazzled my eyes, so the first sensation that came to me was the sound of music, a cheerful tune played on the violin by musicians I could not see yet. Right away, a group of colonial officers bore down on us, waiting to be introduced by the viceroy and to shake our hands. Then it was the turn of priests, city officials, and Aztec nobles. Along the walls, Castilian ladies dressed in fine taffeta stood watching us, periodically whispering to each other behind their lace fans. The air smelled of burning candles and brazen ambition.

When dinner was announced, Mendoza led us to a banquet table, indicating to each one of us where he should sit: Cabeza de Vaca across from Doña María, the viceroy's wife; Dorantes next to her; Castillo across from him; and I next to Dorantes, with colonial officers and Aztec noblemen filling out the remaining seats. The sheer number of forks and knives around my plate perplexed me, forcing me to watch my neighbors in order to know which ones should be used on which food. And the codpiece on my new breeches made me feel particularly uncomfortable. So I spoke little, but bits of conversation from other parts of the table reached me.

The wine is from Valladolid. Have you tried it?

Who can keep up with the price of horses these days?

The trait to look for in these people is loyalty. Loyalty is the thing.

My mother sends her regards, Don Antonio.

My dear, the noise of construction in this city is unrelenting.

After the third or fourth course had been served, the viceroy turned to the subject that, it was clear from his tone, had been exercising him since our arrival in México. He was a native of Granada and spoke with the sibilant sounds of an Andalusian. Señores, he said, we are honored to have such distinguished explorers among us. In fact, the city is wild with rumors about your remarkable journey. Perhaps you may even have heard some of them. I cannot overstate how important it is that you give us an official account of what happened. My deputies will collect your testimony into a joint report for His Majesty, that he may know what happened to the Narváez expedition. I trust that you will make every effort to give a precise account of the dates of your journey and the distances you crossed. Any details you can give about the nature and climate of the land you traversed, the kind and number of people who inhabit it, their languages and their ways of subsistence—all this will be of great help as we seek to pacify the northern territories.

This caught Cabeza de Vaca's attention. Have you a plan for a new mission? he asked.

Not at the moment, the viceroy replied. But the process of securing the northern borders of the empire is ongoing. His tone suggested that pacifying the Indians was a heavy burden, but one to which he had long ago resigned himself to carrying with grace. He turned his goblet of wine between his fingers and, cocking his head to the side, he added, a little sadly: Unfortunately, we have had to contend with a particularly difficult obstacle.

I believe we may have met the obstacle, Cabeza de Vaca said.

Guzmán is a sight, is he not? the viceroy said with a smile. Do you know that his province has become almost completely barren of its Indians? He hands out slaving licenses like a drunk hands out flowers. Perhaps you could include this in your testimony to His Majesty? You could mention in passing, could you not, that Nuño de Guzmán has done a poor job of administering the land and the Indians that were entrusted to him?

Cabeza de Vaca was taken aback by the suggestion to alter his testimony, and unsure how to respond. He looked down at his porcelain plate, where a small game hen, adorned with fried almonds that gleamed like gold, sat untouched on its garnish of laurel leaves. A servant came to refill his glass of wine and still Cabeza de Vaca did not look up or respond.

The viceroy sat back in his chair, suddenly aware that he had pressed the treasurer a little too far. In an indulgent voice, he said: There will be time yet to discuss all of that. For the moment, you need to get plenty of rest. The process of collecting testimony may seem simple, but it is very long and it strains the mind to such an extent that it can be exhausting. Still, it is a crucial step, as I hope I have impressed upon you.

With his fork, Cabeza de Vaca pushed the almonds to the side of his plate. His silence had grown long enough to be awkward, so Dorantes had to intervene. And how long will the testimony take?

That all depends on you, the viceroy replied. Now he narrowed his eyes at Dorantes, studying him like a fisherman considering a lure. Why do you ask?

Don Antonio, Dorantes said pleadingly, we have been away from our families for so long that we are all eager to return to Castile as soon as possible.

I understand, the viceroy said. But the report will not take long. A couple of months, I should think. Until then, of course, you are my guests.

ON THE QUESTION of the official testimony, the viceroy turned out to be correct: it took two full months for his deputies to collect the captains' depositions. The courthouse was being renovated, so the interviews were conducted in a simple office at the church, but in spite of all appearances my companions were not asked for a true confession; rather, they were required to provide a detailed history of the expedition. In telling this history, my companions began to modify its more damaging details. They credited Narváez with all the poor decisions, they omitted the torture and rapes they had witnessed, they justified the thefts of food and supplies, they left out the Indian wives they married, and they magnified their suffering at the hands of the Indians as much as their relief at being found. In this shortened and sanitized form, the chronicle of the Narváez expedition became suitable for the royal court, the cardinals and inquisitors, the governors and officials, and the families and friends they had left behind in Castile.

But no one asked me to testify. I should have been resentful of this, but I was not—not yet. The only thing at once more precious and more fragile than a true story is a free life. This was all I cared about in those days. So whenever my companions came to the guesthouse for visits with their wives, I listened to them recount the day's testimonials with only a mild interest and even some amusement.

That evening, I remember, we were congregated in the living room, drinking warm chocolatl by the fireplace. All of us had grown a taste for this frothy and bitter drink, and enjoyed especially the invigorating effect it had on our moods. On either side of the sofa were round tables with brass candelabras, whose light reflected against the glass panes of the windows. The doors to the courtyard were left ajar, letting in a breeze.

You told the court recorders that we arrived in Aute on the twentieth of July, Castillo said. I thought we were still in Apalache in July.

No, we were already in Aute, Cabeza de Vaca said. I am certain of it.

But that was eight years ago, I said with a laugh. How can you be so sure about the date?

Cabeza de Vaca's reply was as candid as it was serious. I have always had a good memory, he said. His hair had been cut in a way that disguised his large ears and his features had filled out, so that he looked like an older and more handsome version of the treasurer of the Narváez expedition. He had always loved to tell stories, but now his memories of the expedition were entered into the official record, invalidating all others. I realized with a start that I was once again living in a world where written records were synonymous with power. This was true not just of things like dates and places, but also births, marriages, and deaths.

Well, Castillo said, it is impressive that you remember the date so precisely. That it was the twentieth and not, say, the twenty-first or the twenty-second.

Dates do not matter, Dorantes said with irritation. What they really want are clues for drawing a precise map. Dorantes knew that he was in possession of valuable knowledge, and his tone suggested that the court recorders were doing him a grave injustice by asking for it. He was sitting on the sofa, next to his wife, Tekotsen, who rested her hands on the mound of her belly.

Did you feel that? Tekotsen asked suddenly, her voice ringing with excitement. She brought her husband's hand to her belly, so that he could feel the baby's kicking over the voluminous folds of her dress. The priest had told the women that they were to wear Castilian clothes at all times, an order with which they complied, but which they liked to flout in different ways, however small. Oyomasot wore her bone necklaces and Kewaan still had her anklets and deerskin shoes. But Tekotsen followed the friar's rules to the letter, including the one that dictated she should cover her hair with a cap. She had spoken to Dorantes in Avavare, but now she switched to Spanish. Here, she said, moving his hand to a different spot, so that he could feel the kick.

It is a boy, Oyomasot said.

How do you know? Tekotsen asked.

From your shape, Oyomasot replied. See how high you carry?

Dorantes still had his hand on his wife's belly, but his face was turned toward his fellow Castilians. And why should we give away all of our knowledge for nothing? he asked. They will only use it for a new mission. After everything we have been through, we have more right to that territory than anyone else. And if not a territory, then at least proper compensation.

Since the court interviews had begun, Dorantes had been increasingly worried about money. The sale of the emerald arrowheads in Tenochtitlán, a city where such jewels were easily rivaled by an abundance of sapphires, rubies, and pearls, only brought us a few hundred pesos. But the rest of our treasures, which I had placed in consignment in different markets of Tenochtitlán, had found some buyers, and I was confident that

I could raise the correct sum for our passage, or very nearly. Still, this did not relieve his worries about money.

Calm yourself, Cabeza de Vaca said. Even if the viceroy sends a mission to the north, no one can be declared governor of a province without an order from the king.

Dorantes replied: But are we just going to sit here and wait while others take the territory from us?

Oyomasot came to sit beside Tekotsen. Let me try, she said. Maybe I will feel the baby. She closed her eyes in concentration, her lips curved in a smile. My wife wanted a baby of her own, and I wished for one, too, especially because she was so good with children, but God had not yet willed it. Perhaps, I thought, once we left the turbulence of Tenochtitlán and settled into a quiet life in Azemmur, we would be more fortunate.

There, Tekotsen said. Did you feel that?

Yes, Oyomasot replied with a laugh. A good little kick.

Cabeza de Vaca put down his cup of chocolatl and stood up, stretching his arms over his head. There is not much we can do about this until the interviews are completed and we return to Seville, he said.

Speaking of Seville, I said to Dorantes, we still need to have those papers drawn.

Dorantes buttoned down his doublet and stood up. I will do it after we are done with the court testimony. Now let us go, Estebanico. It is time for dinner.

The four of us had been invited to the house of a prominent gentleman, a native of Cadiz who had been awarded a large estate and hundreds of Indians from the king, and who was known for his extravagant parties. There was intense curiosity about us among the nobility. The story of our shipwreck entertained the lords and ladies of New Spain, many of them residents of the capital who had never known the dangers and delights of exploration.

So for two long months, I watched everyone come and go. Father Herminio came to teach the women about the virtues of Christianity; the Aztec servants delivered gifts or invitations to dinner at noblemen's houses; my Castilian companions gave their court testimony; and I waited.

22.

THE STORY OF THE HACIENDA

The viceroy was not the only newly titled man in Tenochtitlán. Hernán Cortés, whose fame in New Spain was unrivaled, had been made Marquis of the Valley of Oaxaca, and he, too, gave a banquet in our honor. It was held out-of-doors, in the garden of the fortress he had erected over an Aztec tribute house in Cuernavaca, twenty leagues south of the capital. Bronze chandeliers hung from the trees that lined the garden, illuminating the tables underneath with a soft, yellow glow. In the center of the garden was a water fountain, around which circled jugglers, acrobats, jesters, and dwarves, each one performing his act before moving to the right, allowing the next performer to entertain the guests.

Cortés was the subject of constant gossip in the capital. Long before meeting him, I had heard about his conquest and destruction of Tenochtitlán, the emperor he had killed, the thousands he had enslaved and branded, the thousands more he had massacred at Cholula, and the soldiers who, weighed down by bars of gold, had drowned in the lake around the city. I was also intrigued by the story of his two sons, both of them named Martín. The first Martín was born to La Malinche, Cortés's guide, interpreter, and concubine, the woman who had made it possible for him to claim the empire of the Aztecs. The second Martín was born nine years later to Doña Juana, Cortés's Castilian wife. But rumor had it that the second Martín would be the one to inherit Cortés's title.

Perhaps because he was such a famous man, I had expected Cortés to be tall, but he turned out to be of average height, a thin and well-built man with small, inquisitive eyes. There was no hint of pride or excessive propriety in his manner, a quality that, oddly enough, reminded me of

Narváez. He seated the four of us around him at a small table, with no
other guests to share our meal or conversation. One of his Aztec servants stood beside us, quietly directing the servers to bring dishes or clear
them. These dishes were a mix of Castilian and Aztec: steamed meat of
wild bird and lizard, leaf-wrapped ground corn, mushrooms in a savory
sauce, two kinds of baked squash, and warm chocolatl served in cups tied
with a gold thread. Cortés ate very little, but he asked us a lot of questions. How are you adjusting to the capital? he began.

Dorantes replied: We were gone for so many years that we thought
no one would remember us. We certainly did not expect such a wonderful welcome in México or so many invitations. I must admit, it is all a bit
overwhelming.

Dorantes had spoken quickly, so eager was he to say something that
would interest or impress the famous Cortés, but now he paused to take
a breath, and Cabeza de Vaca took this opportunity to speak. He said: But
people are making up all sorts of vicious lies about us. They say we have
bewitched the Indians.

Believe me, Cortés said, no one in New Spain understands your situation better than I. The rumors about me that are circulated both in the
capital and at the king's court would make a man of weaker disposition
retire from public life altogether. But one must do one's best in the service of our king, do you not agree? One must trudge on, even as the
rumors swirl.

My companions nodded gravely, as if the marquis had said something
highly perceptive or original. Such was Cortés's fame that even the most
banal observation was met with whispers of awe. Now he said, I hear that
the viceroy has kept you busy.

For a few weeks, Cabeza de Vaca said.

He has collected your testimony? Cortés asked, though something
about his tone suggested that he already knew the answer. He was known
to have spies everywhere in the province, and in the few places that were
outside the reach of spies he had made allies who kept him informed.
After all, he had arrived in this city long before the viceroy and was familiar with many of its officials, whether in the governing council or in the
commercial boards.

Nearly all of it, Cabeza de Vaca said.

The viceroy will be relieved to have this record, Cortés said. Now he leaned forward on the table and his tone grew even more familiar. Of course, men like you and me, who have embarked on expeditions into uncharted territories, know things that recorders never will. It is one thing to write about facing the unknown; doing it is quite another. We are doers, señores. Doers.

It was such a small word, but its effect on my companions was immediate. Cabeza de Vaca seemed particularly sensitive to the flattery; he told Cortés that the viceroy had charged him with taking the Joint Report to Santo Domingo, on the island of La Española, where it would be examined by the imperial court. From there, he would travel home to Castile.

I see, Cortés replied. And what about you two hidalgos?

I am still trying to secure passage to Seville, Dorantes said, but it is more expensive than I expected. Dorantes had found it hard to resist the Spanish taverns of Tenochtitlán, so he had returned to gambling, a habit he had last indulged in Seville, and had already spent his share of the proceeds from the sale of our treasures. As a result, he had been forced to write to his father to ask for money for his passage, but as the date of our travel approached, he seemed less eager to leave. Eight years ago he had dreamed of conquering La Florida and returning to Béjar del Castañar covered in gold and glory; now his homecoming would be without fame or fortune.

Perhaps I can help with your expenses, Cortés said.

How kind of you to offer, Dorantes replied. His voice betrayed his relief and, when he realized it, his cheeks flushed.

It would be my pleasure, Cortés said. A soft wind picked up, rustling the leaves of the tree above us and making the light from the chandelier flicker over our table. The entertainers stepped around the fountain once more, so that masked dancers could perform for us. After watching them for a moment, Cortés said: I hear that your slave is familiar with all the routes to the north, and fluent in the local languages. Is that true?

Merciful God, I thought. Not this again.

Dorantes cocked his head to the side, stunned by the proposition that Cortés's question implied: if he wanted the marquis to help with his expenses, he would have to trade his slave in return. From his reaction, I could tell that the thought had not occurred to him before. But now that it had, he remained silent.

I glanced at Castillo and Cabeza de Vaca, but they both averted their eyes, whether in disbelief or indifference I could not tell, so I leaned forward in my seat. We journeyed for eight years together, I said. My voice came out as a croak and I hated the pleading note I heard in it, although I could not control it. Eight years, I said.

Cortés nodded slowly. Yes, he said, I know. He sounded neither angry nor offended by my interruption. In his eyes, I was a useful cog that had to be procured. Just as he had needed La Malinche for his conquest of México, he needed me as a guide and interpreter for whatever mission he was planning to the north.

The dancers had finished their round and now they moved to the right, to make room for the jugglers, who were dressed in cotton skirts and feather headdresses. Balls of different colors flew up from their hands and whirled in the air at such a pace that the colors blurred. One of them balanced a ball on his nose, while juggling seven metal rings at once. Another lay on his back and juggled a long, thick log with the soles of his feet.

Your Highness is very kind, Dorantes said. But I am expecting to receive some funds from my father soon.

Well, do give it some thought, Cortés said. Let us set aside all this talk of money for now. The native jugglers are about to perform. These two over here, the ones closest to Capitán Castillo, were part of Moctezuma's court, and this one over there I found in a village about one hundred and fifty leagues from here. Watch, señores, watch.

A WEEK AFTER OUR DINNER with Cortés, the Joint Report was completed and Cabeza de Vaca left Tenochtitlán. Though he had been clear about his intent to leave immediately after the end of the testimonials, his departure still struck us as abrupt. We stood, shuffling on our feet, unsure what words to use to bid farewell to a man with whom we had shared our incredible adventure. But he did not seem so troubled; he hugged us amiably and then climbed on the horse he had purchased with his share of the proceeds. It was a magnificent horse, a tall, white mare with a curved profile and a thick mane, the kind of horse that testified to a man's position.

With the reins in his hands, Cabeza de Vaca turned toward us. He looked like a proper Castilian gentleman now, with doublet and cape, breeches and buckled shoes. Dorantes looked on with undisguised envy. It would be awhile before he heard back from his father and, until then, he had to subsist on what remained of his money. What was more, the viceroy had hinted that Dorantes and Castillo should move to the guesthouse with me, because he was expecting guests from Cuba that week and needed the palace rooms for their accommodation.

I remember that it was a morning in fall, but the day was threatening to be hot and damp. The birds that ordinarily sang from the height of the trees around the palace courtyard were quiet. Two sentinels, weighed down by their helmets, breastplates, and weapons, leaned against the open doors of the gate. Between them, through the arched stone gateway, the city square and its passersby were visible.

Do you have the letters I gave you? Dorantes asked.

Cabeza de Vaca patted his saddlebags. Yes. I will deliver them to your father.

Send me word when you reach Veracruz.

I will. And I hope to see you in Castile soon.

God willing.

Cabeza de Vaca nudged his horse, and the next moment he was out of sight. Dorantes gazed wistfully in the distance before turning away. The three of us walked slowly around the palace to the guesthouse, where we were to have lunch with our wives. The departure of our companion, so swift and so sudden, weighed down on us, though we did not speak of it during the meal. Mostly we talked about what to do with the gifts that had been sent to us by various noblemen of the city, and which were kept in a locked closet in the dining room: chiseled silver vases, enameled plates, rolls of fine fabric. These were small gestures of appreciation for the stories we had told at dinners given in our honor. Dorantes wanted to sell the whole lot, although he would have to do so discreetly if he did not want word about his financial troubles to spread.

After lunch, the others retired for a nap, but I remained in the living room with Dorantes, so that I could speak to him about the notary. The sun streamed through the open windows, and, with the house now quiet, the flitting of the insects in the bushes could be heard. Dorantes reclined his head against the back of the sofa and stretched his legs before him. He looked for all the world like a man who had had a long day of labor and was finally getting some well-earned rest. I spoke as calmly as I could manage, even though I had waited for this moment for eight long weeks. Dorantes, I said. The report is done now. When will we go see the notary?

His expression veered from sleepiness to astonishment. He sat up and fixed me with his blue eyes. Do you know that the viceroy offered me five hundred pesos for you? And do you know what I said? He raised his eyebrows in a challenge. I said no.

He looked as though he expected me to congratulate him for this refusal. I opened my mouth to say something, but could think of nothing to say—nothing to say, at any rate, that would not sound argumentative or disrespectful or even amusing to him. If I said, But you promised me, he might reply that I was questioning his word and a quarrel would erupt. If I said, I have waited long enough for my papers, he might ask me what was the rush and what plans I was hiding from him. And if I said, You do not have a bill of sale any longer, he would have simply laughed and replied that it would take only one or two Castilian witnesses to produce a new bill of sale.

I reclined against the back of the sofa, sinking in the overstuffed damask cushions, the room around me fading into a blur of colors. This was not supposed to happen, I thought. Tenochtitlán was supposed to be a new beginning for me. Instead, and almost without my realizing it, Dorantes and I had slowly reprised our old relationship. Once again, he was standing in the sun and I had to retreat in his shadow. Once again, he was the speaker and I was the listener; he was the decider and I was the supplicant. Once again, he was the master and I was the slave.

An Aztec servant came in at that moment to announce that some gifts from Hernán Cortés had arrived. Bring them in, then, Dorantes said. The servant opened the door wide and in walked a pair of greyhounds. They were both male, brindle in color, eight to ten months old. Swiftly they walked around the room, tails wagging, sniffing at our hands and legs and at all the furniture. In disbelief, Dorantes stood up. What am I supposed to do with dogs? he asked. The servant did not reply, for a gift from Cortés could not be returned without causing some offense.

It was the first time I had seen greyhounds in New Spain. Their narrow faces reminded me of the sloughis of Barbary, which are used for hunting hare, but their color was similar to the dogs that the Capoques kept as companions. The two memories, one of Azemmur and one of the Land of the Indians, combined in such a way that they produced in me an even deeper melancholy.

The servant left now and Dorantes sat down again. He was expecting me to say something about his refusal of the money, and my insistent silence struck him as ungratefulness. Now he pressed me for some acknowledgment of his fortitude in facing down the viceroy. With his elbows on his knees, he asked: Who would refuse an offer from Mendoza?

No one.

No one in his right mind, he said. Now he stood up again and went to the glass doors. The dogs followed him there, but he ignored them. With his back still turned to me, he asked: Is there another slave in New Spain who can claim to have been invited to the tables of both the viceroy and the marquis?

No.

Or to have received Communion from the bishop himself?

No.

Or to stay at the viceroy's guesthouse?

No.

Is there another master who allows his slave to go about as he pleases on the streets of the capital?

No.

So why do you want to run off like Cabeza de Vaca? Be patient, Estebanico. The two of us will have more adventures yet.

He returned to sit on the sofa. The dogs came to sniff his hands, but he shooed them away with irritation and turned to his side. A moment later, he was asleep.

THE CURTAINS WERE DRAWN when I walked into our room, cloaking it in a blue darkness. I made my way to the bed on the tips of my toes in order not to rouse my wife. The softness of Castilian bedsheets had eventually tempted her and she had begun to use the mattress. But she was not asleep; she sat up now, in her white nightdress and with her black hair loose on her shoulders. What did Dorantes say? she asked.

Nothing, I replied. In my shame, I could not bear to look at her. I sat down on the edge of the bed and slowly unbuckled my shoes. I felt a great heaviness all over my body; all I wanted to do was lie down and go to sleep and never wake up again.

He made up another excuse?

Slowly, I unbuttoned my doublet. Each gesture demanded great effort.

Why? she asked. Why do you keep believing him?

I lay down on the bed next to her and closed my eyes. The image that came to me was of the shard of clear glass, lying under a thicket of green cactus in the Land of Corn. I had been a free man then, roaming the world that God had made, providing solace to other people and receiving sustenance in return. But somehow I had started a chain of events that had led me to this city, this little room, this very bed. And not only had I lost my freedom once again, I had lost my wife's, too. A horror. An unbearable horror.

Listen, Oyomasot said. She put her hand on my face and kept it there until I opened my eyes. Listen, my love. The more you ask him, the more he will want to hold on to you. What you want is not something that can be asked for, it can only be taken.

On the nightstand was a pitcher, another one of the gifts that had been sent to us by a nobleman after we had entertained him with our stories. Oyomasot poured me a glass of water, wiped the bottom with her palm, and handed it to me. Drink, she said, drink, you are burning up. I took a sip, turned to my side, and fell into a deep, dreamless sleep.

When I woke up, hours later, the first thought that occurred to me was that I had lost everything. I had lost the rustling of the Umm er-Rbi' River, the view of the eleven minarets, the noise of the souq, the taste of figs eaten right off the tree, the pearls of dew that woke me when I slept on the rooftop of our house on hot summer nights. I had lost, too, the endless expanse of green wilderness, the taste of deer I had hunted, the sound of drums around the campfire at night. I had given up my right to go where I pleased, my right to work as I wished, my right to worship as I wanted. I had sacrificed my wife at the altar of my ambition. I had willingly walked back into darkness.

Everything was lost.

But a voice inside me said no—not everything.

I still had one thing. My story. I had journeyed through the Land of the Indians and had witnessed many things that my companions had preferred to revise, embellish, or silence. What had been changed, perverted, or left out was the heart of our history, the part that could not be explained, but could only be told. I could tell it. I could right what had been made wrong. And so I began to write my account. For every lie I had heard about the imperial expedition that had brought me to the edge of the world, I would tell the truth.

23

THE STORY OF THE GUESTHOUSE

On a cold evening in winter, I walked into the ferran around the corner from the grand mosque. The neighborhood's bread trays were stacked in four neat columns along the far wall, each tray bearing a mark that identified its owner in some way: a small design carved on the handle or a colorful fabric for the bread. Orange flames rose inside the gaping oven and, even though I stood by the door to the street, I felt their heat. As I said my salaams, I noticed that the apprentice, a young boy of perhaps twelve or thirteen years of age, was new. Is Mohand not here today? I asked him. But the boy did not answer. He put a fresh loaf of bread on his peel and slid it deep inside the oven, placing it in a row next to the other loaves. Again I asked him about the baker. Where is Mohand? The apprentice turned toward me and, as he did so, his hand brushed against the edge of the oven door. His wails of pain were loud—so loud that they woke me.

For a moment, I was unsure if the cry I heard was an echo from the dream I was having. No, the sound came from inside the house. Beside me, Oyomasot had not stirred. Another moan of pain tore through the silence. I pushed back the covers and rushed to the door. The hallway still smelled of the roast chicken that had been served for dinner, in celebration of the Christian feast of the Nativity. At the other end of the house, the dogs were scratching at the kitchen door, begging to be let in; I had forgotten to tether them for the night. Then Dorantes's door opened and he stepped out in his nightclothes. He stood, silhouetted against the candlelight from the bedroom, looking like a man who had gotten lost on his way home. When he saw me in the hallway, the confusion on his face gave way to relief. Tekotsen, he whispered. Tekotsen is in labor.

I nodded and turned around to get Oyomasot.

The labor lasted all night. I went out to tether the dogs, but they kept barking and jumping and running around in circles, as if they sensed what was happening inside, so I relented and brought them with me into the living room. I found Dorantes sitting by himself, wrapped in a Spanish blanket. If it is a girl, he said, I will name her Pilar. Or maybe Ximena. My aunt is named Ximena.

In the dark, the living room seemed bleaker than ever. I put fresh logs in the fireplace and started a fire. As I worked, the dogs stood on either side of me, and when I sat on the armchair they came to lie at my feet. In just a few weeks I had grown attached to them. Whenever the weather allowed, I took them to the lake, around which they could run free for a while. I enjoyed these walks, for they gave me a good pretext to be out of the guesthouse, where there was constant talk of the future. I needed some time to myself to consider how I might solve my predicament.

Dorantes spoke again. I remember the day my brother Diego was born, he said. I was thirteen. I was with my tutor in the study when one of the servants came to inform me that my mother had gone into labor. My father was in Extremadura that week. Of course, I sent for the doctor, but the doctor was not home either, and the servant had to go looking for him. I was sick with worry; I felt I had been left alone to shoulder the heaviest burden in the world. But in the end, it was the laundress who delivered Diego. I remember she came out into the hall to show him to me, all wrapped up in his linen sheets. He was so small. I was afraid I might break him if I touched him.

What if it is a boy? I asked. What will you name the baby if it is a boy?

Dorantes seemed on the verge of saying something, but in the end he did not reply. He fell asleep after a while and I think I did, too, because the next thing I remember there was a creak as the door opened. It was already morning and the first rays of sun filtered through the windows. It is a girl, Oyomasot said with a smile.

Though my wife looked reluctant to give up the baby, still moist with afterbirth, Dorantes stood up to receive her. How beautiful she was. A round-faced girl with a tiny mouth and long-lashed eyes that surveyed our messy world with astonishment. I kept my gaze averted, but I knew that, like Oyomasot's, it was filled with envy.

Now, with his child in his arms, Dorantes sat down by the fireplace again. Good morning, he cooed. Good morning, little lady.

The girl would be named Ximena María, but everyone would call her María la Mestiza. She would be held and kissed and nursed and swaddled and sung to for days on end, but by the festival of the Resurrection, Dorantes would send her to live in a Spanish convent ten leagues north of the city.

IT WAS AN EARLY SPRING that year. The clouds disappeared almost overnight and the warm weather made the orange trees in the courtyard erupt with early buds. Dorantes had reluctantly begun his preparations for the journey to Seville when Viceroy Mendoza sent word that he wanted to see the two of us. I wonder what he wants, Dorantes said as we walked from the guesthouse to the palace.

At the gates, Dorantes stopped to check that his breeches were properly tucked in and as my gaze fell I noticed on the ground a wooden charm in the shape of a hand. How odd, I thought as I picked it up. Had it been made in Tenochtitlán or had it been brought here from somewhere else? It looked just like the amulets my mother used to wear, except hers were made of metal rather than wood. I pocketed the little charm, thinking it a sign of good luck.

We were ushered into the viceroy's private office, a high-ceilinged room where plumed statues of Aztec warriors watched us from each of the four corners. On the walls were portraits of King Carlos and Queen Isabella, and a painting of the Prophet Jesus with his apostles. The viceroy was sitting on an armchair, his leg in the lap of an Indian servant, who was tightening the buckle of his shoe. The heavy rugs that covered the floors muffled any sound we made when we entered the room, so that neither Mendoza nor his servant heard us. Dorantes had to clear his throat before the viceroy noticed us. He waved the servant away and stood up. Ah, Capitán, he said. It is so kind of you to come.

Thank you for inviting me, Dorantes said.

But I hear you are already leaving us? the viceroy asked.

In a few weeks. I am returning to Seville.

Might we not be able to convince you to stay with us a little longer?

Your Highness is much too kind.

The journey to Castile is long.

Indeed it is.

Mendoza's voice turned grave. And longer yet is the effort to get a grant from His Majesty. It can take years. A decade even. But if you stay in New Spain and serve the Crown in a different capacity, your efforts will be rewarded. I am preparing an expedition to the Seven Cities.

On hearing this name, a feeling of dismay brimmed up within me. I had heard about the Seven Cities months earlier, but thought them nothing more than a legend, the kind of story that could be used to entertain children on a cold winter night. In the eighth century, some people said, when the Moors conquered the kingdom of Portugal, seven bishops fled the continent with their followers and sailed westward across the ocean. They reached a vast, fertile island, where each of them founded a city. These cities prospered so much that they came to be called the Seven Cities of Gold.

Mendoza had all of the gold of Tenochtitlán, I thought, and yet he wanted more. In my younger years, such greed would have seemed ordinary to me, desirable even, but nowadays I found it only distasteful and destructive. It was greed that had led me to leave the notary's life for the trader's life, it was greed that had convinced me to sell men into slavery, and it was greed that had led the three hundred men of the Narváez expedition to perish in La Florida.

Do you remember, Mendoza asked, the story you told us some months ago?

Dorantes and I glanced at each other. We had told many stories of our adventures at the dinner parties to which we had been invited and some of these stories had acquired a few embellishments along the way. So we could not be sure which one the viceroy had in mind.

With a smile, Mendoza said: You said that the Indians in the permanent settlements north of Nueva Galicia often spoke about cities that shine brightly in the sun so that a visitor, standing from afar, must look away from the light reflecting on their gates or risk blindness. These must be the Seven Cities.

Your Highness means to send an expedition?

Yes, but it is a small one. Two friars, some horses, a detachment of Amigos. Nothing too large or complicated. A man of your experience should not find it too difficult.

It is not difficult, Dorantes said cautiously, and I would offer to go were it not for the fact that our ordeal in La Florida and beyond has left me with no desire to explore new lands. Have you considered Capitán Castillo?

Indeed I have. But—how shall I put this?—he seems to me to be a little soft. He was, what, eighteen or nineteen when you left Seville? He has spent nearly a third of his life with the Indians, and it seems to me he is far too biased in their favor.

I know not what to say, Your Highness. Castillo is a faithful servant of the Crown.

Oh, no doubt. He is a good man. I just do not believe he would be appropriate for the mission I have in mind. I thought you would be better suited.

Your Highness flatters me. But, as I said, the thought of exploring new territory is not one I can contemplate for myself at the moment.

Perhaps we might come to a different understanding, then? I am told that the Indian women you brought with you have finished their Christian instruction. They will make appropriate guides for this mission. But I would also need someone who can help the friars and horsemen cross the northern lands in safety, someone with the kind of power you wielded when you lived among the savages. A sort of ambassador, if you will. Someone like your Esteban.

I felt the hair on the back of my neck stand. Was this the stroke of good fortune promised by my discovery of the khamsa? Could it be that the very thing I had once dreaded might allow me to return to freedom?

But Dorantes replied: How generous of Your Highness to think of him. But Estebanico has been with me for ten years now and I am so attached to him I have never considered selling him. As for the women, they are needed to attend to my household, and I prefer for them to stay here in the capital, where they might be able to receive further guidance from the church.

As you wish, the viceroy said. But know that His Majesty will look most kindly on those who serve him in his hour of need.

Mendoza walked us out to the palace courtyard. When they saw him approach, the sentinels straightened up and clicked their heels. A group of swallows were taking turns swooping down into the water fountain for a drink. The sun was high in the sky, and the viceroy tilted his face toward it, soaking up the warmth. Another beautiful day, he said. Then he added, almost as an afterthought: Do you remember Doña María de la Torre? The kind lady in the black silk dress at the banquet last week? She inherited an encomienda from her husband—quite large, fifteen hundred Indians. I would be most pleased to make introductions.

IT WAS A WARM EVENING in summer. Castillo and I were sitting in the patio, under the canopy of white bougainvillea that grew on the gallery rails. From the city square came the faint sound of music, fiddles and drums played for the entertainment of passersby. But the house was dark and quiet; the servants had not yet begun to prepare dinner. Castillo had just returned from a walk to Lake Tezcuco with Doña Isabel, a lady he had met at one of the viceroy's dinners. Now he slipped off his black shoes and white hose, and vigorously rubbed his left foot between the toes of his right, satisfying an itch or a rash. How I hate wearing socks, he complained.

Why wear them if you do not like them? I asked.

He shrugged. I have to. I cannot walk around the capital barefoot, you know.

Something crackled under the lavender bushes and one of the greyhounds at my feet lifted its head, but, sensing nothing, went back to sleep. Did you enjoy the walk? I asked.

I did, Castillo said. Doña Isabel sailed all the way from Castile to be with her husband, the alderman of the city, but not six months later he was killed, leaving her alone in New Spain. She has no family here in the capital, only friends she has made since her arrival.

Like you, then?

Yes. And she is from Tordesillas, not far from Salamanca.

Castillo's face was concealed by the darkness, but from his voice I sensed his excitement at the acquaintance he had made. In the bushes, the grasshoppers began to sing. A candle was lit at the kitchen window, as if the house had opened one eye and was watching us.

What about Kewaan? I asked after a moment.

Nothing will change between us, he said earnestly. This is different.

Everything was different in New Spain, I thought. Cabeza de Vaca had left. Dorantes was rarely home now; he was courting the widow de la Torre, to whom the viceroy had introduced him. The chair that he normally occupied sat between us now, empty. The memory of that day with the Carancahuas, when I had woken up to find he had escaped without us, returned to me all of a sudden. I asked Castillo: Did you ever talk to Dorantes about the notary?

Castillo ran his tongue on his lips. He looked so much older now than when I had first met him and, although he had always been very thin, our prolonged stay in Tenochtitlán had filled out his narrow frame to the point that he had become portly. With his eyes to the ground, he said: I asked Dorantes several times why he would not sign your papers, Estebanico.

And what did he say?

That it was none of my concern.

Reader, I should not have been surprised by this retort, but I was. I think there was still some small part of me that stubbornly held on to the belief that Dorantes had been changed forever by our common experience in the Land of the Indians. We had been hungry together. We had shivered in the cold together. We had worked side by side for the Carancahuas and side by side we had tried to heal the Indians in the Land of Corn. But whatever transformation had taken place within him had slowly been undone by his prolonged stay in the capital, where there was endless talk of money and power.

BY THE TIME the fall season started, Dorantes announced that he would marry the widow de la Torre. Castillo, too, decided that Doña Isabel, and her estate, were a good match for him. The three men I had once thought of as brothers were moving on: they were seeking royal grants, or getting married, or acquiring estates, forgetting everything that we had been through in the north. But I did not have the luxury to put the past behind me. I had made the mistake of once again placing my fate in the hands of another man and I had to find a way out.

I was sitting with my greyhounds by the window one afternoon when Dorantes came in. He began to chatter about the expedition that the viceroy was preparing. It was to be led by a young man named Francisco Vásquez de Coronado, and it would include a friar from France, a certain Marco de Niza, and several hundred Aztecs. The viceroy had once again asked Dorantes to sell me to him so that he could use me as a scout.

And what did you say? I asked.

I refused, of course, Dorantes said.

Outside, the shadows of the orange trees had begun to lengthen; it would be dark soon. The lavender bushes swayed in the wind. Dead leaves eddied across the courtyard.

But the Seven Cities of Gold, I said. What an incredible opportunity! It is, he sighed.

And if the friar and I manage to reach them, just imagine what we will find. You would have a claim to all those riches.

The thought of the Seven Cities silenced Dorantes for a long while. All his fantasies of gold and glory returned to him and he found them hard to resist. Perhaps he could have a second chance at making them come true. Perhaps he could finally receive the rewards that had been promised to him when he was a younger man in Seville. Perhaps he could become famous for a success, rather than a failure.

Turning away from the window, I added: Besides, who could refuse an offer from the viceroy of New Spain?

No one, he replied.

Dorantes was lost in thought, weighing the alternatives that had been presented to him: keep me with him in Mexico, where he faced the daily drudgery of running an estate; or send me to the north, where fortune might smile on him. From above the fireplace, the king of Castile watched us with equanimity, confident in the knowledge that, whatever the outcome, his share was secure.

You are right, he said at last. You must go.

I looked at his face—the scar on his right cheek, the lines around his eyes that had deepened over the years, the gray hair on his temples and beard. Now he started to chew his lower lip. I wondered if he had ever learned to read the expressions on my face the way I had learned to read his. I suspected he had not or he would have realized that I was finally going to set myself free.

COME, I SAID. COME. Oyomasot smelled of lavender—a new scent on her, a scent acquired from living in this guesthouse—but I loved it, for it mixed together the memory of old and new, past and present. From very far away came the sound of horns, celebrating one imperial triumph or another, but in the bedroom it was very quiet, the only sound the ruffling of her dress. I unlaced her corset, but when finally I freed her of it, Oyomasot still turned away from me. What is it? I asked.

Are you sure your plan will work?

Yes.

You have made promises before.

It will be different this time, I said. You will see.

24

The Story of the Return

I left Tenochtitlán in the year 945 of the Hegira. Once again, I was part of an expedition to the farther reaches of the empire, surrounded by a governor, friars, and horsemen. But this time there were no soldiers or settlers—no soldiers because the viceroy did not want to pay their salaries without the certainty of profit, and no settlers because he did not wish to put civilian lives at risk just yet. Instead, he had sent with us more than a hundred Amigos, who would carry supplies, set up our camp, cook our meals, fight any hostiles, and generally do what needed to be done. The Amigos were Aztecs who had allied with the Crown of Castile against other Aztecs—and for this betrayal they had earned the privilege of losing their tribe's true name, replacing it with a common and unthreatening Spanish noun. Whatever their talents, the Amigos could not know what lay beyond the range of mountains that bordered Nueva Galicia; nor did the newly appointed governor, Francisco Vásquez de Coronado, or the two friars, Father Marco and Father Onorato. They were all venturing into the unknown, unaware of the landscape, unfamiliar with the people, and ignorant of the languages.

Except for the forty horses Coronado had brought and the mules the friars rode, most of our company trudged on foot, burdened by baskets of provisions. So our progress was slow. Having been idle in the capital for so long, it took me a while to get used to day-long marches again, but I walked resolutely toward the north, pausing only when the governor complained that it was time for a break from the heat. At such moments, while he dabbed the sweat from his face with a white lace handkerchief, I shed some of my clothing. I took off the too warm doublet first, and later the frilly shirt, and later yet the uncomfortable shoes and tight belt.

Four weeks into the journey, when we had just crossed into the province of Nueva Galicia, we came across a group of Indian slaves, thirty of them shackled together with irons, shuffling quickly to keep up with the two Castilian horsemen who were riding on either side of them. One of the horsemen squinted at us with great curiosity. His face was wrinkled and darkened by the sun, and his hair was white. The other, younger and taller, was indifferent. He chewed on a blade of grass and waited, his hands resting on the pommel of his saddle.

The governor opened his right arm, in a gesture that took in the slaves and their drivers. Where might you be going? he asked.

To the capital, the older horseman said. He wiped his mouth with the back of his hand, as if he had just taken a sip from his flask.

The different groups of Indians, brought here by different groups of Castilians, stared at one another with envy, pity, or contempt. Envy came from the shackled Indian slaves; pity from my wife and others in our party; and contempt from the Amigos, who thought that their station guaranteed they could never be reduced to slavery. I had felt both the envy and the pity at some time in my life, but I could not allow myself the luxury of contempt. I knew only too well how precious and how fragile a man's freedom was.

You must undo their shackles, Father Marco said.

They are slaves, Father, the younger one replied. And then, as if suddenly aware he was addressing a friar, he took out the blade of grass from his mouth. They will run away, he said.

You cannot enslave them, Coronado said.

Who says we cannot?

His Majesty, you fool.

The two men looked at each other across the heads of their slaves. What are we supposed to do for money? the younger one asked.

For a few moments, Coronado watched them in silence. Then he said, I am the new governor.

The horsemen seemed unsure what they were supposed to do with this announcement. They climbed down from their horses and in their dusty clothes approached the governor. Are you taking them from us? the older one asked in a voice that was barely audible.

Coronado looked beyond the men at the horizon. The midday sun was melting the road, the boulders, and the trees into one hazy, indistinguishable mass of brown, yellow, and green. You must remain in your town and build up your settlements, he said. If you remain in your town, I will see to it that you get some help. Then he shook his head, in the weary manner of a man already resigned to the vicissitudes of running an imperial province. Go, he said. Go, before I change my mind.

Before the day was over we encountered another group. Coronado did not give the order to stop this time, and the horsemen moved their slaves to the side of the road so that our procession could pass. For the governor these encounters were already a nuisance, but for me they were a frightful reminder of what I was trying to escape.

IN GUADALAJARA, we were greeted by a terrible thunderstorm. Rain pooled on the only road in the town, turning it into a giant puddle of mud, and the somber clouds that hung in the sky showed no sign of clearing. White flashes intermittently lit our quarters, making the darkness that followed even bleaker. At times, it seemed as if we were stationed in the middle of a dark swamp. To add to my worries, the air in Guadalajara did not seem to agree with Oyomasot; she suffered from constant nausea, which was particularly pronounced in the morning.

Could it be that you are pregnant? I asked her.

The light from the window was on her hair, bringing out shades of red. She turned from the bowl where she had been washing her face and gave me a look of surprise. So accustomed had she become to childlessness that the possibility of a pregnancy had not crossed her mind. It stunned me that the baby we had wanted for so long had chosen this delicate moment in our lives to announce its presence. I put my arms around her and found her trembling. A baby, she whispered.

At last a good omen, I replied. But I resisted saying what I feared— that the risk we were taking was so much greater now. The empire's men were all around us. We could never hope to defeat them with force. We had to use other means.

The weather was not the only reason for our tarry in the town; as the new governor of Nueva Galicia, Coronado had to attend to the complaints of the people of Guadalajara. Of which there were many: the Indians, the settlers said, were either dying of the pox and the measles, or they had run away to join the rebellion of a cacique named Ayapín. The fields remained untilled for lack of labor. Ayapín was torching homes and crops, the settlers said, making it impossible for good, decent people like them to have a single day of peace. And there was no school in the town, so that many of the wives wanted to go back to a more civilized place, closer to Tenochtitlán.

Coronado promised to change all this. There would be no more slavery in the province, he said. The Indians would soon return to work, more lands would be given to the settlers, money would be spent to build the town of Guadalajara. And, of course, this Ayapín character would be captured and dealt with appropriately.

Know this, he said to the alcalde on the day of our departure. The era of people like Guzmán is over. There is a better way to run the empire.

It was a speech Coronado had prepared in the capital and it seemed to me that the more he told it, the more he believed in it: that the empire brought order where there was chaos, faith where there was idolatry, peace where there was savagery, and since its benefits were so indisputably clear, it could be spread through peaceful means. I waited for him to finish telling his tall tales so that we could leave, and go north.

COMPOSTELA WAS IN DISARRAY. Nearly half the houses that had been standing when I was last in the city looked abandoned now. There were few people walking about on the streets and, I noticed, the bathhouse where my hair had been shorn was boarded up. I left Coronado at the governor's mansion and took his deputies and the two friars to the barracks. There, I found the flagpole bare, the gate unguarded, the sentry box empty. I was well inside the courtyard before the sentinels took any notice of me: they were sitting under the shade of the arcade, playing a game of cards with an Indian man. It was Satosol.

The guards rushed to greet the new governor and apologize for their careless protection of military quarters. There were no Indians around here anymore, they explained, and most of the settlers preferred to stay on their plantations rather than in town. Fumbling with their keys, they unlocked the doors to the rooms and let in the governor and the friars. But I stayed behind with Satosol under the arcade. He wore a white shirt, which looked tight over the paunch he had grown since I had last seen him. His eyes flickered with a fierce curiosity. Are the others with you? he asked.

No.

They stayed in the big city?

Cabeza de Vaca went back to his country. Dorantes and Castillo married women of their kind. They have estates now, not far from Tenochtitlán.

Did my sister come back with you?

No, she is still with Dorantes. She had a baby.

Boy?

Girl.

What about my cousin? (He meant Kewaan, the wife of Castillo.)

She stayed behind, too. But what are you doing in the barracks? I asked him. Guzmán had been arrested only a few weeks after our passage through his town, so I knew that the reconnaissance mission for which he had hired Satosol had not taken place.

I still have the room, Satosol said. He pointed upstairs. And look, he said. He pulled out a knife and, by way of demonstrating its sharpness, he pricked his thumb with it. Instantly a bead of blood appeared; he licked it.

But what do you do here? I asked.

Same as you, brother. Whatever needs to be done.

We are not the same. Brother.

Then what are you doing with these new white men?

You ask too many questions.

I had never been close with Satosol, but for the three weeks I stayed in Compostela he shadowed me, asking me where I was going and what I was doing. If I sold my frilly shirt in order to buy paper and ink, he asked me why I had gotten rid of such fine cloth. If I sat down to write by the light of a candle, he asked me when I had become a notetaker like the white men. If I spoke to one of my companions in a hushed voice, he asked me what I was plotting. If I looked for wild garlic in the fields around the town, he asked me if my wife was pregnant. The more guarded my answers were, the more insistent he became, so that I spent much of my time avoiding him altogether.

The reason for our long stay in Compostela was that Coronado was interviewing the settlers to find out why they had abandoned their homes. The town was too far from their estates, they complained, where they needed to remain if they wanted to keep a close eye on their laborers. In addition, the Indians who were slaves were too lazy to work, while those who were free did not pay the tribute imposed on them by law. So Coronado gave orders to build new barracks closer to the estates, awarded more lands to the settlers, told them they needed to treat the Indians better, and said he would return in a few weeks to ensure that his orders had been carried out.

THE FIRST THING I noticed when we arrived in Culiacán was that Melchior Díaz's mustache had become even more elaborate. It reached all the way to his earlobes, its ends maintained in place by means of some mysterious grease. He was standing in the middle of the dusty road, flanked by two of his men, their muskets pointing in opposite directions. To the left, the horse run was empty. To the right, the Indian settlement looked deserted. It was as if all the Indians that had been in Culiacán—both its natives and the captives my companions and I had brought with us—had disappeared. But the garrison looked immutable; it was squat, well guarded, and teeming with Díaz's men. Before he had even dismounted, Coronado asked Díaz why he had not yet captured the rebel Ayapín.

Because someone else will replace him, Díaz said. Someone who might be even worse than him, which I know sounds hardly possible. But believe me, Don Francisco, this rebellion will continue as long as the conditions of the Indians remain the same. Nuño de Guzmán told me . . .

The era of Guzmán is over.

Yes, Díaz said. I was not his most fervent supporter, I assure you.

Peaceful conquest is the new way.

Yes, yes. I myself have been saying this for some time, as I hope Cabeza de Vaca has reported to the viceroy. But I will find Ayapín for you.

I hope so, Coronado said. Otherwise I might have to make some changes.

The blunt threat made Díaz frown. He seemed offended that a man of his age and long experience in the frontier should be spoken to in this way. But he dared not say anything in return and only watched while Coronado handed his reins to a servant and walked into the barracks.

The viceroy's plan called for Coronado to stay in Culiacán for a few weeks, while the friars, the Amigos, and I went on an advance mission to the north. Our task was to bring back a detailed report of the land, including information about its trails, water sources, towns, tribes, and the alliances between them. In short, we were to find out everything we could to facilitate the governor's entrada.

While waiting for the Amigos to prepare supplies for our journey, I took long walks around the outpost with my greyhounds. I had traded or given away all of my Castilian clothes by then and wore a leather coat over a cotton tunic, of the kind made by the tribes that dwelled in Nueva Galicia. Oyomasot, too, had discarded the dresses she had found constricting, especially in her new condition. I noticed that she smiled more easily; she even composed a rhyme when I prepared an infusion of zaatar for one of the Amigos. It seemed as if my wife, and my life, were slowly being returned to me.

When the day of our departure arrived, Coronado came to the gates of the garrison to bid us good-bye. He reminded Father Marco and Father Onorato that they were to take careful notice of everything they saw and that they should not hesitate to send back regular messages with one of the Amigos. For me he reserved a less humble tone. Estebanico, he said, you have been given an important mission, and I trust you will execute it faithfully.

I am ready.

If you find the Seven Cities, you will be treated well and receive many rewards. But if you betray your orders in any way, it is as if you have disobeyed His Majesty himself, and I will find you and punish you in ways you cannot even imagine.

I am ready, I said again.

He put his right hand on my shoulder. Then go with God.

WE ARRIVED at the base of the mountains at the worst time. It was windy and cold and we had to trudge through slippery trails. Behind me, the two friars pulled their mules by the reins, but the animals were slow and reluctant. Then the Amigo porters followed, balancing their baskets on their heads; it was a miracle that none of them fell and killed himself. But my wife's spirits were high, though she refused to take the hand I offered her. I can manage, she said, I can do this. She was just as eager as I to reach the other side.

Only when we reached the Land of Corn did we begin to slow our pace. The trail brought back many happy memories of our time here. One morning, about a week into our march, we came across a macaw-feather trader who recognized Oyomasot and me—he had been selling his wares to the Jumanos during our visit with them. From him, we learned that over the last two years the Indians in this area had been sick with fevers that brought on red spots and vicious welts. Hundreds had died. He was on his way to the settlement of Petatlán, farther north, where he hoped to find a reputable medicine man. So he joined our party as we headed there.

We arrived in Petatlán at midday four days later. It was a beautiful town of about fifty or sixty dwellings, all of them built with mud bricks. Brown and yellow mats hung from the walls, exposed to the sun. At night, they would be pulled down and used as bedrolls. Beyond the houses lay the fields of corn and beans, where workers still labored, tiny figures bent among their crops. In spite of the large number of people in our party, the town elders offered us food and shelter for the night.

While the friars took a nap in their quarters, Oyomasot and I visited the tribe's elders. Of course, we had no cure for the pox that afflicted their people, but we listened to the stories they told us and we shared our own. We described what we had seen in Tenochtitlán, the temples the Castilians had destroyed to erect their own, the slaves with branded faces, and the mission that Coronado was heading. But later that night, when we returned to the lodge where we were staying, we found the two friars waiting for us.

Oyomasot walked past me into the house and left me standing by the door with them, under the light of the moon. Father Marco, the older one, was very tall and had bulbous eyes that seemed to take notice of everything: my clothes, my satchel, even the gourd I carried, which had been given to me as a gift by one of the town elders. The friar spoke Spanish with an accent that hinted of his birth in France. Estebanico, he asked, how far are we from the wealthy settlements Cabeza de Vaca spoke of?

This is one of them, I replied.

Petatlán is one of them? But it does not look the way it should.

How should it look?

It seems much poorer than I expected.

Compared with the camps we lived in for so long, this town is much richer.

Well, I suppose it is all a matter of perspective. Still . . .

Father Marco's gaze drifted away. Coronado had instructed him to send detailed letters from every town we reached and to take note, especially, of any precious ornaments, decorative items, or trading materials that could suggest proximity to the Seven Cities of Gold; he was probably working out what he would write in his next letter to the governor.

The other friar, Father Onorato, was much younger and had never been outside of New Spain. He was watching me with the curiosity and enthusiasm of a young novice on his first day of service. Everything about him suggested sharpness: straight eyebrows, an angular nose, small lips that were pressed together in a disapproving line.

I unslung my satchel and put it down with my gourd by the door. Without waiting for him to ask me about it, I said: We use gourds in our cures.

This was the opening for which he had hoped. It seems to me, he said, that what you do with these Indians is dangerously close to witchcraft.

Do you see me calling upon any evil spirits?

Well, he said. He glanced at Father Marco for support, but the older friar remained silent, lost in his thoughts about wealthy settlements.

I am curious, Father Onorato continued. What did the friars from the Narváez expedition think of your cures? Did they not think them an affront to God?

The friars never witnessed any cures, I said.

There was a long silence, during which Father Marco's thoughts finally drifted from the matter of wealth to the matter of God—few minds can entertain both subjects at once. Now he focused his bulbous eyes on me. Yes, he said. The friars of the Narváez expedition had already been martyred by the time Cabeza de Vaca journeyed here.

Always Cabeza de Vaca, I thought, with not a little bitterness. That man's sterile account of our travels would always be considered the truth—no matter what had happened. I felt a small rebellion bubble within me.

Not all of the friars died, I said. One of them settled with the Indians.

Father Onorato raised a surprised eyebrow. Is that true? he asked.

Indeed it is, I said. His name was Father Anselmo. He was a good man. As for the other friars, one drowned on his raft. And two were eaten.

Eaten? Father Onorato repeated. Do you mean—by cannibals?

Yes, I said, eaten. The look of horror on Father Onorato's face told me that my story needed only a little embellishment. After a moment, I added: their bodies were consumed in different stages and their hearts were saved for last.

Father Onorato's mouth hung open. It did not cross his mind that Castilians like him could partake of human flesh, and I did nothing to correct his assumption that the cannibals had been Indians. I bid him good night and left him standing there.

The elders teach us: be a trickster, and you will survive.

THE NEXT DAY, WHEN WE WERE getting ready to depart Petatlán, Father Onorato declared that his dinner had not agreed with him and that he was much too ill to ride. He wanted to remain in the town until we returned. Father Marco and I went into his lodge and found him on his bedclothes, facing the mud wall.

Arm yourself with patience, Father Marco said, sitting on his knees by his side. The pain will pass.

I cannot ride, the young friar replied. His face remained stubbornly turned toward the wall. He pulled up to his neck his wool blanket, a gray piece of fabric that had many holes along the hem. In a moment, he began to moan.

Father Marco laid his hand on the curled form of the young friar and whispered a prayer. We can stay here until you feel better, he said.

But we have to cover another ten leagues today, I protested.

The light from the doorway fell on a corner of the room, where our hosts had laid a pitcher of water, a bowl of nuts, and a pot filled with fresh peppers. I tried one of the peppers—it was sweet and crisp and made a satisfying sound as I crunched. I leaned against the doorjamb, waiting.

I would rather not cause any delay, Father Onorato said. Go on without me, Brother. I will wait here.

Reluctantly, Father Marco stood up and adjusted his belt over his belly. Let us go, then.

Outside, Oyomasot was waiting for us, the dogs sitting obediently beside her. The Amigos, who had been sitting on their haunches in the shade, stood up at our approach. They picked up their bundles and baskets. Father Marco climbed on his mule and put the satchel that contained his papers in front of him on the saddle, as though it were a child.

We marched for another four days. Except for inquiries about the land or the trail, Father Marco remained quiet. He no longer had the company of one of his Franciscan brothers, and there were no Castilians in our party. He cut a lonely figure, sitting on his black mule while the rest of us were on foot. Behind us, the mountains had faded into a haze.

We reached the town of Vacapa just before sunset. Having heard about our arrival from emissaries sent from Petatlán, the villagers were already waiting for us in the square. Their hooting calls and joy-cries alarmed the friar, and he asked me to take him to his quarters directly.

The banquet that was given for us that night was as long and extravagant as any we had had in the Land of Corn, so that I did not speak to the friar until the next morning. He looked at my new turquoise earrings with disapproving eyes. What is that? he asked.

A gift from the townspeople, I said.

Are you performing your cures again?

I help whenever I can.

He corked his bottle of ink and began to gather his papers. His spirits had dampened over the last few days. Writing a record of our expedition was not as glorious a task as he had expected it to be. Our days were spent on the dusty trail, exposed to the sun or the rain, whichever it pleased God to impose upon us. The conversations were short, the lodgings bare. The work of exploration required patience and persistence, for which Father Marco had no inclination.

If you like, I said to him, I can go ahead of you to the next settlement.

No, he replied. We already left Brother Onorato behind. We must remain together. The governor's instructions were quite clear in this regard.

But think of what you stand to gain.

What do you mean?

You want to minister to these people, but they know nothing about you. Imagine if you were to be preceded by an ambassador who would introduce you and tell the people all you know and all you can do.

I need no introduction.

The fierce Indians who dwell in these parts will be better disposed toward you if you are properly introduced. And your reputation will grow. This is how Cabeza de Vaca used to proceed.

The friar's ambition wrestled with his doubt, but in the end ambition won. How will we communicate? he asked.

I had already thought of a way. I told him that I would go ahead of him to the next town and, as I proceeded, I would ask the Indians about the Seven Cities of Gold. If I heard or saw signs of them, I would send back a group of Amigos with a signal. If the land was poor, the signal would be a white cross the size of a hand. If it was rich, the signal would be a cross the size of two hands. If it was very rich, the signal would be a cross the size of an arm. And if it was richer than that, as rich as Tenochtitlán, then the signal would be a white cross the size of a man.

The friar agreed.

And now, free of him, I marched on. At each town my wife and I reached, I dispatched a set of Amigos, sending them back with a cross of decreasing size, until I had only ten of them left. When we arrived in the Indian town of Hawikuh, I sent back the remaining ten, giving them a cross the size of only one hand.

At last, I was free of the Amigos, who were not amigos. And my involvement with the empire was finally over.

25

THE STORY OF HAWIKUH

With the sun nearly at its nadir, the sky had turned a light shade of amber. The breeze, still warm despite the late hour, diffused the scent of the wild flowers. I lay on the soft grass, with my head in Oyomasot's lap and my ear pressed against the growing mound of her belly. If I stayed perfectly still, I could hear the faint heartbeat of our child. I had waited many years for that sound, for its promise of a new life. From the lake nearby came the croaking of the frogs and the singing of the crickets. It seemed to me as if the entire world were speaking to me, telling me that I was free now, free no matter what happened next, and a feeling of tranquility settled over me.

Listen, I said. Let me tell you a story that you can tell our child. I spoke to Oyomasot in her native language, a language I had had to learn in order to survive, a language that no longer felt alien on my tongue. She looked down at me then and her long hair brushed against my arm, making my skin break into bumps. There was a hint of curiosity in her eyes, but her face was otherwise untroubled and her features moved with grace.

The rays of the setting sun colored the walls of Hawikuh an orange color, the color of the gold that the servants of empire so desperately sought and so rarely renounced. Of all the places I had visited in the Land of the Indians, none looked to me so much like my hometown in Barbary, with its houses huddled together against the light. I thought of Azemmur in the spring, when the fig trees bloom and the fields are a sea of green and white. How I longed to see those fields again, to lie in them and listen to the humming of the bees, to swim in the Umm er-Rbi' again, to sit on a boulder at the edge of the river and watch the shad swim against the current. How I longed to lay eyes upon my mother, to visit my father's grave and whisper a prayer for his soul, to sit by my uncle's side as he built chests or divans. How I longed to be woken in the morning by the call of the muezzin, to be tempted to go back to sleep, and then to feel my brothers' hands gently shake me awake.

None of these things would be mine again, but if my destiny had been to travel west and see this vast, mysterious, beautiful land, perhaps it would be my child's destiny to travel in the opposite direction and see my homeland, which will seem just as vast, just as mysterious, just as beautiful to him—or will it be her? In my mind, I could almost hear my childhood self intone, together with the other boys in the msid, our bodies moving forward and back to the rhythm of Qur'anic verses, that to God belong the east and the west. Whichever way you turn, there is the face of God.

This moment was perfect. It was all I had, and it was everything. I did not care for all the gifts that had been given to me along the way to Hawikuh—lapis, coral, turquoises by the purseload, pelts and furs. All I wanted was the freedom to lie here in the tall grass, under a darkening sky, with my wife beside me. On the other side of the town walls, Ahku, the cacique of the Zunis, was still appraising the news I had brought him and conferring with the tribe's elders about what he should do.

That afternoon, when we arrived at his gates, Ahku came out to greet us. He was an older man and his hair was streaked with white, but he walked about with the posture and vigor of a youthful warrior. He was wrapped in a red blanket, tied with a bone clasp over his right shoulder. Behind him, three deputies stood, watching us with bare curiosity. Their headdresses were modest, made of plain strips of leather, but they wore many necklaces of coral and turquoise stacked together. None of them carried any weapons, for the town was fortified and well guarded.

Ahku led me into his lodge, a handsome, mud-brown edifice with white ladders angled against its walls, leading to the doorways of higher floors. A meal of roasted corn and baked beans was laid out for us in his receiving room, and we ate and conversed with great ease. But when I told him about the white men who were headed his way, he became concerned. What do they want? he asked.

Gold, I replied.

We have no gold.

I know. But they mean to conquer the country even if it has no gold. All of the territories south of here are already under their rule. They force people to till the land and those who refuse or fight them are branded rebels and killed wherever they go.

And how do you know this?

Because I lived with them. I came to this country with them.

Ahku ran a thumbnail on his lips, removing flecks of dry skin in one smooth stroke. His eyes traveled from me to my wife, and back again; I felt as if he were scrutinizing every gesture, every breath, every word. A servant brought a dish of roasted wild fowl and Ahku waited until we had taken a few bites before he spoke again. You said that these intruders are white, but you are black. How do you know so much about them? How do you know their ways or their intentions?

It is true that I look nothing like them, I said, but I speak their language and I have lived among them long enough to know what they mean to do. You must believe me.

Even if what you said is true, why did you come here? What do you stand to gain by warning us?

I gain nothing. I did not make the news, I merely tell it.

Ahku fell silent. He leaned back against the wall, thinking about everything I had said, but his face darkened as he reached his conclusions. Let the white men come if they wish, he said. We have fought intruders before, we can do it again.

At these words, his deputies nodded in agreement. The town of Hawikuh was not a settlement that could be taken without a fight, and they were prepared for it.

But they cannot be fought with weapons, I said. I explained to Ahku that the white men's weapons were far more powerful than anything he had ever seen and that his only means of salvation was to create a fiction.

A story? Ahku asked.

Yes, I replied. Send a group of men, some bearing injuries of battle, to Vacapa. They can tell the friar Marco that the Zunis killed Estebanico.

Ahku laughed. Why do you want us to tell him we killed you? Do you think your tall tale is going to frighten this man away?

It was a tall tale that brought him here in the first place, I said. Nothing else, I was certain, would put a stop to Father Marco's advance. I wanted the friar to go back to Coronado with the news that, not only had he found no gold in the northern territories, but the fierce Indians of Hawikuh had repelled his mission and killed Estebanico in the process. The servants of empire would forget about the Seven Cities of Gold. The people of Hawikuh would be safe. Estebanico would be laid to rest. But Mustafa would remain, free to live a life of his choosing.

What if the white man in Vacapa does not believe your story? Ahku asked.

He will, I said, if the messengers know how to tell it.

Ahku said that he had to consult with the tribe's elders before he could make a decision. All the Indians I had met in this continent decided their affairs by consultation, so this did not surprise me. It was a practice I admired, though I hoped the cacique would make up his mind soon, because the friar was only three weeks away from the gates of Hawikuh.

Whatever Ahku decided, Oyomasot and I would leave in the morning and begin our journey home to the land of the Avavares. We would live out our lives among her people, following the routes her ancestors had taken for centuries, hunting where they had hunted, foraging where they had foraged, trading where they had traded. Our child, too, would learn these traditions. He would learn to welcome guests and fight intruders. Above all, he would learn not to put his life in the hands of another man.

Oyomasot's hand was on my cheek. What story should I tell our child? she asked. I remembered the stories my mother had told me so often when I was a young boy. I had taken them with me when I crossed the Ocean of Fog and Darkness. I had fed on them in the terrible years of deprivation and I had used them to find my way whenever I was lost. I told them when I needed comfort or when I wanted to give it to others. The words pressed themselves against my lips now, begging to come out. I wanted to tell a story to my child, so that he might share the joy or the pain it contained, that he might learn something from it, that he might tell it after my death or after his mother's death, even if only to pass the time. I wanted to tell him a story that he might remember me.

And in this relation I tried to tell the story of what really happened when I journeyed to the heart of the continent. The servants of the Spanish empire have given a different story to their king and their bishop, their wives and their friends. The Indians with whom I lived for eight years, each one of them, each one of thousands, have told yet other stories. Maybe there is no true story, only imagined stories, vague reflections of what we saw and what we heard, what we felt and what we thought. Maybe if our experiences, in all of their glorious, magnificent colors, were somehow added up, they would lead us to the blinding light of the truth. To God belong the east and the west, whichever way you turn, there is the face of God. God is great.

ACKNOWLEDGMENTS

The speech read by the notary of the Narváez expedition in Chapter 1 is a short-ened and modified version of the Requerimiento, a legal justification drafted by the Spanish jurist Juan López de Palacios Rubios in 1513. It was used in every Spanish expedition to the Americas from that year until its abolishment in 1556. It was read to indigenous tribes when they were present, but their presence was not required. The signed document was then sent back to Spain. The text of the Requerimiento is in the public domain, but for an analysis see "The Requerimiento and Its Inter-preters" by Lewis Hanke in *Revista de Historia de América*.

The Narváez expedition was famously chronicled by Cabeza de Vaca in a travel-ogue addressed to and dedicated to King Charles V, and which was later published as *La Relacíon*. An excellent English translation by Fanny Bandelier, revised and annotated by Harold Augenbraum, is available from Penguin Classics under the title *Chronicle of the Narváez Expedition*. That edition has the additional blessing of an introduction by Ilan Stavans.

In researching this novel I have relied on many sources, but I would like to acknowledge, in particular, *The Travels of ibn Battuta*; *The Conquest of New Spain* by Bernal Díaz; *The Karankawa Indians: The Coast People of Texas* by Albert Gatschet; *Crossing the Continent, 1527–1540: The Story of the First African-American Explorer of the American South* by Robert Goodwin; *We Came Naked and Barefoot: The Journey of Cabeza de Vaca Across North America* by Alex D. Krieger; *A Land So Strange: The Epic Journey of Cabeza de Vaca* by Andrés

Acknowledgments

Reséndez; and *The History and Description of Africa* by Hassan al-Wazzan (Leo Africanus.)

Although I have based this novel on actual events, the characters and situations it depicts are entirely fictional. This is especially true of my protagonist, about whose background nothing is known, except for one line in Cabeza de Vaca's relation: *el cuarto [sobreviviente] se llama Estevanico, es negro alárabe, natural de Azamor.* ("The fourth [survivor] is Estevanico, an Arab Negro from Azamor.")

I am grateful to the Lannan Foundation for a residency in Marfa, Texas, and to Hedgebrook for a stay on Whidbey Island in Washington. For their comments on an earlier draft of this book, I owe many thanks to Kirsten Menger-Anderson, Kevin McIlvoy, Maaza Mengiste, Souad Sedlik, and Jane Smiley. Special thanks to Tom R. Kennedy for the long conversation about Hawikuh. I am particularly indebted to my agent, Ellen Levine, whose faith in me is unwavering, and to my editor, Erroll McDonald, whose guidance made all the difference. Thank you most of all to Alexander Yera, who makes all of my work, and indeed my life, possible.